DARK

OF THE

MOON

DARK
OF THE
MOON

P.J. PARRISH

Kensington Books
http://www.kensingtonbooks.com

KENSINGTON BOOKS are published by

Kensington Publishing Corp.
850 Third Avenue
New York, NY 10022

Library of Congress Card Catalog Number: 98-067107
ISBN 1-57566-394-5

First Printing: April, 1999
10 9 8 7 6 5 4 3 2 1

Printed in the United States of America

For Daniel,
who made it happen.
And for Charlotte,
who gave it meaning.

ACKNOWLEDGMENTS

To Phil Ward and Fred Grimm, who helped color
our sketch of Mississippi.

To Robert Terry, who kept us honest and
entertained.

To Heather Montee, for her handholding and
research.

Grateful acknowledgment to Hannah Kahn, for
the use of the poem "To be Black, to be Lost."

And most of all, to Maria Carvainis, who refused
to settle for anything but the best.

Southern gentle lady,
Do not swoon.
They've just hung a black man
In the dark of the moon.

They've hung a black man
To a roadside tree
In the dark of the moon
For the world to see
How Dixie protects
Its white womanhood.

Southern gentle lady,
    Be good!
    Be good!

            —Langston Hughes
              Silhouette

CHAPTER 1

December, 1983

The naked trees snaked upward, black capillaries against a
bleached, predawn sky. The ground beneath his feet was a
mire of dead leaves and copper-colored mud. A cold December
wind wafted through the trees, loosening raindrops from the
needles of the tall pines.

Louis stumbled as his boot sank into a puddle, the suede immediately blanketed by a thin membrane of algae. Cursing softly,
he stepped free and trudged on, grabbing the thin arms of small
trees as he scaled the slippery slope.

He could no longer see the orange vest of the hunter ahead
and he called for him to slow down. Pausing at the crest of the
hill, Louis rested against a fallen tree, pulling up the fleece collar
of his cocoa-brown jacket. He waited for the last man of his trio
to puff his way up the muddy incline.

Despite the freezing temperature, Junior Resnick's porkish face
was flushed and beaded with sweat. His brown jacket, spotted
with mud, looked like a sleeping bag tied around his thick belly.

"Man," Junior said, breathless, "I thought he said it was jus'
a ways out here." He wiped his nose with his forearm. "This is
fuckin' crazy, Louis, plum fuckin' crazy."

Louis allowed himself a small smile. He enjoyed seeing Junior
suffer. Wiping the mud from his trousers with a gloved hand, he
turned away and started down the hill. "We've come this far, we
keep going," he said.

At the bottom of the ravine, he stopped on the banks of a
rippling creek. The sun chose that moment to break through the

heavy gray clouds, shooting eerie streaks of light into the morning mist. Louis heard Junior's footsteps coming up behind him and he motioned for him to stop. A mockingbird's haunting call sent creatures scampering from the brush as the wind whistled softly through the trees. The swirling mist floated over the damp ground, creeping over Louis's shoes. He felt a stir of excitement. It was a fitting day to find a body.

Junior's grunt broke the mood. "How much further?"

"Jus' a ways, guys, up near the swamp," the hunter yelled back.

Louis stepped onto a jagged string of rocks, making his way across the creek, his heart quickening slightly in anticipation. He heard a splash behind him and looked over his shoulder to see Junior shaking water off his boots.

Louis moved on, up a steep hill. Junior began to puff loudly behind him.

"What's the matter there, old-timer? Need a cane?" Louis called over his shoulder.

Junior, a year younger than Louis, showed his annoyance with a slit-eye sneer. Mumbling to himself, he broke off a tree limb, and plucked off the dead branches as he moved on, shaping the branch into a walking stick. "This is crap, Kincaid," he said. "I can't believe you got me out here at six in the morning for this."

A ripple of vexation crossed Louis's face. "This is a dead body. Aren't you the least bit curious? You're a cop, for chrissakes."

"Yeah, a cold and hungry cop."

"Well, this is the first interesting thing I've come across since I've been here."

"Yeah, like you're some veteran or something. What are you, twenty-five? Twenty-six? And besides, you ain't been here but a couple weeks. I bet this here body woulda still been here this afternoon." Junior slipped again. "Fuck," he said, more to the mud than anyone else.

"You didn't have to come, Junior."

"Easy for you to say. Sheriff would ream me good if he knew I let you wander out here alone."

Louis suppressed a sigh and walked on. He wondered what motivated men like Junior to become cops. The man didn't seem interested in police work and he complained about the hours, the paperwork, the pay, and just about everything from the weather to the tires on the squad cars. The only thing he did seem to take pride in was the badge itself. Not what it meant, but the small perks it afforded him around town.

But the remark about the sheriff did remind Louis that Junior had one important function. He was Louis's watchdog, a human buffer, so the nice white folks of Greensboro County, Mississippi, wouldn't get riled when a black cop came ringing their doorbells. And, Louis had to admit, Junior did that part of his job well. In the three weeks Louis had been in Black Pool, Junior had stuck to him like kudzu on a telephone pole.

"You know, you're full of shit, Kincaid," Junior called. "We gets lots of interestin' stuff. 'Member Emmett Jenkins's missing cows? That was a good one and we done solved it."

It had started to rain again. "Yeah, we solved it. The damn cows were lost," Louis muttered. He held back a branch so it wouldn't smack Junior in the face, although he was tempted to let it fly.

"Does it rain like this in Dee-troit, Louis?"

"This time of year it snows. White Christmas and all that."

Junior guffawed. "That's real funny, Louis, coming from you . . . white Christmases. Say, they got colored Santas in Dee-troit?"

The question seemed so genuinely innocent, Louis almost answered. But the hunter cut him off.

"Here it is fellas, right here."

Louis and Junior came to a stop, staring at the orange cap the hunter had left as a marker, dangling from the leafless limb of a poplar tree.

In the eerie silence that followed, the three men gathered their courage. Louis had never seen a corpse before, not one like this. He had seen dead people. A few in silk-lined coffins, their faces powdered and prepped. And a few traffic fatalities. That was all. This was different. Very different.

The body, or what remained of it, lay cradled in the knotted roots of a twisted old oak tree, almost concealed by the thick grass, pine needles and branches. Louis approached it slowly, knelt in the mud and removed his gloves. Gently, he brushed away the dirt. His fingers touched something and he withdrew. An ocher-colored skull protruded from the mud, its eye sockets empty, black caverns.

"Jesus fucking Christ," Junior murmured, standing over Louis's shoulder.

Louis squinted up into the rain, wishing there was more light. The rest of the body was covered with a thin layer of dirt, indicating to Louis a hasty burial. Brushing a forearm across his face, he scratched at the cold mud, his fingers soon growing numb from the effort.

They touched something rough. Louis eased it from under the skeleton. It was the end of an old rope, blackened with decay. A heavier, knotted part was intertwined with the bones in the shallow grave; the other end snaked off into the woods. Louis gave a tug and with a sucking sound, the ground released the rope. When it broke free of the dirt, Louis stood up, clearly defining the noose against the silvery light. The three men stared. They all knew what it was—a lynching.

"Jesus fucking Christ, Louis," Junior whispered, "Jesus fucking Christ Almighty." He took a step back, distancing himself from the noose.

"I'm done here, man," the hunter said uneasily. "Y'all don't need me here, do you?"

Louis shook his head, gripping the rope in his cold hand. His gut tightened. He had only a few memories of his childhood and this place he had left so long ago. This kind of violence, the horror stories of Southern-style justice had seemed just that, stories you saw on TV or in movies. Until now. Suddenly, they were very real and the sensation that moved over him was very frightening.

"What do you wanna do, Louis?"

Louis ignored Junior, following the rope, pulling as he went, letting it lead him to its end. He expected to find it frayed and worn, rotted away. But it was cut clean.

He looked up at the oak, wondering if the tree had served as gallows for the man who lay at its feet, and if so, who cut the rope down. He stood silent for a minute, stiff in the fine spray of drizzle, trying to gain a feel for what had happened. He shivered, feeling a presence in the air. But he could see nothing.

"Louis, I'm cold," Junior whined.

Louis turned and glared at Junior—the pudgy face, spotted with freckles, the unruly wisps of rust-colored hair sticking out from under the sides of the cattleman's hat, puerile blue eyes and a chinless mouth. Junior Resnick was so very stupid, and at that moment, so very, very white. Louis bit back his anger and held out his hand. "Give me your radio."

The strange firmness in Louis's voice compelled Junior to hand it over without question. Louis called the station, waiting patiently for some life on the other end of the radio while Junior drew circles in the mud with his stick.

"Sheriff Dodie here. Who the hell is callin' me so early?"

"I am, sir, Louis. I asked them to call you at home."

"Where's Junior? He with you?"

"Yes sir. We're out on old Road 234, a mile or so off the highway."

"And?" Sheriff Dodie asked impatiently.

"We have something out here. A body."

"Anybody we know?"

"Just a skeleton, sir, if that. Just bones."

"Bones? You sure they human?"

Louis's jaw tightened. "They're human, sir." Louis looked down at the pattern of ovals Junior was drawing in the mud and back at the bones. "It looks like a lynching victim," he added.

There was a silence on the other end of the radio. Louis wiped the dampness from his brow.

"Still raining out there?" the sheriff asked finally.

Louis frowned at the odd question. "Yes, sir. How long do you think it'll be before we can get someone out here?"

"Kincaid, need I remind you it's six A.M. Besides, we ain't got no coroner right now. Got to git Davis from over Sampson County way."

"We'll wait," Louis said. Junior rolled his eyes.

There was another pause. "Then you'll be waiting in that rain until after dinner."

"Dinner?" Louis repeated. "Six o'clock?"

"Dinner, Kincaid," the sheriff said impatiently. "Not supper."

Louis sighed, remembering dinner and supper were two very different things here. Dinner was lunch.

"I'll see if I can roust him," Dodie said. "Y'all wait on the side of 234 and be watchin' out for us."

Louis clicked the radio off and handed it back to Junior, turning to look down at the skeleton. The sky was lighter now and the birds had come alive with the vanishing mist. A cold breeze rippled his trousers. The skull stared up at him. What had the eyes seen last? Pharisaic white hoods or the trusted face of someone familiar?

A sudden gust of wind scattered dead leaves around Louis's feet and over the face of the skull. He looked at Junior, who had ambled over.

"Junior," he said quietly, "do you have any idea what we are really looking at?"

Junior poked at the skull with his stick. "No offense, Louis, but it looks like a dead nigger to me. Nothin' but a poor dead nigger."

CHAPTER 2

The Blazer bounced over the rough terrain, cutting through the brush like a tank. Sheriff Dodie drove, with Junior seated next to him and Louis in the back with Ed Davis, the Sampson County coroner. Greensboro County hadn't had its own coroner since last June, when that man had died of a heart attack and no one had seemed anxious to replace him. Not much was expected of the coroner except to show up and officially pronounce someone dead, all for the grand salary of $25 dollars per body. Junior had said nobody hereabouts wanted the job.

Louis stared blankly at Ed Davis's craggy profile, then turned his gaze out to the trees, lost in his thoughts. He checked his watch. It seemed to be taking an eternity to get back to the scene. Half the day was gone.

"Kincaid, you ever seen anything like this before?" Sheriff Dodie asked, his eyes searching the rearview mirror for Louis's face.

"No, sir."

Junior turned in his seat and squinted at Louis. "Got a good one for you. . . . What did the ni—I mean, Mexican, do with his first fifty-cent piece?"

"Don't start on that shit, Junior," Dodie said.

"He married her. Like that one, Louis?"

Louis turned away, his jaw set, his eyes focused on the passing woodlands. He could feel Junior staring at him.

"Don't suppose you saw many hangings up north, now, did you?" Junior asked.

Louis met the sheriff's eyes in the mirror as he spoke. "Not as many as you do here."

Junior turned back around, sinking into the seat. "Always a smart-ass, aren't you, Kincaid?"

No one answered Junior and the interior of the Blazer fell quiet until Junior's voice broke the silence. "Sheriff, here! Look, there's the marker we done left. Stop!"

The sheriff hit the brakes and the Blazer slid to a muddy stop. The men climbed out and with Louis leading the way, started up the slope. The four were silent as they made their way down the ravine. In the distance, Louis saw the hunter's hat on the poplar tree. Though eager to get back to the site, he slowed his steps in deference to old Ed Davis.

He waited under the tree for the others to catch up. The sheriff stopped, staring down at the bones, his face impassive. Davis came up beside Dodie. He blanched, swallowed hard, then slowly knelt beside the shallow grave. Junior took out a 35-mm camera, preparing to take photographs. Louis pulled a half-roll of yellow police tape from his jacket.

The sheriff, chewing on an unlit cigar, watched as Louis tied the tape to a tree and began to unravel it. "Kincaid, what the hell you doing?" he said finally.

Ed Davis and Junior looked over.

"Roping off the crime scene," Louis said.

"Just what the hell are we protecting?"

Junior snickered and Davis hunched over the bones. Louis looked at Sheriff Dodie, mystified. Shaking his head, Dodie walked over to where Davis was and looked down at the elderly man.

"Ed, how old you guess them bones to be?" he asked.

The coroner looked up. "Could be five, ten or even thirty."

Dodie turned back to Louis. "Now, do you really think it's necessary to do that after so many years?"

"But someone could—"

"Nobody's gonna come out to this swamp and ruin no 'crime scene.' Put the goddamn tape away," Dodie said firmly.

Louis retraced his steps slowly, rolling up the tape, watching the sheriff out of the corner of his eye. A single thought kept running through his mind, the same thought that had flashed into his head the first day he set foot in Sam Dodie's office: What am I doing here?

He had come back to Black Pool for one reason and one reason only: to care for his dying mother. The job with the sheriff's department, well, that had been a lucky break more than anything. Louis let his gaze wander over the forest. He had never been an investigator. Or a detective. He had a college degree and two years' street work as a cop. All he had been looking for was a deputy's job, something to put food on the table. But he had been offered the job as an investigator. Louis never knew why. Maybe the sheriff was impressed with the degree. Louis had readily accepted. How much crime could a little Southern town have?

Louis's eyes drifted down to the skull, now being slipped into a paper bag by Ed Davis. It occurred to him how ironic it was that he had to come to such a godforsaken place to work on his first homicide. Louis shivered slightly in the cold wind. Homicide. . . . This was no ordinary homicide. This was a lynching.

His gaze went back to Dodie and he found himself seeing only one thing—the color of his skin. In his mind, every white man over forty had suddenly become a suspect. The guy at the Texaco station. Had he been there? The old man sitting outside the barber shop. Had he watched it? The man in the pickup who pulled up beside him at the stoplight. Had he been the one who had tightened the noose around the victim's neck? God, he was getting paranoid.

Louis put the tape in the truck and leaned against a tree. He studied the three men. Ed Davis was certainly old enough to have been around at the time of the lynching, but he had lived in neighboring Sampson County. Junior would have been in diapers at the time. Louis's eyes went to the sheriff.

Sam Dodie was a big man, six foot or so, with a broad chest and a convex waistline. He parted his black hair on the side and there was just enough gray at the temples to add distinction to the pitted but comely face. In the short time Louis had been here, he had never seen Dodie in a uniform. He wore his badge on the pocket of a plaid flannel shirt and his gun on a belt that supported faded jeans. He always wore the same soiled red cap, embroidered with the county sheriff's emblem.

Louis estimated that Dodie was in his mid-forties, making him about twenty at the time of the murder, if Davis was right about the age of the bones. He stared hard at the sheriff. He couldn't even begin to guess if Dodie was the kind of man who could take part in a lynching, but the thought of it made the hair on his neck stand up.

Ed Davis's voice shook him out of his thoughts. "Sheriff, look at this. Somebody wrapped him up in something. Looks like canvas or tarp, what's left of it. Probably a good thing, too. Doubt he'd be this together if he was just stuck in the dirt."

Dodie walked closer and squatted by the grave. "Critters didn't get him?"

"Won't know how many bones we lost 'til we piece him back together. Got a chain here, too," Davis said. "Looks like an heirloom."

"Was it around his neck?" Louis asked, sliding between Junior and the sheriff and kneeling next do Davis.

"Can't tell, bones are kind of strewn about."

"May I see it?" Louis asked.

Davis bagged the mud-caked medallion and handed it to Louis. It was about four inches in diameter and heavy. The chain was intact. Louis ran the tips of his fingers over the raised seal on the front.

"Got this, too." Davis slipped a small tattered book into a plastic bag. The cover was black with mold and some of the pages disintegrated when Davis dropped it into the bag. "It was near the rib cage," Davis said, holding the book out to Louis. "Buried with him, I'd guess, probably under his shirt or jacket."

Louis reached for the book, but Junior snagged it first. "This ain't no damn good. Can't read it," Junior said.

"Give it to me, and be careful." Louis said, holding out his hand.

Junior gave the bag to Louis. He studied the front, then gently opened the cover to reveal a patch of yellowed paper on the inside.

"Hard to tell what he was wearing," Davis went on, "but I can tell you what he wasn't wearing."

"What?" Junior asked.

"Shoes."

"How can you tell that?" Junior said, leaning forward.

"Because there aren't any, none in the grave, none nearby."

"Maybe some coon dragged 'em off," Junior suggested.

"Critters drag off bones, not leather," Dodie said.

"His hands were tied," Davis said, handing Dodie a short, circular rope still knotted.

Louis wet his lips and briefly closed his eyes, trying to imagine the horror of the man's last moments. When he opened them, he saw the sheriff looking at him.

"They were all tied," Dodie said to no one in particular. "That's the way it was done."

Louis rose stiffly. "Anything else?" he asked as Davis began bagging up the rest of the evidence.

"Shreds of clothing. Denim, looks like. Lots of discoloration. Can't tell if it's mold or something else." Davis continued to bag what things he could. "Louis, you move that rope there?"

Louis nodded. "Yes, I did. It was under him."

"Figured as much. Got all of it?"

"The end was cut. That's all there is."

Dodie lit his cigar, the acrid smell drifting on the cold breeze. His eyes traveled in a circle around the scene and stopped on Junior. Junior was gazing into the shallow grave, hands stuffed in his pockets.

"Junior, you gonna just stand there? Take some more pictures. Walk around and see what else you can kick up," Dodie said.

"Like what?"

"Bones, you jackass, bones. Turn over some rocks and dirt." Dodie looked back at Ed Davis. "Anything else, Ed?"

"Nothing that I can see. The boys in Jackson can probably tell you more. This will take awhile, but I'll see the remains get headed that way this afternoon."

Davis stood up, using the poplar tree for support. His small, gray eyes met Louis's. "I'm right sorry about this, Louis."

Louis did not know what the coroner was apologizing for, but he nodded just the same. Louis gazed up at the thick limb over which the rope surely had been slung. It seemed odd that the rest of the rope was gone, but it probably wasn't important. Someone had most likely cut it down, unaware that he stood atop a grave. The wind rustled through the tree's bare branches, and Louis put out a hand, touching the trunk, as if it could tell him what happened. But the tree was as silent as the man beneath it.

"Kincaid."

Dodie was calling, but Louis didn't see him with Junior, who was heading back to the Blazer for a shovel. The sheriff called again and Louis followed the voice away from the grave, through some thick brush and trees. He spread some branches, stepping into the thin streaks of sunlight that cut through the threatening clouds. Dodie stood next to a white wooden fence, his body silhouetted against a rolling, yellow pasture spotted with copper-colored cows. Louis could see the smoke from his cigar drifting upward against the darkening sky.

In the distance was a large white house, more of a mansion really, the kind of house seen in the history books on the Civil War. It was shaded by strategically placed pines, and surrounded by a white brick wall. It was at least a half mile away, at the bottom of the sloping meadow.

Louis wandered to the fence and stood next to Dodie. "Who lives there?" he asked, his mind already framing questions to ask the owners.

"That's Max Lillihouse's place. His wife Grace's grandparents built it. Beautiful, ain't it?"

"Yes, it is. Do they own this land here?" Louis asked.

"Yeah." For a second, they were quiet. Suddenly Dodie turned to face Louis. "Now, don't you go bothering them folks, Kincaid. That family has nothing to offer on this, and Miz Grace is the nicest lady I know. Trust me. You stay away from them."

Louis did not reply. He had no intention of staying away from anyone. He was debating whether to share this thought with Dodie when the sheriff spoke again.

"Stupid animals, cows."

Louis directed his gaze back to the slow-moving animals. "No dumber than some people I know," he replied.

Dodie took the cigar from his mouth and looked at Louis as if about to say something profound. "You seem to have forgotten a lot about these people here, Kincaid."

Louis smiled faintly. "White people or Southerners?"

Dodie shrugged. "Both, I reckon. Mostly Southern folk. I need to tell you, I'm concerned about you, Kincaid—you and this case. I don't want to see you going off half-cocked on this thing, if you get my meaning."

"If you mean I should just ignore this, Sheriff, then no, I can't say I do get your meaning."

Dodie relit the stubborn cigar. "Look, I know you probably harbor some bad feelings, and I don't blame you. But you gotta look at it from a different point of view, a policeman's point of view."

"That's what I am doing, sir."

Dodie sighed. "Now, Kincaid, it's not like the folks in this town would consider this a *real* crime. It's just—well, things like this are part of their past, part of something terrible they'd rather forget."

"What about *his* family?" Louis said. "Do you think they forgot?"

Dodie let out a tired breath. "Kincaid, I ain't talking to hear myself talk."

"Sheriff," Louis said slowly. "We need to find out who killed him. We *will* find out who killed him."

Dodie jerked the cigar from his mouth with one hand and the cap off his head with the other. "The Klan killed him, for chrissakes! Ain't that good enough for you?"

"No, it's not," Louis said, his teeth clenched. "And I don't think it should be good enough for you."

Dodie's face reddened and Louis could see his neck muscles tighten, as if he was choking down an outburst. Instead, Dodie pointed his cigar at Louis.

"You've no right to talk to me like that, Kincaid. I don't need some lecture from you on police ethics. You don't know me, and you don't know nothing about nobody here."

Louis stared at Dodie's gray eyes then looked back at the cows. He could smell the manure in the air. It seemed appropriate.

Dodie put his cap back on and stuck the cigar back in his mouth. "For chrissakes, let's find out who the poor bastard was and just give him a decent burial," he said.

"There's no statute of limitations on murder," Louis said softly, without looking at the sheriff.

"I know that, Kincaid," Dodie said. "But if you think these folks, white or black, are going to talk to you about something that happened twenty or thirty years ago, you're dumber than those damn cows." Dodie paused to take a deep breath. "Look, Kincaid, I don't know if we still have Klan here or not, but I reckon we did back then, and a good number of those people are still here. They're retired, they're old, they don't want to remember. I'm tellin' you, it was just the way things were."

Louis turned to face Dodie. "This is a murder, sir, whether it happened thirty years ago or thirty minutes ago. We're police officers. We are obligated to investigate this."

Dodie stared at him, his eyes hard as granite. Louis knew what he was thinking. It was the same thing he had thought about all day, that an investigation would tear the town apart.

Dodie looked away and out at the pasture. The lines around his mouth grew tight, and his eyes flickered just a little as he spoke. "You want revenge because you figure he was black."

"I want justice because he was a man," Louis said.

Dodie did not look at him, but turned toward the Blazer. The cows were moving slowly down the hill. Thunder rattled overhead.

"There is no justice, Kincaid," he said, "not for me, not for you. And not for him."

CHAPTER 3

Louis dipped the knife into the jar, scooped out a glob of peanut butter and spread it across the bread. Before replacing the lid, he ate two or three clumps off the knife, then folded the bread in half, picked up a Dr. Pepper and padded to the sofa. The sound of gunshots from the TV filled the room, followed by a ferocious roll of thunder from outside.

Tugging at the belt of his terry-cloth robe, Louis dropped into the sofa and pulled an afghan over his legs. He swallowed the sandwich in two bites, then climbed off the sofa to turn up the television. *Magnum, P.I.* was on, and Louis settled back to watch as Tom Selleck chased a bad guy down the beach in Waikiki. How simple police work would be if all cases had a well-plotted script to follow. And how nice to do it living scot-free on an estate in Hawaii.

The room was cold from the drafts that squeezed in from around the old windows, and Louis got up to turn on the small space heater. As the coils began to put out a reassuring glow, Louis smelled the stench of burning rust and wondered if the odor might be lethal. He settled back to the sofa. What a way to die, he thought; of poisonous fumes in a run-down Mississippi boardinghouse.

He rented the room from Bessie Lloyd, a widow who leased out the extra rooms in her house to anyone with ten bucks and a job. The old green-shingled house was a stone's throw from the railroad tracks, and every night at dusk the house rattled with the undulations of the passing freight train headed north to Nashville. Louis's second-story room overlooked the street. It was a cozy room, furnished with the basics, including a bed with a tarnished tubular headboard, an ancient rosewood table spotted with water rings and a kitchenette with a minifridge. Bessie had given Louis a handmade quilt. She didn't usually take such personal interest in boarders, but Louis, well, he was special. He needed looking after, she had said. And right now, there was only one other boarder—Louis's mother.

Lila Kincaid lay dying in the room across the hall from Louis. She had cirrhosis, complicated by other conditions, including syphilis. Louis didn't want to believe the doctor when he told him about that part of her illness. It was bad enough his mother had drunk herself near to death. The syphilis was a horrifying reminder of how she'd lived her life, and he had demanded that the doctor keep it secret.

Louis heard Lila cry out over the noise of the television. He closed his eyes, bracing himself to get up. But he heard Bessie's footsteps and dropped back into the sofa, a mixture of guilt and relief washing over him.

He kept telling himself that he had no reason to feel guilty. He was here, wasn't he? He had put his own life on hold to come back to this place he had tried so hard to forget. He was being the devoted son, even if she had been the less-than-devoted mother. But every time he looked at her now, he felt shame, the same shame he had felt as a boy. He had escaped, distancing himself in miles and years from this place and the bad feelings. It was all buried and forgotten. But now, coming back had forced everything to the surface again.

He heard Lila moan and he got up and went into the hallway. He leaned against the doorjamb, watching as Bessie made Lila comfortable among the pillows and covers strewn over the bed. Louis gazed at Lila Kincaid's sunken face. He did not know this woman, his mother. His blurry memories consisted mainly of the stench of stale alcohol, harsh words and bloodshot eyes. The only affection he had received as a child had come later from his foster mother, Frances Lawrence. If there was anyone to call mother, it was her. The fact that Frances Lawrence was white . . . well, that never mattered much to him. He was half white. That was the only thing given to him by a father he had never known.

Half white . . . or was it half black? He was never sure, and didn't really care, unless someone or something forced him to think about it. Here in Black Pool, it seemed there was no question.

He was black. He had found that out on his first day in town when he pulled into the Texaco station. The attendant had ambled out to stare at his Mustang with its Michigan plates and then peered at Louis's University of Michigan jacket. When Louis had asked the way to Bessie Lloyd's place, the man had given him a sneer and some mumbled directions. It was only after Louis had driven around for a half hour out in the sticks that he realized the man had purposely misled him. What he didn't know was whether it was because he was black or just a Yankee. Probably both.

Black or white . . .

Back home in Michigan, he was able to convince himself it really didn't matter. But he knew it did, subtle as it was. Louis could see that look of curiosity cross a stranger's face as he tried to figure out his race. The frank stares he would get when someone tried to reconcile his brown skin with his pale gray eyes. The box—check one—on his college application that asked: White, Black, Asian, Hispanic, and, at the bottom, Other. He had left it blank.

Bessie came out of the room, closing Lila's door softly. Her face was coal black, with full cheeks and large, white teeth. Her hair was a mass of black ringlets and she always wore brightly colored muumuus over her ample figure. The sparkle in her eyes kept Louis wondering what secrets she held.

"You hungry?" she asked.

"No, ma'am."

"Y'all don't eat enough, Louis Kincaid. You need to put some meat on those bones. I cook for you and you sit up here and eat . . . peanut butter," she said, wiping a smudge of it from the corner of his mouth.

Louis smiled. "I don't want to be any trouble."

"And you don't do nothin' but work," she went on. "You're a good-lookin' man, Louis, and if I was twenty years younger, I'd put you on a plate and sop you up with a biscuit."

She let loose a hearty laugh, and Louis joined in.

"You need a good woman," she said, "somebody to fill your belly and warm your bed. You want I should find you someone?"

"I can do my own finding." Louis grinned. "Thank you."

"Jus' tryin' to help." She turned to go down the stairs.

"Bessie," he called, "I need to ask you something."

She paused, hand on the railing, waiting.

With a look back at Lila's door, Louis took a few steps closer to Bessie. "You knew my mother," he said. "You knew how she was, how she treated me. Why did you call me to come here, Bessie? I have nothing to give her."

Bessie shook her head slowly, and something in her expression made Louis feel ten years old. "You're wrong there, Louis Kincaid," she said. "All good sons take care of their mamas. It don't matter what she done or what you feel. You jus' do what needs to be done." She started down the stairs but turned, her face set in a frown. "A black man who turns on his mama ain't nothing but a nigger." Without waiting for his response, she went down the stairs, leaving him standing alone.

He stood there for a moment, taken aback by the admonition in her voice. Finally, he went back to his room, closing the door softly. The room was warmer and he took off his robe, sitting on the edge of his bed in his boxer shorts and T-shirt. A part of him was angry at Bessie for trying to make him feel guilty. He had to come back. In the end, it had been his decision. But God knows, he sure felt out of place here.

It was strange. Here he was, surrounded now by more people of color than ever in his life, yet he felt like a visitor to an alien planet. But in a way, these people, the blacks who shared this neighborhood, were no more his people than Lila was his mother. Maybe he was the one who was the alien.

He went to the window and idly parted the thin curtains. He gazed down at the street, busy with traffic coming and going at the four-way stop. Rusted old cars with black plastic covering broken windows cruised in front of the house. Children played in tattered, open jackets. Despite the cold weather, they wore shorts and laceless sneakers over bare feet. Michael Jackson's *Beat it* blasted from a passing car filled with teenagers.

On the corner was a two-story building with a large metal sign on the roof that read TINKER's GENERAL STORE. Faded advertisements on the side for Coca-Cola and Lucky Strikes, told him the store had been there for decades. Kitty-corner to Tinker's was a ramshackle gas station with two pumps, covered by a rusted aluminum awning. Weeds poked through cracked cement. Next to that was a weathered mobile home, flat tires still attached, children playing outside on discarded furniture.

The scene was typical of small towns across the South. He had learned that much during the drive from Michigan. The thought, mingling with memories of the bones in the shallow grave, left him depressed. What a haunted place Mississippi was, the air thick with ghosts and history. He gazed down at the street. Even on these four corners, there was history—enough to write a book.

History . . . history. He straightened, frowning slightly as the realization hit him. He had been thinking about what the sheriff had said; that no one would talk to him about the lynching. He had been trying to figure out where to start his investigation, and here it was, right under his nose. If he wanted to find out about Black Pool's history, all he had to do was step outside. He threw on some jeans and a navy-blue University of Michigan sweatshirt, and hurried down the steps of the boardinghouse.

The sun was setting through the remnants of stormclouds, and the black branches of the trees stretched up into the pink sky. The cool air felt good on his face as he jogged across the street to Tinker's General Store.

The coffee-skinned girl behind the counter eyed him as he came in. Louis had been in the store several times for peanut butter and Dr. Pepper, but had never spoken to her except to say thank you.

Louis strolled to the back, looking around. There were fresh vegetables piled in a cooler against the back wall. Lima beans—called butter beans here—greens, sweet onions, okra and, of all things, artichokes. Next to that was a shelf lined with small hardware items such as nails, screws, and lightbulbs.

He stopped at an old metal drop-in cooler and slid back the door. It held small white cups and he reached it and picked one up. It was light and he lifted the lid slowly. It was just dirt. Oh, man . . . a worm. Earthworms. Christ. He put it back and moved on.

He passed a cooler full of soda pop: Southern Lightning, Mountain Dew and Dr. Pepper. Then came the milk, eggs and butter. Louis noticed there was no beer or wine. That was unusual for a convenience store, but then again, this wasn't a convenience store, it was a country general store.

He made his way back to the counter. Next to the register there was a huge jar of pickled pig's feet and a display of Red Man chewing tobacco. Behind it, amid the usual NO CREDIT and NO

CIGARETTES SOLD TO MINORS signs, were homemade clocks, carved out of what looked like the middle of a tree. They were all different, some with blooming magnolias painted on them and others with shellacked photos of the Mississippi River or country streams. They were quite beautiful, Louis thought, and he found himself wondering how much they cost.

His eyes fell upon a needle-stitch with a solitary flower embroidered in the middle of a white cloth. Underneath it said, BLOOM WHERE YOU ARE PLANTED.

The young girl finished waiting on a woman, then came out from behind the wood counter. Her oversized black sweatshirt hung to the knees of her scrawny legs. She wore black spandex pants and tiny slip-on shoes. Her hair was pulled back into a ponytail that sprouted into a bouquet of finely woven braids, each fastened with a different-colored clip.

"You need some more Jif?" she asked, hand on a hip that jutted to the side.

"Is the owner here?" Louis asked politely.

"Who wants to know?"

"My name is Louis Kincaid."

"You're that cop. You workin' for the sheriff," she said, her brown eyes narrowing. "My granddaddy ain't done nothin'."

"I didn't say he had. I just want to talk to him."

"He don't got nothin' to say to you, either."

"How about if we ask him that, okay?"

The girl spun away. "Can't get no peace. If it ain't white ones, it's black ones. We don't take kindly to *any* color cop, you know that, don't you? You hear what I'm telling you, mister?"

"Teesha, mind your tongue," said a baritone voice from the back doorway. A large man filled the door, his face the color of pumpernickle bread, his body clad in bib overalls. A frayed straw hat shadowed weary eyes behind wire-rimmed spectacles.

Louis extended his hand. "My name is Louis Kincaid."

"I know who you are," Tinker said, ignoring the outstretched hand. "What do you want?"

"I just want to talk to you, if you have time."

Alfred Tinker nodded to his granddaughter and she went back behind the counter.

"On the porch?" Louis offered.

"Suit yourself."

Tinker followed Louis to the porch, and when Louis sat down in one of two wooden rockers, Tinker remained standing. Louis looked up at him. "Please, sit down."

"You're in my chair."

Louis slid over to the other chair. Tinker sat down and the rocker began to squeak as he put it in motion.

"Mr. Tinker, I'm a police officer—"

"I know who you are."

"Well, okay, the other day—"

"I know about the bones too."

"Then maybe you can help me." Louis leaned forward.

"With what?" Tinker stared at the cars coming and going at the stop sign.

"I need some information about the past, Mr. Tinker, and I was hoping, since it's obvious you've been here for some time—"

"And what makes that so obvious?" Tinker interrupted. "The fact that my name's on a run-down store in the worst part of town?"

"No, I didn't mean that. I mean— I meant . . . I assumed you were well established in Black Pool, grew up here, that's all." Louis sighed. "Mr. Tinker, about the body—"

"I can't help you with your dead man."

Louis waited but Alfred Tinker continued to stare at the street, rocking.

"Then tell me about the sixties," Louis pressed. "What was it like here then?"

"If you don't know that, you should be ashamed to call yourself a black man."

"I'm not sure I call myself anything, Mr. Tinker."

For the first time, Tinker looked at him. The stare was so cold that Louis looked away.

"I know what I read about the sixties," Louis said after a moment.

Tinker returned his gaze to the cars. "The *Man's* version, Mr. Kincaid, the *Man's* version."

"All versions," Louis said.

The rocking stopped suddenly. Alfred Tinker faced him again. "And what did you learn? If you learned anything at all, you learned some things don't change."

"One thing can change, Mr. Tinker, right here, right now."

"How?"

"With the man who died."

Tinker resumed rocking. " 'Liberty and justice for all,' right?"

"You could call it that."

"*You* call it that."

Louis stared at Tinker's profile. He ran a hand over his eyes and leaned forward. "Mr. Tinker," he said softly but firmly, "a man was murdered, a black man. What do you want me to do? March around in front of the state capitol with a protest sign? I am trying to do something, in my own way, by talking to you. I'm a policeman. This is how we get things done."

"You're a token, Mr. Kincaid. You're living in a white man's world, breathing his air, working for *his* justice. You don't know about us. You don't even know about yourself."

Louis was so stunned he couldn't think of a reply. He stared at the old man with a mix of anger and frustration. He rose slowly. "I believe there's such a thing as justice," he said.

Tinker gave him a soft, mirthless laugh. "You should have marched with King. He was a dreamer, too."

"Dreams can become realities."

"*Reality, justice, history* . . . just words. You want to know about history, just look around you. This is reality, this pestilence spreading like cancer. This"—he said, motioning toward the run-down street—"is your history."

"I need your help, Mr. Tinker, I need to know what things were like then."

"Things don't change, Mr. Kincaid. When you've been here long enough, you'll understand that. You'll understand the fear. You'll feel it, living inside you, always there, like footsteps that follow you home at night."

Louis shook his head. He was getting nowhere. He rose and started down the steps, then stopped and looked back at Alfred Tinker. "You don't think I'll find out who did it," he said. "You don't think I'll solve it."

"You might find out who the dead man is," Tinker said, "and you might even find out who killed him. But you'll never solve it, Mr. Kincaid. Because what you're trying to solve isn't a crime. It's a state of mind."

"So you're saying I'll never find out the reason."

"You look for reasons where none are to be found. You'll never find the answer because you don't know the question."

Louis was tired of Tinker's ambiguities. "I don't understand," he said with a sigh.

The steady squeak of the rocking chair blended with the sound of crickets and passing cars. "You will," the old man said, "when you hear the footsteps."

After a restless night of dreams filled with Alfred Tinker's ramblings, Louis rolled out of bed, feeling as if he had gotten no sleep at all. He went about his perfectly choreographed morning routine. He turned on the radio, which poured out the usual local news, highlighted by death notices, times of funeral services, and the lunch specials at the River Bottom Cafe. After a quick shower, he dressed, ignoring the crisply pressed khaki uniform in favor of gray slacks and a white dress shirt. He was tying his tie as he hurried down the front steps of the boardinghouse at exactly eight-thirty.

The station was quiet, as usual. Mike, one of the other day-shift deputies, hovered over the latest issue of *Fish and Game* with Junior, both men sipping coffee from Styrofoam cups. The third deputy, Larry, sat at a corner desk, legs up, thumbing through *Hustler*, one of the dozen skin magazines from the cache he kept in a bottom drawer. No one looked up or said hello, but Louis had gotten used to it by now. In the three weeks since he joined the Black Pool sheriff's department, the other deputies had kept their distance, never openly hostile but never friendly, either. Sheriff Dodie had told him there never had been a black man on the force before, offering it as something of an explanation that Louis should understand and accept.

Louis often found himself missing the easy camaraderie he had enjoyed back in Michigan. He had been one of only three black cops there, and while the force had its share of bigots, he had never felt the sting of being an outsider. The bond among cops somehow transcended color. It was not the same here.

Louis went to the coffeepot and poured himself a cup. He glanced back at the three deputies with a vague feeling of unease. It wasn't that he feared these men; he just had no way to relate to them. Junior was stupid but not dangerous. Mike was young, green-as-grass, and would probably be friendly if he weren't so influenced by Larry. Larry . . . he was a piece of work. There was something about the man that brought a knot to Louis's gut. Larry was fairly quick-minded, but there was a tension about him, like something inside was wound too tight. Louis sensed a meanness in the man, a meanness that went soul-deep.

"Well, lookie here."

Junior was standing at the window, parting the venetian blind to look out at the street.

"Hey, Larry, your girlfriend's back," Junior said, his voice childishly taunting. Larry looked up from his magazine.

"It's Miss Abigail Lillihouse," Junior said. "Come home for Christmas from college."

Larry didn't get up, but his neck craned to the window.

"Goddamn, she's lookin' good," Junior went on, whistling. "Those pretty little boobs jigglin' in that pink sweater. Larry! Quick, she's leaving! Why don't you go ask her for a date?"

"Fuck you, Junior," Larry said, from behind the magazine.

"Larry has the hots for Miss Abigail," Junior said to Mike, grinning. "There was a picture of her in the paper couple years ago, when she was Homecoming queen, and I caught Larry in the john with it, pounding his pud."

"I said shut up!" Larry shouted. Mike stopped snickering. Louis looked up. Larry shot up from the chair, threw Louis a cold look, and bolted from the office. Junior and Mike looked at each other and shrugged. After a moment, they were lost again in the pages of *Fish and Game.*

"Junior," Louis said, "any word from the lab in Jackson?"

A voice came out of the huddle. "The report's on your desk."

"What about the M.E.?"

"The what?"

"The medical examiner."

"Oh . . . they ain't done with the bones yet."

Louis sighed. "Sheriff in?"

"Nope."

"Any calls?"

"Nope."

"Anything happening?"

"Nope."

Louis set the cup down on the old pine desk. The desk's edges were rounded with age and the scarred top bore testimony to years of cops' doodles. Louis pulled on the top drawer, looking for a letter opener and as usual, the drawer stuck. He hit the top to release it, thinking for the hundredth time what he wouldn't give for some decent equipment. Even a fax machine would help bring the department into the 1980s.

He gave up on the drawer and picked up the heavy manila envelope. He tore off the top, then carefully took out the chain and the book that had been found at the grave, still secured in plastic and labeled.

Now, why had the lab sent back the evidence along with the report? He looked back at Junior, tempted to ask him if this was standard procedure for the Mississippi state crime lab when dealing with a rural area. But he didn't want to admit he didn't know procedure. Most labs stored their own evidence until the city or county needed it for trial. But then again, most departments worked within their own jurisdiction, with the lab being part of the process. This place . . . well, that was another story.

He put the necklace aside, grabbed his glasses from the pencil holder and started to read. The shreds of clothing had traces of blood. The threads of the pants were denim, the shirt cotton. The necklace turned out to be silver, but it was severely tarnished and chipped. They had cleaned it, but the embossing was still undistinguishable. He set the report down and picked at the necklace with a paper clip, but his efforts were futile. The necklace needed to be in the hands of an expert.

He was very careful extracting the book from its protective wrapping. He laid it gently on the desk, pulling the gooseneck lamp closer. Then he sat back, looking at it. It bothered him the lab had sent this back so soon. How could they be done with it so quickly?

"Junior," Louis called out, "do we have latex gloves?"

"In the first-aid kit, over there."

Louis rose and opened a cupboard. He found the kit and dug out a pair of surgical gloves. As he went back to his desk, tugging them over his hands, Junior followed.

"What's with the gloves?" Junior asked. "They already done looked at it. What difference do gettin' prints on it make now?"

"I don't know," Louis said softly, studying the book. Even under the bright light, the cover was unreadable. The report said the lab had been unable to raise the title. But then, the entire report was peppered with one word: *Unknown*.

It seemed an odd size for a book, about eight inches in height and five inches wide, and not very thick, maybe a hundred pages total. Bits of frayed material suggested the cover might have been light gray or beige.

Louis could hear Junior breathing behind him. He glanced over his shoulder. "Don't you have something to do?" Louis asked.

"I guess the sheriff must've told them not to worry about this stuff, eh?" Junior said.

"What do you mean?" Louis asked.

Junior shrugged. "They don't usually send stuff back unless someone says we done closed the case."

Louis felt his muscles tense. Closed? Already? He turned back to the report. *Unknown. Unknown. Unknown.* He couldn't imagine a lab being so incompetent as to not come up with anything better than this. Had Dodie told them to just slide it through? Was it over before he could even get started?

He sighed and gingerly opened the book. The spine cracked softly. The first few pages were cemented together by mold and threatened to fall apart in Louis's fingers. He knew he should leave further examination to an expert but someone else might not look deep enough. He focused his attention on the middle of the book, where he was most likely to find a legible page. He picked at the brittle pages with a paper clip and finally found a page of readable script. It was less than half a page, but it was something. Eagerly, he examined the words.

> *Ask night how*
> *To be   lost*
> *   the feeling of cold*

Farther down the page, he could make out more words.

> *day   feels to be light*
> *Exposed so all may see,*
> *   sharp of   the sun*
> *The glare of intensity.*

More mold and dried mud. The edge of the page crumbled like ashes in his trembling fingers.

> *fears that torture the dark,*
> *And days*
> *Ask me how   to be both*

That was all there was. Louis scribbled the words on a legal pad, then he sat back. Junior was reading over his shoulder.

"Now what are you doing?" Junior asked.

"Trying to decipher this."

Junior peered at the book. "What is that shit?"

"A poem. Or bits and pieces of one."

"A poem? What's a dead guy doin' with a poem? It don't make no sense."

The phone rang and Junior returned to his desk. Louis leaned back in his chair, locking his hands behind his head. What was a poor black man doing with a book of poetry? And who had buried him? Certainly not a sentimental Klansman. Louis stared at the poem's broken words, wishing he had paid more attention to his college literature classes. Well, Junior was right about one thing. It didn't make sense.

"Jesus fuckin' Christ!"

Louis looked over his reading glasses. Junior was standing, clutching the phone, his face so white the freckles looked like measles.

"Somebody get the sheriff on the horn," Junior sputtered. "Jesus fuckin' Christ, we got us another one."

CHAPTER 4

"Man, oh man, two bodies in less than a month," Junior said, wheeling the Blazer around a sharp corner. Louis braced himself as the truck squealed off the asphalt, its rear tires kicking up dirt from the shoulder.

"Junior, slow down."

Cow-splattered pastures flew by. An armadillo waddled across the highway ahead of them, coming within inches of being another Mississippi roadkill.

"Hey," Junior said, deliberately swinging the car to scare the poor thing. "Why did the chicken cross the road?"

Louis gripped the armrest. "Okay, why?"

"To show the armadillo it could be done." Junior cackled at his own joke.

Louis smiled. True enough.

The siren wailed, an unnecessary formality since on a Sunday morning there were probably more armadillos than people on the county road.

This body, they knew, was fresh. The hunter who called it in had been nervous and the details were sketchy. The hunter, named Wilbur Hardage, was waiting for them at his farm ten miles east of town. When they pulled into his long, fenced drive, Junior finally killed the siren and slowed to a respectable speed. He skidded to a stop on the man's gravel drive. Wilbur Hardage, still dressed in his camouflage jumpsuit, hurried over to the Blazer and climbed in back.

"Which way?" Junior asked.

"Take this here road down thataway and keep going till I tell you to stop."

Staying on Wilbur's farm, Junior drove across the pasture, and plunged the Blazer into a wooded area much like the land where they had found the first body, only drier. Louis and Wilbur gripped their seats as Junior bounced the Blazer over rocks and streams.

"Junior, for crying out loud, why are you so anxious to see this one when we couldn't drag you out of bed for the first one?" Louis asked, bracing himself against the dash.

"Now I got a real taste for it, ya know? Kinda excitin'."

Wilbur called for him to stop as the Blazer leaped into a small clearing, and Junior slammed on the brakes. The Blazer did a 180 before jolting them to a stop. Louis took a deep breath and pushed open the door.

Sunlight streaked into the small clearing from behind high clouds, warming the crisp morning air. Louis slipped off his jacket, leaving it on the seat. He grabbed his bag and closed the door. Wilbur was walking toward the center of the clearing, Junior on his heels. Louis called for them to wait.

He hustled to catch up to them and then saw the body. The man lay spread-eagled in the yellowed grass, face-up, a rifle just inches from his right hand.

"Stay back," Louis said, moving closer, careful of his steps as he scanned the ground. He knelt by the body. He swallowed hard to bury the bile rising in his throat and took short, steadying breaths.

It was a white man, fortyish, with gray hair and a chubby face. The eyes were still open. He wore standard hunting apparel, camouflage shirt, hat, pants, and a thin tie-around orange vest. There was thick mud on the heels of his black boots. In the center of his forehead was a round, black hole, about the size of a dime. The cap was tipped back off his head, stuck in the blood that had coagulated beneath the skull. Parts of the hair and scalp lay globlike on the grass.

Louis touched the corpse's skin. It was cold. He bent down, put his nose to the barrel of the rifle and sniffed. It did not appear to have been fired.

"Junior, grab the camera and the tape and call this in," Louis said. "I want Davis out here within the hour. No Sunday bullshit this time, either." Still on his knees, Louis looked around the pasture. The man's head lay toward the forest they had just driven through. His feet lay to the north, fifty yards from where the forest resumed. Louis looked up at the trees and back at the dead man.

Junior came up behind him and caught sight of the hole in the man's head. "Oh, man," he muttered. "That's terrible, that's really god-awful, Louis. I guess maybe I ain't got a taste for this shit after all."

Louis glanced up at him, surprised at the display of emotion. "You can't do anything for him," Louis said quietly. "Rope off the clearing."

He turned back to the body. The man had fallen backwards, shot from the trees to the north. The wall of pines that circled the clearing was thick and dark.

"Louis," Junior said. "I called for Davis. He's on his way. Reckon we'll need an autopsy on this one?"

Louis nodded as he circled the body.

"You want a *real* medical examiner?"

Louis stared at him. "As opposed to what?"

"As opposed to old Doc Reichard."

Louis couldn't believe what he was hearing and his expression must've showed it.

Junior hesitated. "I guess that means you want a real one. I'll call the funeral home."

"What for?" Louis asked.

Junior stepped forward, seemingly pleased to be explaining something techical. "Rotatin' mortuaries," he said. "Each gets a turn when we get a dead body, you know how it goes. The body goes to whoever's turn it is and then some guy from Jackson comes up and does his stuff."

Louis hung his head.

"Detective," Wilbur called from the truck. "You think someone got 'im by accident?"

Louis hesitated, forcing his attention back to the body. The wound was from a large-caliber gun, .30-.30 maybe. A likely caliber to hunt with but how the hell could another hunter not see someone in the clearing? There wasn't a tree or bush within fifty feet of the body. But then again, the shooter could've been a good distance away, back in the trees, unaware his shot claimed a life.

"Junior, you alive yet?" Louis called.

"I'm okay, Louis. I got the tape."

"Start with the perimeter. The trees form a neat circle. And watch your step. I'm going to those trees over there." He stood up. "Mr. Hardage, do you recognize this man?"

"No, sir."

"I do," Junior said, looking away from the body, unrolling the tape. "I didn't realize it at first, but it's Earl Mulcahey."

"He got family?" Louis asked.

"Wife, two kids, grown now, in school, over at Mississippi State. I grad-jeated high school a few years before his son, Leverette. Louis, this is gotta be an accident. I mean, ain't nobody wanna kill Earl."

Louis walked toward the north trees, following a set of worn tire tracks, scoping the grass for anything of significance. He tried to stay in line with what he perceived as the path of the bullet, checking his progress over his shoulder. He reached the thicket and ducked into it, turning every few feet to maintain eye contact with the body. It would be impossible to find a casing in this brush. He could be off only by inches and miss it. And with all the hunters who frequented these woods, it would be impossible to determine anything specific. But still he looked.

About fifteen feet into the forest, still in line with the tire tracks, he came to another clearing, this one much wider and longer. A different set of tracks spanned this area, stopping at the edge of the forest where he stood. These were fresh. The grass around them was smooth and untouched. He ventured out a few feet. He would cast these tracks, he decided. It had not rained since Friday and they appeared to be the freshest set.

He looked up. In the tree above him was a platform, what hunters called a deer hide. He backed up to get a clearer look at it. It was just large enough for two people. He reached up and grabbed a limb, hoisting himself up. It wasn't until he climbed his way to the platform that he saw the one-by-twos nailed to the other side, forming a tenuous stepladder.

Louis kneeled on the small structure, facing the first clearing, alert not to touch anything. He could just make out the spot where Junior and Wilbur stood. Louis could see the bright yellow tape Junior was draping around the scene. Louis turned to face the larger pasture. He could see a highway off in the distance.

Louis climbed down and walked back to the body. Junior was taking pictures now and Hardage was sitting in the truck.

Louis stood at the head of the body and walked away from it, measuring his steps, stopping to look back at the hide and at the body several times. The head was blown open so wide in back, the bullet must have passed straight through. Where was it?

Louis did a light search of the area, stepping around any footprints, but saw nothing. Maybe the bullet was embedded in the ground. Perhaps it would turn up when the search team came out. Hardage called to him from the truck window. "Detective, I think somebody's callin' you on the radio."

Louis walked back to the Blazer and keyed the mike. It was Larry.

"Louis, a fellow by the name of Jacob Armstrong's on the line. Says he's an M.E. outta Jackson. Says your labwork and the report on your bones are in. Do you want him to overnight it, or will regular mail do?"

Louis paused. He thought of the skimpy report on the book and medallion. Maybe if he went to see this guy Armstrong at the state lab, he could find out more. He glanced at his watch. "Tell him I'll drive down to pick it up later today," he told Larry. It was early. Once he was finished with the Mulcahey scene, there still would be plenty of time to make the trip to Jackson.

The road to Jackson was wet and slick. Rain sprinkled the Blazer as it whipped along the Natchez Trace, once an ancient trail, now a blacktop lined with heavy shade trees and spotted with sneaky state troopers. Louis turned on the red light to avoid unnecessary delays.

Junior lit a cigarette. Louis looked over and sighed. "Please open the window."

"It's rainin', and it's fuckin' cold," Junior replied. The smoke curled around the car with nowhere to go. Louis cracked his own window and the smoke slithered out.

"Why we going down here anyway?" Junior asked.

"I told you, I want to talk to him in person."

Junior shook his head. "You don't really think you're gonna solve this bones case, do ya? Sheriff don't think so, you know. He tole me jus' the other day, he said, 'That old Louis there, he gots high ideas about this case, but he's wrong.' "

"Oh, he did. What else did he say?"

"Jus' that you got these fancy ideas about gettin' your name in the papers and all. Nobody really cares about some long-dead nigger. No offense, Louis."

"Junior, what do you have against me?"

"You think I got something against you 'cause you're black. You're wrong there. Black folks, they have rights, too. They have a right to go to school and git jobs. They—you—whatever, are just part of our society, see? We get along all right, but it's a lot easier if everybody, you know, keeps their place, Louis."

"And where's my place, Junior?"

"That's just it, Louis. Folks like you, maybe they ain't got no place. Cain't hang with us, cain't hang with your own. That's what we keep tryin' to tell you folks. You're a living example of what happens when you break God's laws of nature. Now, black folk in general, I got no problem with. I mean, black folks gotta have someone who can walk into their part of town and kick ass, without gettin' his head shot off." Junior paused, ruminating. "I got no problem at all with black folk 'cept those that think it's okay to mix. That's what my daddy taught me, and that's the way it should be. If'n I ever had a son, I would teach him the same thing."

"What if you had a daughter, Junior?"

"Whatcha mean?"

"What if you had a daughter who found herself a black man?"

Junior shrugged. "Well, I'd just have to shoot the fucker, Louis."

God knows, the bastard probably meant it, Louis thought.

The car fell silent. For the rest of the drive to Jackson, the only sound was the rain beating on the windshield. Downtown, Louis found the county building and parked. They hustled through the rain to the entrance.

They found Jacob Armstrong in the medical examiner's lab. He was young, not much older than Louis, dressed in green scrubs and white Nikes. His sandy-blond hair matched an amateur goatee, and he had eager blue eyes behind brown horn-rimmed glasses.

"Glad you could make it, Mr. Kincaid," Armstrong said, rising from his stool as they came in. "I don't have a lot of time, but I know you're in a hurry. You know how long these things take sometimes, especially this type of—"

"You mean a lynchin' like this?" Junior interrupted. He stuck out his hand with an air of self-importance. "Officer Resnick."

Armstrong peeked over his glasses at Louis then tentatively shook Junior's hand. "No, not the style of killing, but the age of it," he said. He looked back at Louis and smiled. "Most of the staff is wrapped up in that big case on the Gulf, triple homicide, so this kind of fell in my lap. I'm new, proverbial low man on the totem pole, and usually end up twiddling my thumbs on the big ones. But I found your case fascinating."

Louis followed Armstrong across the room, glad the bones had fallen into the hands of someone who cared. Junior yawned and leaned against the wall, stuffing his hands in his pockets. Armstrong stopped at a box. Inside were the bones, ready to be shipped back to Greensboro County. Louis reached in and picked up a long, discolored one, gently holding it in his hand.

Armstrong smiled. "There is nothing quite as disquieting as the feeling that comes when you hold another human's bone in your hand, is there?"

Louis turned. "No, there isn't. He was black, wasn't he?"

Armstrong looked at Louis oddly. Louis fingered the curve in the femur, then glanced at Junior. "You guys have straight ones," he said.

"Is that how come you all can jump higher?"

Smiling, Armstrong moved on to the report. "Although I can't prove it, I'd say you were right on the cause of death," he said. "It would seem to be a hanging. The neck wasn't broken, though. The rope had minute particles of human skin. Even found a strand or two of African-American hair. It was a male, probably fifteen to twenty years of age, about five-ten or -eleven." He was reading off his report. "One arm was broken—my guess is at the time of death—and he had a deep wound in the skull. And a fracture along the jaw. The teeth were in good shape at the time of death, which also indicates a young man: wisdom teeth unerupted. No dental work. Didn't need any. And . . . oh, we have a congenital anomaly in the left hand."

"Like a deformity of some kind?" Louis asked.

"Yes, present from birth," Armstrong said, "At first glance, the third and forth digits would appear as if they ended at the knuckle." Armstrong adjusted his glasses to read the report. "Other bones were missing, but that's expected in wilderness bodies. The clothes ..." Armstrong paused. "Or rather the threads, were unremarkable. Denim pants, judging from the studs, and a cotton shirt. T-shirt material, I think. I don't believe he was wearing a jacket. The zipper or buttons would have been here. By the way, that tarp saved us a ton of evidence, you know. So, if the T-shirt is any indication, he was probably killed in the warmer part of the year."

"How long ago?"

Armstrong sighed. "To be sure, you'd have to do a carbon-date on him."

"I don't guess there's a university here with that capability?" Louis asked.

"No," Armstrong said. "It's Washington or nothing. And last I heard, the turnaround is four to five weeks. We can send something and try it, if you want."

"Yeah, do that," Louis said.

"That cost money, Louis?" Junior asked.

"No, Junior. Slow as it is, it's free." Louis turned back to Armstrong. "Mr. Armstrong, what's your guess?"

"My guess is twenty years or better."

Twenty years. 1963 . . . 64, Louis thought. Not a good period to be poking around in. "Anything else?" Louis asked.

"I was hoping for a wallet or keys. Or even jewelry. But no such luck. No ID whatsoever."

"Just the necklace and the book, " Louis said.

"I didn't handle that. You have the report on that yet?" Louis nodded. "Nothing there, either."

"Too bad. Nothing here that would help you identify him. Most of the marks on the bones were perimortem." Armstrong looked back at Junior. "Inflicted at the time of death. I'd guess the guy was pretty healthy before he was murdered."

"Did you run any tests that could determine disease or any other unusual condition?" Louis asked.

"No, we didn't. We could, but I doubt it will show anything."

Louis sighed, thinking about the vagueness of the lab report on the book and medallion. "I was just hoping for more."

"Listen, I just had a thought," Armstrong said. "I know a woman in Florida who does forensic sculpting. You know, reconstructing a face from the skull."

Louis turned to face him, excited. "I'd like to talk to her."

Junior rolled his eyes. "Louis, man, the sheriff—"

"Don't worry, I'll take responsibility. Can you give me her name and number?"

"You take all the names you want, Louis," Junior said, "sheriff ain't never going to approve this move, no sir." Junior nodded at Jacob Armstrong. "You ship those bones right back to Greensboro County, and Louis and I are outta here."

Armstrong looked at Louis then back at Junior. "Well, what is it going to be, gentlemen?" he asked finally.

Louis jerked his detective shield out of his jacket pocket and slammed it on the stainless-steel counter. "I'm in charge here and I say the skull gets a holiday in sunny Florida."

"Look here, Mr. Armstrong," Junior said, pushing himself off the wall and coming forward, "Louis here don't know it, but that badge don't mean shit. You do yourself a favor and just pack them bones up nice and neat and Fed-Ex 'em to Black Pool."

Armstrong bit back a smile. "Sorry, Deputy. Last time I watched *Hill Street Blues*, detectives outranked deputies. I'll call her today, Mr. Kincaid, and arrange it. I should tell you, sometimes this takes quite a while. And it can be expensive. Like I said, this isn't a high-profile case."

"I understand," Louis said. "And thanks for your help."

They were barely out the glass doors before Junior grabbed Louis's shoulder. "What the hell you think you're doing?" he demanded.

Louis shrugged out of his grip. "My job," he said, hurrying down the steps.

"Your ass is in big trouble now, Kincaid," Junior called after him. "I don't know where you get off thinking you can do what you want here."

"I'm an investigator."

Junior caught up. "In name only. You think the sheriff would have given you this job if he'da known who you were?"

Louis stopped, his hand on the car door. "What do you mean?"

Junior hesitated, pulling his hat down against the rain.

"Junior, what are you talking about?"

"Nothin'."

"Don't tell me, 'Nothing.' Dodie knew who I was. I sent him a résumé. I was interviewed."

"Yeah," Junior said uneasily, "over the phone."

Louis stared at Junior over the top of the car. Junior wouldn't meet his eyes.

"He didn't know you was black," Junior said.

Louis turned away, shocked. Slowly, the shock gave way to fury. What the hell difference did it make? Shit, he knew what difference it made. He had just forgotten where he was.

He jerked open the car door and got in. Junior slid into the passenger seat. The rain grew into a downpour, beating down on the windshield.

"He didn't know, Louis," Junior repeated. "I mean, it's not like you talk black and all."

Slowly, Louis wiped a hand across his wet face, struggling to contain his anger. " 'Talk black' . . . Jesus," he muttered.

"And then when you got here, well, what could he do?" Junior went on. "When you walked in, in that fancy suit, we all thought you was some N–double-A–CP lawyer."

Louis said nothing, his mind traveling back to that first day.

"Then when Uncle Dodie found out, man, I thought he was gonna shit," Junior said.

"Junior, shut up."

Junior sighed. "I'm jus' tellin' you how it is, Louis."

Louis put both his hands on the steering wheel, staring out at the gray county building, misshapen by the rain. "This place stinks, Junior, you know that?"

Junior looked hurt and scratched his temple. "I don't think it's so bad, Louis. I like it here. I was born here."

Louis started the car. "So was I," he muttered. He swung the car out into traffic, heading back to the freeway.

"Louis?" Junior said after a few minutes.

"What?"

"Don't tell the sheriff I done tole you."

Louis glanced over at him. "Why not?"

Junior shrugged. "I don't know. I jus' don't want him to think I can't keep a secret."

CHAPTER 5

It was near eight by the time they got back. Louis dropped Junior off at the station then headed back to the boardinghouse. As he slowly drove through town, he replayed in his head Junior's remarks. He was tempted to quit, to say, The hell with the whole thing. But the fact was, he couldn't afford it.

As he drove, he thought about the string of events that had led him to the job. After Bessie had called him about Lila, he had gone to his lieutenant to ask for a leave of absence from the force. "Your mother . . . that's tough, man," his lieutenant had said. Louis hadn't told him the truth, that he didn't know the woman. He said only that Lila wasn't expected to live long. But the truth was, neither he nor Lila's doctor really knew how long she would last. Could be months, the doctor had told him by phone.

It was Bessie who suggested that Louis look for temporary work in Black Pool. "Call your cousin Charles," she told him. "He works for the mayor. He know where the jobs are."

Louis hadn't known he even had a cousin. He called Charles Devlin, asking about police work. Charles sidestepped, offering information about the logging company and the city sanitation department. It was only after Louis pressed that his cousin said he had heard about an opening in the Sheriff's Department. Louis fired off his résumé and within a week got a call from Dodie.

"We're a small department here, Mr. Kincaid," the sheriff had told him over the phone. "I gotta say, I don't know what a law officer needs with a college degree." Nonetheless, Louis could tell by the man's voice that he was impressed. "But we're looking for some new blood, a new attitude, and a fresh approach. The fact that you was born here, well, that's a nice plus now, isn't it?''

Dodie had offered him the job as the Greensboro County Sheriff's Department's first investigator. The title meant that while he wouldn't have authority over the other deputies, he would have more decision-making power as far as the police work went. And the pay was higher, Dodie said proudly, $150 a week—although he cautioned Louis not to mention that fact to the others. The pay was ridiculously low, but Louis was willing to overlook that. His dream was to be a detective, and that could take years on a large force in the North. A stint as an investigator, even a short one, would look good on a résumé.

He could still remember vividly the first day he walked into the sheriff's office. He wasn't a fool; he knew things would be different in the South. A black guy back on the force in Ann Arbor had worked in Birmingham and had warned him that "it took some getting used to," but that the other cops had treated him with respect.

Louis sensed something very different that first day in Black Pool. First there was the stunned look on Mike's face when he told him who he was. Then came the hard stares from Larry and Junior, stares that immediately told him he was not merely a stranger here—he was an intruder. Junior had disappeared into the sheriff's office, and Dodie had kept him waiting a half hour before finally asking him to come in. Dodie's expression was harder to read, but Louis could almost imagine his thoughts: *Oh shit, what am I going to do?* They got through a few moments of small talk so painfully awkward that Louis fully expected Dodie to tell him to turn around and go home. But finally, the sheriff had thrust out a hand and said grimly, "Welcome to Black Pool."

Louis pulled the Mustang to a stop at the curb outside Bessie's house. Man, he was smarter than this. He should have realized things would be worse in a place like Black Pool. There was racism in Michigan; there was certainly racism in the South. But he should have known that the smaller the town, the greater the magnification would be.

Louis cut the engine, his mouth twisting in a rueful half smile. Dodie had said he wanted new blood, a fresh attitude. Well, he certainly had gotten it. Hell, it didn't matter. These weren't his kind of people and this wasn't his kind of place. He didn't plan to spend one day more in Black Pool than he had to. But for now, he and Dodie were stuck with each other.

Bessie was still awake and called to him when he came in. He hung up his damp jacket on the hall tree and went into the living room.

Bessie called it "the parlor," and it was a warm room, like the rest of the house, even though the children who had filled it with laughter were long gone. Tiffany-style lamps illuminated the corners and sheer Priscilla curtains billowed over each window. Rugs that had seen the feet of Bessie's grandparents covered the polished hardwood floors.

Bessie was sitting in her usual chair, reading the newspaper. "You look tired, Louis," she said, setting the paper aside. "Come sit with me for a while."

He dropped into a lumpy sofa. Bessie got up and padded off to the kitchen, returning with a cup of coffee for him. He thanked her, gripping it in his cold hands.

"Your mother was awake today, Louis. She asked for you."

He took a sip of the coffee. "I'll go see her . . . in a while."

She hesitated, as if she wanted to say something. Finally, she went back to her chair and sat down. The room was silent except for a muted clang from the furnace deep in the basement.

"Louis?"

"Hmmm?"

"It don't do no good to keep things bottled up inside you."

"I'm not bottling up anything, Bessie."

"Then why you avoiding talking to your mama, Louis?"

He didn't answer. When he looked up, it was right into Bessie's eyes.

"I knew you when you was just a child," she said gently. "I've known your mother since we were little. What happened to you was a sorry thing, dear Lord, but you can't carry all that anger, you just can't."

Louis looked away.

"She needs you now," Bessie said softly.

He shook his head slowly. "Well, I needed her once, too, Bessie. And where was she? Hiding in a bottle."

"Louis . . . Louis."

He set the coffee cup on the table, feeling a wave of fatigue wash over him. It had been a long day, first finding the new body and the trip to Jackson and back. He didn't mean to be abrupt with Bessie, but he didn't want to talk about Lila now.

"It wasn't easy for you, Louis, I know that," Bessie said.

"I don't believe in looking back, Bessie," Louis said.

"I know. But everyone's got a past, some more hurtful than others, and it ain't healthy to run from it. If you do, it'll just keep following you around, like a ghost." He could feel Bessie's eyes on him. "There comes a time, Louis, when a person's gotta just stand his ground and face it," she said.

When the furnace went off, the drafts quickly took over the old house. Louis shivered slightly.

"You want more coffee?" Bessie asked.

Louis shook his head slowly, staring into the cup. It was several moments before he spoke.

"What was he like, Bessie?"

Bessie didn't have to ask who Louis was asking about. She shook her head derisively. "Jordan Kincaid was trash, Louis, jus' like all Lila's men. Your sister Yolanda's daddy was trash, too, I suppose. He done took off, too."

Louis sat back against the cushion. Bessie's bare honesty hurt, yet somehow brought him relief at the same time.

"Why?" Louis said softly. "Why, in the fifties, in a place like this, did a black woman get herself hooked up with a white man?"

" 'Cause she didn't know no better. Or maybe she did and she just didn't care. But it didn't work, Louis. Neither of them could take the meanness." She paused, looking at Louis sadly. "Jordan Kincaid wasn't your father in any real way, Louis. He hung around long enough to seed you and then he was gone, like he had gotten a taste of her and then he went on to the next one. That man left you nothing but a cross to bear." She smiled slightly. "That and those gray eyes of yours."

And the name Kincaid, Louis thought, even though he knew that Jordan and Lila were never legally married. Interracial marriages had been illegal in Mississippi in the fifties, and remained so until 1967. Louis carried the name Kincaid because that's what Lila had put on the birth certificate. She used the name Kincaid to this day, just as he did, even though he had been raised by the Lawrences.

Empty spaces, there were so many empty spaces in his memories. And questions, so very many questions. He had managed to keep the questions buried all these years, but the spaces were getting harder to ignore.

"What happened when he left?" Louis asked.

Bessie shook her head. "I can't say, really. When Jordan came into the picture, your mama changed and we kinda lost touch. A black woman and a white man, it just wasn't done, and there was a lot of meanness . . . a lot of meanness."

Bessie paused. Louis waited.

"Things got worse after you was born, and neither of them was strong enough to take it. Jordan left, and your mama was never the same after that, Louis. I think maybe she just gave up." Louis thought about his sister Yolanda and his brother Robert. He thought about Frances Lawrence and her willingness to accept a strange child into her home. "Why were we taken away from Lila?" he asked Bessie.

Bessie shifted her bulk uneasily. "Things was real poor for you children. Lila was drinking and wasn't fit to tend you. It got so bad, we just couldn't help no more. Yolanda went to your aunt Jenny, and Robert was took in by your mama's grandma, till she passed, and then by a friend."

Louis looked deep into Bessie's eyes and knew the answer to his question before he asked it. "Why was I the only one put in a foster home?"

Bessie heaved a huge sigh. "I don't know how else to say it, Louis." She paused, rubbing her hands. "It was 'cause you was half white."

His eyes held hers for a moment, then he lowered his head, resting his elbows on his knees. "You were ashamed of me," he murmured. "Weren't you?"

"No, Louis," Bessie said softly. "We wanted the best for you. We just didn't know what else to do."

"Yeah . . ." he muttered.

Bessie slowly got up from the chair. She went to the bookcase, pulled out a large volume and came back to sit down beside Louis. "I want you to see this," she said, spreading it open on her knees.

From out of the old photo album, the face of a beautiful woman looked back at Louis. In the sepia-toned photograph, he could see the sparkle in her dark eyes, a lovely seductiveness in her smile. A satin ribbon curled downward to her shoulder from black curly hair.

"Your grandfather had this taken when Lila was eighteen," Bessie said, running her hand over the plastic covering. "He wanted to send it off to magazines and movie studios, but there was little call for black actresses back then. I remember he said it cost him three weeks' pay. It's yours, if you want it."

Louis stared at the photograph. He did not remember his mother like this. It was too stark a contrast to the sloppy drunk he knew. He took the book from her and closed it gently. "You keep it, Bessie," he said. "You obviously see more in it than I do."

He stood up, and Bessie grabbed his hand. "Things was hard back then," she said. "People get tired and selfish and do weak things."

She paused, her eyes soft. It almost looked like pity, and Louis felt both touched and uncomfortable. "You have strong convictions, Louis," she said. "And that's good in a man. But a man gotta have forgiveness to go with that. Let God do the judgin', Louis, not you."

Louis looked down at her hand holding his own. "I don't know why I'm here, Bessie," he said softly.

"Jesus knows, Louis," Bessie said. "Jesus has brought you here for a reason. And if you open your heart, he will show you that reason." Her fingers tightened around his. "Your mama is dying. Now is the time for forgiveness. Pray with me, Louis."

He looked down into her face, then gently pulled his hand away. His eyes went toward the staircase. "Is she awake?"

Bessie shook her head. "The medicine has put her to sleep. She'll ask for you again in the morning."

He felt suddenly tired to his bones. He nodded and took a step away. Hesitating, he bent awkwardly to kiss Bessie's cheek. "Good night," he said.

He went quietly up the stairs and paused outside Lila's door. Hearing nothing, he went into his room, closing the door behind him.

Junior knocked on the door and then stuck his head into Dodie's office. Dodie was on the phone and looked up, a pained expression on his face. He covered the mouthpiece with his hand.

"What you want?" he asked in irritation.

"We gotta talk, Uncle," Junior said.

Dodie frowned and motioned for Junior to sit. He turned his attention back to the phone.

"Yeah . . . yeah . . . I heard ya, Walt," he said. He reached for his cigar and propped the phone on his shoulder while he fumbled for his lighter. "I don't need you hollerin' at me about this." He ran a hand over his eyes. "Yeah . . . I won't." He hung up loudly.

Junior propped his feet up on the sheriff's desk and leaned back in his chair. "That the mayor?" Junior asked.

Dodie gave him a long, withering look. "He's riled about those damn bones. Wants to know what we're doing about them."

"We ain't doing nothing," Junior said, pulling a toothpick from his shirt pocket.

Dodie looked at him oddly, then went back to searching for his lighter.

"Listen, Uncle, we gotta talk about Louis. It's important."

"Not now."

Junior let the chair thud back to the floor, and leaned forward. "You gotta do something about him, Uncle. I'm telling ya, he threatened me."

"I can't see Kincaid threatening nobody."

"Well, when we was in Jackson, he pulled rank on me, right there in front of everybody."

"You were probably provokin' him, Junior." Dodie started rummaging through a drawer. "Now, I keep telling you, Kincaid is here, whether you, or me—or anybody in this town—likes it or not. So I want you to just shut up and deal with it, for the time being at least."

Junior got up from the chair. "But you should have seen the way he talked to me in front of that lab guy—"

"And I suppose you did nothin' to make yourself look like an ass, did you?" Dodie said sarcastically. "I suppose you conducted yourself like a fine professional jus' to show those Jackson boys that we're not the hicks they think we are."

"Uncle Dodie . . ."

Dodie jerked open another drawer, still looking for the lighter. "I don't need you jawing at me about Kincaid, Junior," he said, cigar clenched in his teeth. "Need I remind you that this is an election year. The sheriff is an elected official of this town. You know what I'm saying, Junior? No Sheriff Dodie, no Junior."

Junior leaned forward, jabbing a finger at Dodie. "I never thought I'd see the day when a member of my own family would let a nigger walk all over him," Junior said angrily. "I'll tell you something, Uncle, you don't put him in his place now, it'll be Sheriff *Kincaid* next fall."

"Don't you point at me!" Dodie slammed the drawer shut, making Junior jump back from the desk. "Goddamn it, where's my fuckin' lighter?!" he thundered.

A tap on the glass made Dodie look up at the door. Dodie could see the outline through the frosted glass.

Louis poked his head in the door. "Good morning, Sheriff. Figured you'd want to see me."

"Yeah, come in. Sit down, Kincaid." He glanced at Junior. "You too."

Junior slumped into a chair. Louis hesitated, then sat down. The sheriff set the cigar down in the ashtray.

"All right, Kincaid, what's this about some lady in Florida drawing some picture?"

"She's an artist who can reproduce what she feels is a likeness of a victim based on the skull," Louis began. "I've heard about the technique before, and that it can be very accurate. I thought it was worth a try. Junior disagreed. He thought you'd be upset about the expense."

The sheriff looked over at his nephew and ran his fingers through his hair. "How much is this gonna cost?"

"They're supposed to let me know. If necessary, sir, I'll be happy to partially reimburse the county for any extra expense."

Dodie shook his head. "Not necessary. Maybe it's time we got with this state-of-the-art stuff. I'll allow it. But next time, I expect to be asked before we go sending our dead halfway across the country."

"But Sheriff," Junior sputtered, "this is stupid. This is just a dead—"

"Junior, shut up," Dodie said. He looked back at Louis. "Now look, Kincaid. I told this to Junior here, and I'll tell it to you. I don't ever want to hear about my men—of any goddamn rank— going into another jurisdiction and arguing about how we do business. You understand?"

Louis nodded.

"Now get back to work."

Junior stormed out. Louis heard the outside door shut a few seconds later, relieved that he would not have to deal with Junior today. He would go home and pout, all on county time.

Louis rose slowly from the chair.

"Sheriff, thank you for okaying this. It means a lot to me."

Dodie looked up. "It seemed like the right thing to do," he mumbled. "But you run things like this by me from now on, you hear?"

Louis nodded. He turned to leave, spotted something on the floor and picked it up. He set the battered Zippo lighter in front of Dodie. "You were looking for this?"

Dodie picked up the lighter. "How long were you out there listening, Kincaid?" he asked without looking up.

"Long enough."

Dodie leveled his hard, gray eyes at Louis. "Things ain't always what they seem to be, Kincaid," he said. "You remember that and you'll be okay here."

Louis started for the door then turned. "Sheriff, I don't want to be here any more than you want me to be here. But as long as I am here, you'll get my best work."

The two men stared at each other. "Fair enough," Dodie said finally.

"Didn't know they even made those things anymore," Louis said, nodding at the Zippo.

"It belonged to my daddy," Dodie said.

Louis glanced at the four-by-six-foot Confederate flag over the book shelves to the right. Dodie followed his gaze.

"So did that," he said. He flipped the Zippo's top with his thumb, lit the cigar and met Louis's eyes.

"And I just never saw no reason to take it down," he said.

CHAPTER 6

As Louis drove around the bend on County Road 234, the sunset caught his eye and he slowed to take it in. The orange sun glowed, like he imagined a UFO might do, simmering on the horizon. He realized suddenly that he couldn't remember the last time he had even noticed a sunset. Always too busy, always moving too fast. At least that's what Frances Lawrence always chided him about. From running fast on the high-school track team to finishing college a semester early. "Louis," she used to say, "one day you're going to find you rushed right through life."

Funny she should come to mind right now, he thought, smiling slightly.

He pressed the accelerator and the old white Mustang shot down the road. The Lillihouse home came into view and he slowed as he passed between two white brick pillars that guarded the open iron gate. He cruised up the circular drive and got out of the car, taking in the mansion with one sweep of his eyes.

It was a storybook home, the kind you saw in movies. White brick, fronted by a wide porch with pillars that supported an iron balcony on the second floor. Vines, naked from winter's chill, climbed the outside of the home.

He couldn't shake the uneasy feeling that rippled through him as he stood in the gravel drive, staring up at the proud house. He wasn't sure if it was the affluence or the power that the house represented that intimidated him. Maybe it was the sense of history that shrouded it. He lifted the elaborate gold knocker, embossed with the Lillihouse name, and tapped it lightly against the door.

He looked out at the expanse of lawn as he waited. The sheriff would ream him a new asshole if he knew he was here bothering old Mrs. Lillihouse. Especially after he had promised to keep Dodie informed of everything he did. But sometimes, he told himself, knocking again, you had to do what you had to do.

It was several more moments before he heard movement on the other side. Someone was peeking out the peephole and he smiled obligingly. When the door did not open, he sighed, pulled out his shield and held it up to the tiny hole. The lock clicked and it swung open.

"Yes, Officer," said the woman.

She was not young but she was still beautiful. Her honey-colored hair was drawn away from her face and twisted around her head, held by a silver clip. Her long-lashed eyes were the color of a clear Mississippi sky, complemented by a light brush of crimson on her cheeks and lips. Only the lines around her eyes betrayed that she was somewhere past forty.

"Mrs. Lillihouse?" Louis asked.

"Yes. What can I do for you?"

"My name is Louis Kincaid, ma'am. I'm from the Sheriff's Office and I'd like to talk to you for a few minutes, if you have time."

She gave him a small frown of puzzlement then stepped back to let him into the foyer. The floor was a black-and-white checkerboard marble and a statue of a half-naked Greek god frowned at him from its pedestal in the corner. Grace Lillihouse closed the heavy door softly and led the way to the living room. Glancing up at the chandelier, Louis followed her through an archway into a large room, accepting her offer to sit down. It was a library or sitting room, done in understated pinks and greens, with bookcases recessed into the dark paneled walls. Over in one corner, nestled in a bay window, was a grand piano. He could pick up the faint scent of lemon furniture polish and hickory.

"It's about the body, ma'am. . . ." he began.

"I assure you, I can be of no help with that." She slid into a green damask wing chair, the skirt of her satin lounging-robe flowing around her tiny ankles.

"I was hoping you might be able to—well, give us some information perhaps, since the body was found on your land, ma'am."

"I can offer nothing, Officer. The whole thing was quite a shock."

Louis waited. But Grace Lillihouse just looked at him blankly, with a slight tilt to her head.

He cleared his throat. "We estimate the body to be about twenty–to–twenty-five years old," he continued.

"Such a young man. . . ." she said wistfully.

"I meant twenty years in the ground, but he *was* a young man as well. Probably fifteen–to–twenty."

Grace folded her hands in her lap and looked into the fireplace. Louis could see the flames reflected in her eyes. She looked like she was going into a trance. "Do you have any idea who it is?" she asked quietly.

"Not yet. Mrs. Lillihouse, were you living here in the early sixties?"

"Yes, but I was only a girl, Officer."

"But were you living here?"

"Yes, I was born in this house." Her voice wavered slightly. She continued to stare at the flames.

It struck him that Mrs. Lillihouse was like a porcelain doll; she sat so stiffly he thought her face would crack. He had to get her to relax somehow. He glanced around the room, debating how to continue. He locked eyes with a portrait above the fireplace. It was of a striking man with silver hair and gentle eyes. Louis thought he resembled the actor Jimmy Stewart.

"Handsome man," Louis said. "Your husband?"

Her eyes moved to the oil painting. "My father," she replied.

Louis sensed a bitterness in her voice and decided to drop the subject. He continued to look around. To either side of the fireplace were recessed cherrywood shelves, crowded with books of all sizes and colors. The two green damask wing chairs sat within warming distance of the fire, sharing a round, glossy antique table with a crocheted doily. There was a small crystal lamp and a porcelain figurine of a long-skirted girl with golden curls, arms outstretched as if awaiting a lover. Daintily-printed pink flowered wallpaper added a homey touch to the room, but there was still something empty about it. The house reminded him of a mansion you had to pay money to tour.

His eyes fell on the piano. A slender Baccarat vase sat atop it, holding two white lilies. Maybe if he could get her to talk about herself, she'd relax a little. "That's a beautiful piano," he said. "Do you play, Mrs. Lilllihouse?"

Her gaze drifted to the piano and away. "No," she said.

He suppressed another sigh, his eyes going now to the shelves of books over her head.

She noticed and seemed to emerge from her gloom. "Do you like to read, Officer Kincaid?" she asked.

"Yes, but I never have the time. I've hardly opened a book since college, and I've been pretty busy since I've been here. How about you?"

"Not as much as I would like." She smiled. "Do you have a favorite author?"

"No, ma'am, not really."

Grace moved to the bookshelves. He waited politely, wondering if he should keep her talking about books; it seemed to loosen her up a bit. He thought about the poem.

"Do you know anything about poetry, Mrs. Lillihouse?"

"Some. Why do you ask?"

Her back was still to him as she ran her fingers along the spines of the books.

"We found an old book of poetry with the bones."

Her hands paused at a book. "Really?" She pulled the book and carried it to him, looking more like she was floating rather than walking.

"You might like this one. Have you read it?"

He looked down as she placed the book in his open hands. *The Golden Apples* by Eudora Welty. He hadn't read it.

Grace smiled. "You'll like this," she said. "I have never read a book that gave a better feel for the texture of Southern life."

"Thank you. I'll try to find time to read it."

"Don't forget to return it to me."

"No, ma'am." He put the book under his arm.

Grace studied him. "You're not from the South, are you?"

"I was born right here in Black Pool. But I was raised in Michigan."

"Is it a culture shock for you? I mean, do the blacks here live differently than those up north?"

He was surprised by her candor. "People in general live very differently here than 'up north,' as you call it. Here, they're very . . ." He searched for an appropriate word.

Grace finished his sentence for him. "Traditional."

"I suppose you could put it that way, ma'am." He heard his

voice, which sounded so strangely formal that he almost smiled. There was something about Grace Lillihouse that forced graciousness.

"Mrs. Lillihouse," Louis began, "do you remember ever hearing anything about a killing or maybe about someone who disappeared from around here, about twenty-five years ago? Talk among the men, maybe a rumor?"

"Of course not," she whispered. "We didn't talk about things like that. Things like that happen to other people."

He let the comment go. "Do you have any idea why someone would have chosen to bury this man on your land?"

Her lips drew into a tight line. Her long robe was iridescent in the flickering light of the fire, and her face took on an amber glow. She looked very young at that moment. Transfixed by her quiet beauty, he found himself staring. There was a gentleness about her that put him both at ease and on edge.

"Officer," she said, "we have over twenty thousand acres. We could have a hundred bodies buried out there and not know it. Maybe at the time it just seemed like a good place to bury someone."

"Mrs. Lillihouse, it's important to me to give this man his just due. I don't think he was given much of a chance in life, and I think we owe him that."

She tilted her chin upward and turned to him, about to speak when a door closed loudly in the hall. A voice echoed from the foyer.

"Mother?"

Grace Lillihouse's beauty paled in comparison to that of the young woman who entered through the archway. Louis got up from his chair.

Bright green eyes dominated her pale, heart-shaped face. Long, silky auburn hair bounced off her shoulders as she tossed her knapsack to the floor. She wore an oversized banana-yellow sweatshirt that slipped casually off a slender shoulder. Black leggings detailed shapely legs.

She moved across the pale pink carpet and greeted her mother with a cool kiss. Louis guessed she must be the daughter Junior had been kidding Larry about. He tried to remember her name, but couldn't.

She gave him a quick look of curiosity before turning to her mother. "The library was deserted. I was able to get a lot of studying done," she said, rubbing her neck. She faced Louis and smiled, drawing Grace forward.

"Abby, this is Officer Kincaid. This is my daughter, Abigail, Officer Kincaid. She's a student at the University of Florida."

"Louis Kincaid," he said, offering his first name and his hand. "Christmas break?"

She looked down at his hand and then took it tentatively. She gave him a shy smile. "Yes. And long overdue," she added. "You're a policeman?"

"Sheriff's Office."

She met his eyes, looking up at him from under wispy bangs. She had a spray of faint freckles across her nose. "What brings you to see Mother?

"He's asking me some questions, Abigail," Grace said, "about that poor dead man they found."

Abby's smile faded. "You found him down by the swamp. That's our land. I used to ride through there."

"The man's been buried for more than twenty years," Louis said. He glanced at Grace Lillihouse. "I was asking your mother if she remembered hearing anything that might give us a lead to his identity."

Abby turned to her mother. "Do you?"

"Of course not. Abby, go put your things away and change your clothes."

"Mother, I would like to stay and talk to Officer . . . ?"

"Kincaid."

"I took a criminology class last semester," she said to Louis. "It was fascinating."

Grace's eyes hardened in a silent reprimand. Louis felt a slight tension creep in between mother and daughter. "Abigail, you have things to do upstairs," Grace said firmly.

Abigail started to protest, but seeing Grace's expression, she sighed and ambled toward the knapsack. As she hoisted it up, she looked back and gave Louis a small smile. " 'Bye," she said.

Louis watched her hurry up the steps, a faint smile on his face. He guessed she was about nineteen . . . a very young nineteen. When Abby had disappeared from the top landing, he turned back to Grace.

Her eyes were like rocks and her message was crystal-clear.

Good God, she thought he was hitting on her precious daughter. It was time to go. Hell, he had probably gotten as much as he could out of Grace Lillihouse anyway. He swallowed and let out a deep breath.

"Thank you for your time, Mrs. Lillihouse. If you think of anything, please call me. Anything at all."

She did not reply and Louis went to the door with the feeling she would be on the phone to Sheriff Dodie before he was out of the drive.

"Officer."

He turned. Grace stood rigid and her hands were balled into little fists. Suddenly she looked older. "Don't come here again," she said.

Grace Lillihouse was a puzzle. But then, Louis had come to think all Southern women were strangely paradoxical. Grace Lillihouse looked so delicate, yet he could sense a steely strength to her. She was all charm and refinement, but the moment she imagined that he was interested in her daughter, she had turned colder than a stone. Something told him there was more to her coldness than wanting to protect her daughter. Maybe she had something to hide. Maybe she was just slightly nuts. He wasn't sure. But his instincts about people had always been good, and right now they were telling him that there was something in that big white house that just wasn't right.

About a quarter mile down the road, he slowed the car to a crawl. He was not far from the place where he and Junior had first left the road to get to the bones. When he reached the spot, he pulled to the side of the road and turned off the ignition. It was quiet, except for the chirping of some birds.

He thought about what Grace Lillihouse had said, that a hundred bodies could be buried out here and no one would know it.

He got out of the car, looking around. The land on the east side of the road ran on for several miles, spotted with farmhouses and pastures. The land on the other side of 234, where the body had been found, was dense woodlands owned by Max Lillihouse.

Twenty thousand acres . . . a lot of friggin' land.

He frowned slightly, as the question that had been nagging at him for days pushed to the front of his mind. Why here? Why had the victim been killed in this particular place?

Even today, a black man had little business in this part of the county. Louis knew that the nearest house owned by a black family was miles away in Cotton Town. Twenty years ago, a black man probably had even less reason to be on this road.

It just didn't make sense.

He suddenly remembered something Grace Lillihouse had said, that maybe, at the time, it just seemed like a good place to bury someone.

Louis looked back in the direction from which he had just driven. He could see the big white house. It was only about a half mile or so away. Walking distance.

So what do you do if you want to kill a man? Drag him out to a familiar spot, a spot you could keep an eye on and protect. A place nobody would likely to be in, except you.

A light went on in the second story of the white house. He knew that he would have to question Max Lillihouse. But for now, the answers he needed weren't in that mansion. Maybe they were to be found in less obvious places. He got back in the car and started slowly down the road. After a minute or so, he passed a sign, nearly obscured by weeds. He braked and backed up. A faded sign pointed the way down a copper-colored dirt road to Cotton Town.

He glanced at his watch. It was still early. He swung the Mustang south down the mud-rutted road.

A few miles down the road, Louis slowed the car. Cotton Town could have been picked up and set down on the edge of almost any fair-sized Southern town. Most places like Black Pool had a Cotton Town, a patchwork quilt of old homes set around a focal point of a general store, church, and gas station.

Plywood shacks listed under lopsided tin roofs. Clotheslines laden with laundry were festooned from yard to yard. Skinny dogs pulled against their chains, barking at children who romped in their red dirt playgrounds.

Louis brought the car to a stop in front of a house where a man sat on a porch. It was dusk, and curious eyes peered through open windows and from porch swings as he got out of the car. Some children ran up to the white Mustang and peeked inside. Louis watched them for a few seconds and then waved to the man studying him from the slanted porch. The man nodded cautiously. Louis walked through a broken gate and stood several feet from the porch, respecting the man's territory. He introduced himself and waited for the man to respond.

"What do you want?" the man said finally.

"Information."

"What kind?"

"I'd like to talk to someone who's been here a good many years."

"No one here wanna talk to you." The man stood up. The combined stench of stale whiskey and urine drifted to Louis, and he took a step back.

"I really need some help."

The man glared at him from beneath a green baseball cap. The brown skin on his forearms was scarred with sores, and his overalls were held together by multicolored swatches.

"I can be trusted," Louis said finally.

The man pointed toward a house farther down. "Buford might talk wit ya. He likes to talk. He'll talk to damn near anybody. That's his place, the green one."

Louis thanked him, and walked through the sand and across the faded asphalt road to Buford's house, a flat green, shingled structure with several poorly constructed additions jutting out the sides. The additions were only partially completed, large sheets of thick plastic serving as walls. There was a pack of children playing around an old pickup seat in the front yard. Louis stepped on the porch and knocked lightly on the screen door.

Two dogs jumped at the screen, batted away by a big woman who came to the door. She was at least fifty, with midnight-black skin and a nest of rust-colored hair that resembled shredded steel wool. She folded her big arms across her breasts hanging low against her belly.

"May I speak to Buford?" Louis asked through the screen.

"Who are you?"

"Louis Kincaid. Sheriff's Office."

Her brows knitted. "I'll fetch him. See if he wants to speak with you. You stay put, mister."

Louis waited. He watched the kids play, small faces peeking at him from behind an old pickup seat. The woman returned and slapped open the screen door. "Buford says he'll talk to you. C'mon in and have yerself a seat. He's a 'comin'."

Louis stepped inside and scanned the small musty room as he waited. On the wall were pictures of Ernie Banks and Jackie Robinson and a frayed Chicago Cubs pennant. An ancient Zenith sat directly in front of a stained chair. The worn couch was covered with an old sheet. A man appeared in the doorway of a narrow hall and Louis watched as he teetered toward his chair.

Buford was as dark and wrinkled as a prune, with a thin patch of white hair. Although his teeth were yellow and his fingernails brittle and cracked, there was something pleasant about the man. Buford's bones cracked as he sat down, and he turned to the woman in the kitchen. "Lottie, the Cubs on yet?"

"Buford, it's December," came the irritated response. "I keep tellin' ya. Baseball don't start till spring. You wanna watch sports, you watch basketball. That's all that's on that damn TV."

Buford mumbled something and looked at Louis. "Who the hell are you?"

"Detective Louis Kincaid. I would like to talk to you."

"Turn off that damn TV, would ya? I hate goddamn basket-ball."

Louis obliged him, and returned to his seat next to Buford. "I'd like to ask you a few questions."

"What about?"

Louis explained about the body and its location. "Best estimate is that it's been there since the early sixties. I'm hoping to find someone who's been around a good number of years and see if they remember anyone disappearing around then."

"Good Lord, son, you say this man was hanged?"

"Yes, sir."

"Can't recollect anybody just up and vanishin'...'cept maybe . . .'"

Louis leaned forward.

"There was a young'un, let's see . . . maybe that was 'sixty-seven, -eight. Can't recollect the name of the family. Jus' a young'un, he was. I'll think of it, sonny. I will. I think he lived out in Sweet-water. Nice boy . . . had a weird hand."

Louis almost jumped to his feet. "Which one?"

"Right, I'm thinkin'. Strange lookin' thing. Looked like his fingers were cut off."

Wrong hand, but it was easy to confuse. "I need his name."

"I'm thinkin', I'm thinkin'."

Louis sighed, trying to be patient. He pulled the plastic bag containing the medallion from his pocket. "I have this, too."

Buford took the plastic bag and squinted at it. "Lottie! Bring me my glasses, would ya?"

Lottie brought a pair of wire-rimmed spectacles and Buford struggled to get them on. Then he peered at the medallion. "This here didn't belong to no black boy."

"Is it of religious significance?"

Buford shook his head. "No sir, don't believe so. Looks like something maybe been passed from granddaddy to son, and so on."

"Would it have been a gift?" Louis asked.

Buford pushed his lips together and contemplated the question. "More likely stolen. Probably what got him kilt. I tell ya what, there's a jeweler in town called George Harvey. He mighten tell ya more about it."

"We figure the man we found was fifteen to twenty years old."

"That'd be 'bout right. This was a young'un, he was."

"What about this town of Sweetwater? Where is it?"

"Gone. Burnt up. I only 'member him 'cause he went to my church, Charity Baptist."

"The same Charity Baptist in town?"

"Nah, the one I'm talking about burnt to the ground. Folks don't go theres no more. Fact is, all of Sweetwater was burnt. No folks left out that way now."

Louis put the medallion away and rubbed his face. "Sir, can you think of anyone else who lost somebody mysteriously?"

"Nope, lots of folks disappear. They just go. Cain't tell what happen to them."

"People just don't disappear." Louis doubted his own words. His own father had just "disappeared." "It's important to me you try to remember the boy's name."

"I'll git it, I'll git it."

Louis waited a few minutes but Buford looked more like he was falling asleep than thinking. Louis stood up, sighing. "If you think of anything else, please call the Sheriff's Office," Louis said. "Talk directly to me and not anyone else."

.

"I don't have a phone, sonny. Y'all hafta come back and see me."

"Will do." Louis shook his hand. Buford nodded sleepily and laid his head back. Louis said good-bye to Lottie and her dogs, and stepped outside. It was dark now, and colder. The kids in the street had gone inside and the neighborhood was empty, except for a couple of teenagers with a boombox on the corner. Louis could feel the vibrations of their music against his chest.

It was five-fifty when he swung into the parking space in front of Black Pool Jewelers. He bounded from the car, and pulled open the glass door to the store. Jewelry stores had always made him uneasy, like he didn't really belong. Once, when he was twelve, he and a friend were in a store like this, and the owner, a nervous white man, ran them out with a baseball bat, thinking they were going to rob him. Louis had gone looking for a gift for his foster mother. After that, he always thought of jewelry stores as places that existed only for the wealthy. This one, with its gold-plated glass cases and thick green carpeting, seemed no different.

A man in the back office spotted him and came toward the counter. "May I help you?" the salesman said.

"Yes, I'm looking for George Harvey. Is he in?"

"George Harvey is in. That's me."

George Harvey had a round face, oily gray hair, and lots of gold on his fingers. Louis pulled the necklace from the bag and laid it on the counter.

"My name is Officer Louis Kincaid, from the Sheriff's Department. What can you tell me about this?"

George looked at it carefully, turning it over and over in his stubby fingers. Louis stared at the top of his bald head for almost a minute before speaking. "Anything you can tell me?"

"It's very old. And it's real silver. Where did you get it?"

"Off a dead body. I was hoping it might help identify him."

"The bones you cops found?"

"Yes. The bones."

The jeweler shook his head. "I don't see how this could help. Surely there's someone around who can identify the dead man."

"Well, all we have is an old skull, Mr. Harvey, and I don't think it would do much good to show folks a Polaroid of that, do you?" Louis smiled.

George did not look up from the medallion and replied flatly, "I suppose not."

"Any chance of tracing it?" Louis asked, shifting his weight impatiently.

"I don't see how." George laid it on the glass. "It's just an old relic."

"You don't recognize it, then?"

He shook his head. "Never saw it before in my life."

"And you've been here a long time?"

"Almost ten years. My grandfather ran the store before me."

Louis put it back in his pocket. "Thanks anyway." When he got to the door, he turned. "Say, you don't suppose a Civil War expert or somebody like that could trace it, do you?"

"I doubt it."

"Thanks again, and if you think of anything, give me a call, would you?"

The jeweler nodded. "I will, Officer."

After Louis had left, George Harvey looked at his watch and walked to the door, locking it. Then he pulled the blinds, and returned to the counter. Standing in the darkened room, he picked up the phone and dialed a familiar number. When he heard the voice on the other end, he hesitated.

"This is George," he said. "He has the medallion."

CHAPTER 7

Sheriff Dodie turned from the window. "He went to see Grace Lillihouse?"

Junior propped his feet on the sheriff's desk and slipped the toothpick in and out of his mouth. "That's what I hear. I also hear Miz Lillihouse wasn't none too happy 'bout it, either."

Dodie frowned. "Christ, now I suppose Max'll be calling."

"When you gonna put the reins on Louis, Uncle? He's way outta line here with this case. Somebody oughta get hold of that boy and explain how things is done down here. Seems to me, Sheriff, that's your job, if'n you ask me."

"Well, nobody's asking you, Junior, so shut up. Git him in here."

Junior dragged his feet off the desk and slowly stood up. "You gonna send him out to Earl's place? Ethel's been wantin' to know about the autopsy."

"I reckon it oughta be done in person."

Junior opened the door and hollered for Louis. Sheriff Dodie sat down behind his desk and removed his red cap, slapping it against the blotter. Louis appeared at the door, and waited. The sheriff motioned him in.

"Y'all want me to stay, Sheriff?" Junior asked.

"Nooo," the sheriff said, agitated, "I don't want you to stay. Git outta here. Louis, you sit down."

Junior banged the door closed, and the sheriff waited until his shadow disappeared from behind the frosted glass before speaking.

"I understand you paid a visit to Miz Lillihouse yesterday," he said, slipping on his cap and leaning back in his chair.

Louis nodded.

"What the hell for?"

"To ask questions."

Dodie shook his head. "I told you—"

"I know what you told me," Louis replied, leaning forward, spreading his palms, "but how can I conduct an investigation without asking questions?"

"There's just a proper way to go about it."

"I'm going about it the only way I know how. I ask questions."

"Well, you're asking the wrong people, Kincaid."

"Oh, it's the right people. Maybe the wrong questions, but the right people."

Dodie took a deep breath. "Leave the Lillihouses alone."

"I can't promise that."

"Goddammit, Kincaid, do you know who you're working for?"

"The people."

"Don't get smart with me."

Louis set his jaw. "I wouldn't dream of it."

Dodie pointed toward the outer office. "There're plenty of guys out there who would've given their mama's left tit to have your job. Larry almost quit when I hired you for it instead of him."

Louis watched the sheriff chew on his cigar.

"Kincaid, things aren't the same down here as you might be used to," Dodie said. "You'd better start understanding that. You gotta take things slow and easy-like. People don't like change here much. You gotta go about it a different way."

"A different way or no way at all?" Louis asked.

Dodie blew out his smoke, long and slow. "You're pushing me, Kincaid."

Louis leaned forward in his chair. "Look, Sheriff, you and I both know your bringing me here was a mistake. But I'm stuck here, and like I told you before, I will do you a good job." He paused. "I believe that things can be better, and being a cop is the only way I know how to do that. That's why I became a cop in the first place. I'll try to do things the way you want, but I won't compromise the law. I can't work like that."

Dodie leaned his head back against the chair. "That's a nice speech, Kincaid," he said, "a real nice little speech."

Louis could feel his heart beating hard in his chest. The ceiling fan squeaked slowly above his head. Louis looked at the Confederate flag and back at Dodie, trying to calm himself.

Dodie was staring at him with narrowed eyes. Slowly, he reached over and ground the cigar out in the ashtray. He picked up a folder and tossed it across the desk toward Louis.

"Got the report back today on Earl Mulcahey," he said. "We've ruled it accidental."

Louis snatched it up and scanned it quickly. "Sheriff, we haven't even had time to investigate this yet. I haven't even looked at it."

"District Attorney Bob Roberts looked at it and says it looks accidental to him. That's good enough for me."

Louis hesitated. A medical examiner's report sent right to the district attorney? Jesus, did Dodie have any authority in this place? A better question was, did he himself have any? Louis suppressed a sigh. Now was not the time to argue. Hell, it probably was a hunting accident.

"Earl's widow needs it for the insurance," Dodie said. "Earl probably had a bunch. He sold it for a living. I want you to take a run out there and give Ethel the news."

Louis rose, taking the report. He was glad to have an excuse to get out of the office.

"Louis," Dodie called after him, "take Junior with you."

Louis walked back to his desk and called to Junior that they were heading out to the Mulcahey place. Junior was talking with Larry in the corner, and waved a weak acknowledgment. Louis picked up his radio and headed toward the door, stopping at the glass to wait.

Along the wall, from the front door to the sheriff's office, was a row of eight-by-ten photographs of former sheriffs. The gallery started in 1911 with a sour-looking, bulbous-nosed man and went all the way to 1976 when Dodie had assumed Greensboro County's most elite law-enforcement position. This was the first time that Louis had looked at the grim white faces that he passed every day. Most of the photos were in stark black-and-white, making the cops look like extras from *The Maltese Falcon*.

His eyes settled on one man, and at first he didn't know why until he read the name: Jedidiah S. Dodie. He had served as sheriff from 1951 to 1959. Louis glanced at the sheriff's closed door.

"You ready, Kincaid?" Junior asked, knocking him slightly as he brushed past.

Louis nodded and followed him out into the brisk sunshine.

The Mulcahey home was a pale yellow ranch-style farmhouse shaded by sprawling oak trees. It brought back to Louis one of his few good memories of Black Pool, the drive on Sunday to church when he was very small. Just vague memories of sitting in the back of someone's rattling car, face pressed to the window, the tight collar of the thin cotton shirt squeezing his neck. They had to drive past the white part of town to attend the Good Hope Community Church, and they had passed many of these houses. Simple, neat little places with covered porches, manicured roses and swing sets in the backyard. Places that looked like the people who lived in them were happy.

Ethel was a plump sparrow of a woman with brown hair and a colorless face. She had gentle eyes, a mother's eyes. She held the screen door for the officers and directed them toward the living room. There was a radio playing quietly from the kitchen. Louis let her sit down before speaking.

"We've officially ruled your husband's death accidental. I need to tell you, Mrs. Mulcahey, how sorry we are for your loss. I don't know what else to say. Sheriff Dodie sends his condolences as well."

Ethel nodded dully. "I still can't believe it. We were married twenty-eight years ago tomorrow. Twenty-eight years." She paused, shaking her head. "You know, that man went hunting for twenty years and never shot anything. Our boy bought him that rifle last year for his birthday . . . told him maybe it would help him finally get something." Ethel began to cry. "I just don't understand how this could happen."

Louis shifted, disquieted by the woman's tears. "Mrs. Mulcahey," he said gently, "did your husband know anyone who would want to hurt him?"

"No, no one. Earl was a good man."

"That's true, Louis," Junior said. "Everybody liked Earl."

"I just wish someone would come forward, even if it was accidental. I just would like to know," Ethel said, wiping her eyes with an embroidered handkerchief.

Louis used the time to study the room. There was a cluster of framed pictures on an end table, the largest showing Earl and

Ethel smiling, their arms around a pretty young woman and a handsome young man. The daughter and son, had to be. He looked around. There were more family pictures scattered about, on the mantel and on the walls. A needlepoint of a pond and a duck hung near the door and an afghan was spread over the back of the sofa. He was sure Ethel Mulcahey had done both with her own hands.

"Ma'am," Louis began, "is there anyone here with you, to stay with you?"

"The kids will be back shortly. They've gone into town." She continued to dab at her eyes. Louis glanced at Junior, who looked ready to cry himself.

"Junior, go out to the truck and tell the sheriff we'll be heading back soon," Louis said.

Without a word, Junior quickly left the house. Louis heard the screen door bang shut and moved to the sofa where Ethel sat, tentatively reaching for her hand. He wasn't sure she would let him take it, but she seemed to welcome the touch. She continued to cry, and after a few seconds, she leaned against him, holding the handkerchief to her face, sobbing openly. He held her silently, rocking gently back and forth, listening to the music from the radio, staring out her front window at the barren oak trees.

The scene with Ethel Mulcahey had left Louis depressed. Back on the force in Michigan, when he was a rookie, he had been given the assignment of "breaking the news" to loved ones. They had called him the Messenger. He hated the job. As often as he had done it, he had never gotten used to it.

It wasn't right, he thought as he pulled out of the Mulcaheys' drive. Even if poor old Earl had been accidentally shot by another hunter, it wasn't right that his death just be brushed off. Louis had considered asking Ethel Mulcahey more questions, but she had been too upset. Besides, a part of him was glad to put the Mulcahey death out of his mind so he could concentrate on the bones. And frankly, Dodie wouldn't have appreciated him bothering Ethel any more than necessary, and the last thing he needed from Dodie was another ass-chewing.

What he did need was a drink. It was seven o'clock, he was off duty and it had been a pretty shitty day. And though he didn't want to think about it, he felt very alone.

Louis dropped Junior off at the station and then drove back through town. He had seen a bar out on Highway 19, and that's where he headed now, suddenly determined to at least get a healthy beer buzz going.

He pulled into the lot of Big Al's, between two dusty pickups. It was a low-slung nondescript box of a building, with Budweiser signs sending out reassuring red neon glows into the dark night. He had already cut the engine when he noticed the brown Blazer parked near the door.

Shit, it was Dodie's.

Louis debated whether or not to go in, then decided that going back to his room with a six-pack from Phil's Fast Trip would make him even more depressed. He pulled himself out of the Mustang and into the crisp night air.

The smell of smoke, stale beer, and frying grease engulfed him as he walked into the bar. It was dark as a cave, but he could see the heads of the men turn toward him. He felt himself stiffen. From off in the corner came the *ping-ping* of a pinball game.

For a moment, Louis didn't move. Then, slowly, the men turned back to their drinks. Louis spotted Dodie's broad red-flannel–clad back, and went slowly up to the bar. Dodie didn't turn around, but his eyes followed Louis in the mirror behind the bar.

"Heineken, please," Louis said to the skinny man behind the bar.

"What?"

Louis started to repeat his order but changed his mind. "Beck's, then."

"Huh?"

"Bud," Louis said with a sigh.

The bartender slapped a napkin and the brown bottle down on the bar. Louis watched as the foam bubbled out and trickled down the long-necked bottle. He took a drink. It was ice-cold and tasted great. He took three more drinks before he finally looked around at his surroundings. Two burly men in parkas sat hunched over drinks at the bar staring at him, and four others were huddled at a table. A man was slouched by the pool table, eyeing Louis as he chalked his cue. In the corner, a sweaty young man wearing a Skoal cap was thrusting against the pinball machine with an almost sexual ferocity, cursing under his breath. Louis's gaze went to the back of the bar where a hand-lettered sign announced FRESH

BOILED CRAWFISH. Another smaller one hung over the cash register that he had to squint to make out. It showed the cross of the Confederate flag and the words *You Got Your X, I Got Mine.*

Louis took another sip of beer. His eyes drifted up into the forlorn gaze of the deer head above the bar, and he raised his glass in a subtle toast. There were blinking Christmas lights strung across its antlers. When he looked down, he met Dodie's eyes in the mirror. With a sigh, Louis picked up his beer and went over to stand next to Dodie.

"Can I buy you a beer?" he asked.

Dodie poured the last of his Dixie into a glass. "Sure, why not," he said, without looking up.

Louis motioned to the bartender, who set another bottle before the sheriff and then slunk off, his eyes glued on Louis.

"So, that's Big Al?" Louis asked, nodding toward the emaciated bartender.

"Never been any Al that I known of," Dodie said flatly. "That there is Dwayne."

A moment passed. Louis watched as Dodie reached into a bowl of steaming crablike things and picked one up, shaking off the juice before he brought it to his mouth. With his thumb, he popped off the head and tossed it aside. Then he put the open neck to his lips and sucked out the juice.

"What in the hell are you eating?" Louis asked, wrinkling his nose.

"Boiled crawfish."

"Bald crawfish?" Louis repeated.

"Yeah, boiled crawfish."

Louis looked back at the sign over the bar. *Boiled* . . . not bald. Jesus.

"Ain't you never had crawfish?" Dodie asked.

Louis shook his head.

"Try one."

"No thanks."

Dodie plucked out another crawfish, peeled off the soggy shell, then popped the small piece into his mouth. He pushed the bowl at Louis. "Try one," he said firmly.

Louis hesitated, and out of the corner of his eye caught Dwayne looking at him. Hell, why not? He grabbed one and looked into the bug-eyes, curling his lip. "I can't do this."

"It's dead."

Louis positioned his thumb at the neck and tried to pop the head off. It didn't budge.

Dodie leaned closer. "A real man bites off his first head."

Louis heard the bartender snickering and glanced around. A few others were watching him and he felt suddenly like he was onstage. It was a test, some sort of Southern ritual, probably.

Louis bit off the head and removed it from his mouth, laying it on the bar. It was spicy, Cajun-flavored. Closing his eyes, he sucked out the juice. God*damn*! It felt like his mouth was on fire. His throat constricted and he reached for his beer so quickly, he knocked it over. It rolled off the bar and he gasped for air to cool his burning mouth.

"Jesus Christ, what's in that?" he whispered hoarsely.

Another Bud suddenly appeared in front of him and he drank nearly half of it before he set it down. Then he heard the chuckling.

"Straight Tabasco and Cajun Joe's hot sauce. They simmer for two days in that," Dodie said.

Louis wiped his watering eyes and gulped down more beer. The laughter had softened and he met Dodie's eyes.

"So," Dodie said. "What did you think?"

Louis smiled slowly. "I think I'll stick to lobster, thanks."

Dodie's smile faded. "They ain't all that hot. Depends on how you cook 'em."

Louis nodded, noticing the other men had turned back to their business. He wasn't sure if their laughter had been cruel or friendly. It made him uncomfortable and he looked down at his bottle, thinking about his argument with Dodie earlier about Grace.

"Look, Sheriff, about Mrs.—"

"We don't need to be talking about this no more, Kincaid," Dodie interrupted. "You hearing what I'm saying?"

Louis held up a hand. "Okay, okay," he said. As he took a swig of beer, he caught sight in the mirror of the men at the table. The pinball freak had finished his game and had joined his buddies at the table. They were all staring at him. It was getting on his nerves. He could feel his muscles clenching.

"Kincaid."

He met the sheriff's gaze in the mirror.

"Sit down," Dodie said quietly.

Louis slid onto the stool next to the sheriff. "What? Am I the first black man to come in here?" Louis said under his breath.

"Nah, it's cuz you asked for that foreign shit beer," Dodie muttered.

Louis stared at the sheriff's profile for a moment, then smiled. "Yeah, forgot where I was for a second."

"You seem to do that a lot."

Louis waited, but Dodie just stared straight ahead, somberly slugging down his beer. "This place is the only bar around for fifty miles, 'cept for the joint out near Cotton Town," Dodie said finally. "They don't get many blacks coming in here. Ten years ago, you wouldn't even been allowed in here."

Louis took a quick drink. "The laws changed."

"Yeah, well, laws change. But sometimes people don't. That's all I've been trying to tell ya."

The pinball freak got up and went to the jukebox. A second later, Johnny Paycheck's twangy voice filled the dank room. *"Take this job and shove it / I ain't working here no more . . ."*

Louis watched the men in the mirror. They seemed to be sizing up Louis in a new light now that he was drinking alongside the sheriff.

"You see Ethel?" Dodie asked.

"Yeah . . . she's in bad shape."

Dodie finished his beer. "Never did have the stomach for doing that part of the job," he said, shaking his head.

Louis was debating whether to mention his experiences back in Michigan when a woman came up to the bar on the other side of Dodie. As she put a five on the bar, she glanced over at Louis. Her heavily mascaraed eyes lingered longer than necessary before she turned away. Louis stared back. She was probably twenty-five or so, and pretty in a hard sort of way. Too much makeup, but a nice smile. She paid for two beers and Louis watched her as she sauntered back to the pool table, her tight black skirt riding up slightly over her shapely butt.

"Pick your tongue up off the floor."

Louis looked back at Dodie. "Was it that obvious?" he asked.

"Forget it," Dodie said. "She's a whore."

Louis snuck another look back at the pool table. She leaned over to make her shot and wiggled her ass. "I knew that," Louis said finally.

"Like hell you did," Dodie said with a grin.

Louis took another drink. He felt the knots slowly starting to unloosen in his neck and shoulders as the alcohol worked its way into his bloodstream. His body felt as if it had been coiled like a spring for weeks now.

"Relax," Dodie said. "Have another beer."

Any other time, any other place, he wouldn't have. But he did now. And the first sip of the second icy-cold Bud tasted even better than the first bottle had. The music stopped and started again, this time Kenny Rogers, and Louis found himself mouthing the words to "You Picked a Fine Time to Leave Me, Lucille."

" '. . . *Four hungry children and a crop in the field . . .*' "

Dodie sang softly.

Louis smiled. "You've got a good voice," he said.

"Yeah, I can hum a tune or two."

"I always wished I could," Louis said.

"What?"

"Sing." Louis took a deep drink. "When I was younger, my mother—my foster mother—used to tell me that I ought to be able to sing. She told me it should have come natural, like dancing or basketball."

Dodie gave him an odd look.

Louis smiled. "My foster mother was white."

"That didn't bother you?"

Louis smiled. "We have a unique relationship. We can kid about anything. Anyway, I can't do any of the three."

Dodie smiled. His eyes wandered over the Christmas lights as he sipped his beer. "You ever been married, Kincaid?" he asked.

"No." Louis set his empty bottle out and signaled for another.

"My wife's name is Margaret," Dodie said. "She's the only woman I ever had. We've been married twenty-nine years."

"Quite a feat, one woman in your whole life," Louis said. "Ever wonder if you missed anything?"

"Sure. Every night," Dodie said. But then he chuckled.

Louis took a long, cold drink of the fresh Bud, thinking back to high school and college. From the age of thirteen he had been aware that he could draw looks from the girls. As he grew older, the girlish glances turned into seductive come-ons from women of all kinds, and he found himself with no shortage of companionship.

"But I don't have no regrets," Dodie added.

"Wish I could say that," Louis said softly. It had to be the beer. He never talked to anyone like this.

Dodie glanced at him. "At your age? Hell, if I was your age, I'd be grabbing all I could. It don't last long, believe me."

Louis ran his fingers down the wet bottle. He closed his eyes.

She had been nineteen. She had fallen in love with him, she said, but all he had really wanted from her was the sex. Hell, he had been just twenty. That's all any kid wanted at that age. Two months into the relationship she told him she was pregnant. Frightened and selfish, he denied it was his. But he knew it was.

Louis took a drink, letting the cold beer slide down his throat. A week later, he heard she had aborted the baby and dropped out of college. He never saw her again.

Louis shook his head. "I was twenty," he said, "and very stupid."

Dodie nodded. "Who isn't at that age? The point is, did you stay stupid?"

Louis sighed. "Somewhere out there, there is a woman who hates my guts. I made a mistake and I only cared about how it would affect my life, like hers didn't matter. I don't ever want to make anyone feel that way again."

"She turned you cold," Dodie said.

"Not cold. Just cautious," Louis said.

Dodie poured the last of his beer into the glass. "What was her name?"

"Kyla."

Dodie looked at Louis's bottle. "Buy you another?"

Louis nodded and Dodie motioned to Dwayne. Louis heard Dodie grunt. "Jesus Christ, there's Max."

Louis looked around, his eyes not really focusing. "Who?"

"Max Lillihouse," Dodie said, looking away.

Like everyone in the bar, Louis turned to the door. The man was just standing there in the open doorway, like a king surveying his realm. The cold blew in around him, standing his sparse dark hair on end. It was illuminated by the streetlight outside like a gaudy crown around his otherwise bald shiny head. He wasn't very tall, but with his barrel chest and commanding posture, he seemed to fill the room. As he came closer, Louis could see his ruddy face and his dark beady eyes, unnaturally bright even in the dim light. Louis found himself smiling at the absurd sight. Christ, the man was wearing a burgundy velvet dinner jacket with black satin lapels and a bow tie. He was carrying a white shopping bag with the distinctive blue Gayfer's department-store logo. This was too bizarre. He didn't look like the kind of man who came into a joint like this, but he had the distinct look of belonging.

Max Lillihouse came up to the bar, several feet from where Louis and the sheriff sat. "Give me a Chivas and water."

Max cheerfully acknowledged the two men in the parkas by first names, then turned, recognizing Dodie. "Sheriff, good to see you," he said with a broad grin. He slapped a fifty down on the bar. "Couple bottles of Chivas and a fifth of Bacardi," he told the bartender.

"Having a party, Max?" Dodie muttered.

"Just the annual thing. You know."

Louis watched the exchange. He had a hunch that the sheriff didn't know. He somehow couldn't see Dodie being invited to the Lillihouse mansion.

Max came over to stand next to Louis. "Sam, why don't you introduce me to your new man here?"

Dodie introduced Louis. When Max held out his hand to shake, Louis saw the flash of gold on his wrist and fingers. "Welcome to Black Pool," Max said.

Louis nodded politely. The man was like his handshake, overly hard with not a touch of sincerity. He thought suddenly of Grace Lillihouse. The same steeliness, covered with a veneer of gentility, was in the wife as the husband.

"Interesting time for you to be in our little town," Max said.

"How so?" Louis asked.

"The bones, of course."

"Yeah."

Dwayne brought the three bottles of booze and Max put them in the shopping bag. Max's gaze moved to Dodie. "Sam, why don't you come by the house tonight?"

Dodie looked up. "What?"

"It's been a long time since you've been there," Max said, smiling. He had big white teeth. Louis suddenly had a vision of Max Lillihouse as a young man, handsome, probably a football player. Louis realized that Dodie hadn't answered and was just staring into his beer.

"I bet it's been ten years since you've been up to the house," Max said. "What do you say, Sam?"

"It's been twenty years since I've been up to the house, exceptin' on business, Max," Dodie said flatly.

Max seemed unperturbed. "Then it's time," he said easily. "C'mon, I'll give you a ride."

Max looked directly at Louis and paused. "Both of you," he added.

Dodie couldn't conceal his surprise. "We'll pass," he said. "Thanks anyway."

Max leaned closer. Louis could smell the booze on his breath. "Look, Sam, I'd really like you both to come. There'll be some people Mr. Kincaid here should get to know."

Louis wanted to go. He was ready to meet some people and wanted to know more about Max Lillihouse. And he had enough beer in him to give him whatever courage he needed to set foot back in that house. He nudged the sheriff and Dodie shot him a look.

Max watched them both for a second then picked up his scotch and slugged it down. He tossed three dollars on the bar and hoisted up the shopping bag. "Well, if you change your mind, you're welcome to come. Merry Christmas, Sam."

After he was gone, Louis leaned over. "I would have liked to have gone."

"I know you know where it is," Dodie said.

"I'd feel better if you came with me."

Dodie turned to look him straight in the eye. "Kincaid, I have no idea why Lillihouse invited me—or you—to his damn party. I don't like that house and I don't want to think about the last time I was there."

Louis thought about asking him why but then just sighed. "Sheriff, I have no life here outside work. I'm bored. I don't want to go home. What's a few minutes? It's Christmas."

Dodie stared at him for a second then shook his head. "All right," he said, picking up his red cap. "But don't say I didn't warn you."

CHAPTER 8

The Lillihouse mansion looked like some magic fairy-tale castle. Thousands of tiny white lights covered the gate, the pillars, the front door and the wrought-iron balcony, all reflected in the brilliant sheen of the dozen or so cars parked outside.

Louis could hear carols playing as he swung the Mustang to a stop in the driveway. He glanced down at his jeans and University of Michigan jacket. It wasn't the appropriate attire, but then maybe he wasn't exactly the appropriate guest. He smiled. A part of him was going to enjoy this, the part with all the beer floating around inside, probably.

The sheriff had gotten out of his Blazer and was standing at the bottom of the porch, staring up at the lights. "Well, the eats'll be good, anyway," he said under his breath. "Come on, let's go."

When the door opened, Louis blinked in the blaze of light. Then the smells assaulted him—pine, cinnamon candles, a hickory fire. He stepped into the foyer with Dodie. Fir garlands were woven into the staircase and draped across the archway. Lights twinkled from every corner. And there, beyond in the living room, was a twenty-foot fir tree heavy with glittering lights, ornaments, gold garlands and giant pink bows, coordinated to match the pale carpeting. Presents were heaped high beneath. Swimming in the lingering haze of the beer, Louis thought it was all so overdone, so lavish, so absurdly beautiful, that he laughed.

Dodie looked at him oddly. "What's so funny?"

"Man . . . So this is what Christmas is supposed to look like." Louis chuckled again.

The maid took their jackets and they stood awkwardly in the

foyer, looking into the living room. The other guests were a kalei-doscopic blur, the men's black dinner jackets standing out in sharp contrast to the women's colorful dresses and sparkling jewels. A waiter in black wove his way through the chattering crowd with a silver tray of canapes. Another brandished a tray of fluted cham-pagne glasses. Louis glanced over at Dodie, who was standing stiffly, hands stuffed in his pants. The man looked so thoroughly ill at ease that Louis almost regretted asking him to come.

"Sam Dodie!"

Max came to the foyer, smiling broadly. "So you decided to come after all." He gave Dodie a slap on the back. "Good, good! Come on in, let's get you a drink. You, too, Mr. Kincaid."

Max led Sam to the inner sanctum, with Louis trailing behind. When they got the bar, Max pressed a glass of bourbon into Dodie's hand, but Dodie just looked at it and set it back on the bar. He asked the silver-haired bartender for a beer. Louis ordered a club soda. He felt suddenly sober, and he wanted all his wits about him.

He looked around the crowd. Had he imagined it or had there been a sudden but subtle decrease in the volume of conversation as they entered? More than a few people had paused in their conversations to stare. Others had been more discreet but no less curious.

Two men approached the bar, both in dark suits. One was tall and thin, with slick grayish hair plastered back over knobby ears. His eyes looked like blue marbles embedded in plastic skin. He had no lips and elongated yellowish teeth. Louis recognized him as Walter Kelly, the mayor.

The other was shorter, with charcoal-colored eyes and wavy black hair that needed a trim. Although he had a babyface, the horn-rimmed glasses added some maturity and intelligence. His suit was not custom-made like Kelly's. It was strictly off-the-rack, Sears all the way.

"Well, Sam, I didn't know you were going to be here tonight," Kelly said, with a forced smile.

"I didn't either, Walt," Dodie said tersely, picking up his beer. Kelly was looking at Louis and Dodie let him stare for several seconds before speaking. "You know Kincaid."

"Good evening, Officer," Kelly said coldly.

Dodie leaned against the bar and nodded toward the shorter man. "This here's Bob Roberts. He's district attorney hereabouts."

Louis shook Roberts's hand, which was soft and sweaty. Louis discreetly wiped his hand on his jeans.

"Sam has been filling me in on your case," Walt Kelly said. "It must be pretty near impossible to investigate a death that happened so long ago."

"It's not easy," Louis said with a smile.

"In fact, as I was telling Sam just yesterday, I don't know if it's the best use of manpower."

Louis's smile faded. "We do have a couple clues."

"An old book and a necklace," Kelly said with a smile. "Not much."

The medallion . . . damn. He had almost forgotten that he had an appointment in the morning to show it to a Civil War expert in Vicksburg. Louis glanced at the sheriff. He would tell him later.

"Well, I intend to keep going until I find something," Louis said.

Kelly cocked an eyebrow. "A little advice here, Kincaid. There are many ways to go about something. I do not want to see this whole thing blown up into a public fiasco-type affair, you understand me? Keep things under wraps. Be subtle. In a few days, put it away and go on."

"Things like this aren't resolved in a few days," Louis said.

"You'd be surprised, Kincaid. We'd like to see this wrapped up, right, Bob?"

The district attorney looked up at Kelly slowly, swirling the ice in his glass. "Right."

"We don't want things to drag on more than they have to, right, Sam? We have the taxpayers to consider. A lengthy investigation is money, Kincaid. Money, this county doesn't have." Kelly was staring at Dodie now.

There was a short silence, broken finally by Max Lillihouse clearing his throat. "Walt, there's someone I want you to meet—"

Walt Kelly set his empty glass on the bar. "Well, Merry Christmas, Sam," he said with a smile.

"Same to you, Walt."

Louis watched the three men drift off into the crowd, then turned to Dodie. "Nice guys," he said.

Dodie caught the sarcasm in Louis's voice. "Yeah, a regular Three Musketeers." He looked at the bottle in his hand and set it down. "You get a bill yet from that artist lady?"

Louis shook his head. "Sheriff," he said. "I've got to go down to Vicksburg tomorrow."

"What for?"

"I want to show the medallion to this man I found who knows about Civil War relics."

Dodie stared at Louis for a moment. Louis bit back his urge to argue his case. "Take Junior," Dodie said finally.

Grateful, Louis nodded. He thought about Walter Kelly, wondering if the two men got along. Dodie didn't report to the mayor, but based on the subtle dynamics he had seen at work tonight, you'd sure think otherwise.

Louis raised his glass to drink. Over the rim, he saw a woman in a green dress coming down the big staircase. She paused halfway down, spotting Louis. She smiled broadly and started toward him. At first he didn't recognize her, but as she drew closer, he blinked.

It was Abby Lillihouse. She was wearing an emerald-green satin gown that hugged her slender waist and fell full over her hips to the floor. The neckline was low, revealing her shoulders and the soft swells of the tops of her breasts. Her shiny red hair was swept up, a few tendrils framing her small face and curling down her neck. As she came toward him—no, floated toward him—she seemed to be giving off sparks of light.

Earrings . . . it was the earrings, he saw now. Emeralds set with small diamonds. He stared. Jesus, she was beautiful.

"Hello there." Her voice was the same—soft, high, and girlish. But the girl, the one in the yellow sweatshirt, was gone. This was a woman.

"Remember me?"

He shook himself out of his stupor. "Of course. Abby, right?"

She smiled. Her perfume wafted up to him. Flowers . . . What kind? Lilies? Roses?

Abby turned to Dodie and smiled. "Hello, Sheriff. How are you tonight?"

"Fine, Miz Abigail, just fine."

Louis looked over Abby's shoulder. Max was coming toward them, and he wasn't smiling. Louis stepped back slightly as Max swept Abby into the crook of his arm.

"Doll Baby, don't you look pretty tonight? Give your daddy a Christmas hug."

Flushing slightly, Abby allowed herself to be crushed to her father's chest. "Where's your mama?" Max demanded.

"With the Potters, I think."

"Why don't you go get her. Tell her Sam Dodie's here."

With a weak smile, Abby extracted herself from Max's arm. As she walked away, she gave Louis a shy smile over her shoulder.

Max watched her go. "She's a beauty, ain't she?" he said, nudging Dodie.

"She's grown up real fine, Max, a real lady," Dodie said, glancing at Louis and seeing his lingering gaze. He nudged him as Max turned back to the bar to have his glass refilled. The clinking of ice drew Louis's gaze from Abby and he watched as Max motioned for the bartender to fill it to the brim.

The man had been drinking before he came into Big Al's, and now he was half in the bag. He stared at Max's nose. With a pang of sadness and anger, he recognized the veined redness of a longtime alcoholic.

"Mr. Kincaid," Max said suddenly. "My wife tells me you were by here the other day. You were asking her some questions."

Louis could feel Dodie's eyes on him. "It was just routine."

"That's exactly what I told her." Max took a drink of scotch. "I feel I should apologize for the way she, well, overreacted."

Louis looked at Dodie. "No apology needed, Mr. Lillihouse, except maybe from me. I didn't mean to upset your wife."

"Shit, don't worry about that. Mama gets upset if the maid farts." He twirled the ice around in his glass. "But as you've probably found out, we Southerners here are a pretty private bunch."

Dodie sighed. "He ain't figured that out yet, Max."

Louis ignored Dodie. "I have had a hard time finding people who are willing to talk about the past," he acknowledged.

"Ah, the past. . . ." Max gave a cold chuckle. "Not many people like to talk about that. The past is just that. It's over, totally irrelevant, and certainly not worth digging up."

"Well, I've got a murder to investigate, Mr. Lillihouse," Louis said. "A lynching, to be exact. I think it's worth 'digging up.' "

Max stared at Louis for a moment, then his eyes darted away and he suddenly smiled. "Well, here comes Mama at last."

Grace Lillihouse came up to stand by her husband's side. She gave Dodie a smile, more of politeness than warmth. "Hello, Sam, it's been awhile."

"Yes it has, Miz Lillihouse." He shifted from one foot to another. "The house looks right pretty."

"Thank you." She looked at Louis. "Merry Christmas, Officer Kincaid," she said crisply.

No smile of any kind for me, Louis thought wryly.

"Same to you, Mrs. Lillihouse," he offered. The four of them stood awkwardly for a moment, then Grace put her hand on Max's sleeve.

"Max, Joan and Freddie are—"

"In a minute, Mama," Max interrupted. "I want to talk some more to the detective here."

Grace leaned toward Max, whispering, "I asked you not to call me that."

Max glared at her and she backed away, embarrassed. She gave Louis a nod and a small smile to Dodie. "Give Marsha my best," she said.

"Margaret," Dodie said, but Grace was already gone.

Max pointed at Dodie's empty hand. "Let me get you another, Sam."

"I've had enough, thanks."

"Mr. Lillihouse," Louis began, wanting to pick up the conversation again. "I'm curious to know what you think *is* relevant about this case."

"Nothing, far as I can see," Max said with a shrug. "We all have things we don't like to think about. Don't you?" When Louis didn't reply, Max went on. "Those bones should stay buried, just like the bad part of the South's past they represent. It's a new era."

"You want people to forget," Louis said.

"Yes," Max said, his eyes locked on Louis's. "And they always do. If you let them."

Louis smelled flowers. Abby had come up behind him. He didn't turn around, but he watched her as she came to stand next to Max. For a second, he found himself looking for a resemblance between father and daughter. It was there, barely, in the high forehead and thin noses. He realized Abby was looking at him. The room felt suddenly too full, of smells, sights, sounds.

He looked back to Max. He had a fresh glass of scotch in his hand and he was staring hard at Louis.

"Mr. Kincaid," Max said. "You are a young man and you aren't one of us."

Louis felt himself tense but decided to let the remark go.

"You can't possibly know what it was like," Max went on. "You have only the things you've read in books and the stories passed down to you from your people. Mississippi is not what a lot of people might want you to believe. It's not just crosses burning on lawns and men in white robes." He took a big gulp of scotch.

"Daddy . . ."

Louis looked over at Abby. The sparkle was gone from her eyes, replaced by a cloud of wariness. Louis watched as Max reached back and grabbed the bottle off the bar and quickly refilled his own glass.

"It's a beautiful state with good family traditions and Christian people. Don't judge us, Mr. Kincaid," Max said, raising the glass with one finger pointing at Louis. Some of the scotch sloshed out of the glass and down onto Abby's skirt. "Don't judge us just because you've read sad stories by some writer, some Langdon Hughes or—"

"I'm not judging, Mr. Lillihouse," Louis interrupted. "But I'm not forgetting, either. You might want to forget your history, but I can't." He paused. "By the way, it's *Langston* Hughes."

Louis glanced at Dodie, who was staring at him.

Abby had taken a step away from her father. Her cheeks were flushed with humiliation, her eyes sad. "He's just doing his job, Daddy," she said softly, brushing lightly at her dress.

Max looked down at her, his eyes snapping. Then, quick as a flash, he smiled. Then, incredibly, he laughed. He wrapped an arm around her shoulder. "Well, I guess you're right, Doll Baby, I guess you're right."

Max looked back at Louis. "Well, you go ahead and do your job, Mr. Kincaid." His arm tightened around Abby. "But I don't think you're gonna like what you find."

Louis stared at the fingers locked on Abby's bare shoulder and understood exactly what the gesture meant. He took a long swallow of the club soda and set the glass on the bar.

"Thank you for having me. I'd better get going."

"I'll walk you to the door," Abby said quickly, breaking loose of Max. Louis turned on his heel and headed to the foyer, knowing Abby was following, wishing she had the sense not to.

"Sir," the maid called.

He turned and saw the maid holding his jacket. He took it from her and pulled open the heavy front door. The cold night air was like a sudden splash of water on his face after the stuffiness of the house.

"Mr. Kincaid—"

He kept walking, not sure why he was so angry.

"Louis!"

He stopped and turned. She came up to him, her breath forming white clouds in the still cold air. The Christmas lights twinkled off the diamonds. Her perfume came to him again. Lilacs, it was lilacs.

"Abby, get back inside. It's cold," he said.

He turned and started toward the car. He heard the crunch of her shoes on the gravel behind him. He turned.

Her lips were on his, sudden and hard, almost knocking him backward. Her arms flew up around his neck. For a second, he was too shocked to react, but then he pulled back and took hold of her wrists.

"Hey, hey," he said softly but firmly. He gently pulled her hands down. She stood, head bowed, not meeting his eyes. He held her wrists up between them.

"Abby . . ."

When she finally looked up at him, her eyes were bright. Was she going to cry? He couldn't tell. But suddenly, the woman had disappeared. The young girl was back.

Say something, he thought. *Say something, and make it the right thing.* But before he could, a voice boomed out from the porch.

"Abby? Abby, you out there?"

It was Max. Louis looked up to the porch, thankful the parked cars hid them from his view.

"Go," he said softly. He let go of her wrists and took a step back.

"Go," he repeated.

She stood there for a moment, her hair haloed by the lights. Then she turned and was gone. From inside the mansion came the sound of laughter, floating above the carols.

CHAPTER 9

Louis adjusted his sunglasses and tried to concentrate on the road as he drove. But his head was clouded with the scent of lilacs and the lingering taste of Abby's kiss.

It had been a kiss sugared with the candor of a child. But beneath it was the spice of a woman's yearning. He knew he had done the right thing by stopping it. Despite her appearance, Abby was too young, and the last thing he needed right now was her infatuation. He hadn't imagined that look of abhorrence on Max Lillihouse's face, and he knew he needed to pay attention to what Dodie had said in the bar about forgetting where he was. He had a job to do. And getting involved with someone like Abby Lillihouse would be more than a distraction. It could be downright dangerous.

But still . . . he couldn't get the picture of her coming down the stairs in that green dress out of his head. He sighed. *Keep it level, Kincaid, keep it level.*

He tried to reach the coffee cup in its console holder. "Hey, Junior . . ."

The lump in the passenger seat grunted sleepily.

"Hand me my coffee, will you?"

With an exaggerated sigh, Junior sat up, popped the lid off the coffee and handed it to Louis. Louis took a sip, watching the road through the steam rising from the coffee.

"Where are we?" Junior said, squinting out at the bright morning sun.

"Coming up on some place called Bovina. Which exit should I take?"

"Vicksburg ain't got but two." Junior lit a cigarette and took a deep drag. "I don't know why I had to come. I hate long drives. I don't get overtime for this, you know."

Louis frowned. "Open the damn window."

Junior did, and the smoke snaked out. "And I don't know why we had to go all the way to Vicksburg to see this guy," Junior went on.

"I told you. He's an expert. I'm hoping he can tell me something about the medallion."

"Yeah, right. Where'd you find him, Louis, in the Yellow Pages under 'Civil War'?" Junior laughed at his own joke.

Louis glanced at his watch. Vicksburg was six hours round-trip from Black Pool, which is why he had dragged Junior out at seven in the morning. He wanted to be back early enough to stop off at the Black Pool Library. It would be closed tomorrow until after New Year's and he wanted to try to track down the poem in the book found with the bones. He knew it was a huge long shot, but he had no other leads.

"Sheriff know we're goin'?" Junior asked.

"Yes, Junior. I would think the sheriff knows damn near everything I do."

"Did he chew your ass for goin' to see Miz Lillihouse?"

"Yeah, he took a bite or two." Louis pulled a folded piece of paper from his shirt pocket and tossed it in Junior's lap. "Look at those directions and tell me where to get off."

"If you need my help to get off, then you got some fuckin' problems that I can't even begin to help you with!" Junior cackled again.

"Just tell me which damn exit to take."

"This here one." Junior settled back against the door, frowning. "Goddamn, Louis, you got *no* sense of humor."

Zachary Taylor's home was located just outside the graceful old river town of Vicksburg, at the top of a steep, green hill. Taylor was a descendant of the former president and had earned a reputation as an expert on Civil War–era relics. Louis had found him by calling the Vicksburg Historical Society.

As they pulled up to the house, Louis had the feeling of stepping back to the 1800s. It was an elegant, flagstone mansion surrounded by an iron fence. A brick path curled from the gate to the massive wooden door, shaded by evergreens and pines. They were greeted by a housekeeper who led them silently to a study.

The study was paneled in blackened oak with hand-carved window frames set off with lace valances. Impressive leather furniture sat on glazed hardwood floors. But Louis was drawn to the dozens of paintings and black-and-white photographs that crowded the walls. Slaves picking cotton, patrician men on sleek black horses, pale women in hoopskirted gowns lounging on verandas, black women staring out from ramshackle porches. A Confederate battlefield littered with dead, a battalion of black soldiers leading an assault on Fort Wagner in South Carolina, Lincoln riding in a carriage to his inauguration. Family, wealth, poverty, despair, victory, horror, hope. It was all there on Zachary Taylor's walls.

"Good afternoon, gentlemen," Zachary Taylor strutted into the room, sticking out a stiff arm in a friendly greeting. Taylor himself looked as if he were locked in a time warp. He had a tiny silver goatee and mustache and wore a natty smoking jacket of Scottish plaid. "How was your trip?"

"Long," Junior said, standing near the door.

Louis pumped Taylor's hand. "It was fine, sir. Thank you for seeing us on such short notice."

"No bother at all. Make yourself comfortable, please."

"This is quite a room," Louis said. "It must have taken you a long time to amass a collection like this."

"And lots of bucks, too, eh?" Junior added.

"My grandfather was a Union captain," Taylor said, "who fell in love with a Southern lady named Annabelle Pierce. She wouldn't leave her home, so he settled here. I was twelve when I found his diary among some old things. That got me started." He smiled. "Then I discovered the attic. My mother's family built this home in 1789 and two centuries of history were stored up in this attic. I used to be a teacher, but I'm retired now." He spread his arms wide. "This is what I do now."

"Quite a hobby," Louis commented.

"It's no hobby, Mr. Kincaid, it's my life." He pulled at his goatee. "Now, let's see what you have," he said eagerly.

Louis pulled out the medallion. "I've been told it was made in the 1800's."

Taylor took the medallion out of its plastic bag and went to his desk. "Interesting," he murmured as he examined it under a jeweler's glass. "Is this the only piece you have?"

"What do you mean?" Louis asked.

"This is part of a collection, you know."

Louis came over to the desk. "A collection?"

"Three pieces—with a ring and a bracelet. Wealthy families had them made by silversmiths as kind of a substitute for a family crest. The medallion and ring were worn by the man of the house for such affairs as weddings and funerals. The woman wore the bracelet. Each one was unique as each family designed its own. They were worth hundreds of dollars at the time. Very expensive for the day."

"Were they common?" Louis asked.

Taylor shook his head. "Only a few hundred were made. I myself have seen only a few pieces and just one complete set."

"Can it be traced?"

Taylor shrugged. "This one is in very poor condition. Where did you find it?"

"In the ground," Louis said.

"On a dead nigger," Junior added. "No offense, Louis."

Taylor spun around and stared at Junior. "You, sir," he said coolly, "may wait outside."

"What?" Junior said.

"You may wait outside," Taylor repeated. "The uncouth and ignorant have no place in my home." He called to someone named Tilly. A large man with arms black as oil and thick as his thighs appeared in the doorway. He wore a Hawaiian shirt that stretched tight across his powerful chest.

"Tilly, escort this gentleman to the porch. He wishes to wait outside."

"Now, wait a minute here—" Junior stammered. He looked over at Louis, expecting him to intervene. Louis merely shrugged. Tilly's massive hands clamped down on Junior's shoulder, and Junior twisted away angrily. "I can walk, thank you."

When they were alone, Taylor smiled. "Don't worry about your friend, Mr. Kincaid, Tilly won't harm him." He shook his head. "Frightening, our tolerance of inferior professionals."

Louis smiled. "I always thought the community gets the police force it deserves."

"Perhaps. Now, back to your article. Your best chance of tracing it would probably be if someone were to recognize it. Perhaps someone in your town may know it."

Louis shook his head. "No luck so far. No one's claiming it."

Taylor pursed his lips. "Well, in a way, that doesn't surprise me."

"Why's that?" Louis asked.

"Well, let's just say that owning one of these medallions isn't exactly something to be proud of."

Seeing Louis's frown, Taylor beckoned him to come closer. "I'll start at the beginning. See this design in the middle? All the medallions had them and all the designs were different." Taylor pointed to a cross and a flag. "Except for this, of course. They all had a cross and a Confederate flag."

Louis squinted through the glass. "What's that third thing there?"

"Ah, that's what's interesting. Every medallion featured a third element, unique to itself, and it was meant to represent the family trade. Your medallion here shows a sword, so my guess is this medallion belonged to a family of soldiers."

"So the sword represented family, and the flag represented the Confederacy," Louis said. "Then what did that cross represent?"

"Segregation," Taylor said without blinking.

Louis set the jeweler's glass down carefully on the desk.

"But not in the way you might think, Mr. Kincaid," Taylor said.

"I don't know how else you can think of it," Louis said with a wry smile.

"In the Old South, in the years before the war, most people thought of segregation as an accepted fact of life. For the wealthy, those who kept slaves, segregation was simply a matter of ... well, property." Taylor pointed at the medallion. "That cross was a symbol of a certain way of life. A symbol, if you will, of a way of thinking about your place in it." Seeing the look of dismay on Louis's face, Taylor added, "Some people derive great security from knowing their place in life. Which is why so many Southerners felt so lost after the war ... and why some still do."

"I suppose," Louis muttered. "You said the medallion was valuable in its time. So what did you mean when you said it isn't something to be proud of?"

"Symbols can change meaning," Taylor said. "The swastika was an ancient Sanskrit symbol that meant 'auspicious' before the Nazis corrupted it." Taylor raised his hand in a V-fingered salute. "This meant 'victory' in war before the hippies changed it to 'peace.' "

He picked up the medallion. "After the war, these fell out of favor. I think people just packed them away in trunks and tried to forget them. But early in this century, a curious thing happened. They started to surface again, worn again by rich men, but men who were different from the original owners, men who saw a different symbolism in them."

Taylor looked directly at Louis. "You see, these men didn't understand the old traditions and the reasons behind them. These were men who aspired to the gentility of the Old South but who were, at heart, simple racists."

Taylor rubbed a finger over the medallion's crest. "These became a sort of perverse symbol of a new brotherhood, like a secret handshake or some arcane ritual. To those who understood its significance, owning one of these was as meaningful as putting on a white robe—but more socially acceptable."

Taylor held out the medallion. Louis took it, looking down at the tarnished silver. "If you were looking for its owner, where would you start?" Louis asked.

Taylor hesitated. "I would start with an old family, one with historical pedigree. Look for a family with a political background, maybe wealth. But keep in mind, Mr. Kincaid, that the piece could have been stolen during the war or long after. It may be very far from its original owner. Probably is." Taylor smiled. "I'd be glad to take it off your hands. Give you a fair price."

"It's not mine, Mr. Taylor."

Taylor nodded. "I'd guess that it didn't belong to your victim, either."

Unless he had stolen it, Louis thought. Is that why he was killed, because he had stolen a necklace? Louis's eyes drifted up to the photograph of the slaves in the field. What a stupid thing to die for—a piece of tarnished silver.

Abigail swung her yellow Firebird into the parking lot of the library and turned off the ignition. She sat motionless, a heaviness pressing down on her, making any movement, even the simple act of breathing, difficult.

The parking lot was almost deserted and it was very quiet. But she could still hear the cries. She shut her eyes. And she could still see her mother's face. Her hands, gripping the steering wheel, began to shake.

It had started about one in the morning, right after the last guest had left the party. She had heard her father's voice echoing in the foyer downstairs, yelling at the maid to get out. Then a crash, as a tray of glasses fell somewhere in the house. Then more shouting, her father's voice thundering through the house as he called to Grace. *"Mama! Goddammit, where the hell are you?"*

He had found her sitting in the dark library.

Abby shut her eyes tighter as a hot flush of shame washed over her. Why hadn't she gone down there when she first heard her mother's cries? Why had she just huddled there in her bed like a coward as her father hit her mother? Oh, God, why didn't she do something?

A deep shudder shook Abby's body and she leaned her forehead against the wheel. No . . . Why didn't *she* do anything? Why didn't her mother do something to defend herself? Why did she let him hit her?

Hot, silent tears flowed down Abby's face. The hurt was back, oozing up to the surface, like blood from a wound that had never healed. The memories came back, memories of hiding under her bed as a child, listening to the breaking glass, the shouting profanity and her mother's cries. She could remember the makeup and long sleeves her mother wore to hide the marks and bruises, the stories she told to friends, putting up a face to the world that everything was all right. Her mother was so good at covering up, so good that Abby was almost able to pretend along with her. And then, as the years passed and the beatings lessened, Abby began to believe that everything really was all right. He still drank heavily, especially on holidays, but at least the beatings had stopped.

Then, last night happened. What had triggered the beating last night? The hurt was back, and with it, the old anger she felt toward her mother for letting it happen again. Why? Why? Why? It was the one word she kept coming back to. Why did she let him treat her like that? What was wrong with her?

This morning, her mother had not come down for breakfast. When Abby knocked at the bedroom door, Grace's tremulous voice came to her, telling her not to worry, that she just had a headache. Abby had tried the door but it was locked, and she had known it was to keep more than just her father out. Elaborate lies, long sleeves, and locked doors. Even Abby was not allowed in.

Slowly Abby raised her head and opened her eyes. "Oh, Mama," she whispered. "Why?"

Abby stared out the windshield of the car. She had come to the library partly as an excuse to get out of the house. She had often come here when she was younger, whenever things got bad at home, losing herself in picture books of foreign countries. Such simple tricks of escape no longer worked, but the old library still felt like a refuge.

Abby looked down at the textbooks on the seat. School was her escape now, as far away as she had been able to manage. Her father had dismissed her need to go out of state as a silly notion, but she had stood her ground. She had escaped, temporarily. But the seed of defiance still hadn't grown into any real confidence. Her father talked often of how he expected his "Doll Baby" to come back home after graduation, settle down and marry some nice local boy. Abby gathered up the books and got out of the car. Being home this week had made her realize that she was, in her own way, still as much a prisoner as her mother was.

The library was quiet, only a handful of people bent over books or roaming the aisles. Mrs. Jenkins, the elderly librarian, greeted Abby as she came in. Abby smiled and waved a hand in acknowledgement. She had known Mrs. Jenkins since she was nine, finding solace in her warmth just as she had always found her escape in the library. Mrs. Jenkins always seemed to know when something was wrong at home and often invited Abby into her office for cookies and tea. But today, Abby just couldn't face the sweet old woman. She went quickly to a table and slipped her knapsack off her shoulder. When she looked up, she spotted a familiar face across the room.

Louis was sitting at the first table, his head bent over a book. She stood there, the sting over her rejected kiss still fresh. As if he felt her eyes on him, Louis looked up in her direction.

His gaze was steady but he didn't smile. She forced herself to walk to him with a determined step. She took the chair across from him, meeting his eyes.

"Don't worry," she said under her breath, "I won't do anything to embarrass you." She gave him a tentative smile.

Louis closed his book and smiled back. "More studying?" he asked, nodding at the textbooks. He thought about bringing up last night, but it was probably best to stay on neutral ground.

Abby nodded. "I've got a term paper due in philosophy." She cocked her head to read the title of the thick book Louis had been reading. "Poetry?" she said.

"I'm looking for a specific poem," he said, "something to do with the case."

"Oh."

Louis studied her face. She looked pale and tired. Her eyes were red, as if she had been crying. He hoped it wasn't over what had happened between them—or not happened. Maybe he should bring up last night.

"Abby," he asked, "is something wrong?"

She shook her head. "Nothing's wrong." She smiled again, but it had a false brightness. "You know," she said, "maybe I can help you. Find your poem, I mean. I'm majoring in English lit."

"I could use some help," he said.

Her green eyes locked on his for a moment, and he resisted the urge to look around the room to see if anyone was watching them. Then, suddenly, her eyes brimmed with tears.

"Abby—"

She quickly lowered her head. She dug in her knapsack, pulling out a pen and a pad of bright pink paper. She scribbled something, folded it and slid the paper across the table. She looked up, her eyes bright and pleading. Then with one quick move, she gathered up her books and knapsack, rose and ran toward the door.

Louis stared after her, stunned. He reached out and picked up the paper. He unfolded it and read what she had written.

I have to talk to you about last night. Meet me on Road 490 at the turnoff to the lake in 20 min.

He stared at the paper. Her name was embossed at the top, so serious, like business stationery—but on hot pink paper. It made him think of a girl playing dress-up. With a sigh, he folded the note and put it in the pocket of his jacket, hung over the back of the chair.

Damn, he didn't need this. He didn't think he had put out any signals toward Abby. Not intentionally, anyway. Where had she gotten this idea that he was interested? Jesus, he needed to talk to her. To say something. She was a beauty, but he shook his head, thinking of one of Bessie's expressions: When trouble comes knocking, don't go answering that door. Going out to that lake would only bring more trouble.

He returned the poetry book to the shelf, then wandered through the aisles, trying to figure out where to go next with his investigation. The medallion, in its plastic, was heavy in his pocket, and he thought back to what Zachary Taylor had said that morning, about looking for its owner among old, prominent families. Well, the Lillihouses sure fit that description, and the body had been buried on their land. But where was the connection? And where was the "why" of the murder?

He found himself in the back of the library, standing before a door with a sign above it that read Local History. He peered though the glass at the dark room. He opened the door and flicked on the light. It was musty and deserted. There was a microfiche machine off in the corner. There were shelves filled with large books and newspaper binders.

"I'm sorry, you'll have to leave now."

Louis spun around. It was the dour elderly woman who had been behind the main desk when he came in. "Pardon me?" Louis said.

"You'll have to leave," she said. "We're closing."

"Oh . . . sorry." With a look at the room, Louis switched off the light and closed the door. He'd have to come back; this might be worth pursuing.

The woman accompanied him to the front door and locked the door behind him. Louis stood on the steps for a moment, looking at the sun sitting low in the sky. He glanced at his watch, realizing he was hungry. Then he thought of Abby, out at the lake, waiting for him.

Shit, he couldn't just leave her sitting out there. He had to go. He headed to the Mustang, but just as he was getting in the car, he heard the squeal of tires and a too-familiar voice.

"Louis! Sheriff wants you," Junior called from his patrol car.

Louis looked down the road, in the direction of the lake, then back at Junior. "What for?"

"How the hell do I know? Sheriff said get you and get you now."

He couldn't possibly reach Abby, and she would think he was even more of a jerk. Damn. "Junior, you go ahead," he said. "I need to stop somewhere first."

"No, sir. Sheriff said to bring you now, that it's important and can't wait. I'll follow you."

Louis let out a long breath. "All right. Let's go."

Louis's mood didn't improve when he got back to the station and saw that Dodie was waiting in his office with Walter Kelly. It could only be bad news.

Louis tossed his jacket in a chair and shook Kelly's hand. Junior followed him in uninvited and stood against the wall. Dodie tilted back in his chair, chomping on his unlit cigar.

"Sit down, Kincaid," Kelly said, dragging up another wooden chair. Louis obeyed and waited. Kelly remained standing, tugging at the lapels of his slate-gray suit. Louis noticed he had the peculiar habit of sucking in his cheeks with each breath.

"We have great news for you," Kelly said. "We've identified your John Doe."

Louis's eyes darted from Kelly to Dodie and back again. "Who is it?"

"A man by the name of Willie Johnson."

Louis held back a smile. Good move. Pick the most common black name in the South. Unverifiable.

"He was a dirt farmer up in Tanner County," Kelly went on. "The sheriff up there, Vance, remembered a fellow getting into some trouble a few years back. He'd been arrested and tossed in jail, and—well, sorry to say, son, the administration at that time was real poor in the community-relations department, and I regret to say that the young man mysteriously met his death after he was abducted from the jail by a mob."

Louis had trouble keeping a straight face. "How did you identify him?"

"Dental records."

"You're kidding." Louis suddenly remembered Jacob Armstrong's words. *"No dental work."*

"Kincaid, this is not a kidding matter," Kelly said. "You seem pretty ungrateful another county had to do your legwork for you. Sheriff Vance spent a lot of time on this, researching old records, talking to folks."

"Time?" Louis repeated. "*I* spent the time. And if you're trying to tell me some poor old dirt farmer actually had teeth, let alone dental records that were kept all these years, then you must think I'm pretty damn stupid." Louis stood, snatching his jacket off the chair.

Dodie motioned for Louis to sit back down. "Kincaid, calm down."

Kelly threw Dodie a look that silenced him immediately. Louis slid back into the chair, staring at the wood floor. Tension ate away the next few seconds. Finally, the mayor spoke.

"Look, Kincaid, we all know you have a chip on your shoulder to overcome."

"What?"

"Well, you're young and you're black," Kelly said. "And you've got a bleeding heart. Not a good thing in a police officer."

Louis bristled but remained silent.

"Now, you've been whinin' about these goddamn bones for weeks now," Kelly went on. "Sheriff tells me you spend your time visiting Civil War historians and reading damn poetry."

"Mayor—" Dodie said.

Kelly's head snapped toward Dodie. "Shut up, Sam, or it'll be your ass on the line here instead of his. If you had done your damn job, I wouldn't have to do it for you."

Dodie fell silent again, his face set in stone. Louis glanced at Junior, who was picking at his nails with the toothpick he usually kept in his mouth.

"Those bones have been identified, and his name is Willie Johnson," Kelly said. "Now, you gather those bones together, order a damn casket, and let's get this sucker buried."

"Mayor," Louis said, "I have to tell you that—"

"You don't have to tell me nothing. You got that?"

Louis thought about telling them what Zachary Taylor said about the medallion's symbolism and Jacob Armstrong's observation but remained silent. What good would it do?

Kelly reached for his long wool overcoat. "Sam, I'd like the service scheduled for January fifteenth."

"Martin Luther King's birthday," Louis said softly.

Kelly looked at Louis. "It is? Well, all the better. We'll play it for all we can. Plan the whole kit and caboodle—local paper, maybe even some of those Jackson reporters. Get some fancy black reverend to come do a nice talk on this poor bastard. It's over, as of now."

Kelly buttoned his coat. "Now, Sam," he said, "I expect a real nice memorial, you understand? I'll talk to y'all when I get back from Gulf Shores."

The door squeaked closed behind Walter Kelly. Louis stared blindly out into the street behind the sheriff's head. Dodie rubbed his face.

"Sheriff, this man isn't who they say he is," Louis said softly.

"What difference does it make?"

"It makes a big difference . . . to me," Louis said firmly.

Dodie eyed Louis for a second then turned to Junior, still propped against the wall. "Leave us alone," he said.

Junior moved toward the door, eyeing the bright pink paper he had seen fall from Louis's jacket. He scooped it up discreetly, slipping it in his pocket.

Louis waited until he left then leaned forward in the chair. "Listen, Sheriff, I'm not unreasonable. I don't expect to find out who murdered this man, but I do expect to find out who he was. That's the least I—we—can do for him."

"Leave it be, Kincaid. It don't matter who he was as long as he gets a proper burial."

"It matters," Louis said, raising his voice. "He was a man, he had a name. It matters!"

Dodie eyes snapped. "Get the damn chain and book," he said deliberately, speaking as if to a child, "and take them over to Wallace-Pickney and let Stan know what's goin' on with this memorial and all."

Louis stood up. "It's not right, damn it. It's not right and you know it."

" 'Right'? 'Right'?" Dodie said, glowering at Louis. "Sometimes you just gotta forget 'right' and do what's necessary."

Louis stared at Dodie, shaking his head. "I don't get it," he said. "You let me go to Vicksburg. You let me get that forensic sculpture done. You give me rope, like you want me to solve this thing, and then you keep jerking me back."

"Unfortunate choice of words, Kincaid," Dodie muttered.

"Whose side are you on?" Louis said.

Dodie's steely eyes stared up at him. "There ain't no sides. Just what's best for everyone involved."

"What's best? Or what's easiest?" Louis said.

Dodie stood up. "The case is closed, Kincaid. *Closed.* You got that?"

CHAPTER 10

Louis closed the book: *Attack on Terror—The FBI in Mississippi.*
He had read it before, as part of his black history course in
college, and before leaving Michigan had decided to bring it along
and reread it. He realized now that the book had been just words
before. Now . . . now he was living it.

He laid the book aside and rubbed his eyes. Lila murmured
and he looked over at her. He had been sitting by her bed most
of the evening as he read, but she hadn't stirred. He felt a heaviness
in his chest as he stared at her. Her skin was like tight leather
stretched across her hollow cheekbones. Thin strands of gray-
black hair fell limply over the pillow. There was a small pile of
photographs on her chest that rose and fell with each shallow
breath she took.

Bessie had put the photographs there. They were snapshots of
Louis's family. Bessie said that Lila, early on in her illness, had
often asked for them. Lately Lila had not been lucid enough to
see them, but Bessie still put them there every evening.

Louis pulled his chair closer to the bed and picked up the
photos. He sifted slowly through the blurred black-and-white
images. Yolanda, his older sister, standing on the porch, her hip
thrust out, arm elongated against the wooden post, her adolescent
face staring smugly at the camera. His brother Robert standing
with Lila in the dirt in front of their home. Lila wore a shapeless,
flowered frock and Robert was barefoot and shirtless in denim
pants.

Louis came to the last picture. He cocked his head, staring at
the man. It was Jordan Kincaid, his father. He was standing in
the shadows of a porch awning, wearing only baggy overalls and

a straw hat. Louis held the picture to the light, rubbing his father's pale face with his finger as if that would clear away the shadows created by the wide-brimmed hat. He could remember someone telling him, when he was small, that Jordan was blond, with powerful shoulders and an easy smile. He wasn't sure who it was who had told him. It might have been Yolanda. She would have remembered Jordan. Louis had no memories of the man, but then, Jordan Kincaid had not even stayed around long enough to see his son take his first step. Louis did remember the social worker, though, who came six years later to take them away. Yolanda had been fifteen, Robert about eleven, and he had been only seven.

Sitting in the quiet now, he recalled a faint memory of Yolanda hugging him before he climbed into the strange blue car. He never saw her again. When he was sixteen, he received a letter from her, but by then the memories of how she had mothered him when Lila couldn't had faded and he didn't miss her anymore. He had a new life.

He did not know where either Yolanda or Robert was now. Bessie said she thought they might be living down near the Gulf Coast, but she hadn't heard anything about them in five years. Frances and Phillip Lawrence had always encouraged Louis to keep in touch with his aunt Jenny. It had only been through her that Bessie had been able to find him.

Louis stared at the clapboard house in the first picture and compared it to his home in Michigan. The Lawrences had a nice house, a yellow brick trilevel with a big yard and neatly trimmed grass, a blue Doughboy pool in the backyard. He learned to swim in that pool. The house had been warm, with lots of rugs and padded furniture. He had his own room, decorated with sports awards from school and Detroit Tiger souvenirs. He loved baseball. The three of them had made every opening day for five years. Nineteen sixty-eight, the year Detroit won the Series, was his first year with the Lawrences. What a time to be a nine-year-old boy whose parents had season tickets!

He turned to look again at Lila. He was surprised to see her looking back at him. She was awake.

"Louis . . ." she whispered.

He lowered his eyes. She had said his name once before, but only as part of incoherent ramblings. He waited, tensed for another one, guiltily hoping to hear Bessie's footsteps on the stairs.

He felt something warm touch his fingertips, and looked up. There was a clarity in Lila's eyes that he had not seen before.

"Louis . . ." Her fingers closed around his. They were warm. "We had no time," Lila whispered.

Louis leaned closer. "What?"

"We had no time . . . to know each other."

Louis looked back at the floor.

"Louis, look at me."

He forced himself to meet her eyes.

"You came back to see me die," she said. "Why?"

He swallowed dryly. "I don't know."

"I did wrong. I did wrong with you and Yolanda and Robert. I know that. I did wrong. . . ."

Louis wanted to run from the room. Her fingers gripped his, surprisingly strong. He closed his eyes.

"Louis . . . talk to me."

Louis gritted his teeth, fighting back tears. "Why?" he said. He took a shaky breath. "Why the booze?"

Lila's eyes welled up. "Don't . . ."

"Why?" Louis whispered hoarsely.

" 'Cuz it was all I had," Lila said.

"You had us," he whispered.

Tears fell down Lila's hollow cheeks. "It wasn't enough."

Louis pulled his hand away.

"I done things wrong," Lila said, crying. "I done things wrong and God ain't gonna want me up there with Him."

Louis shut his eyes. It was quiet, except for the sound of Lila crying. Louis could hear Bessie down in the kitchen making dinner. She was singing softly.

"Louis . . ."

He looked back at Lila. Her eyes glistened in the thin light, pleading up at him.

"Louis, I need to know you don't hate me."

He averted his eyes. He wanted desperately to run, get out of the room, away from her, away from this place.

"I guess you can't find no words," Lila said. "You never could find words too easy."

His mind was screaming. *You weren't there, you weren't there to hear me.*

"You was my baby," Lila said weakly. "You was so pretty, you with them sad gray eyes. . . . Lordy, did we get the stares."

From the darkness of his swirling mind, the old images came now, the images of her drunkenness, her meanness, the overwhelming feeling of shame. All of it was flooding back to torture him, like those blurred snapshots. God, wasn't there one good memory? Wasn't there one thing to hang on to?

Suddenly the tears came. He couldn't stop them. They fell, warm and silent, down his face. He felt her touch on his hand again.

"Hush, baby . . . hush," she whispered.

He watched as her eyes slowly grew cloudy. The moment had passed, the lucidity gone as quickly as it had come. Lila closed her eyes, and after a few moments, her breathing deepened and Louis knew she was asleep again.

He picked up the photographs and placed them on her chest.

Bessie took Louis's plate and scraped the food scraps into the sink. Louis sat back in the chair with a sigh. He was so tired. First the long drive to Vicksburg, then the mayor's news about Willie Johnson, then the scene with Dodie. Any energy he had left had vanished up in Lila's room. He had barely touched the dinner Bessie made, but she sensed something was wrong and for once had not nagged him to eat. He wanted to do nothing more than go upstairs and crawl into bed.

"You want pie, Louis?" she asked gently.

"No thanks, Bessie." He took a sip of coffee.

"You didn't come down when things was hot. I hate giving you leftovers. Lots of folks was asking about you. Charles was here."

Louis picked up the coffee cup and over the lip, stared at the twinkling lights on the Christmas tree in the parlor beyond. "I don't think she has long," he said quietly.

"I suspect that's so," she said, nodding sadly. The furnace kicked on, sending a rumbling through the house. Bessie put her hand on Louis's shoulder, but said nothing. The gesture brought an unexpected catch to Louis's throat.

He stood up and caught sight of the sink piled high with the dinner dishes. "Want some help with those?" he asked.

Bessie smiled, shaking her head. "Get some sleep, Louis," she said.

Louis nodded. He went up the stairs and with a glance toward Lila's door, went into his room. He was just pulling off his shoes when he heard the phone ring downstairs. Bessie called out that the call was for him. He went out to the hall to pick up the extension.

"Is this Kincaid?" someone said. It sounded like a white man.

"Yes. Who's this?"

"You need to take another look at Earl Mulcahey's 'accident.' "

"What?"

"I think Earl was murdered."

"Who is this?"

"Never mind. Just check on it." The phone went dead.

Louis turned and hollered down the steps for Bessie. She came around the corner, her eyes wide. She had been listening on the extension.

"Bessie, did that man tell you who he was?"

"No, he didn't," she said. "What you gonna do, Louis?"

"I'm not sure." He rubbed a hand over his face. What the hell was that all about? He sighed tiredly and looked down at her. "I've got to go into work for a while, Bessie."

"Louis, you're so tired. Can't it wait?"

But he was gone, closing his door behind him. He was dressed and on the road in ten minutes. As he drove back to the station, his mind was trying to reassemble the facts about the Mulcahey case. It was all there in the file, and maybe he had just missed something. But then again, maybe the call was just a prank. He kept seeing Ethel's wan face in his mind. In any case, he owed it to the Mulcaheys to at least have one last look.

The station was deserted, except for Larry who was at his usual dispatcher post. Larry looked up as Louis walked past, but reburied his face in the *Hustler* without a word.

Louis retrieved the Mulcahey file, grabbed a cup of coffee and went back to his desk, switching on the small lamp. He put on his reading glasses and hunched over the file, trying to concentrate. The Chipmunks sang out from the radio on Larry's desk.

He spread it all out on the desk, the various reports and photos of Earl's body and the surrounding woods. He went to the ballistics report first.

It said Earl had been killed with a .30-.30 rifle bullet, but without the bullet Louis knew it was just a guess. A hundred other shells had been found around the site, but few of that caliber. Louis sifted through the other reports. The fiber and fingerprint results were not back, but the cast of the tire tracks found near the body were. They had been made by a wide radial tire with crisp new tread. Car tires, not truck or four-wheel-drive tires, as Louis would have expected.

"Hey, Kincaid, what you doing here?" Larry called out.

"Just checking on something."

"Fuckin' New Year's Eve, and I'm sitting here on my ass waiting for the drunks to let loose," Larry said, as he turned the pages of the magazine. "I hate being on nights."

Louis turned his attention to the photos of the body. He took off his glasses and pinched the bridge of his nose. This was useless; he was too tired, and there was probably nothing to see anyway.

Larry let out a low whistle. "Man, look at that beauty."

"No thanks. I gave up skin magazines in high school," Louis said without looking up.

"It's a gun, asshole," Larry said, holding out the page.

"Didn't know they advertised in porno magazines."

"Sure they do." Larry was shaking his head in admiration of the ad. "Remington 700 DBL. My friend Max has one of these. $600 bucks, Jee-sus. 'Course, the scope is extra. That's a month's pay for me." Larry looked over, a sneer creeping across his face. "I don't make the big bucks like you do."

Louis said nothing.

"The old lady would shoot me if I spent that kind of money on a rifle."

Louis found himself reading the same words over and over, and he wished Larry would shut up.

"You hunt, Kincaid?"

"No, I hate the sight of blood."

Larry laughed. "I thought maybe you guys hunted coons."

Louis looked up slowly and leveled his gaze at Larry. "No, that's something we leave up to you nice Southern boys."

Larry didn't move, but Louis could see the veins bulge in his neck. He turned back to the file, to one close-up photograph of Earl's head. The bullet wound was dead-on in the center of the forehead. If you were aiming at a man to kill him, you'd sure go for the center of the head. Louis frowned, staring at the photo. He reached for the ballistics report. There it was; the bullet had entered Earl's head at a downward angle of twenty-five degrees.

Damn. Louis took off his glasses. Earl hadn't been shot by some hunter prowling around nearby. He had been shot from somewhere high above ground level. He had been shot from the deer hide.

"Shit, I was up there. Why didn't I see it?" Louis whispered. He knew why. He had been too busy worrying about the bones and too eager to get back to them to argue with Dodie about Earl Mulcahey.

Someone had to have climbed up to lie in wait, as if stalking an animal, and then deliberately aimed at Earl's head. But why? Who wanted to kill Earl Mulcahey? The guy was a family man, a town saint, for chrissakes, if you believed what everyone said.

Louis grabbed a piece of blank paper and a pen. He wrote *angle* on the page. The problem, he realized, was that he had been going at this from the wrong angle. He had assumed the shooter was on the ground when he was in the trees. And he was assuming everything he had heard about Earl Mulcahey was true.

Everyone had secrets to hide, and often you had to search below the positives on the surface to find the ugly, buried negatives. The negative . . . that's where the motive was. That was one of the first things he had been taught back at the academy.

He felt a little embarrassed for having shelved this case too soon. He should have caught some of this.

Louis wrote *Earl Mulcahey* at the top of the page. Then he wrote a list: *family problems, business problems, money problems, enemies.* By all testaments, Earl had none of these. Louis glanced over at the file. There was a handwritten note attached to the front, in Dodie's chicken-scratch scrawl: *Ethel needs autopsy report.*

Louis set the pencil down and let out a tired sigh, thinking of Ethel's teary face and that portrait of the smiling Mulcaheys in her living room.

He picked up the pencil again and wrote, *insurance $$$.* And then three more words: *Why? Why? Why?*

"Cra-zy . . . I'm crazy for feeling so lonely . . . "
Patsy Cline was warbling from the Blazer's radio.

"That's what I must be—plumb crazy for letting you drag me out here," the sheriff said, glancing over at Louis as he drove.

"I needed you to see this," Louis said.

They arrived at the site where Earl Mulcahey's body had been found. Louis got out of the Blazer first, pulling a four-foot piece of cardboard and an orange hunter's vest from the back of the Blazer. He draped the vest over the cardboard and propped it against the truck. Then he grabbed a long leather case and started off across the field, leading Dodie to the deer hide.

Dodie looked up at it. "You're not expecting me to climb up there, are you?" he asked.

Louis grinned. "Need a boost?"

"Hell no." Dodie grabbed a branch and hoisted himself up onto the boards nailed to the trunk. With a few more grunts and groans, the sheriff made it to the platform, dropping against the plywood floor. Louis scaled it quickly and knelt beside him. He pulled the rifle from the case.

"Kincaid, what's the point of all this?"

Louis handed him the rifle. "Aim at the truck."

The sheriff took the rifle and aimed it. "I can't see the truck. I can only see that stupid piece of cardboard."

"Why can't you see the truck?"

" 'Cause it's the same damn color as the ground."

"But you can see the orange vest clearly?"

The sheriff picked up the rifle and looked through the scope. "Yeah, I can see the orange vest. What I still can't see is your point, Kincaid."

"Whoever shot Earl was up here. And he could see that orange vest down there as clearly as you can." Louis told him about the bullet-entry angle. "It was no stray hunter's bullet that hit Earl in the center of his skull. It was a carefully aimed bullet, shot from a scoped rifle by a very good shooter." Louis sat back on the platform. "Earl was murdered, Sheriff."

Dodie peered through the scope awhile longer, then lowered it. When he took the rifle away from his eye, his face was ashen.

"I got a call last night," Louis said. "Someone called to tell me Earl's death wasn't an accident."

Dodie shivered slightly as a cool breeze cut through the trees. Louis gazed at his rugged face, waiting for a reply. For a long time, the chirping of the birds remained the only sound. Finally Dodie spoke. "Why would anyone murder Earl?"

"Money."

"Money?"

"You said Earl had a lot of life insurance. I checked. He had over a million in life insurance. Double for an accident."

Dodie whistled. "But, Ethel . . . no way."

Louis sighed. "I know. I had the same thought. What about the son, Leverette?"

"Kincaid, I don't like this one bit."

"Sheriff, it's the oldest motive in the world."

Dodie said nothing. He just sat there, staring at the orange vest off in the distance.

"I've been thinking about this for a couple days, Sheriff, ever since the call," Louis said. "I went back and rechecked the files, all the interviews. Earl went hunting most Sundays, always in one of three spots. Leverette was here for Earl's birthday, even bought him a new gun case. It was only natural Earl would want to take it out for a test run. Do you think it was hard to figure out where he'd go . . . and then *bang*, and you're a rich man."

"Hard to believe a man could sit up here, staring down the scope of a high-powered rifle and lie in wait for his own father." Dodie paused. "But the money. . . . Ethel gets it. Or did you check that, too?"

"She gets half a million, the son gets a quarter, the daughter a quarter. We've dusted everything here for prints. Let's see what comes up." When Dodie didn't say anything, Louis added, "I think you'd better put a stop to the insurance payment, until we're sure."

Dodie nodded and gazed out over the woods. Louis started to pack the rifle back in its case.

"Kincaid."

"Yeah?"

Dodie didn't turn around. "Good work."

"Just doing the job," Louis said.

Dodie continued to stare out at the pine trees, focusing on the orange vest. "Well, I guess we reopen the case," he said. "Earl's dead, but he deserves that much."

Louis hesitated, then zipped up the rifle case. "Sheriff, so does that man in the grave," he said quietly.

Dodie turned. "Don't start on that, Kincaid."

Louis shook his head in frustration. "You're willing to reopen one case but you won't reopen the other. Why? Is it because Earl was white?"

"Don't insult me, Kincaid. This ain't no racial thing here," Dodie said.

Louis sighed. "Then what is it, Sheriff? Is it because everybody here knew and liked Earl Mulcahey, and the other man was unknown and forgotten for twenty years?"

Dodie uncrossed his legs, trying to get comfortable on the small platform. "Look, Kincaid, the cases are just different, that's all. There's a . . . point to finding out who killed Earl. I don't see anything coming out of digging up that other poor bastard's past, except maybe hurt." He shook his head. "I'm telling you for the last time, Kincaid, let it go."

Dodie's voice was firm but calm. The cold breeze picked up, making Louis pull up his collar. "Look, Sheriff," he said. "Just give me a little bit of time to look into some things. The memorial service isn't for two weeks yet. And Kelly will be out of town—"

Dodie's eyes hardened. "I ain't goin' behind Walt's back on this." He stood up. "And I don't want you going behind mine."

Without another word, the sheriff started back down the ladder. When he reached the bottom, he looked up.

"You got that, Kincaid?" he said.

Louis looked down at him. "Yeah, I got it," he said. He watched Dodie trudge off toward the Blazer. Damn, he had taken a gamble and lost. He had bet on his instinct that there was something not quite right between Dodie and Kelly, something he could use as a wedge to urge Dodie over to his side.

He had hoped, too, that the fragile bond that he had sensed forming between himself and Dodie was more than something born of his beer-clouded imagination that night in the bar. But Dodie could not be his ally. He knew that now. Sam Dodie was like Black Pool itself—or any little Southern town. Accepting on the surface, but closed up tighter than a fist when an outsider really tried to get inside.

Picking up the rifle case, Louis started down the ladder. If he intended to keep going on the bones case, he would need help. And whoever it was had to be an outsider, just like him.

The sheriff dropped Louis back off at the courthouse. Louis

stowed the rifle in the trunk of his Mustang and was about to go into the station when he saw Abby and Grace across the street, standing outside J.C. Penney.

They seemed to be arguing. Abby was waving her hands and Grace kept shaking her head. Finally Grace stalked off to a silver Monte Carlo parked at the curb. She waited a few seconds, but when Abby didn't get in, Grace started the car and drove off.

Louis watched Abby, who stood there with a deep frown clouding her face. He leaned against the car, crossing his arms. He needed to talk to her. And no matter how much he denied it to himself, he wanted to talk to her. At the very least, he owed her an explanation for not showing at the lake. He cut across the street, dodging a car. She looked up to see him coming and turned quickly to head the other way.

"Abby, wait—"

She kept going until he caught up and grabbed her arm. When she turned around to face him, her eyes were so solemn he at first didn't know what to say. He had expected anger, not the wounded look she was giving him.

"I'm sorry," he said finally, "for not meeting you at the lake."

"If you didn't want to come, you should have said so," she said.

He hesitated. It would only hurt her feelings more if he told her that he hadn't wanted to go. "You ran out so quickly, I didn't have time to say anything," he said. "Besides, right after you left, I got called back to the station on business."

She was wearing some kind of short fur jacket that set off her red hair. Her green eyes peered up at him from under wispy bangs, dubious but then trustful. He tried not to smile. God, she was so guileless. So very . . . young. He had a vision of her walking on campus at rowdy University of Florida, a lamb among the fraternity-house wolves, and wondered why in the hell a man like Max Lillihouse let his beautiful daughter out of the house, let alone out of state.

"Really, it's the truth," he said. Now he did smile.

She didn't smile back. Instead, she glanced around the street. "Can we go somewhere?" she said.

He was taken aback. "Why?"

She shrugged. "Just to talk. There's this coffee place way out on Highway 12. No one would see us there."

Louis suppressed a sigh. This was getting sticky, and he had to put an end to it before she got any more ideas than she already had. "Okay, coffee," he said, "at McDonald's."

"But everyone will see us there."

He steered her toward the Mustang. "That's exactly the idea."

In a few minutes, they were sitting in his Mustang in the McDonald's parking lot. The car was filled with the scent of lilac perfume and steaming coffee.

"This is so romantic," Abby said with a smirk, stirring her coffee.

Louis let himself laugh. "I have to stay near the radio. I'm still on duty." He debated whether to use her remark as an entrée into a talk about no romance, but it seemed too brisk and he didn't want this to be preachy. His impression was that Abby was the type of young woman who took everything to heart, be it her father's boorish drinking or a rejected kiss.

She rescued him. "How's the case going?" she asked.

"It's been officially closed," he said, looking at her over his cup. He paused. "Although I don't think it should be."

"Why?"

"Because I still have some leads I should follow. And because I think the dead man deserves . . . I don't know, justice of some kind."

She was looking at him thoughtfully. She seemed to have brightened up some after that argument with her mother. "So you have some clues?"

Louis thought about the medallion in his jacket pocket. He reached for it and handed it to her. She cupped the necklace, still wrapped in plastic, in her small hand. "It's heavy. Is this the necklace you found with the bones? I read about it in the newspaper."

Louis nodded.

She looked at it for a moment longer then handed it back. "I heard Daddy talking on the phone the other night. He was saying that dragging all that stuff up now wouldn't do anyone any good."

"What do you think?"

She looked troubled. "I don't know. He's probably right. Daddy is usually right . . . about most things."

There was something in her voice that made him feel a little sad. Abby Lillihouse was probably a lot smarter than he was ready to give her credit for. But growing up in a place like Black Pool, steeped in Old South traditions, and wrapped in the cocoon of wealth provided by her doting daddy, there wasn't much chance she could learn to really think for herself. No amount of university sociology classes could change that.

"I mean, Daddy is right about one thing," Abby said. "It was in the past. Things have changed. We've come a long way."

"Abby," Louis said gently, "if things have changed so much, why did you want to take me out to some coffeehouse in the middle of nowhere?"

She looked at him then brought up her cup to drink. Her hair formed a curtain, hiding her face from his sight. The smell of lilacs was everywhere in the car. For a brief moment, he found himself wishing they were somewhere else, far away from Black Pool. He found himself remembering what her lips tasted like.

The abrupt crackle of the radio chased the thought away.

"Louis? Louis, you out there? This is Mike."

Louis picked up the mike. "Yeah, Mike."

"Sheriff wants to know where you took off to."

"Uh . . . 10-7, McDonald's."

Louis glanced over at Abby. She was staring out of the passenger window. It was fogged-over from the heat of their bodies.

"Got a call for you, Louis."

"Patch it through."

The feminine voice came on moments later. "Detective Kincaid? This is Marsha Burns from Tampa."

Louis straightened, setting his coffee on the dash. It was the sculptor. "How are you? Is the head finished?"

"That's why I called. Someone called me the other day and said you didn't need me to finish it. I was told that you found out the man's identity."

"Who told you that?"

"Your sheriff, I believe. How in the world did you identify him?"

"We—" He stopped. Their conversation probably was being monitored back at the station. "Uh, we got lucky. Listen, Miss Burns, can I call you back? I can barely hear you."

Abby looked over with a slight frown, knowing Louis could hear just fine. Marsha Burns told him to make it quick. Louis repeated her number and hung up.

"I've got to go, Abby," Louis said, turning in the seat to face her.

She looked up at him. "Will I see you again?"

He took in a deep breath. "I don't think that would be a good idea," he said softly. He saw disappointment cloud her eyes. "Maybe in a different place or time, it would work, but . . ." He was saying more than he should. "I don't think it's a good idea."

Her eyes held his for a moment then she looked away, nodding briskly, biting her lower lip.

"Can I drive you home?" he asked.

She didn't look at him. "No, I think I'll stay in town for a while. I . . . I have things to do here." She opened the car door and got out quickly.

"Abby—"

"Good-bye, Louis." She closed the door. She ran across the parking lot. He wiped the foggy windshield with his sleeve and watched her go.

He got out of the car and went to the pay phone inside McDonald's. He dialed Marsha Burns's number and waited until she came to the phone.

"I couldn't talk over the radio, Miss Burns," he told her. "The truth is, we haven't identified him. There are some people here who want this body buried and this case closed. I need you to finish the head."

"I can't do that, Detective," the woman said. "Your sheriff told me that the case is closed, and when I'm told to stop, I stop. I'm not getting paid to continue, and I can't do this pro bono. I'll send back what I have."

Louis shifted the phone to his other ear. "Look, Miss Burns. In two weeks, those bones will be buried. A nameless corpse will be buried. Please, Miss Burns. I need to know who he was."

"I'm sorry, Detective, but I can't help you."

"Miss Burns—"

"I have to go. Good-bye."

"I need a face!" Louis said, raising his voice. But she had already hung up.

Louis slammed the phone down and it bounced out of its cradle. He did it again, his frustration exploding into impotent fury.

Finally he turned, breathing heavy, to look square into the disgusted eyes of the black girl behind the counter.

"Well, I sure hope you get that new face, mister," she said, " 'cuz that one you got is lookin' damn ugly right now."

Louis just stared at her then finally broke into a laugh. Jesus, he was going nuts. This case, this place, was making him nuts. But he wasn't going to give up. He had decided that much up in the deer hide. He wasn't going to give up until either every last damn lead—or he himself—was exhausted.

Early the next morning, Louis was waiting on the steps of the library when the elderly woman trudged up with her key. Louis gave her a polite "Good morning, Happy New Year," but she still eyed him warily as she let him in.

He went straight back to the Local History room. He switched on the fluorescent light and it took several minutes to finally flicker on. There were no windows and the room had the cramped, mildewed smell of an old basement. An old iron radiator in the corner heated the small room to an unbearable stuffiness.

Louis quickly took off his coat and draped it over a chair. He wandered down the shelves, running his index finger along the spines of the books. *Greensboro County Book of Vital Statistics*, *The History of Black Pool*, *Northeast Mississippi's Prominent Families*.

On a wide shelf near the back were huge land and plot maps, and stacks of newspaper binders that protected the brittle issues of the weekly *Black Pool Journal*. He brushed the dust off the top one and read the embossing. 1973.

He opened the book, supporting the large cover with his left hand while turning the pages with his right. He had no idea what he was really looking for. The headlines were typical of small-town news: politics, deaths, club news, high-school sports. The dusty binder was bulky, and after a few moments he set it aside. He paused, sweating, and pulled off his sweater before moving on.

He stopped before a wall of books, some with leather-bound covers, others held together with plastic coils. Interesting.

He pulled one down. The cover said, *The Carlson Family History*. Louis opened it and skimmed the first few pages. Somebody had written down, for all to read, the Carlson family tree and all the honors and noteworthy events that had happened to the family members throughout history. Louis put it back. There were more than a hundred of these books. It floored him that families actually did this. Who the hell cared?

He pulled out another one, then another, working his way up the alphabet to Lillihouse. There it was. Strange, it was a cheaply prepared xeroxed copy, bound in plastic. Louis took the book to a worn leather chair with a split seat.

The Lillihouse book began in 1810 with hyperbolic prose that made even the criminals in the family sound exciting and noble. It went on through the generations, citing births, deaths, marriages, and various accomplishments. The Lillihouses were a plantation family, originally from Georgia. They had settled in the northeast corner of Mississippi fifty years before the war, and were well established by 1860. Like many others, their land and wealth was pillaged, and after the war they struggled to regain the lifestyle of the past. The text credited Great-Grandfather Milton as the savior of the family, having overcome the ruinous conditions of Reconstruction. It took forty years but he became a prominent businessman by establishing Black Pool's first gasoline automobile sales yard, specializing in "previously owned" models.

Louis smiled. The original used-car salesman.

Milton Lillihouse had several children, but only one boy. That boy was Franklin Lillihouse, Abby's paternal grandfather. Louis was hoping to find a military man in the family tree to match what Zachary Taylor had told him about the medallion. But all the Lillihouses were landowners, bankers and local businessmen, as Max was. Not a Medal of Honor in the bunch, including old Milton himself.

There was a listing for Abigail Elizabeth, born April 17, 1964. She was the only child of Max Lillihouse and Grace Ketcher. A vision of the grand old Lillihouse home came to Louis's mind. Dodie had said Grace's father built the mansion. That made it owned by the Ketcher family, not the Lillihouses. Maybe he should be looking up Grace's history.

The Ketcher family book was a large, expensively bound volume that dated back to the early 1600s. This volume had a professional touch. Louis smiled to himself. Apparently Grace's family had been the one with the money. Old Max must have married into a good thing, if the quality of his family's book was any indication.

Louis flipped through the pages of the Ketcher book. There was plenty of Confederate gray and more than a few military men, including old Colonel Ketcher himself, Grace's father. The more recent pages had a multitude of photographs, and Louis found one of Max and Grace's wedding dated October 2, 1956.

They made a striking couple, standing before a half-circle of twelve bridesmaids. Grace looked lovely, her blonde hair done in the bobbed style of the period, her dress and long veil ending in a pool of satin and lace around her feet. In his white morning coat, Max was a broad-shouldered, handsome man—just as Louis had expected. Louis studied their faces, intrigued by the contrast he saw. Max was beaming proudly. Grace was somber, almost sad.

There was another couple in the picture. Walter Kelly and his wife, Maisey. Maisey had these big Liz Taylor eyes and wore a dress too tight for a wedding. Mayor Kelly was reed-thin, with not much more hair than he had now.

Suddenly Louis froze, his eye riveted by one small detail. Around the mayor's neck was a chain. A heavy chain, with a medallion on the end.

He let out a long breath. Jesus, it was the necklace.

CHAPTER 11

L ouis sat in the car in the library parking lot, staring at a xeroxed copy of the wedding picture. The librarian had not allowed him to check out the Ketcher family book, so Louis had made several copies. His heart was racing. Finally he had some proof, something to link someone with the dead man. And not just anyone. Walt Kelly, the goddamn mayor.

He peered at the copy, trying to make out the medallion. It was possible that it wasn't the one found in the grave. No, it was too close for coincidence. Taylor had said only about a hundred medallions were made. What were the chances of two in the same little town? Louis let out a deep breath. Questions, nothing but questions. But the real question now was, what to do with this information?

There was no one on his side, no one he could trust. He knew he had to tell Dodie about this, but he couldn't be sure just where Dodie stood with Kelly. He needed more information first, about both men.

He thought suddenly of his cousin Charles. He worked in the mayor's office as a clerk or something. Maybe he could shed some light. Louis headed the Mustang back to the square.

A half hour later, he and Charles were sitting in a cafe near the courthouse. Charles had been pleasantly surprised when "Cousin Lou" showed up at the office to ask him to lunch. Charles was a tall, sinewy man, about forty, with gray-specked hair and the longest, most graceful hands Louis had ever seen on a man. They looked like he imagined a violinist's hands might be. By the time Charles was digging into his pecan pie, Louis had gotten Charles through all the small talk and was eager to pump his relative for answers.

"So, how long have you worked for Walt Kelly?" Louis asked.

"Going on fifteen years," Charles said. "I was the first black man hired by the county. Started as a sweeper, and now I'm an administrative assistant." He drew out the last two words proudly.

"Is Kelly a good man to work for?" Louis asked.

Charles shook his head. "I suppose. If you lay low and keep your nose clean. That man, he runs this town. He's . . ." Charles searched for the right word. "He's not *mean*, exactly, but, you know, not the kinda man you wanna piss off."

"Yeah, I got that impression myself. How long has he been mayor?"

"Since '76. Before that he was a councilman. His family's always been big in politics."

"How does he get along with the people he works with?" Louis picked up his coffee cup. "Like the sheriff, for instance."

"Dodie? He and the mayor get along good. They's different, but alike, and they scratch each other's back, like everybody 'round here, know what I mean?"

Louis smiled. "Not really, Charles. This place is a mystery to me."

Charles chuckled. "Suppose it is. Well, I remember the election in '76. Kelly had it locked up for mayor. His daddy had been a congressman, and Kelly, well, he just had all the right stuff . . . went to Ole Miss, dressed real fine, talked so smooth, saying he'd bring progress to Black Pool. I remember all the signs he put around said, 'Walter Kelly: Symbol of the New South.' " Charles gave a wry smile. "Shit, I voted for him myself."

"And Dodie?" Louis prodded.

Charles shook his head. "Well, he was different. A real roughneck. Didn't even finish high school." He leaned close. "Rumor was he got Margaret Sue Purdy knocked up, so he dropped out to go to work." Louis waited while Charles munched on pie. "Sam wanted to be sheriff real bad cuz his daddy, Jed, had been sheriff. But Sam, well, he wasn't exactly a chip off the old block, and everybody knew it."

"What do you mean?" Louis asked.

Charles's expression turned cold. "Let's just say Jed ran things tight, real tight. And the white folks liked it that way."

"But Dodie got elected," Louis prodded.

" 'Cuz of Kelly. I think Kelly was afraid of the other guy who was running, thought maybe he couldn't keep him in line the way he could Sam. So one day, there was this big old ad in the paper saying Walter Kelly wanted Sam Dodie as sheriff, said he'd do the job as good as Jed did. So Sam got to be sheriff, riding right in on his daddy's coattails."

"And Walt Kelly's endorsement," Louis added.

"Yeah, and Sam's been paying for it ever since."

"What do you mean?" Louis asked.

"Well, Kelly's on the board, you know."

"Board?"

"Board of commissioners. They oversee the sheriff's budget and stuff. Sheriff can't spend a dime or take a shit without their approval."

"Who else is on this board?"

"Well," Charles said. "There's Fred Turner. He owns McCabe's Sportin' Goods. And Kurt Franck. He's a big wheel at the loggin' company. Stan Wallace, the funeral guy, and Max Lillihouse."

Louis signaled the waitress for more coffee. After she left, he pressed on.

"Any other history between Dodie and Kelly?"

"History?"

Louis wasn't sure where to go. Except maybe to the two powerful fathers. "What about their fathers? They get along?"

Charles shrugged. "Well, Kelly's old man, Albert, the congressman, I remember when I was a kid, seein' a picture in the paper of him standin' on the steps of Valley College, keepin' the black students out. As for Jed, well, he was like John Wayne, and if you was black you just had to jaywalk and you went to Jed's jail." Charles shook his head. "We used to joke that Albert wouldn't let us in and Jed wouldn't let us out."

Louis had a sudden vision of the two fathers in white robes. "So they were friends," Louis said.

"They was different, different jobs, come from different kind of folk, but it was like they had the same brain, know what I mean?"

Louis nodded. "Tell me something, Charles, you notice any-thing weird going on at work lately?"

"What you mean?"

"Extra visits, private conversations . . . anything weird?"

"Just all that plannin' for your bones, Louis."

Louis frowned, thinking. There were no secrets in small towns. "What do you know about Kelly's personal life?"

For the first time during the lunch, Charles stopped eating. "What you gettin' at here, Lou?"

"Well, who's he hang out with?"

Charles set his fork down, the pie suddenly ignored. He leveled his eyes at Louis. "You didn't invite me to lunch just to get to know me, did you?"

Louis hesitated. "Look, Charles . . ."

"You're questionin' me," Charles said, stabbing a finger at Louis. "I know what you're doin'. You're interrogatin' me." He shook his head disparagingly. "Jesus, my own flesh and blood."

"Charles, I'm sorry. I should have been more honest."

"Shit . . ." Charles was frowning, more from disappointment than anger.

Louis sighed. "I'm stuck on this case, Charles, and I don't know where to go. I thought you might know something about Kelly." He paused. "I'm sorry," he repeated, genuinely contrite.

Charles pursed his lips. "Well, I'll forget it, but only cuz you's family." He picked up his fork and poked at the pie.

Louis hesitated then leaned forward. "Give me an honest opin-ion, Charles," he said in a low voice. "Could Kelly or his father be involved in something like a lynching?"

Charles met Louis's eyes. "You talking 'bout the bones?"

When Louis nodded, Charles looked around the cafe and leaned close. "I heard some shit, a long time ago. I really can't say for sure about Kelly, but I know for a fact that old Jed liked to go out ridin' at night."

Louis was silent, his mind working, trying to fit the pieces together. He felt Charles's eyes on him.

"Why you doin' this, Lou? Even if Kelly did do it, you ain't never gonna prove it."

"You're probably right," Louis said quietly. "But I don't believe the man is who they say he is."

"You ain't the only one," Charles said. "Lots of folks think it's a big joke, havin' a funeral for some guy, some Willie Johnson. He was killed by the Klan, and it's like them tryin' to make it all right now, when we know it ain't never gonna be."

"I didn't think you cared about the dead man," Louis said. "I didn't think anyone here did."

"Well, maybe we do, but we just don't see no sense in talkin' about it. You don't understand, Cousin, is that it's plain-ass *painful* to talk about it. I lost my daddy in a church bombin'. You know that."

Louis let his shoulders drop. "I'd forgotten. I'm sorry." He sat back in the booth, feeling deflated. He still had no sense of whether he could trust Dodie. And he sure as hell couldn't do this alone anymore.

"Charles, I need help."

"You done said that and I done told you all I know."

"I mean outside help. Who do you know in Jackson?"

"Jackson?"

"With the FBI."

"The FBI? Are you fuckin' crazy?" he whispered. "Do you know what would happen if you went behind everybody's back to the FBI? Man, they'll be findin' *you* hangin' from a tree and me next, if they knew I helped you."

Louis never thought about the Feds until he read the book about their infiltration into Mississippi Klan activities. But he was getting desperate.

"Charles, you must know someone."

"I can't do this, Lou."

"You can, damn it."

Charles slumped back against the booth. Louis leaned forward, his voice low. "Charles, there comes a point when you got to quit being scared. You owe it to this dead man to help him, however you can."

"I don't owe some dead guy nothin'."

"Charles, black men have died countless faceless men like this one, have died. Your own father, for God's sake. I'm not asking for much, just a name."

"Man . . ."

"If I don't do this right, I'll just end up pissing everyone off," Louis said. "I need someone who'll give me some help without coming in directly. Please."

Charles sighed. "I know a guy, Lou."

"What's his name?"

"Winston Gibbons. He used to come around here a few years back. We had coffee a few times. I'm pretty sure he still works for the Feds in Jackson. Man, Louis, you sure you know what you're doing?"

"No, I'm *not* sure, But I have to do something."

Charles leaned forward. "I'm scared for you, Lou."

Louis was surprised by his cousin's concern. "I'll be all right, Charles."

Charles frowned. "You gotta know. The mayor's got muscle all over this state. If Kelly is involved in this, you watch your black ass, man." He shook his head. "You watch it real close."

Winston Gibbons was a short, light-skinned black man, with a thin mustache and closely-cut hair. His office was immaculate and well furnished, with only one sentimental touch: a photograph on the wall of two boys with fishing poles. Louis sat across from Gibbons, fidgeting with his tie. Gibbons leaned across the massive desk, folding his hands.

"I'm afraid I don't have much time, Detective. Charles said you needed some help with something. Good man, Charles. You say he's your cousin?"

"Yes."

"Well, what can we help you with?"

"I need some information on Klan activities in my area during the late fifties, early sixties."

Gibbons's eyebrows came together and he unfolded his hands. "Why would a small-town officer need information like that?"

Louis told him about the bones. Winston listened attentively without speaking. "What do you intend to do with this information?" he asked when Louis was finished.

"Find the murderer."

"Murderers, more likely," Gibbons said. "Detective, if this was indeed Klan, and if by some chance you could put faces to the event and names to the faces, do you realize how futile it still would be?"

"Yes. But I have to try."

Winston rocked in his chair thoughtfully. "You could be playing a deadly game."

"I know."

"What sort of assistance do you expect from our end?"

"Not much right now. I'd like to go it alone for a while longer. Just somewhere to start."

Gibbons smiled. "I was a clerk for James Thomas, an agent assigned here during the sixties. I saw many things, Detective, too many things. I saw a lot of hatred go unpunished and a lot of bravery unrewarded. It made me sick, but it also made me strong." He paused.

"There are a lot of ghosts in this South," Gibbons said. When Louis did not reply, Gibbons smiled. "I'm not nuts, Detective, but they are here, trust me. It's a feeling in the air. You can't hear them or see them, but they're there. They live with their pain, a pain we can never understand."

Louis thought about the eerie feeling he had experienced by the grave.

"My brother Wayne died in Montgomery," Gibbons went on, "beaten to death by the cops. That's us in that photo up there. I keep that there to remind myself of why I do what I do."

"So you always wanted to be in law enforcement?" Louis asked.

"Oh, I wanted to be a lawyer when I was a kid," Gibbons said. "But that was out of reach, so I tried to get into law enforcement. Too many walls there, too, so I headed up to Cleveland, got my degree and went to work for the FBI as a clerk. I just wanted to be part of the process. Then came the summer of '64 and everything changed."

"When did you become an agent?"

"1979."

"Ever regret it?"

"Not for a minute. I have the utmost respect for the law, and those who enforce it with honesty and integrity."

Louis leaned forward. "Will you help me?"

"Certainly," Gibbons said.

As Louis drove back to Black Pool, he thought about the events of that afternoon. Gibbons had asked him to wait in a nearby restaurant for the information he had requested. He had eaten two full meals, drunk six cups of coffee and read the *Jackson Clarion-Ledger* front to back by the time the woman came in to deliver a manila envelope. He had been tempted to rip it open right then, but the waitress was looking at him strangely and he headed home.

Now he was on the Natchez Trace Highway, the only light coming from the dash. He looked down at the envelope on the seat. Unable to resist any longer, he swung onto the gravel shoulder and cut the engine. He fiddled with the overhead light, and it blinked erratically and stayed off.

He reached down to the passenger-side floor and retrieved a book of matches Junior had dropped. He ripped the envelope open. On the first page was a paragraph followed by a list of names. He struck a match, straining to read.

Detective Kincaid:

I have enclosed whatever information we have on your county and a list of people implicated in Klan activities during the years 1950 to 1965. Keep in mind that in the fifties the Klan felt little need to exercise its influence because racial restraints were already in place by the government. The names you will see come only from undercover reports. No charges were ever filed. Sorry it is not more complete. Greensboro was not an area of high Klan activity. Please keep in contact. I'm very interested in your progress. My agency will be happy to assist in any way. Be careful, my friend.

—W. Gibbons

The first few paragraphs were a short summary of activities of the era, mostly dealing with the church bombings, fires, and street violence that erupted as the sixties began. There wasn't as much as Louis expected. But the summary, from a document dated in 1965, made his pulse quicken.

Although Greensboro County is not an area of rampant violence, there seems to be one common link in all activities: the acquiescence of the Sheriff's Office and its refusal to cooperate with any investigation. From 1951 to 1959, Sheriff Jedidiah Dodie permitted the beatings of Negroes arrested and detained in Greensboro County. The succeeding sheriff, Joseph Millard, continued this policy to a lesser degree until 1964. To date, the Greensboro County Sheriff's Department is believed to be responsible for the mysterious deaths of three Negroes.

The match went out. Louis let out a long breath, thinking about the dank cells back at the office. How many black men had been tortured there? How many murdered? Good God, had the unknown dead man been killed in one of those cells, too, then taken out to the woods and hanged so it looked like a Klan murder?

Louis lit another match. The report went on to list possible Klan members of the era, and the first name to hit him was Jedidiah Dodie. His cousin Charles had been right. There were more names, none of whom meant anything to him. But then one name sent a shiver through his bones. Walter Kelly. No goddamn wonder he wanted the case closed! Louis's stomach turned over as he had a vision of Walt Kelly and Sam Dodie yanking the rope higher and higher.

But then something clicked in Louis's head. What had Jacob Armstrong said about the bones, that they were twenty years in the ground—*at least*. Without the carbon test, the age of the bones couldn't be dated accurately, and the test wasn't due back for weeks. The lynching could have happened *thirty* years ago. Maybe that was why nobody missed the dead man. Jesus, was he chasing the wrong men? Were the fathers the murderers or were the sons? Was Dodie trying to protect himself or his father's memory?

He heard a tap on the window and he jumped, dropping the match. It went out, engulfing the car in darkness. He hadn't seen or heard another car. Was it a hitchhiker? He rubbed the condensation off the window and peered out. A face stared back. He opened the window an inch.

A police officer stood outside, his eyes visible in the small crack of the window. "Get out of the car."

Louis looked in his rearview mirror. "Why aren't your lights on?"

The officer backed up and put a gloved hand on his gun. "Just get out."

Putting his hands carefully on the wheel, Louis took a deep breath. "Take it easy, I'm a police officer," he said. Slowly, he opened the door and got out, raising his hands in the air. The Mustang's headlights illuminated the empty stretch of road ahead.

"Move away from the car."

"I'm a cop."

"You think we care what the hell you are?" The policeman reached in and turned off the headlights, plunging the highway into darkness. The faint light of the cloud-covered moon gave a silvery glow to the officer's white face. Louis looked around, his heart pumping faster. This was all wrong.

"My badge is in—"

"Shut the fuck up!"

Louis heard distant footsteps on the pavement and another cop appeared from the darkness, his gun drawn. Louis's mouth went dry and he took in short, nervous breaths. He was going to die and his only thought was, *Not here, not on a Mississippi highway, not for nothing.*

The first officer thrust him toward the car, banging his head against the hood roughly. He frisked him, jerked out Louis's gun and tossed it in the front seat of the Mustang. The other officer, who was searching the car with a flashlight, shouted something back Louis could not understand.

"Look, fellas—"

The officer twisted, slamming his nightstick against Louis's jaw. He tumbled against the car, tasting blood. He licked it away, glaring at the cop through the darkness. He wore a beige uniform, much like his own. On his hands were black leather gloves. He wore no badge.

The other policeman climbed out of the Mustang, papers in hand. Louis inhaled thinly and stole a glance at them through the darkness. Another violent lunge of the nightstick hit his rib cage, bringing him to his knees. He cried out, but it only brought another blow, a sharp jab between his shoulder blades. He fell to his hands and knees, writhing.

He stayed there for several moments, pressed against the rear tire. The asphalt was cold, and he could feel gravel through the knees of his pants.

He did not move. He heard the roar of the engine as the car peeled away. It was an unmarked dark sedan. He watched the taillights fade into the distance, and breathed a sigh of relief.

Every breath rattled his ribs. Fire shot through his lungs. Using the door handle, he pulled himself erect and fumbled to open the door. How had they known where he would be? Who had sent them?

As he slid into the seat, he pushed his gun over. His breathing became more regular and the pain eased slightly. His eyes began to focus as he wiped the blood off his mouth. The papers were gone. It didn't matter; he could get other copies, and he had seen what he needed to see. A name he could link not only to the necklace, but to the Klan. Just like Zachary Taylor had said . . . politics and power. Walt Kelly was guilty as hell. He knew it. But how did he prove it?

CHAPTER 12

L ouis leaned closer to the mirror, wincing as he dabbed iodine on the cut near his lip. Two days had passed since the night on the Trace, but his lip was still badly swollen and deep purple.

He reached for his shirt. There was only one reason those cops would have followed him and taken the report. Someone had sent them. Someone was worried, enough to steal evidence and scare him just enough to make him back off. But who? Kelly? Dodie? And how did they know where he was?

Louis gingerly slipped on the shirt, wincing over what he suspected were bruised ribs. He sat down to put on his shoes. He hadn't slept well, plagued by his aching ribs and his racing mind. It was a fact that Kelly had a medallion. It was a fact that he was once a Klan member. It was a fact that he wanted this thing over with, the victim buried. But how to connect the pieces? And where did Dodie fit in?

Groaning, Louis rose from the bed. The rising sun began to filter through the curtain. He had called in sick yesterday, hoping after two days' rest he'd feel—and look—better. But the cuts and bruises were too damn ugly to hide. He might as well go in early and face Dodie.

It was bitterly cold outside, colder than he expected, and he hurried to his car. He paused, seeing the light on in Tinker's store. A real cup of coffee, that's what he needed. And maybe one of those sprinkle donuts Mr. Tinker baked each morning.

He was surprised to see Tinker behind the counter instead of Teesha. Mr. Tinker greeted his first customer of the day with a cool nod as Louis walked in.

"Got coffee this morning, Mr. Tinker?"

"Always do. You know that."

"I'd like a donut, too."

The big man took the lid off the plastic case. "What's your preference?"

"Sprinkles."

Tinker grabbed a napkin and set the donut in front of Louis. "Coffee's over there."

Louis walked over to the pot and filled a large Styrofoam cup. He had never smelled fresher coffee than the stuff Tinker made.

"I'm surprised you're not dead yet," Tinker said.

"So am I."

"Folks say you're still asking a lot of questions. Thought they identified those bones."

Tinker rang up his breakfast. Louis put a dollar down as he bit into the donut, wincing as he wiped his mouth.

"Let me ask you something, Mr. Tinker. You've heard about the memorial service for this man, right?"

Tinker nodded.

"You planning to attend?"

"What for?"

Louis shrugged. "Pay your respects to a dead man."

"It doesn't mean anything to me. It's their conscience they're cleansing, not mine."

Louis finished the donut and sipped the coffee. "I agree. That's why I'm still asking questions." He tossed his empty cup in the trash and headed for the door.

"Good day, Mr. Tinker." Louis paused near the screen door. "If you ever decide you can help me, I'm still listening. I'm in this alone. I sure could use some help from someone in this town."

"I've no help to give you."

Louis nodded. "I understand."

Tinker's eyes narrowed slightly and he called to him. "What happened to your face?"

Louis smiled wanly. "I heard the footsteps."

There was no one in the station when Louis got there. He went to the coffeemaker in the corner and started a pot, then went to his desk and sank slowly into his chair, holding his side. Maybe his ribs were more than bruised; maybe he should have listened to Bessie and gone to the hospital for X rays. He sighed. He felt bad for lying to her about the injuries. He told her he had tripped on a rug up in the hall and fallen down the stairs, and she had promptly thrown the braid rug out, blaming herself. But there was no way he could have told her about the beating.

Louis felt a ripple of anger toward the anonymous cops out on the Trace. Goddamn cowards. He glanced at the phone, debating whether to call Winston Gibbons. He needed to get another copy of the FBI Klan report, but he'd wait on that, too. He didn't want to have to tell Gibbons what had happened if he could help it.

He noticed the large envelope sitting on his desk and picked it up. It was the Mulcahey case fingerprint report from the lab in Jackson; it must have come on Saturday when he was out. Louis snagged his reading glasses off the pencil holder and opened the envelope.

The door banged and Junior strode in, going to the coffeemaker. "You're here early," Junior called out. "How's the stomach?"

"Huh?" Louis grunted, lost in the report.

"Your stomach. Mike said you was sick."

"Oh, fine. Just a bug."

Junior sipped his coffee, grimacing. "Man, you make shitty coffee, Louis," he said.

Louis turned to reply but Junior had drifted off to the bathroom, newspaper under arm, for his morning routine.

The lab had lifted eleven different prints and numerous partials off the deer hide. They had matched seven. Louis ran his finger down the list. His own name was there along with others Louis assumed were random hunters. And yes, there it was: Leverette Mulcahey had left a palm print the size of Mississippi on the metal ledge that partially enclosed the platform. Leverette's prints were on file for an arrest two years ago. Louis shook his head. Stupid kid had stolen two six-packs of beer from Phil's Fast Trip.

Louis closed the report and took off his glasses. A quarter of a million dollars was a very tempting motive for a young man. Louis tried to open his drawer. It stuck again and he hit the top of the desk to loosen it.

"Goddammit, Kincaid, get that thing fixed or I'm going to burn it."

Louis looked up to see Dodie coming in. He watched as the sheriff stopped off at the coffeepot. Louis stared at Dodie's broad back, his head filled with the image of a big man in a white hood.

But whose face was under the hood, Jed Dodie's or his son's? And who was Sam Dodie? Was the man who had bought him a beer in the bar capable of pulling a noose around the neck of a black man?

Dodie turned and stopped by Louis's desk. "What the hell happened to you?"

"I was stopped on the way home from Jackson Friday night."

Dodie came closer, pulling off his cap. "Stopped?"

"I pulled over to the side of the road, and two friendly patrolmen happened by. I guess they thought I looked suspicious."

Dodie reached out and turned Louis's face to the light. Dodie's hand was rough. Louis felt himself flinch involuntarily.

"Cops did this?"

"Yes." Louis pulled away.

"Say who they were?"

"No, and I didn't get a good look at them. It was dark, and it's kind of hard to see when you're kissing the pavement."

"What county were you in? I can make some calls."

"I'm not sure they were even on duty. They weren't wearing their badges, I saw that much."

"You sayin' they did this intentionally?"

"I don't know," Louis said flatly. "Maybe they just like to go joyriding after dark and harass niggers."

Dodie put his hands on his hips. "They take your gun?"

"No. Professional courtesy, I guess."

Dodie slipped his cap back on. He suddenly looked very tired. Louis studied his face. His surprise and his distress seemed genuine. If those cops last night had been tailing him, they hadn't been sent by Dodie.

"I want you to stick close to Junior for a while, Kincaid."

"I don't need a bodyguard. And even if I did, he'd be my last choice."

Dodie pursed his lips. "Okay. But you be careful, you hear?" He motioned to the report. "What's that?"

"Print report from Jackson on the Mulcahey case. Guess whose prints showed up on the deer hide?" Louis said. "Leverette Mulcahey's."

Dodie's mouth drew into a line. "Leverette's a hunter, he's bound to have prints up there."

"Maybe, but that's a damn good cover when you think about it." Louis got up slowly, careful to hide the fact his ribs were killing him. Dodie didn't need more reason to give Junior a baby-sitting job. "I think I should go out to the Mulcahey place to talk to Ethel about some things."

Dodie nodded. "I guess it's time to talk to Leverette, too. He hasn't gone back to Starkville yet. Saw him in town yesterday."

"He goes to MSU?" Louis asked.

Dodie started toward his office. "Sure does."

Louis got up and went to the file cabinet, intending to put the print report in the Mulcahey file. When he opened the drawer, his eyes lingered on the John Doe folder. Then he frowned.

"Sheriff? Where's the envelope that was in here?"

"What envelope?" Dodie called out from his office.

Louis rummaged through the drawer. "The big one with the necklace and poetry book in it."

"It's over at Wallace-Pickney."

Louis looked up to see Dodie standing at the door of his office, cigar clamped between his teeth. "Mike took it over yesterday."

"Why?" Louis said.

" 'Cuz I told you to do it and you didn't."

Louis looked back at the John Doe folder, with the big red CLOSED stamped on the front. He shoved the file drawer and it banged closed. With a quick look at Dodie, Louis started to the door.

"Kincaid," Dodie called out "What in the hell were you doing in Jackson?"

"Visiting a goddamn friend," he shot back without turning.

The basement was damp, and Louis knew that if he was cold, then Ethel Mulcahey, sitting there in her thin sweater, had to be shivering. He glanced around the sweet-smelling knotty-pined basement. A few sheets of paneling and an open box of vinyl tile sat off in one corner by the bar. A corner of the basement had been partitioned off for a workroom and Louis could see rows of shiny tools hanging on pegboard and a professional-looking saw bench. Earl must have just finished the remodeling.

At the other end of the basement stood two handsome gun cabinets, and two more gun racks hung on the wall nearby. All were full of long-barreled guns. Louis went over to them.

"I can't believe it," Ethel murmured. "Who would want to murder Earl?"

Louis looked back at her. She looked as if she was going to cry again. She had already cried once upstairs when he told her that they suspected Earl's death was not accidental. When Louis had asked her if there were any guns in the house, she had managed to compose herself and bring him down to the basement. But now, she looked pale and very fragile, like she might break into pieces at any moment.

"Mrs. Mulcahey," he said, "do you know which gun Earl used most often?"

She shook her head. "He was a kind man," she said vacantly, "he would never hurt anyone."

Without touching them, Louis examined the rifles, disappointed to discover none was a .30-.30. "Do you have any other guns?"

"No."

"Does your son have any with him, up at school?"

"I think so. He's not supposed to, but I think he took one with him."

Louis stared at the shiny blue barrel of the shotgun. "Mrs. Mulcahey, did your husband and Leverette ever argue?"

She looked up at him. Then she smiled slightly, like only a mother could. "Sometimes. Leverette wanted to quit school and start his own business, a laundromat. He wanted his father to back him, but Earl said not until he finished school."

Louis turned to look at her. "How much of an investment was it?"

"I'm not sure. I never paid much attention to finances."

"The life insurance . . . do you know how much that was?"

"Only because they called. Earl's policies are worth about a million dollars." She shook her head. "That seems like a lot."

"Are you the beneficiary?" Louis knew the answer, but he tested her just the same.

Mrs. Mulcahey seemed embarrassed. "No, Leverette gets about a fourth, as does my daughter."

The basement was quiet for a moment. Louis's eyes traveled over the sleek guns. When he turned back to Ethel Mulcahey, he saw something in her teary blue eyes. She knew what he suspected.

"We are a close family, Detective," she said softly. "Leverette could never do what you're thinking."

"I have to ask, Mrs. Mulcahey."

The dampness was seeping through to his bones. He suggested they go back upstairs. Ethel moved slowly, in a broken sort of way. Louis felt sorry for her as he followed her up the narrow stairs. At the top, as they entered the kitchen, Louis stopped, hearing a car. Mrs. Mulcahey went to the window and parted the curtains. "That's Leverette now."

Leverette Mulcahey was a tall, dark-haired boy who walked with the blocky swagger of an athlete. He wore a burgundy Mississippi State sweatshirt and snug jeans over strong, slender legs. He came up the steps and Louis met him on the porch. For a second, they eyed each other, then Leverette's shoulders drooped and he moved to the wooden swing and sat down. Louis let the screen door slam shut.

"Leverette . . ."

"Isn't it bad enough Dad's dead? Do you have to keep coming around?"

"I need to ask you some questions," Louis said.

"About what?"

"Well, we told you it was an accident—"

"It was no accident," Leverette murmured, looking down at the porch.

Louis waited, but when Leverette said nothing more, Louis asked, "What do you mean?"

Leverette shook his head. "I just never thought it was an accident." He scuffed his tennis shoe against the porch, setting the swing in slow motion.

Louis watched the young man carefully. "Leverette, did you call me?"

Leverette blinked a couple of times. "Call you?"

"On New Year's Eve."

Leverette frowned. "Why would I call you?"

Louis leaned against the post, watching him. Leverette let his eyes fall again to the porch. Louis had to tell him.

"We think your father was murdered," Louis said. He hesitated. "Leverette, I have to ask you some questions."

"About what?"

"Do you have any guns in your dorm?"

His eyes shot up, then darted away, steady on the warped boards of the porch. "I can't believe this."

"Leverette, do you have any guns with you at school?"

He shook his head.

"These questions are just routine, Leverette."

He looked up. "My dad has a million in life insurance. And now you're asking me about my guns. Sure, routine. . . ."

"Where were you that morning?" Louis asked. "Your mother says you were home for the holidays, but no one knows where you were."

"I went for a walk."

"At seven A.M.?"

"Sure. Why not?"

"Leverette, I need a better story than that."

Leverette looked up finally. His eyes were defiant but there were tears brimming his dark lashes. "That's all I got, Detective."

Louis watched as Leverette twisted his hands and then put his face into them. He leaned his elbows on his knees, rocking in the swing. Louis's instincts, all his training, had told him never to trust anyone. People could con you out of anything. The most sympathetic old woman could be a cold-blooded killer. But Leverette was tough to read.

"Thank you, Leverette."

He looked up, surprised, but did not reply. He returned his face to his palms.

Louis stuck his head in the door and thanked Ethel, and left. He stopped off at two neighbors' but his questions about the Mulcaheys didn't unearth much that was new. One man told him the son came home once a month or so, and yes, he did go hunting with Earl frequently. But his wife volunteered that the whole family got along and she had never seen a hint of trouble between Leverette and his father. He got the same story from the neighbor on the east side. If Leverette Mulcahey had intended to murder his father, he hid his plans well.

As Louis headed back to the station, he called Mike on the radio and asked for Dodie.

"He's busy," Mike said.

"Well, tell him we have to get a search warrant for Leverette Mulcahey's dorm at MSU."

"Gotta get Judge Eucher for that, Louis. Might take awhile."

Louis frowned. He had forgotten that the judge rotated between counties and was seldom in his office.

"Hey, Louis," Mike said. "A package just came for you from Florida. Whatcha do, order some grapefruit?"

Florida? Then he realized it had to be from Marsha Burns, the sculptor. She had said she was going to send back the unfinished head. He told Mike to just put it on his desk. Another lead stifled by Dodie.

When he got back, Larry and Junior were there, joking around while Mike lounged at the dispatch desk. Louis looked at the box on his desk with dismay. He opened the box halfheartedly and read the note sitting atop the plastic peanuts.

Dear Detective,

I couldn't help but think about what you said on the phone, and I decided that money or politics shouldn't interfere with the execution of justice, no matter how long overdue. I finished the head as quickly as I could. I hope this helps you.

Sincerely,
Marsha Burns

Louis let loose with a laugh that drew looks from the deputies. "I love you, lady," he said.

He dug through the layer of peanuts and carefully lifted the heavy gray bust out of the box. He set it down on the desk and took a step back.

A face stared back at him, a young face, about eighteen. It was thin and chiseled, with high cheekbones and a high forehead. A long nose, and heavy, but curiously delicate-looking lips. A jutting, almost defiant jawline, and almond-shaped eyes.

Louis stared at the face sadly. He had been handsome. Somehow Marsha Burns had also managed to give the hard clay bust an oddly touching expression of sadness mixed with hope.

Junior and Mike had come up to stand quietly behind Louis. "He sure looks sad," Mike said.

"You'd be sad, too, if they hung you," Junior said. Junior let out a snicker. "And they might just do that to you, Kincaid, you don't quit playing footsie with Abigail Lillihouse."

Louis's head jerked around in shock. "What?"

Junior's smile faded. "Lou—"

Louis grabbed the collar of Junior's shirt, cutting him off, and slammed him against the desk. "I'm going to say this one time, and one time only," Louis hissed. "Keep your ignorant opinions to yourself. No one here is interested in what you have to say. Especially about Abby Lillihouse. Do you understand, you stupid redneck?"

Louis let go of his shirt, and Junior stumbled slightly, color rising quickly to his chubby cheeks. He glanced back at Larry and Mike with embarrassment. Mike's mouth hung open and Larry started motioning toward Louis with his fists. Junior moved forward, thrusting his face nose-to-nose with Louis.

"You want a piece of me, Kincaid? Well, come on, dammit, let's go!"

Louis turned away in disgust.

Junior bobbed around to face him, thrusting out his chest. "You think you're a real big man, now, don't you? You think you're better than all of us! Well, come on, big man!"

"Stop it, Junior," Mike called weakly.

"I'm fuckin' tired of your attitude, Kincaid!" Junior yelled, raising his fists. "You're so smart, you're so damn much better than us! Now you even got a white woman to fuck!"

Louis reacted so quickly that it was not until he felt Junior's flesh against his fist that he realized he had hit him. The punch landed on Junior's jaw, sending Junior tumbling off the side of the desk, dragging the ink blotter, telephone, and cardboard box with him. The phone cord trapped the bust, pulling it off the desk.

Louis stretched to catch it, but missed. A second later, Junior tackled him, throwing him to his back. He straddled him, pinning him to the floor. Larry leapt forward, hunkering over the desk, watching as Junior drew back his fist, raising it over his head.

A gunshot pierced the air.

Junior's fist froze in mid-air and he sat up, breathing heavily, his lip bleeding. Louis shoved him off and used the desk to hoist himself up. All faces turned toward the door to the sheriff's office.

Dodie jammed his gun back in his holster, glaring at everyone. Without a word, he turned and disappeared back into his office. The door slammed shut, sending a shudder through the walls.

The room was quiet as a graveyard. Louis looked up at the ceiling, watching the dust from the bullethole rain down onto

Larry's desk. He looked at Junior, who was panting like a walrus, then down at the floor. The bust lay in the corner, broken into large pieces.

Louis wiped the corner of his lip and tried to pull in a deep breath. He winced in pain, his hand going to hold his ribs. He picked up the box and went over to the broken bust. He knelt down and carefully put the pieces into the box and slowly got up. Without looking at any of them, he walked out.

"Jesus, Junior," Mike said quietly. "Why'd you have to do that? Louis—"

"Mike," Junior said, "go get the first-aid kit, will ya? I'm bleeding to death here."

Mike began opening cupboards. Larry came up to peer at Junior's split lip. "He gotcha good. Better go put some cold water on that."

Junior trudged off to the bathroom, slamming open the swinging door. Larry squeezed in behind him as it squeaked shut. He followed Junior to the cracked mirror.

"Fuck," Junior said softly. "Look at me. That Kincaid's got no sense of humor."

"How the hell did you know about Abigail?" Larry demanded. "What?"

"Abigail," Larry demanded. "How'd you know?"

Junior wet a paper towel and dabbed at his lip. "I followed him. After I found that note I showed you."

"What note?" Larry said, irritated. "I don't remember no note."

"I showed it to you. That note she wrote him that was in his jacket."

Larry came up next to Junior. "You never showed me no note." Larry turned away as the door popped open and Mike stuck his head in.

"You still need these?" he asked, holding out a can of Band-Aids.

Larry slapped the door shut on Mike's arm. "Get the hell out of here." Mike's head disappeared and Larry spun back toward Junior. "You sure about this?"

Junior smiled. He wasn't sure by any means, but this was too much fun to stop now. "The son of a bitch hit me, didn't he?"

"I don't believe it," Larry muttered, running his hand through his hair. Junior watched him in the mirror. Larry's jaw went so tight that Junior could see the blood vessels pulsating. They rippled all the way into the thin brown hair at his temples.

Junior smiled slightly, watched him. "Kind of grates ya, don't it?"

"Fuck you."

"Don't go getting mad at me. It ain't my fault she won't go out with you." Junior snuck another look at Larry's face in the mirror. Man, he was pissed.

"You gonna tell Max?"

Larry started shaking his head. "Fuck, no. I ain't being no dead messenger. Not me."

The bathroom was quiet as Junior turned off the water. Larry was so damn easy to rile. "Hey, Larry," Junior said with a smile. "Can't you just see it? That black hand on her little ass. That nigger cock in her juicy little pussy . . . in and out . . . in and out . . ."

"It ain't true, I know it ain't true," Larry muttered.

God, this was fun. Junior turned and gave Larry a big smile. "I'm telling you, it's the fuckin' truth. Louis and Abby are doing it."

"Shut up, Junior!"

Junior jabbed a chubby finger at Larry's chest. "Face it, Larry ol' boy, your dream girl is fuckin' a nigger."

CHAPTER 13

L ouis closed his eyes, but sleep would not come. It was late, well after midnight. He could feel the cold air slipping through the cracks of the window, and he pulled the quilt up over his shoulder. The night sounds from outside—tires, boomboxes, horns—all seemed magnified in the darkness of the small room.

He opened his eyes, then with a sigh pushed back the quilt and swung his legs over the side of the bed. It was no use; he was too keyed-up to sleep. His eyes drifted over the the cardboard box on the table that held the pieces of the broken clay bust.

Ignorant assholes. Fucking ignorant redneck assholes posing as cops. He was tired of all of them. The cops who had beat him. Junior and his stupidity. And Dodie with his excuses that things were just different here. Well, fuck them all, those cowards on the Trace, Larry, Junior, and especially Dodie. Fuck him and the horse his robe-wearing father rode in on.

He tried to pull in a deep breath but winced in pain. He rubbed his hands over his face. He wanted all this to be over with. He wanted to go home.

There was a noise outside his room. The hall light went on, sneaking under his door. A few minutes later, there was a knock on his door.

"Louis?" Bessie called out softly, then opened the door, sticking her head in. "Louis?"

"I'm awake," he answered.

"It's time, Louis."

"Time for what?"

Bessie opened the door, and the light spilled around her large body, making him blink. "Lila has to go to the hospital," Bessie said. "I can't do no more. It's in God's hands now."

"Okay, I'll be right there." Louis reached for his jeans and shoes. For a few seconds, he sat in the cool darkness of his room, his shoes dangling in his hand. Then he forced himself to get dressed.

The hallway was cold. Bessie was coming out of Lila's room and looked up at him sadly. "Want I should call an ambulance or do you want to take her?" she asked.

Louis avoided her eyes. "Call an ambulance," he whispered.

Bessie picked up the phone and Louis went to Lila's room. He could smell death. He turned away and waited for Bessie.

"They won't be long," she said. "You go downstairs. I'll tend to her."

Louis nodded and walked slowly down the stairs. He stood in the vestibule, staring blankly out the front door into the darkness. He couldn't seem to arrange his thoughts. He felt an urge to try and fix things before she died. But he didn't know how to even start. What could he say to her now? It was too late to say anything.

He heard the siren and saw the red lights as the ambulance pulled up to the curb. He stepped out onto the porch. Lights went on up and down the street. Two paramedics hurried up the walk with a gurney and looked at Louis questioningly. He held the door open for them. "She's upstairs," he said. "There's no hurry."

They glanced at each other.

"She's dying. Just make her comfortable."

They nodded and went inside. Louis stayed on the porch. Something inside was telling him to go to her, hold her hand, be with her to say something reassuring. But he couldn't move. He shivered. Jesus, he had dealt with death so many times, comforted dozens of strangers. Why couldn't he go to her?

"Louis? You ready?"

"What?"

"To go to the hospital. Are you ready?" Bessie asked.

"I'm ready," he murmured.

Greensboro County Hospital was a small building with a long asphalt drive and an emergency entrance lighted by red neon. It had only two floors: people were born and made well on the first; the desperately ill and the dying were taken to the second. The walls were pale yellow and the tile floor was painted gray. It was cold. Footsteps echoed in the empty halls, punctuated by the *ping* of the elevator.

They put Lila in a single room that overlooked Highway 17 and Phil's Fast Trip. Louis moved immediately to the window and took solace in the darkness. He watched the light over Phil's blink on and off for several minutes before he felt Bessie tug at his arm.

"Can I go get you a cup of coffee, Louis?"

He nodded.

There was a pain in his chest, a deep physical ache. He leaned against the windowsill. Why couldn't he deal with this? He didn't care about this woman. He didn't owe her anything. Why did it hurt so much?

He went to the bed. She was unconscious. As he looked down into her worn face, the memories came creeping back again and he couldn't stop them. Yolanda's screams. Shards of brown and green glass on worn linoleum. The feel of a roach running across his back in the cold of night. Hunger gnawing on the walls of his stomach like a crazed animal. The awful brew of smells in her bedroom: whiskey, sweat, musky sex, and that dimestore Evening in Paris perfume.

He wanted to cry, to feel the rush of relief that tears would bring. But nothing would come. Tired, he was so tired. Tired of fighting it, tired of pretending. He had pretended for so long to feel nothing. He had told himself he *should* feel nothing, that it was easier to feel nothing. But it was the *nothing* that hurt now. Not the anger, the bitterness, the sadness or shame that had been wound so tight inside him all these years. It was the emptiness, the *nothing*, that hurt the most now, cutting into him like a dull knife digging deep in his chest. He shut his eyes tight. He felt dizzy and grabbed the cold steel rail of the bed to steady himself.

"Please," he whispered. "Please, God . . ." He was praying, something he had not done in years. But he didn't know what he was praying for.

Then he felt it. It started with a faint feeling of warmth. Warmth at the back of his neck, like the kiss of an afternoon sun. Then came the scent of flowers, adrift on a spring breeze. He could see himself, in a field, sitting in a blanket of wildflowers.

She was next to him. She was sober, wearing a blue-and-white-checked dress and a wide straw hat. The wind snatched the hat from her head and she laughed as it lifted up into the blue sky like a kite.

Laughing, she was laughing. He was laughing. God, he remembered now. It was Aunt Laurelie's house; they were sitting behind her house, the one with the ducks. He had loved going there.

Mama . . . Mama? Why do I look different?

Because you are special.

What makes me special?

Because you are dusted with angel dust.

Like that powder on your dresser? Is that why I'm not dark like you?

Yes, baby. . . .

Where'd it come from, Mama, where'd the angel dust come from?

From God. . . . God sprinkled you with his dust to make you beautiful and strong.

Does God sprinkle dust on everybody?

No, baby, only those that's gonna need it most.

Louis stared down into Lila's face. Something inside him broke suddenly, something in his chest tore apart. The tears began, and he let them fall down his face. He couldn't stop them, so he let them come. Wave after terrible wave swept over him, threatening to pull him under. But then he felt it; something moving through him, like a warm current flowing through his chest that encircled his heart in an embrace. Then, quickly as it had come, it was gone.

The tears slowed. Finally, with a deep, shuddering breath, he opened his eyes and looked down at Lila. She was gone.

He reached over and picked up her hand. It was hard and deep brown against his smooth tan one. He brought it up slowly and pressed it to his cheek.

The birds swarmed overhead, black specks against the gray-pink morning sky. Louis sat on the picnic table, watching the flock as it wove and dipped as one great mass, darting first one way and then turning sharply to go in another direction. Every so often, the birds would settle down in the trees to rest until something would send them back in flight on their restless, weaving route.

It was cold. Louis zipped up his jacket and hunched his chin down into the collar. He had left the hospital about four and had driven aimlessly in the predawn gloom before coming to the park. He had been sitting on the bench for the last hour, letting his thoughts and emotions drift. They would wander, aimless and fretful for a while, then settle into a calm before swirling again. Lila was there, hovering on the edge of his consciousness. But strangely, his pain had lessened. She was free of hers now, and it was as if she had taken most of his with her.

Louis heard the crunch of tires on gravel and turned to see a yellow Firebird pull in. It was Abby. He turned away, stuffing his hands deeper into his pockets.

She came up to stand behind him. "I saw your car." She hesitated. "Is it okay that I stopped?"

He turned. She was wearing jeans and a denim jacket. She had a funny-looking denim hat with a red flower pulled down over her ears. Her red hair tumbled out beneath. He nodded and looked away, back out at the distant trees where the birds had gathered again.

"What's wrong?" she asked.

"My mother passed away this morning."

"Oh . . . I'm sorry. I shouldn't have intruded," she said in a small voice. "I'll leave you alone."

"No, stay," Louis said quickly, reaching out to touch her sleeve. "It's okay. Stay, please."

She climbed onto the table to sit beside him. "I didn't know you had family here," she said.

"I was born here," Louis said. "But I've been gone a long time."

"Did you come back because of your mother?" Abby asked.

"Yes. She was dying. It was expected."

Abby was silent. "Were you close to her?" she asked after a while.

"I didn't know her. She wasn't . . ." He paused. ". . . a very good mother. I was taken away from her and raised by foster parents."

Abby was quiet again, then asked, "Did they love you?"

Louis nodded. "Very much."

"That's good," Abby said quietly. "That's . . . very good." He heard her sniffling and turned. She was wiping her nose from the cold, like a kid might. "It's sad, though. Families should be together. But things get in the way sometimes, I guess."

Louis looked off into the trees, not really wanting to talk about families.

Abby touched his arm. "Are you going home now?"

"Yes. Soon." He sensed the disappointment in her voice but decided not to say anything in response. He wasn't about to share Junior's mean gossip with her.

"What about your case?" Abby said.

Louis stared off at the birds. "It's over." He looked down at the ground. "Probably just as well."

"But why? I thought it was important to you."

"It is—was. I don't know."

Abby pulled off her hat and held it between her hands. "I've been looking through my books for the poem," she said. He looked over at her. Her cheeks were bright pink from the cold.

"Thanks," he said. "But there's no need now. The case has been closed."

She sat quietly for a moment. "I don't think you should give up," she said. "I mean, you care too much about it."

He looked over at her, surprised. "Maybe that's the problem," he said. There was something in her eyes that pulled at him and he looked away. "In any case, I'm done here. I'm going home."

"Home," she said softly. "It sounds different when you say it."

The blackbirds took flight again, continuing on their frenzied journey. Louis and Abby both looked up.

"I've got to go," Abby said quickly, sliding off the picnic table. She pulled the denim hat down over her hair. "Louis, I don't think you should give up," she said.

"Abby, no one cares about that man."

"You do," she said. "But if you don't want to do it for him, then you should just do it for yourself."

She turned and hurried off to the Firebird, before he could say anything.

Louis stood staring at the empty bed. Bessie had already cleared everything from Lila's room. There was nothing in it now that spoke of sickness and death. The bed was freshly made, the white chenille spread pulled tight, a quilt carefully folded over the footboard. The room smelled strongly of pine disinfectant.

Louis turned away and went into his own room. At the cupboard in the tiny kitchenette, he got out the jar of Jif, but it was empty. He debated whether to get dressed and go over to Tinker's, but with a weary sigh, decided not to. He pulled a Heineken from the refrigerator instead, twisted off the top and took a swig. It was his second already, on an empty stomach, but he didn't care. He stood in the kitchenette, looking around at his room. His suitcase lay by the bed. He had pulled it out of the closet earlier, intending to start packing. But he realized it wouldn't take that long; he was leaving Black Pool with nothing more than he had brought in. Tomorrow morning, he would go in and give Dodie his resignation.

His eyes fell on the cardboard box on the kitchen table. He went over to it, staring down at the pieces of the broken bust. He was going to miss Bessie, but he was glad to be getting out of this place. There was nothing to keep him here now.

The phone rang out in the hall. A moment later, Bessie yelled up the stairs that it was for him. Tightening his robe, Louis padded out to pick up the extension.

"Louis?"

"Abby?"

"I think I found it."

"Abby, it's past eleven—"

"I found the poem, Louis."

He rubbed a hand over his face. "The poem? You found it? Where?"

"Right here at home. In a book here in our library." She sounded excited. "I'll bring it over. I can be there in fifteen minutes."

"No," he said quickly. "No, don't come over here."

There was silence for a moment on Abby's end. "Louis, I'm not afraid."

Jesus, she was talking about coming into the black part of town, not about being with him. Louis shook his head. "Abby, listen to me," he said. "I don't want to give anyone a reason to talk."

"About what?"

"About you . . . about me and you."

"That's crazy, Louis," she said. "For God's sake, I'm not a kid. Look, I'll be there in fifteen minutes."

"Abby!"

But she had already hung up. Louis put the phone back in its cradle with a frown. Damn it, there was no way to stop her. He dressed quickly and went downstairs. The blue light of the old television flickered from the dark parlor. He looked in with a sigh of relief. Bessie had fallen asleep in her chair, snoring along to Johnny Carson's monologue. Louis went to the front door to wait for Abby.

He saw her Firebird pull up, and when she came up to the porch he opened the door before she could ring the bell. "Get in here," he whispered. "And be quiet."

He ushered her past the parlor and up the stairs to his room, closing the door behind her. Abby was looking around the small room, and Louis resisted the urge to apologize for his humble surroundings. He saw her looking at the suitcase by the bed.

She turned to him. "I have the poem," she said, holding out a book. "It's called, 'To Be Lost, To Be Black.' "

He looked at her then took the book and opened it to the page she had marked. His eyes scanned the poem, fitting the missing words into the puzzle that had been turning around in his head for weeks. Then he read it again, slowly this time, now digesting the words as a whole, as a poem.

" '*Ask the night how it feels to be dark,*' " he read slowly. " '*To be pitch, to be black, to be lost.*' " His voice trailed off.

Abby came up and took the book from him. She sat down on the edge of the bed and read in a soft, melodic voice.

" '*Ask winter, the feeling of cold, the bitter edge of frost. / Ask day how it feels to be light, exposed so all can see, through the sharp lens of the sun, the glare of intensity.*' "

Louis listened, mesmerized.

" '*With the fears that torture the dark, and days that are rimmed with pride. / Ask me how it feels to be both exposed and doubly denied.*' "

He had drifted away somewhere for a moment and he struggled back. She was sitting there on the bed, looking up at him, her green eyes somber. He shivered.

"It's cold in here," he said. He went to the space heater and turned it on. He stood facing it, hugging himself as he waited for the coils to heat up, his arms folded over the thin cotton of his T-shirt.

"Louis . . ."

He felt her breath, warm at his ear.

"Louis, is something wrong?"

He shook his head slowly.

"Louis?"

He felt the gentle press of her hands on his back and he closed his eyes. He was afraid to turn around, afraid of the aching loneliness and need inside him and what it might lead him to do. He was afraid of her and her sweet willingness.

He turned. She was so close. She was so beautiful. He could smell her, a womanly musk, a faint scent of wine on her breath, and the lilacs. Her eyes were dark with her desire, her lips parted slightly in anticipation of his.

He cupped her face in his hands. So soft, so sweet, so beautiful. He would lose himself in her, drown himself in her, extinguish all the pain and emptiness.

He kissed her, softly, savoring the fruited taste of her mouth. She hesitated ever so slightly, then responded with a kiss more urgent than his own. She moved against him, fitting her body into his, her arms wrapping around his neck.

Oh God, it felt so wonderful. To hold someone, to be held by someone.

She drew back, took his hand and led him to the bed. She sat down and with shaking fingers, unbuttoned her blouse and took it off. She was wearing a lacy pink bra; her breasts were full, her pale skin dimpled from the cold. She looked up at him, her eyes pleading.

He lay down beside her, cradling her against his chest. He kissed her collarbone and she trembled. He touched her breast and she gave a low moan, arching toward his hand.

"Make love to me, Louis," she whispered.

There was something in her voice, a strange quiver, that made him pull back slightly to look at her. Her hair was a red fan against the white pillow, her face opalescent in the sparse glowing light given off by the heater. Her eyes burned up at him, with desire, but something else, a slight look of fear.

"Abby . . ."

"Please, Louis."

She lifted her head to kiss him but he pulled away. His head was filled with a cacophony of emotions. *Take her, take her, she wants you. It doesn't matter now, you're leaving, nothing matters now.*

He felt her hand moving up the inside of his thigh and he moaned, closing his eyes. Take her . . . and then go. It doesn't matter. She doesn't matter.

"No," he whispered.

He reached down and took her hand, removing it from his thigh. He looked down into Abby's face. "No," he said softly, "this isn't right."

She stared up at him for a moment, then turned her head away abruptly, closing her eyes. He raised himself up on his elbow and she quickly crossed her arms over her chest, shielding herself from him.

"Abby ..."

A tear made its way down her cheek and across her nose. She wiped it away angrily. He touched her arm, but she shrugged it off and sat up, turning her back to him as she grabbed her blouse.

Louis swung his legs over the side of the bed and sat hunched over, eyes closed. He felt the bed move as she shifted to sit on the opposite side. It was several moments before he realized she was softly crying. He went around to the other side of the bed and sat down next to her. She wouldn't look at him; she just sat there crying. Finally he drew her into his arms.

"I thought you wanted me," she said.

"Abby, don't."

"I thought ... I thought you would want me more if I acted more, more ..." Her voice trailed off into tears.

Louis suppressed a sigh. He started to stroke her hair, but then stopped, knowing somehow that it would seem parental and that the last thing she wanted right now was to be treated like a child. The fearful expression that had clouded her face just moments ago came back to him in that instant and he closed his eyes as the realization struck him. God, he was stupid.

"Abby," he said softly, "you're a virgin, aren't you?"

She hesitated, then nodded. She had stopped crying but still lay nestled against his chest. Finally, she pulled back, wiping her face and smoothing back her hair. She let out a long, shuddering sigh.

"I wanted you to be the one," she said softly. "I've dreamed about it, and saved myself even though all my friends were screwing around like crazy. I wanted it to be perfect." She lowered her eyes. "I wanted you because I knew it would be."

Louis smiled slightly. "I'm flattered."

She looked up suddenly, eyes flashing. "Don't make fun of me."

Louis touched her cheek. "I'm sorry. I meant that I really would have been flattered to be your first."

"Then why not?" she said, her eyes tearing.

Louis shook his head. "Because it isn't right . . . at least right now. We would be using each other, Abby, just to fill up some gaps inside us. I'm too damn lonely right now, and you are—" He was going to say *"too young and too desperate"* but stopped himself. "You are just not ready."

She picked at the tufts of the chenille bedspread. "I suppose you've had hundreds of women," she said.

"Hundreds . . ."

A car honked down in the street below, drawing Abby's eyes briefly to the window and then back to Louis. Her tears had washed away the makeup she had so carefully applied and her hair was tangled. The silk blouse was wrinkled and she had buttoned it up lopsided. Louis slowly undid it and buttoned it up right. She held her breath until he finished, and then let it out in one big sigh.

"I'm so embarrassed," she said, not looking at him.

"Don't be."

"I had a couple glasses of my mother's sherry before I came over here."

Louis smiled. "I don't recommend drinking before your first time. I got drunk my first time and I can't remember a thing. And it should be a moment in your life that you don't want to forget."

Abby's eyes held his. "I wouldn't have forgotten."

Her face was lifted toward his and he wanted to kiss her in that moment. And a part of him, the cold nub inside him that had warmed to her touch, was urging him forward.

He leaned over and kissed her forehead. Her scent swirled up to him, and he shut his eyes, memorizing it. "You'd better go," he said softly.

She nodded and got up from the bed. He helped her on with her coat and she pulled a velvet hat over her ears. As she picked up the poetry book, her expression turned forlorn, and he realized that she was trying to find a way to say good-bye.

"When are you leaving?" she asked.

"I don't know. I'm resigning tomorrow. Soon after."

"When I came here tonight, I was hoping I could convince you to stay . . . for me." She looked down at the poetry book in her hand. "I thought that if that didn't work then maybe this would." She held the book out to him.

He shook his head. "I don't need it anymore."

She nodded sadly. "I guess not." She went to the door, opened it and turned back to him. "Good-bye, Louis," she said softly.

"Good-bye, Abby," he said.

She closed the door softly. He stood still, listening to the retreat of her footsteps down the creaky stairs. He waited for the thud of the front door closing and the sound of her car engine starting before he went to the window. He stood, his arms wrapped over his chest against the chill, watching until the red taillights of her car disappeared.

CHAPTER 14

The brown Blazer pulled up to the curb in front of the station just before Louis swung his Mustang into a spot nearby. Louis watched as Dodie climbed out of the Blazer and paused to zip up his jacket against the morning cold. He hadn't intended to tell Dodie about the resignation at that moment, but it seemed better to get it over with here outside, away from the others. He got out and hurried after Dodie.

"Sheriff, wait."

Dodie turned, pulling a fresh cigar from his pocket and slipping it between his teeth. "Mornin', Kincaid."

"Sheriff," Louis began, "my mother died Monday and—"

Dodie took the cigar from his mouth, frowning. "Monday? That why you didn't come in yesterday? Why didn't you say?" He hesitated then patted Louis's arm awkwardly. "Shit, Kincaid, I'm right sorry. You need more time, you take it."

"No, wait, Sheriff, I don't—"

"Sam!"

Louis turned to see Bob Roberts hurrying over to them. He must have just come from the courthouse next door; he wasn't wearing an overcoat.

"Sam, I gotta be in court in fifteen minutes and I'm tied up the rest of the day," Roberts said. "So if you wanna do this Mulcahey thing, it's now or never." He stood there, bobbing up and down, flapping his arms across his chest.

"Fine with me," Dodie said, and started into the station. He turned to Louis. "Kincaid, you'd better sit in on this, too—if you don't mind."

Junior was waiting for them in Dodie's office, his face a rare picture of doom. He had spread the contents of the Earl Mulcahey file out on Dodie's desk.

"Junior, get me a cup of coffee, will ya?" Dodie said, hanging up his jacket. "Bob?"

The district attorney shook his head.

"What's this about, Sheriff?" Louis asked.

"Eucher put a rush on that search warrant you wanted and the boys up in Starksville found a .30-.30 rifle in Leverette's dorm," Dodie said. "I wanted Bob to go over the rest of this to see if we've got enough to arrest him."

Louis dropped into a chair. He watched as Roberts sifted through the material on the desk, knowing what the DA was probably thinking. The rifle, combined with the rest of the evidence—the prints from the deer hide, the insurance policy, and the statement of one neighbor who overheard father and son arguing about money—all made for a strong case against Leverette Mulcahey.

"We still can't match the rifle," Louis said weakly.

"Leverette lied to us, Louis," Dodie said. "The kid hid the damn rifle in his dorm."

"He's got no alibi, either," Junior said.

"But—"

"I bet if we brought him in and scared him a little, he'd fess up," Junior interrupted.

"That's called badgering and coercion, Junior," Louis said. "It's against the law." He shook his head. "Sheriff, I just don't know about this."

"The kid's getting a quarter million bucks," Junior said, sliding off the windowsill and pointing to the policy. "Pretty damn strong motive."

"People do strange things for money," Louis replied, "but I just don't see it in Leverette."

Dodie was looking at Louis carefully. Then he turned to Roberts. "What do you think, Bob?"

"I think we've got enough here." He kept glancing at his watch.

Louis sighed, shaking his head.

"Kincaid, what's the matter with you?" Dodie said. "You're the one who started all this."

"I know, I know."

"Look, Sam," Roberts said, "I can't be dickin' around all day on this. Let's get moving. The mayor wants this thing wrapped up *now*. People think there's a crazed sniper out there. It's killing the hunting season."

Louis looked up at Roberts. What an idiot. He looked back at Dodie and started to say something. But what was the point? He looked at the floor, elbows on knees.

"Too bad," Roberts said, shaking his head. "He seemed like a nice kid."

"Bob," Dodie said, "maybe we should let Kincaid here look into this a little more."

Roberts shook his head impatiently. "We've got enough to arrest him. Just do it, Sam." He leveled his gaze at Dodie. "Okay?"

Dodie hesitated then looked at Junior. "Go get Mike and get over to Ethel's," he said quietly. "Try to keep it low-key, you hear?"

Roberts gave everyone a quick good-bye and left, Junior hurrying out after him. Louis remained seated, watching Dodie as he settled into his chair, took out the Zippo and lit his cigar. The fetid smell of the El Producto filled the room, making Louis wince. It was time to tell Dodie he was leaving.

"Sheriff—"

"Now, don't start harpin' on me, Kincaid," Dodie said quickly, raising a hand. "If Leverette's innocent, I'll be the first one there to unlock the cell door."

"No, it's not that. I need—"

The phone rang, cutting him off. Dodie jumped on it. "Gonna be one of those days," he muttered. Louis watched as Dodie waited, drumming his fingers on his desk in irritation as the secretary on the other end took her time putting the call through.

"Yeah, Walt, what is it?" Dodie said flatly. Dodie's eyes narrowed. "Christ, Walt, the damn service ain't till Saturday. Can't this wait?" He let out a disgusted sigh and slammed the phone down. He rose, grabbed his jacket, and without looking at Louis stomped out of the office. "Goin' to the mayor's office," he called out to Junior.

Louis got up and went out to his own desk. He had to get over to the funeral home and make arrangements for Lila, but he wanted to wait until they brought Leverette in. He didn't know why, really. There was nothing he could do or say now that would make a difference. He sat down and idly surveyed his few personal items. Not much to pack up. His eyes fell on yellowed paper taped to a corner of the scarred desk. It was the incomplete poem. He picked at the Scotch tape and peeled it off.

He leaned back in the chair, closing his eyes. He hadn't slept well, kept awake by the same thing that was troubling him now: the gnawing feeling of defeat deep in his gut. Today, Leverette Mulcahey would be thrown in jail for murdering his father. Even if he were proven innocent, the stain of the accusation would always be there. And Saturday, the bones of another innocent man would be buried, his identity lost forever. Louis crumbled up the yellowed paper and threw it in the trash can.

They brought Leverette in soon after. Louis watched as the young man trudged in, his hands cuffed behind him. He was put straight into a cell to be held until he could be taken upstairs for processing. Louis went back to the cellblock.

Leverette was slumped on a bunk, eyes closed.

"Leverette . . ."

His head shot up. He got up and came up to the bars. His dark hair was disheveled and his eyes were liquid with fear, but they were locked on Louis's with a desperate fierceness. Louis couldn't think of anything to say.

"I didn't do this," Leverette said. "I loved my dad."

"It'll be all right, Leverette," Louis said weakly. "You'll get a lawyer and—"

"No!" Leverette said. "It won't be all right! I didn't do this. No one believes me." His hands, gripping the bars, were shaking. "I'm scared," he whispered.

Louis swallowed hard. "Leverette, a lawyer—"

With a cry, Leverette spun away. He crumbled down onto the bunk, holding his head in his hands. Louis watched him for a moment then turned and slowly walked back into the office.

Ethel Mulcahey came in at that moment and saw him. She was wrapped in a gray coat and had tied a scarf haphazardly over her hair. Louis saw that she was still wearing her bedroom slippers. She stared at him, her eyes glistening beads in the pleated white cushion of her face.

Louis went over to her. "Mrs. Mulcahey—"

"Go away," she said hoarsely. "Just go away and leave us alone."

Her eyes welled and she turned away. Louis watched as Mike led her into the cellblock, then he picked up his jacket and left.

As he sat on the small white bench in the foyer of the Wallace-Pickney Funeral Home, Louis thought about all the times he had been in such places. Twice for cops' funerals and once for a little boy who had been killed by a drunk driver. But this was different. This time he was burying his mother.

It was quiet, except for the muted organ music coming from the parlor down the hall. Louis laid his head back against the wall, closing his eyes. A door opened and he looked up.

A man was coming out of the office, gliding across the white tile floor as if he were on ice skates. He was tall, with deep-set, hollow eyes and thin blond hair that he combed from the left ear to the right to cover his baldness. His suit had a sheen to it, as if it had been pressed too often.

"I'm Mr. Wallace," he said. "You wanted to see me?"

Louis stood up and introduced himself.

Wallace shook Louis's hand tepidly. "You work for Sam Dodie," he said, making it a statement rather than a question.

"Yes, but I'm not here on police business," Louis said. "I'm here to make arrangements for my mother."

"That's not possible."

Louis stared at Stan Wallace in confusion. "I don't understand."

"I'm sure you don't," Wallace said, his nostrils flaring as he drew in a deep breath. "We cannot accommodate your mother."

As Louis stared at Stan Wallace's pallid face, he felt the muscles in his shoulders flex involuntarily. Suddenly Wallace's pinched face went fuzzy. The organ music drifted in and out.

"Excuse me?" Louis said.

"We only take white people."

The words had been spoken so casually that at first they didn't even register in Louis's brain. Then, very slowly, they did, one word at a time, each cutting him, not like a knife but like a razor, so clean, sharp, and quick that he didn't feel the pain, just the gap it left. A sensation shot through him, something so foreign that it took him several seconds to realize what it was—sheer, cold rage.

"You can't do that!" Louis hissed.

Wallace blinked quickly. "Sue me."

"What about Willie Johnson?" Louis said between clenched teeth. "He's black."

Wallace shrugged. "We're making the arrangements for the memorial service but he won't be brought here. The city's paying for it so it's not a funeral . . . per se. It's business. Strictly business."

Wallace's words seemed to ricochet around the sleek walls. Louis felt his right hand clench into a fist and for one second in his mind he could see it landing in Stan Wallace's face. He could feel the give of the man's doughy flesh, the satisfying sharp jolt of bone against his knuckles. He closed his eyes, pulling in a deep breath, trying to quell the fire inside his chest. When he opened his eyes, Wallace was looking at him with strange mix of apprehension and smugness.

Wallace tilted his head back and his nostrils flared once again. "I suggest you try Collins Funeral Home."

"I suggest you go fuck yourself."

Wallace's mouth formed a small O and he took a step back. The man was afraid of him, afraid of what the "crazy nigger" was going to do. Louis wanted to laugh. His mother was dead, goddamn it, and this fucking piece of shit wouldn't bury her. A sound gurgled up from inside him, the beginning of a laugh, but it caught in his throat and came out as a small cry.

Louis turned quickly and hurried to the door. He jerked it open and slammed it—loud enough, he hoped, to wake the dead.

Louis closed the front door softly.

"Louis? That you?"

"Yeah . . ."

Bessie came through the parlor into the hall. Her hands were covered with flour. "You're home early."

He hung his jacket on the hall tree. "There wasn't much for me to do at the station," he said flatly. He didn't meet her eyes. He had told her last night that he was leaving soon. She was taking the news badly.

"You don't look good," Bessie said, wiping her hands on her apron. "Come in and sit with me. I'm making chicken and dumplin's."

Louis followed her into the yellow kitchen and dropped into one of the chrome–and–yellow vinyl chairs. The small room was fragrant with the smells of cooking. His stomach growled suddenly. He had forgotten to eat all day. Bessie put a glass of milk in front of him. He grimaced; he never had liked milk, but Bessie kept trying to pour it down his throat as an antidote to the Heinekens she knew he kept up in his room.

"Leverette Mulcahey was arrested today," Louis said, leaning back in the chair.

"For what?" Bessie asked from the stove.

"They think he murdered his father."

"Lordy, lordy," Bessie clucked. "Do you?"

Louis stared at the milk. "No," he said softly.

The kitchen fell silent.

"What time is that service Saturday?" Bessie asked suddenly.

"It starts at nine." Louis looked back at her. "You planning on going?"

Bessie shrugged as she stirred the stew. "I will if you want me to, Louis. I'll go for you. But truth be told, I think it's all a big put-on. I jus' got a feelin' about it, a bad feeling, that the man they's puttin' in the ground ain't who they says he is."

Louis stared at Bessie for a moment. "Me too, Bessie," he said softly. "Me too."

He turned back and put his head in his hands, resting his elbows on the table. There was a thud on the table. He looked up. It was a bottle of Heineken.

Smiling wanly, he took a long swig, closing his eyes. A moment later, Bessie set a plate of the thick chicken and gravy in front of him. She sat down opposite him. He took a bite of a dumpling. It was delicious. The kitchen was silent again as he ate.

"Louis," Bessie said finally. "You ain't said nothin' about your mama since she passed."

"There's nothing to say," he said softly.

"I know better than that. No matter what, she was still your mama and it still pains you, I can see it on your face."

"Bessie," Louis put the spoon down and sat back. "I . . . I'm not sure what I feel. I just know it doesn't seem fair."

"Nobody ever said things is fair, Louis. Life ain't fair."

Wallace's thin face flashed in his mind. "I went over to Wallace-Pickney today," Louis said. "You know what happened? They refused to take her. *Refused*. I . . . I wanted to kill him. For a split second, I *could've* killed him."

Bessie reached across the table and took his hand. "I told you, Louis, just go over to Collins."

"I can't do that."

Bessie frowned. "Why not? Most of us folk don't want nothin' to do with Wallace-Pickney. We got our own, always have. It's jus' as good."

"I know, but I kept seeing that picture of her, and I kept thinking about how stinking awful things were for her most of her life. And I just wanted her to be there. I wanted to have flowers and—"

"Louis," Bessie said firmly, "Collins done got flowers."

"I know, but—"

"Louis Kincaid, you's a snob. Collins was good enough for my husband and half my kin. Why isn't Collins good enough for your mama? What's so bad about Collins Funeral Parlor?"

Louis ran a hand over his eyes. "It's not the same."

"What's not the same?" Bessie asked, her voice rising.

Louis looked up at her. "It just . . ."

"It's just that's it's *black*, isn't it? Louis Washington Kincaid, you ought to be ashamed!"

He could not look at her. He stared fuzzily into the gravy. He looked up to apologize but she was gone. He was alone in the kitchen. He lowered his head to his arms. He was so very tired.

Bessie slammed a glass frame down in front of him and he jumped.

"This is my great-granddaddy Preston Everard Roberson," she said. "He was born a slave but he was the smartest man I ever knowed. You know what he taught me? He taught me that being black done mean one thing. You can't walk alone."

Louis took the frame and stared at the photograph.

"My granddaddy, his daddy, and all the black men before and after them, they're all in there inside you, Louis," Bessie said, more softly now. "They're inside you and every black man who walks the earth, them and their pain. You can't escape it. You can't deny it. It's a heavy load to carry, but it's what makes us strong."

She took the frame back. "It's what makes us different from them."

He looked up at Bessie, his eyes welling with tears of shame. Her face softened and she sighed deeply. She came to him, stretching out her arms. Louis wrapped his arms around her waist and buried his face in her breasts. She held him, rocking him gently.

The face called to him.

He had tried to ignore it, but finally, he had gone to the closet and got out the cardboard box containing the broken pieces of the clay bust. He had carefully set them on the table and for an hour sat looking at them.

Now he picked up the largest chunk. It was the eyes, with a part of the nose intact. He stared into the blank gray orbs.

"Who are you?" he whispered. "Who are you?"

The phone rang out in the hall, unanswered. Bessie had gone to the Piggly Wiggly. Louis let it go, listening to its plaintive ring, fifteen, twenty times. Finally he got up and went out to the extension in the hall.

"Lloyd residence," he answered, slumping against the wall.

"Louis Kincaid?"

He straightened. The voice sounded familiar. "Yes. Who's this?"

"I can't say right now. You arrested the wrong guy in Earl's killing."

Jesus. It was his mysterious caller. "How do you know? Who are you?"

"I can't tell you yet. I'm afraid."

"Of what?"

"Of getting killed. They'll kill me."

"Who's 'they'?"

"The others. . . ."

Louis shifted the phone to his other ear. "Why are you calling me?"

"I need to make sure someone else knows."

"Knows what? What have you done? Did you kill Earl?" Louis asked.

"No . . . no." The voice hesitated. Louis could hear the man's raspy breathing. "I can't go to prison."

"Look," Louis said, "I can't promise anything. I'm a cop, not a district attorney."

"But you can talk to him."

"I could."

The other end of the phone was quiet a long time. Louis tried to stay calm.

"All right," the caller said finally. "I'll meet with you, but first you go to Roberts and see what you can do."

"Wait! Don't hang up."

"I'll call back."

"When?"

"Saturday night, at ten."

"Look, I need something concrete, something I can tell Roberts to make him listen."

"All right, all right. . . ."

Louis's mouth was dry and he was tense from his toes to his ears.

"Earl was killed because of the lynching of that guy y'all are burying on Saturday," the voice said.

Louis fell back against the wall softly, stunned. "How do you know this?"

"I was there."

CHAPTER 15

Leverette was walking toward him. His shoulders were huge and misshapen, covered with a burgundy shirt. Across his chest was a white number 15. He was wearing handcuffs. There was blood running from his head.

He came closer, along the two-lane road. Cars, big white cars, flew by, buffeting his body from side to side. The burgundy football jersey began to fade, turning to checkered flannel. Then it began to fall away from his body in shreds. Leverette held up his hands. The cuffs had turned into rope. His face started to darken, as if someone was shading in a pencil drawing, turning tan . . . brown . . . black. The cars kept coming, white cars with shiny chrome bumpers.

Leverette's face was just a blur now, smudged. . . . It came closer, but it wasn't Leverette anymore. It was his own face. And it was mouthing two words, over and over: *Help me, help me.*

Louis jerked awake.

The room was black and cold as ice. His heart was hammering and he was bathed in sweat. He sat up, pulling in a jagged breath. The sound of a car going by in the street below filtered up to him. Slowly his heartbeat returned to normal.

Jesus . . . First ghosts, and now nightmares.

He threw back the quilt and swung his legs over the side of the bed. The cold of the wood floor on his feet felt reassuringly real. He stood up and went to the kitchenette. He threw open the refrigerator, blinking in the light as he looked for a beer. None. He closed it and sank back against the counter. Damn, he had to get out of this place before he went crazy.

He looked at his suitcase, sitting on the floor in the corner, piled high with his clothes. The face in the dream came back to him and he closed his eyes against it. He pushed himself away from the counter and went to the window, snapping back the curtains. The street was quiet, deserted, the sky brushed with pale pink in the east. Louis leaned his head against the cold pane.

He saw the light come on in Tinker's store and knew it was six. Too early to get up. But he was too keyed-up to go back to sleep. He showered and dressed, pulling on khakis and an old beige knit shirt. Downstairs, he grabbed his sheriff's jacket off the hall tree and quietly let himself out the front door.

Tinker's store was warm, the coffee smell pungent. Louis started across the creaky wood floor toward it just as Tinker emerged from the back with a tray of donuts.

"Good morning, Mr. Tinker," Louis said as he poured coffee into a to-go cup.

Tinker nodded politely. "Mr. Kincaid."

As Louis went to the counter to pay, Tinker took a sprinkled donut from the tray and set it on a napkin before Louis.

"You have a good memory," Louis said.

"I have an excellent memory," Tinker replied. He selected a plain donut for himself and moved to the coffee machine, picking up the pot of hot water. He brought a cup back to the counter, and Louis watched as he unwrapped a teabag. Dipping it into the water, he looked up at Louis and spoke softly. "Bessie told me about Miss Lila. My sympathies," he said.

"Thank you," Louis said. He finished his donut in two bites as Tinker went about straightening the gum and candy around the cash register.

"All packed?" Tinker asked suddenly.

Louis looked at him over the rim of the cup. Bessie must have told him that, too. "Not all the way," Louis said, glancing at the donut case. Tinker lifted the lid and Louis got another.

"Your case is solved, then?"

Louis shook his head. "Far from it."

Tinker's expression remained impassive, but Louis could sense something behind it. Anger? Disappointment?

"There's no sense in keeping at it," Louis said, feeling the need to explain. "It's their town, their crime. They can handle it however they want now. I'm finished banging my head against the wall." Louis bit into the donut.

"So you're giving up," Tinker said.

Louis looked Tinker square in the eye. "I have no choice. It was hopeless to begin with. You were right." He took a sip of coffee.

"I was right?"

"You said things don't change. You said I couldn't make a difference."

"Perhaps I was wrong. I am, occasionally."

"You weren't wrong. No one cares. No one was willing to help me." Louis said, shaking his head. "I even dreamed about it last night."

"Dreams cannot be interpreted by those who experience them. Dreams come from deep inside. Their true meaning is often fantasy or desire, not reality."

Louis stared into the coffee. "Yeah, sure. Name one person in this town who gives a damn what I do."

"Willie Johnson . . . or whoever he is."

Louis hesitated. He was about to say, "He's dead. He can't do anything anymore," but he didn't. The unknown man was not dead. He had spoken to him that first day in the woods and he hadn't stopped since. Louis studied Tinker's face as the old man took off his glasses and cleaned them with a handkerchief pulled from his overalls. Tinker glanced up, leveling his soft brown eyes at Louis.

"Mr. Tinker, that man can't help me," Louis said.

"Then you must help yourself."

Oh man, why did he bother to come over here? Louis wadded the napkin and tossed it in the trash can. He should know better than to get sucked into the old man's reedy muck of musings.

Louis put two dollars on the counter and picked up a copy of the *Black Pool Journal*, tucking it under his arm. "I'm leaving, Mr. Tinker. There's nothing more I can do." He started toward the door.

"Mr. Kincaid," Tinker called out. "You know your Shakespeare?"

Louis paused. "Some."

" 'To be or not to be, that is the question,' " Tinker recited. " 'Whether 'tis nobler in the mind to suffer the slings and arrows of outrageous fortune, or to take arms against a sea of troubles, and by opposing, end them.' "

Louis smiled bitterly. "You're quoting a weak man who couldn't decide what to do."

"That's what most people think," Tinker said without smiling. "But that's not how I see it. I think those words are really a call to action, spoken by a man who has made a decision and plans to see it through, no matter what."

Louis shook his head, pushed open the screen door and stepped out on the porch. It was light now and he breathed in the cold breeze, watching the cars coming and going at the stop sign. He let out a sigh. Call to action . . . shit.

He started down the steps and the paper slipped from his arm, scattering in the wind. Louis hustled after it, grabbing the front page. He rose and looked at the headline: CITY PLANS SYMBOLIC TRIBUTE TO SLAIN MAN.

Beneath it, there was a photograph of the pencil sketch that Marsha Burns had sent with the clay bust. The caption said: *Willie Johnson.*

Louis crumbled the paper and stuffed it in a nearby garbage can. It wasn't right. Goddamn it, it just wasn't right.

He went back up the steps and jerked open the screen door. He stalked to the counter. Tinker hadn't moved, and Louis looked at him calmly.

"All right," he said. "I'll stay. I'll stay and finish this."

"I never asked you to stay, Mr. Kincaid."

Louis was shaking his head. "But people aren't going to like it," he said firmly. "They're going to have to face the ugly parts of their past instead of running away from them."

"We all need to do that sooner or later, Mr. Kincaid," Tinker said.

Louis stared at him. There was something new in Tinker's eyes, a hint of empathy, a glimmer of compassion perhaps. Tinker went over to the coffee machine and returned with a fresh cup for Louis. Louis thanked him and leaned back against the counter.

Through the window, he could see a small knot of children bundled in tattered parkas, lining up to get on the yellow school-bus. He took a drink of the bracing coffee.

"I'm going to have to do things my way, even if it means going behind the sheriff's back," he said, more to himself than Tinker.

"Your sheriff—is he a good man?" Tinker asked.

"I don't know. He seems to want to close his eyes to the whole thing."

"Then show him something he can't ignore."

"I don't know if I can trust him," Louis said. "Sometimes he seems like he's capable of being a cop, of doing what has to be done, but then . . ." He shook his head. "I just don't *know* him."

Tinker went over to the vegetable bin, pulled something out and came back. He held an artichoke up in front of Louis's face.

"I don't sell many of these," Tinker said. "People come in and say, 'Tinker, what the hell is that ugly thing?' They say it's too much trouble to eat, too hard working through all the tough leaves to get to the good piece inside. But it's worth it, what's inside." He tossed the artichoke in the air and caught it, smiling.

Louis stared at the artichoke in Tinker's large hand, then laughed softly. Tinker set the artichoke on the counter. Louis sobered, looking at him.

"This could cost me my career, Mr. Tinker," he said.

Tinker nodded. "You could leave. You have that choice."

Louis shook his head. "No," he said. "Not anymore."

After leaving Tinker's, Louis drove straight to Ethel Mulcahey's house. He sat in the driveway, looking at his watch. It was only seven-thirty, probably too early to bother her. He didn't even know if she would open the door after the way she acted at the station yesterday, and he didn't really blame her. But he had to try.

The drapes at the living-room window pulled open suddenly and Louis saw Ethel. She spotted his car, stood frozen in the window for a moment then moved away. Louis got out and went up to ring the bell.

He stood waiting for several minutes. He was just about to give up when she opened the door, just enough to look out at him.

"What do you want?" she said flatly.

"Mrs. Mulcahey, please give me a minute," he began slowly. "I want to talk to you about Leverette."

"Did Sam send you?" she asked.

"No, I'm here on my own." He hesitated. She looked worn-out, like she hadn't slept. "Mrs. Mulcahey, I don't think Leverette is guilty. I want to help him."

Ethel's eyes scanned his face. She clutched the lapels of her pink robe tighter around her neck.

"Please, Mrs. Mulcahey," Louis said softly but firmly. "I need to talk to you."

She disappeared and a second later, the door swung open. Louis came into the entrance hall. Ethel was walking away, toward the living room. He shut the door and followed her.

She had sat down on the edge of a chair, hunched over like a sick bird on a perch. Louis took the sofa across from her. The sun streamed in through the big window, falling full on her wan face. She looked terrible.

Ethel looked up at him as if coming out of a trance. "I'm sorry," she said, "I'm usually dressed by now but . . ." Her voice trailed off. "You said you think Leverette is innocent."

Louis nodded.

"Then why was he arrested?"

Louis wasn't sure what to tell her. He considered telling her what had been tumbling through his mind since the mysterious man had called him last night. But the only thing he had been able to deduce from the caller's confession was that Earl had been killed because of the lynching. If Earl had played a part in it, he didn't want to be the one to tell Ethel. But somehow Earl and the mysterious caller were involved. And Walt Kelly was, too, if the picture of him wearing the medallion meant anything.

"I need you to tell me about Earl," Louis began. "About what he was like when he was young."

Ethel frowned in confusion. "What does this have to do with Leverette?"

"I can't tell you exactly. Please, Mrs. Mulcahey, just trust me. This will help Leverette."

She sighed deeply. "All right, what do you what to know?"

"Start when you met. . . . Anything."

She told him they had known each other since childhood, Earl's family living close by her own, and that they had started dating in high school.

"Who were your friends in high school?" Louis asked.

"I had many friends, but Earl didn't," she said. "Most of the boys thought he was . . . a sissy, I guess you would say. Earl was a quiet boy. He liked to read. He didn't play sports. He wanted so desperately to be a part of the crowd but, I suppose, Detective, he was what the kids nowadays call a nerd." Ethel seemed to drift off for a moment.

"Did he hang around with anyone?"

"I . . . I don't really remember." She ran a hand over her face. "Would you like some coffee, Detective?"

Louis took her invitation as a sign she was warming up to him. He was filled to bursting with Tinker's coffee, but he accepted anyway.

She was gone a long time. When she returned, she was carrying a cup and a large, dark blue book.

"I found our annual," she said softly, sitting down next to him. "Perhaps it'll refresh my memory." She handed him the coffee, which Louis set on an end table.

The annual's cover was embossed, *1955, Black Pool High School.* Ethel opened it and turned the pages to the senior-class photos.

"Oh, I haven't seen these faces for years." A small smile came to her lips. "Look at me . . . how silly I was, my hair in one of those funny poodle do's."

"You looked lovely, Mrs. Mulcahey."

She didn't seem to hear him. "And look, there's Walter Kelly."

Louis studied the senior picture of Walter Kelly closely. The eyes were deep and dark, the lips thin and unsmiling. He looked like a prick even then.

"Did Earl graduate with Walter Kelly?" he asked.

"Yes, but they weren't friends. Walter ran with a different crowd, a wilder crowd. Walter and Max Lillihouse were best friends."

Ethel pointed to another photo on the opposite page. "That's Maisey Beth Hill. Now she's Maisey Kelly, of course, Walter's wife."

Louis caught the slight tone of admonishment in her voice. "So that's Black Pool's first lady," he said.

Ethel looked at him. "She was a wild one, that girl was. Pretty as a picture but she . . . Well, let's just say, she flaunted herself. And not always—and my apologies for this, but there's no other way to explain it—on our side of town. She liked to, as we called it, 'go down the hill.' That's what we called the black part of town—'down the hill.' "

Louis looked at the picture of the pretty brunette.

"Of course, I don't think Walter ever knew. But us girls did,"

Ethel went on. "I'm sure he found out after they were married, but by then it was too late. He was stuck with her."

Ethel moved on, her finger moving across the young faces to Max. "That's Max. He's sure put on a few pounds since then. Fat as a pig now."

She flipped back a few pages and pointed to a picture of a pretty blonde. "That's Grace."

Louis focused on the portrait of Grace Ketcher. She had a seductive smile, but artlessly so, as if she were oblivious to the power of her beauty. Just like Abby.

"Grace was so lovely," Ethel said wistfully. "She placed first in the Miss Magnolia Pageant, you know, when she was just sixteen years old. She could've had any boy she wanted."

Louis had to ask. "Then why did she marry Max?"

Ethel sighed. "I really don't know. She was a year younger than me, and we were friends, but not really close. She was kind of shy, really didn't date much, even though all the boys had crushes on her." Ethel paused. "Especially Max. He wrote her notes and stuck them in her locker. He used to go out to her house all the time with the excuse he was there to work on the colonel's car. Grace couldn't stand him. I was surprised when they got married. It seemed so sudden."

Had old Colonel Ketcher held a shotgun to Max's head? Louis thought back to the Ketcher family book, remembering the dates. No, Abby had been born eight years into the marriage. Louis stared at the picture of Grace in the annual. The contrast between this sweet, ponytailed girl and the sad woman in the wedding picture was unsettling.

Ethel resumed turning the pages of the yearbook, a faraway look on her face.

"Mrs. Mulcahey," Louis said, "was there a relationship between your husband and Walter Kelly at any time, before or after school?"

"Nothing to speak of."

"What about Max?"

"Heavens, no," Ethel said softly. "Max beat Earl up one day over something he said to Grace. Earl hated him."

Louis had a sudden thought. "What about Sam Dodie? What was he like?"

Ethel's brows knitted together, then she turned to the first part of the book, to the photographs of the freshman class. "There he is," she said, pointing.

Louis leaned closer and studied the picture. God, he looked like a typical hayseed farmboy. Dark hair parted and slicked to his head, a sprinkle of freckles. He wore a checkered cotton shirt and overalls straps were visible across his shoulders. A far cry from Kelly's snappy crew cut and cardigan, or Max's ducktail and dress shirt.

"Sam was a couple years behind us," Ethel said. "His sister Emily was in our class. She was salutatorian, went to Ole Miss, I think. Sam, well, he wasn't at all like Emily. He wasn't too good at school, or much of anything, really. He was the baby of that family."

Louis took the book from Ethel and studied the small face.

"He was a quiet boy, a hard worker," Ethel went on dreamily. "I remember once when he was a bag boy at Cecil's Grocery, my mother left her wallet there and Sam found it and showed up at our house that night to give it back. He walked all the way over, five miles. Wouldn't even take a tip for his trouble."

She paused, her eyes distant. "I think Emily was ashamed of him. She didn't like having him around. And the other boys, the older ones, Max, Walter, Stanley . . . they used to tease him about his clothes." She smiled, sadly. "He was the waterboy on the football team the year Max made All-State. They made fun of him behind his back."

"He dropped out of school, right?" Louis asked.

Ethel nodded. "To marry Margaret Sue Purdy. We all knew they had to get married because she was pregnant. But no one talked about it." She sighed. "She lost the baby at birth. They never had any more."

Ethel took the yearbook from Louis and closed it. "I was happy for Sam when he was elected sheriff. It was like . . . like he finally did something right. His father was pretty hard on him, hard on Emily, too, but she was tougher than Sam and she moved away." She gave Louis a hopeless kind of look. "I think Sam was a disappointment to his father."

Louis leaned back on the sofa. His gaze went up to the large framed photograph above the fireplace. It was of Ethel and Earl with their two children, taken when the kids were young teenagers. Earl's hand rested protectively on Leverette's shoulder.

"You didn't drink your coffee, Detective," Ethel said. "Can I get you a warm cup?"

"No, no thank you," Louis said with a smile.

Ethel seemed somewhat revived. Louis wondered if the reminiscing had done her some good.

One thing was still nagging him. There still was no strong connection between Earl and Walter Kelly. If they had been together at the lynching, what was the bond?

"Mrs. Mulcahey," Louis said. "You said that Earl had no relationship with Walter Kelly. Are you sure? Did Earl sell him insurance?" When Ethel shook her head, Louis pressed on. "Maybe some business dealings of some kind?"

"The only business deal I ever knew about was the one Earl had with Max," Ethel said.

Louis frowned. "Max?"

Ethel nodded. "I remember it clearly because I tried so hard to talk Earl out of it."

"What was it?"

"Earl sold Max a big piece of land, about thirty acres, I think." She shook her head. "It had belonged to Earl's family and they owned it free and clear. It had a beautiful redbrick house on it with this long drive that stretched deep into the woods. Even had a pretty little stream running through it. When Earl's parents passed on, I thought we'd move out there, but Earl said no. He sold it right after."

"But why did he sell it?"

"He never said. All I know is that Earl wanted to sell it and Max Lillihouse wanted to buy it." Ethel frowned slightly at the memory. "Heaven knows, he didn't need it. He already had the thousands of acres that Grace's father left them. I guess he wanted it because it butted up to what he already had. Max was always greedy that way."

Something went off in Louis's head. "A stream?" he repeated. "Mrs. Mulcahey, was it the same land where the bones were found?"

"The bones?" Ethel's face clouded over. "You mean that poor man you found out in the woods?" She seemed to be trying to think. "I don't know. . . . Why, yes, I think so. Just off Road 234."

Louis's mind was spinning, trying to put it together. "Did Earl ever tell you why he didn't want to live on his parents' land?"

"No. I didn't ask, either. I really wanted that house, Detective, and I was kinda angry with him about that for a while." She sighed. "Earl had this place built for me soon after, though. It's too big, really...."

"Did you have any black workers on the farm?"

"Well, Earl's father had workers. We all did. But I don't think I could remember any."

Nothing fit. None of the pieces were coming together. Louis thought back to his talk with old Buford, trying to remember any details about the missing young man. "Did any of them have a strange hand?" he asked.

Ethel shook her head. "Detective, I don't really remember."

"But you remember a black community called Sweetwater?"

"Oh, of course. No one lives there anymore, though. After the fires, everyone moved out. There was some trouble there then. Lots of trouble."

Louis hesitated. "Mrs. Mulcahey, I have to ask something that may offend you, and please, don't get angry. When he was young, could your husband have been involved with the Klan?"

Ethel just stared at him for a moment. Then her eyes grew moist. "Detective, my husband was the kindest man you could know, to any color human being."

She stood up, and went to an adjoining room that looked to be a study or office. She came back and held out a plaque to Louis.

"This was given to Earl in 1980, from Washington Carver Junior College," she said. "It's in appreciation for the yearly scholarships he sponsored for underprivileged students."

Louis took the plaque, stunned. "Washington Carver's a black college," he said.

"Yes," Ethel said. She took the plaque from Louis and, pulling down the sleeve of her robe, she gently rubbed it clean of smudges. Then she hugged it to her chest, looking down at Louis.

"Detective, please," she said softly. "I loved my husband. And I love Leverette. What does all this have to do with my family?"

Louis looked up at her. "I don't know, Mrs. Mulcahey. But I promise you, I intend to find out."

CHAPTER 16

After leaving Ethel, Louis headed back to town, not sure what his next move was going to be. He had been looking for a connection between Earl and Walt Kelly but had come up short. He hadn't anticipated the link between Earl and Max. But where was it all leading? One thing was certain. He couldn't let the medallion be buried with the bones tomorrow. He headed to Wallace-Pickney.

Stan Wallace let him sit a half hour in the foyer before he came out of the office. "I thought you understood my position," he said crisply.

"I'm here on official police business," Louis said dryly. "I have to pick up the medallion and the book that were found with the bones."

"I was told they were to be placed in the casket," Wallace said.

"The sheriff changed his mind. In a felony case, evidence has to be retained for ninety days before being released." Louis had made it up, but he was betting that Wallace didn't know. He was praying, however, that he wouldn't call Dodie.

"Well, perhaps I should call Sam—"

"Look, Mr. Wallace," Louis said with an exaggerated sigh, "I have the authority to take what I need."

"I would like to deal with the sheriff directly, so if you don't mind, I'll just call him."

"I do mind, and I'm asking you to hand those items over, or I may place you under arrest for obstruction."

Wallace's eyes narrowed and his thick lids fluttered over little black pupils. "You wouldn't dare."

Louis pointed to a group of people in a nearby parlor. "Mr.

Wallace, I am in a hurry. How do you think it would it look to disrupt all those nice people doing their mourning over there when I haul you out of your own funeral home in handcuffs?"

Wallace was quiet. Louis knew he would call Dodie later, but he didn't care. For better or worse, he had chosen his course and couldn't go back. He'd deal with Dodie somehow.

Finally, Wallace motioned for Louis to follow him to the back. Without a word, he gave Louis the medallion and the book, still wrapped in plastic, and retreated back to his office.

Outside, Louis paused. So what was his next step? He had to find out somehow if Kelly was the owner of the medallion. But how? He turned the plastic-wrapped medallion over in his hands. Was it even possible to compare the original medallion with the one in the photocopy? Gibbons . . . he'd call Gibbons. If anyone would know, he would.

He drove to a pay phone and dialed the FBI office in Jackson. Luckily, Gibbons was in. When Louis told him what he needed, the agent told him that the state crime lab in Atlanta was his best bet. "It's faster than going through our Washington lab, but it'll still take weeks. It always does," Gibbons added.

"Damn," Louis murmured. "I don't think I have weeks, Mr. Gibbons." Stan Wallace probably had already called Dodie.

Gibbons hesitated. "Listen," he said. "Why don't you overnight the stuff to me, and I'll see what I can do? I've got a buddy in Atlanta who owes me one."

Louis smiled. "I'd appreciate it, Mr. Gibbons, whatever you can do." Louis thought of the poetry book. "I'd like to send another item, too. The first lab wasn't able to do much with it."

"What are you looking for?"

"I don't know. It's an old book. Blood, prints, anything at this point would help, believe me."

He thanked Gibbons and hung up. On the way to the post office, he fully expected to hear Dodie's voice come blasting over the radio, but he heard nothing but Junior and Mike's banter.

As he watched the woman at the post office pack the items into an overnight mail envelope, Louis felt a twinge of trepidation. He was taking a big chance sending the items off. If something happened to them, he'd never solve the case. And technically the medallion and book were evidence, property of the Sheriff's Department. There would be hell to pay if they were lost in the mail. Hell, there would be anyway, once Dodie found out what he had done. But at least they couldn't be buried now.

Back in his car, Louis debated his next move. He went back over his conversation with Ethel in his mind, especially her comment about Max and Walt Kelly being friends. Maybe it was time to go back to the library, to the newspaper files. Maybe he could find something pertinent about Kelly, Max . . . or Earl.

At the library, he stopped at the door of the Local History room. He wanted to make a couple more copies of that medallion picture to replace the one he had sent to Gibbons. He scanned the shelves. Johnson, Jessup, Longwood . . . no Ketcher. Damn, the book was gone. He stared at the gap between Jessup and Longwood. It occurred to him suddenly that there might also be a Kelly family book; he hadn't thought to look for one before. But if one existed, it, too, was missing.

Louis left the history room and headed to the microfiche machines in the corner. Issues of the *Black Pool Journal* went back to 1903. Louis randomly chose the 1975–76 reel. He sat, turning the handle slowly, watching the months creep by, the trivial news of a small town spilling out from the pages.

He stopped on the 1976 election. It was big news, just as his cousin Charles had said. Walter Kelly was the overwhelming favorite for mayor; an editorial predicted he would be a "fine mayor who will see many years as a public servant." There was also a two-column spread about Kelly's endorsement of Sam Dodie to be the next sheriff. Louis read it, somewhat circumspectly now, thinking about the freckled kid in Ethel's annual.

History continued to unveil itself in reverse as Louis continued back through the years. Louis found himself getting sidetracked, lost in the news about civil rights. The articles from the mid-sixties spoke of marches, Freedom Fighters, and "invaders from the North." There were editorials denouncing the Klan tactics of violence. He read with interest the words of the *Black Pool Journal's* editor, written in November 1961:

> As citizens, we need to make clear that we do not commend nor condone this practice of vigilantism that seems to have permeated our fair county. The perpetrators of this unwanted and heinous propaganda are less than citizens, less than men. Although we agree that there is a need to maintain our

traditions and our way of life, the acts of a few cast dark shadows on the attitudes of many. This piracy of human decency needs to be stopped before it contaminates the entire community. The *Black Pool Journal* makes a public plea for the guilty to put away their weapons and come forth, as members of the community, and lawfully work with us to ensure the continuance of a segregated Greensboro County.

Louis stared at the screen, a tired feeling washing over him. Now he was beginning to understand what Tinker had meant when he said it was a state of mind. And Dodie was right. People here didn't think lynching was a real crime. At least, not twenty years ago.

He scrolled back through the years, moving through the fifties now. A photograph of a vaguely familiar face caught his eye and he paused. Jesus, it was Jed Dodie, and he was shaking J. Edgar Hoover's hand. The story said that Jed Dodie had singlehandedly captured a federal fugitive hiding out in the Toccopola Swamp. Louis stared at the photograph, trying to see a resemblance between father and son. There wasn't much.

Slowly, he moved on. A small headline, tucked in the corner of an inside page, caught his eye. It said: UNIVERSITY ORDERED TO ACCEPT NEGRO. The University of Alabama had been ordered by a federal court to readmit a Negro student named Autherine Lucy. She had been suspended earlier, her admission blamed for causing race riots on campus. Upon her return, angry crowds had thrown rocks and eggs at her, and the university had been ordered to provide her with protection.

Louis was numb. All the black-history classes in the world had not prepared him for what he was feeling now. The library was overheated and stuffy. He closed his eyes.

He did not hear Abby when she came up behind him. When she touched his shoulder, he jumped.

"Louis," she whispered. He looked up at her. She was clutching a pile of books. "I thought you were gone," she said.

He shook his head. "I'm staying, for a while at least."

A slow, shy smile spread across her face. He looked over at the desk. The old biddy was looking at them.

Abby slid into a nearby chair, depositing her books on the table. "I'm so glad you decided to stay," she said softly.

"Abby—"

"I know, I know," she said quickly. "Don't worry, I won't throw myself at you again." She smiled, mischievously. "At least not here."

When he didn't smile back, she sighed and looked at the screen of the microfiche. "What are you reading?" she asked.

"Just some old newspapers."

Abby leaned over him to read, her fragrant hair shielding her face. Louis leaned back in his chair, partly to put some distance between them and partly to stretch. He had been at it for three hours and had found nothing of any real use. He had no idea where to go next—except to Kelly himself. Maybe it was time to just confront the man with what he knew about the medallion, simply to see what his reaction was.

After a moment, Abby sat back. When she looked at Louis, her eyes were serious. "Why are you doing this?" she whispered.

He looked at the screen then back at her, frowning. "What?"

"Are you looking for some reason to hate us?" she asked.

Her directness startled him. "No," he said slowly. "That's not it at all." He thought of Max at that moment, and about what Abby's reaction would be if Max turned out to have had a part in the lynching. He had a vision of Max at the Christmas party and he wondered if Abby could see him as he was. Could any child really see his or her father clearly?

Abby looked at him oddly, then reached over and switched off the machine. "Louis, let's get out of here," she said.

He shook his head again, sitting forward. "I have to keep going."

"Why? What do you think you'll find? More articles about how terrible we were?"

"Abby, I don't need newspaper articles to know that." He switched the machine back on and the page fluttered back to life. Jesus, why was he snapping at her? She wasn't the enemy. She hadn't put a noose around some poor man's neck.

She stiffened, momentarily speechless. "That's cruel, Louis Kincaid," she said quietly.

"Abby, look, I'm . . ." He paused. "Listen, you'd better leave. Please."

The hurt look in her eyes, mixed with the naiveté and absolute incomprehension, was unnerving.

"Is that why you don't want to be with me?" she asked.

"What?"

"Because I'm white?"

Jesus, he didn't need this, not right now.

"Why do you have to be a black man?" she said. "Why can't you just be a man?"

He stood up. "I've got to go," he said slowly.

"Louis—"

He grabbed his jacket and walked away stiffly.

Abby watched him hurry to the entrance. She wanted to follow him, but she wasn't sure what to say. She sat back in the chair, angry, hurt and confused.

"Abigail?"

She looked up into the eyes of Mrs. Jenkins, the librarian.

"Are you all right?" the old woman asked. "Was that man bothering you?"

Abby straightened. "No, no, Mrs. Jenkins, he wasn't. I'm okay, really I am."

The librarian looked at her dubiously, then smiled. "How's your mother, dear?" she asked.

"Fine," Abby said, not returning the smile. "She's fine. Thanks for asking, Mrs. Jenkins."

The old woman patted Abby's shoulder then went back to the front desk. Abby sat back in the chair with a sigh. Her eyes drifted to the microfiche screen. The small headline floated up to her. UNIVERSITY ORDERED TO ADMIT NEGRO.

She leaned forward and brought the page into focus, reading the story. There was a picture of a young black woman in a dark wool coat, carrying schoolbooks. She was a college coed, about the same age as herself. Abby stared at the photo of the young woman. What was it like, to be told you couldn't have something you wanted, just because your skin was a certain color? She thought of her father in that moment, of their argument last night at dinner. He wanted her to quit school and come home. *"That place is filling your head with stupid ideas,"* he had told her. She had cried, pleading with him not to pull her out. He had finally consented to let her finish the semester. His final words echoed in her head. *"Then it's time for you to come home and settle down with some nice boy who'll watch out for you."* Abby had looked across the dining table at her mother, hoping for support. But Grace had just sat there.

Abby stared at the photo of Autherine Lucy. With a sigh, she idly scrolled the page forward. A familiar face rolled in front of her and she stopped.

It was her mother. It was a photograph of her mother at the age of sixteen. Grace Ketcher had just won the 1955 Miss Magnolia Pageant. She was standing in the middle of twenty other young women, all wearing floor-length formal gowns. Her mother was wearing a banner and a crown and was holding a bouquet of roses. She had a beaming smile on her face.

Abby stared at the picture in quiet awe. Her mother looked so beautiful and happy.

A sudden notion seized her and she hit the PRINT button on the machine. She would take the story home to her mother. She had seemed so distant lately, so sad; maybe the story would cheer her up.

When the page came out of the machine, she folded the paper, put it in the pocket of her jeans and switched off the machine. She did not notice the small headline at the bottom of the page:

COLORED BOY MISSING

CHAPTER 17

Abby paused at the top of the staircase. Music . . . piano music. Maybe it was the maid; she often played the radio when she cleaned. But then again, she always listened to the country station, never classical.

Shifting the load of books in her arms, Abby went down the stairs to the library. She stopped abruptly at the entrance.

Grace was seated at the piano. She was playing a melancholy tune that Abby did not recognize. Abby stared at her mother; she hadn't seen her play for years. She never played when her father was around. But this afternoon, he had left abruptly and hadn't returned. Who knew where he was? Abby sighed. It was Friday. He was probably out boozing, getting a head start on the weekend.

Grace had her eyes closed, a small smile playing at the corners of her lips. She was swaying slightly as she played, the setting sun filtering through the big bay window, turning her hair to gold. The sight of her mother like this was so unexpected, so lovely, that Abby felt tears sting her eyes. When was the last time she had seen her mother look like that?

A distant memory pushed its way forward. It was that day— she had been only twelve—when the two of them had driven to Jackson to visit Aunt Ellie. The three of them had gone out shopping and there had been a street festival of some kind, with booths of food and artists selling their work.

Grace had walked toward the festival, as if magically drawn there. Abby remembered feeling surprised; her mother never lingered in such places. Grace had walked up to a man who was playing the piano. "Days of Wine and Roses"—Abby remembered it clearly. Grace had stood at his side, as if mesmerized. He finished, and got up for a break. And then something even more extraordinary happened. Grace sat down at the piano, and in that perfect white linen dress and pristine white gloves, she had put her hands on the keyboard and played.

She played "Moon River." Abby remembered it so well. She had just seen the movie *Breakfast at Tiffany's* on television and she remembered how sad Audrey Hepburn had been looking for that damn cat in the rain. Her mother never watched movies. Her mother never paid attention to popular songs. But she played "Moon River" that afternoon, sitting in the sunlight, played it like it was the saddest song on earth.

The house fell silent. Grace had finished. She looked up, as if coming out of a trance, and saw Abby standing at the library entrance.

"Don't stop," Abby said. "Please."

Grace said nothing. She closed the keyboard and rose stiffly. She stared at Abby in such a way that Abby felt herself coloring, but she didn't know why. She went quickly to the bookshelves and began replacing the books she had taken out last night in her search for the poem. She hesitated as she slipped the poetry book back in its place, thinking about Louis.

He was leaving, and she was heartbroken. She was so confused, and desperately wanted to talk to someone about it. She wanted to talk to her mother. But she had long ago forgotten how. Something had happened to Grace years ago, the warmth driven out of her. And Abby was left with the feeling, especially lately, that if she pressed too hard, her mother would crack into a million pieces, like one of her precious Sèvres porcelain dolls she collected.

"Abigail, we have to talk."

The solemnity of Grace's voice made Abby turn.

"Where were you last night?" Grace asked.

"I went for a drive."

"You came home after twelve. Where were you?"

Abby averted her eyes. "Nowhere."

Grace went to one of the green wingback chairs and sat down, arranging her blue silk gown around her legs. "Sit down, please," she said.

Abby was taken aback by her mother's odd tone. "Okay," she said cautiously, sitting down in the matching chair.

"Sometimes we do things because we feel it to be right," Grace began in a slow, deliberate voice. "Or we may do something without thinking about how it can affect others. But in reality, we end up causing more pain than we could ever imagine."

"I don't understand," Abby said.

Grace's blue eyes focused on Abby. "We must be careful not to let our emotions get the best of us, not to do anything before we understand each and every consequence."

Abby stiffened. Her mother knew about Louis.

"Abigail," Grace said. "Do you have something you want to tell me?"

Yes, yes, I do. . . . I need to talk to you, the voice inside Abby whispered. But the censuring look on her mother's face kept her silent. She and Louis had done nothing to be ashamed of, but it was obvious her mother thought otherwise.

Abby got up and went to the window. "No," she said quietly. She stuck her hands in the pocket of her slacks. Her fingers found the piece of paper there. She pulled it out, unfolded it and looked at the photograph of her mother as a teenager. She glanced back at Grace, who was still looking at her, with an odd, slightly sad expression.

"Mother," Abby said, going back to her. "I found this yesterday. I thought you might like it."

Grace took it gingerly, staring at it for a moment. "Where did you get this?" she asked, looking up.

"From the library. I thought—"

Grace crumpled the paper.

"Why'd you do that?" Abby said.

"That was a long time ago."

Abby was confused. "Can I have it back, then? I'd like to keep it."

Grace rose abruptly and tossed it toward the fire. It hit an andiron and bounced to the hearth, and Abby sprang after it.

"Mother, what's wrong?"

"Abigail, I know what you've been doing with Detective Kincaid."

Abby let Grace's words hang in the air. Slowly, she refolded the paper and put it back in her pocket. She sat back on the carpet, looking up at her mother.

"What?" she said calmly. "What exactly is it you think I'm doing?"

"How could you?" Grace said. "How could you be so, so . . ."

"What? Irresponsible? Immature?" Abby countered. "That's what you've always told me I am."

"No, no," Grace said, shaking her head. "How could you be so inconsiderate?"

Abby gave a small bitter laugh. "Inconsiderate? Of who? You? Is that all that's bothering you, Mother? You're worried about what your friends might think about me and Louis?"

Grace winced slightly at Louis's name. "You're being stubborn," she said.

Abby got to her feet, shaking her head. "Stubborn? Just because for once I'm trying to think for myself?" Damn, she didn't want this to happen. She didn't want to fight with her mother. But Grace had no right to accuse her of anything, and no right at all to look down on Louis.

"Abigail, even if you do not understand, *he* should."

"Oh, he does, Mother," she said quietly.

"Then leave it be. You have no idea what you're doing."

"But I'm not doing anything!" Abby said, raising her voice. She turned away. "God, I can't believe this."

"Abigail, look at me," Grace said evenly. "You don't understand how disastrous this can be. For God's sake, he's a black man!"

"So what?" Abby spun around and she regretted the words as soon as they came out of her mouth. "At least he doesn't hit me."

Grace drew back, as if slapped. "How dare you judge me," she said angrily.

Tears welled in Abby's eyes. "I'm not judging, Mother, but I don't understand! You let him hit you, and then you tell me I can't be with a good man, a man who's done nothing but be kind to me!"

Abby stopped, frozen by her mother's shattered face. She closed her eyes, her shoulders drooping. She hadn't meant to hurt her. She had wanted to talk to her, to tell her about Louis and her feelings for him. "Mother . . ." she said softly.

Grace was staring vacantly at the fire. Abby leaned back against the shelves.

"Your father won't stand for this," Grace said quietly.

Abby wiped her face. "I haven't done anything wrong," she said softly. "Why can't you believe that? Louis wouldn't—"

"Don't do this, Abigail," Grace interrupted. "Don't do this to yourself."

Abby shook her head. "You just don't understand." She turned and started out of the library.

Grace watched her daughter go up the stairs, her pale blue eyes desolate as a November sky. "I understand more than you think," she said softly.

Louis wiped his hands on his pants and stepped back to look at his work. The clay bust was back in one piece again, albeit with long ugly cracks running across its cheeks and chin. Louis put the cap back on the Elmer's glue and tilted his head to look at the bust's face.

"Hello, stranger," he said.

Bessie came up to his open door at that moment. "Louis, who you talkin' to?"

Louis grinned. "I don't know, Bessie."

Bessie came into the room and stared at the head. "That your dead man?"

Louis nodded, sliding into a chair and resting his elbows on his knees. Bessie came up and touched the top of the clay head. "Sorry, sorry thing. Making this head kind of brings him alive, don't it?"

Louis nodded. "It makes him harder to forget."

"Louis," Bessie said, facing him. "I'm glad you stayin' on for a while longer. It'd be right fittin' if you stayed for good."

"One day at a time, Bessie."

"I understand. Sleep good, Louis."

" 'Night, Bessie."

Louis heard the door to Bessie's room close. Louis went to his bed and lay down, arms folded under his head, listening to the night sounds of the house. A police siren wailed faintly in the distance. Probably Junior chasing a speeder. A short while later, he heard Bessie's usual snoring.

He was just dozing off when he heard the phone ring and he jumped to the hall to grab it before it woke Bessie up. His heart beat faster in anticipation of another call from the mystery man. But it was only Mike calling from the station.

"Louis? That you?"

"Yeah, Mike, what's up?"

"Hold on, got another call."

Louis sighed, summoning patience.

"Yo, I'm back," Mike said. "Sheriff said to call you. They need some help at the jewelry store."

Damn, he didn't want to deal with this routine shit right now. "Can't Junior handle it?"

"Sheriff says git you, so I'm gittin' you."

"All right, what happened?"

"There was a prowler report out near Cotton Town."

"What does that have to do with the jewelry store?"

"Nothing, I reckon. But that's where they were comin' from."

Louis felt his jaw tighten. "Mike, what are you talking about?"

"The squad cars, that's where they were comin' back from when the call came in. This here thing at the jewelry store looks like a burglary, but we don't know yet. Somebody called it in."

"Did the alarm go off?" Louis asked.

"No, somebody heard the shot."

"Dammit, Mike, make some sense here for me. What shot?"

"The shot that done killed George Harvey."

Louis looked up at the black moonless sky, then back to the front door of Black Pool Jewelers. The front door, its lower glass panel smashed, was propped open while deputies went in and out. As Louis watched, they brought the body out, strapped to a stretcher, covered with a blanket. They loaded it into the ambulance and slammed the door.

Louis had already been inside. The store was a mess, a glass case smashed and a bunch of gold jewelry strewn around. The cash-register drawer was open and empty, but the large safe in the back was apparently untouched. Louis looked up and down the deserted block. He doubted there had been any witnesses. The store was situated on a side street, well off the main square, and besides, no one hung around downtown Black Pool late at night. The town rolled up its sidewalks after dark.

Louis looked back in the store, where deputies were taking photos and lifting prints. It had to be an amateur job. A pro would have known that George Harvey put the expensive stuff in the safe every night and wouldn't have bothered with a handful of gold chains. A pro would have known that the place had an alarm. Something was not right. Louis frowned. It was things like this that made him feel inexperienced, even stupid, at this detective stuff.

Dodie came out of the store, the heels of his boots echoing in the quiet. He lit a cigar, the Zippo illuminating his face as he sucked in the smoke.

"Kincaid, what's this world coming to?"

Louis sat down on the open tailgate of a pickup truck and shook his head. He pulled up the collar of his jacket against the cold, wishing he had thought to wear a hat and gloves. Shit, it was cold.

"I don't like what I'm seeing here," Dodie went on. "I reckon maybe I'm getting too old for this job."

"It's the rest of the world catching up with your little town, Sheriff."

"I 'spose so." He looked back at the open door. "Damn kids."

Louis glanced up. "You think kids did this?"

"Who else would leave half the take on the floor?"

"Maybe they didn't really want it."

"Then why break in?"

Louis didn't reply. He shook his head thoughtfully, staring at the smashed front door.

Junior came up at that moment, holding a baseball bat by its nub end. "Hey, I found this in the weeds," he said.

Dodie took it carefully by its end and examined it. "This was George's," he said. "He kept it behind the counter, just in case."

"Lot of good it did him," Junior said.

Dodie held out the bat to Junior. "Give this to the fingerprint guys. And don't touch it!"

Louis had risen from his spot on the tailgate and was standing, hands on hips, staring at the broken glass on the pavement.

"Sheriff? Come here a minute."

Dodie came up to his side. "See anything weird about this glass?" Louis asked.

Dodie looked down at the shattered glass, fanning out in a wide swath from the door. He shook his head. "Nope."

"There was no sign of forced entry on the back door, was there?" Louis said.

"No," Dodie said, frowning. He looked back down at the glass, and when he finally looked back up at Louis, it was with a stunned expression. "I'll be damned," he said, pulling the cigar from his mouth. "Whoever was in here tonight used that bat to break the glass to get out."

Louis nodded. "There's hardly any glass on the carpet. It sprayed outward."

"So whoever killed George had a key," Dodie said.

"Or was let in," Louis added.

Dodie shook his head. "Damn, I can't believe anybody 'round here would kill George just for some lousy chains."

Louis was quiet for a moment. He went to the door and examined the jamb and the remaining glass. The door itself was alarmed, set to be triggered if opened, just like the one in back. But the glass itself didn't seem to have any of the imbedded sensors common to more sophisticated systems. But how much security did a small-town jeweler like George Harvey figure he had to have?

"The alarm didn't go off," Dodie said, as if reading Louis's thoughts. "We got a call after somebody heard a shot."

"And what was the response time?" Louis said.

"Twelve minutes."

"Long time. . . ."

The sheriff nodded.

Louis looked over at Dodie. "They catch that prowler out near Cotton Town?"

"No, there was nobody."

Louis smiled wanly. "I bet that was an anonymous call, too, wasn't it?"

The sheriff stood silent, looking inside the store.

"Kincaid," he said after a moment, "you think this was made to look like something it ain't? You think somebody wanted George killed and set him up?"

"Possible," Louis replied. "Maybe he agreed to meet someone. Either way, this stinks, Sheriff."

Dodie threw his cigar to the street and squashed it out. "I'm headed home. You need any help out here?"

Louis shook his head. "We're about finished. Go on, you got a big day tomorrow."

"Oh yeah. The service. Aren't you going?"

When Louis didn't reply, Dodie added, "Mayor expects you there, you know."

Louis bit back his response. Damn, he wished he could trust Dodie.

"Kincaid, I'd appreciate it if you'd show up," Dodie said.

Louis met his eyes. "I'll be there," he said.

Louis watched him get into the Blazer and drive away. Mike and another deputy were putting their equipment into the car and the store was deserted now. A light still burned in the back, dancing off the shards of glass on the floor.

Louis went in and stood in the middle of the store for a moment, trying to envision what had happened. Whoever had come in had entered through the untouched back door. George had been found slumped against the safe, a fair-sized bullet wound just below the knot in his tie. There was no apparent sign of a struggle, but an autopsy would reveal more.

Louis's eyes fell on the register. It was closed now, but he knew that nothing had been found in it. But what store owner kept money in a register after closing? Louis surveyed the interior of the store, focusing on the smashed glass display case. Only one case broken, hardly anything taken. So what was the invader after?

Louis went to George Harvey's desk. It was a clutter of papers, handwritten notes, and a few jeweler's tools. A closed wallet lay on top of some papers. Louis frowned. Why hadn't the robber bothered to take it? And a bigger question: How had this been missed by the deputies? He took a pencil and flipped the wallet open. The Mississippi driver's license said George Hammond Harvey, 276 Flowers Street, Black Pool, Mississippi. He was forty-six years old.

Louis used the pencil to flip through the plastic sleeves of credit cards, his annoyance over the deputies' oversight growing. He would have to take the time tonight to bag these items. Odd that the wallet was lying out on the desk to begin with. Had George been getting ready to pay somebody something?

Louis picked up a small pair of jeweler's tweezers and picked through the bill pocket. A couple twenties, a ten, and some ones. And a small piece of paper. Louis used the tweezers to pull it out and he peered at the small numbers penciled on the paper, wishing he had thought to bring his glasses.

"Damn it," he muttered, picking up a magnifying glass.

The numbers popped out at him. At first they didn't register, then Louis stiffened.

It was Bessie's phone number.

It was four-thirty in the morning when Louis got back to the station. Larry looked up from his magazine. "What are you doing here?"

Louis kept walking to the back room, jerking open the door that separated the four jail cells from the rest of the office. The broken lock rattled against the metal door. An inmate in cell number one opened his eyes, awakened by the sound. Louis kept walking, Larry at his heels.

"Kincaid, where you going?"

"To see Leverette."

Louis stopped before Leverette's cell. Leverette's sleeping body was hidden in the shadows and all Louis could see was the gray jail blanket that covered him.

"Leverette?" Louis called out.

The blanket moved. Leverette moaned softly.

"Leverette!"

Leverette's head appeared. "Who . . . ?" he whispered hoarsely.

"You okay, Leverette?" Louis asked.

Leverette slowly propped himself up on one elbow, squinting out at Louis. He coughed.

Louis looked at Larry. "What's wrong with him?"

Larry shrugged. "Got a bug, I guess."

Leverette coughed again, a deep ragged sound.

"Open it," Louis said to Larry.

"What for?"

"I want to talk to him."

"You can do that from out here."

"Open it!"

Larry crossed his arms. "I don't take orders from you."

Louis shoved past him and went to the empty desk where the jail sergeant usually sat. He yanked open the top drawer and pulled out a ring of keys. He came back, dug in his pocket, and threw some bills at Larry. "Go get him some cough medicine."

Larry's face clouded over. "Ain't nothin' open this time of

night," he said tersely. "And I ain't your slave, Kincaid." Larry glared at him then turned and stalked out.

Louis picked up the money and unlocked the cell. Leverette looked up as Louis came in.

"Leverette, you all right?" Louis asked. But even in the dim light coming from the hall light, Louis could see that the young man was not well. He was pale, with reddened eyes.

"Detective," Leverette said weakly. "Can I have some water?"

Louis went out to the office and returned with a cup of water. Leverette drank it in slow sips. "Throat hurts," he whispered. He pulled himself up and sat hunched on the bunk, gripping the coffee mug of water.

"Leverette," Louis began. What could he tell him? *"I think you're innocent"? "In a few days, you'll be free"?* No. That was premature and he didn't want to raise false hopes. Not yet. But Jesus, the kid looked awful. "Leverette, I want you to relax. Everything will be all right. Give it some time."

Hell, he had no time. Louis knew that. And he knew there would be no bail. Judge Eucher never gave bail in a capital murder case.

Leverette just sat there. He'd be behind bars until Louis could prove his newly formed theory—that Earl was killed because he knew something about the bones. If he couldn't do that, Leverette would rot away in this jail for months.

Leverette raised his head to look at Louis. "Detective, would you do me a favor?"

"Sure, Leverette."

"Could you check in on my mom? I'm a little worried about her. I don't think she's feeling well. My sister went back to school and Mom's all alone."

"I'll do that, Leverette."

Leverette handed Louis the mug of water. He shivered and pulled the blanket tighter over his shoulders.

Damn it, damn it all to hell, Louis thought. This just wasn't right. The kid wasn't going to go anywhere; he wasn't a damn flight risk. He should be home with his mother until he needed to be in court.

Louis stood up. "Come on, Leverette," he said.

Leverette looked up slowly.

"Come on, I'm taking you home." Louis helped Leverette to his feet.

Leverette seemed dazed as Louis led him out of the cell and down the corridor. He blinked in the bright light as Louis brought him out into the office. Larry looked up.

"What the fuck . . . ? What you think you're doing, Kincaid?"

"Taking Leverette home." Louis took off his University of Michigan jacket and draped it over Leverette's shoulders. They started toward the door.

Larry shot to his feet. "You can't do that!"

"He's sick and he's not going to run away, Cutter. I'll take full responsibility for him." Louis started toward the door, his arm around Leverette.

"Kincaid! You hear me? Stop!" Larry scrambled around the desk to the door, blocking their way.

"Step aside," Louis said calmly.

"Fuck you," Larry said, bracing his arm across the door.

Louis shoved Larry's arm away and pushed open the door, holding it as Leverette shuffled through.

Larry took a step backward and glared at Louis. "You're in trouble, boy," Larry yelled. "This here is contempt of court! Sheriff's gonna have your ass for this one!"

Louis tossed the cell keys back on a desk as he followed Leverette out the door. "Tell him to get in line," he said.

CHAPTER 18

Louis stepped out of his car and reached for his deputy sheriff's jacket. Today, he wore the crisply pressed county-issued beige uniform with plain brown tie. He put on the brown cattleman's hat. He seldom wore it but it seemed appropriate for a funeral.

The sky was thick with low-hanging gray clouds and there was a sharp chill to the air and a misty rain. He started up the damp, grassy slope, walking toward the gravesite.

A green-and-white canopy covered the grave, with several rows of folding chairs arranged in front of it. Printed across the canopy was the name Wallace-Pickney. Louis tasted something bitter as he looked at it.

The mourners—or maybe they would be better described as spectators, Louis thought—were milling around on the grass. They were dressed for grieving, the women in their best black dresses and hats, the men in somber suits. A few umbrellas waggled like colorful fishing bobs in the sea of dark clothes and faces.

Louis spotted Tinker standing apart under an oak tree and he walked over. Tinker's face remained impassive as Louis approached. Tinker wore a panama hat and an old dark wool suit with baggy black pants. His tie was thin and knotted poorly, but his height and demeanor lent him his usual air of distinction.

"Detective Kincaid."

"Mr. Tinker. How are you?"

"I'm well, thank you."

"I'm surprised to see you here. I thought you weren't interested in this man." Louis said.

"I'm curious, that's all."

"About what?" Louis asked.

Tinker almost smiled. "About how all this is gonna wash out."

Louis leaned back against the tree, his eyes on the lectern that had been set up in front of the rows of chairs. He watched Walter Kelly, who was standing in a knot of other suited men. There was one woman in the group, standing at Kelly's side. She was tall, with harsh black bouffant hair. Despite the gloomy day, she wore large sunglasses and a black sheath that was too tight across the hips, accentuating the little pads of fat around the top of her thighs. She said something to Kelly, then wobbled away, the heels of her pumps sinking into the wet ground, giving her a drunken gait. Louis wondered if she was Kelly's wife.

"How's the case going?" Tinker asked, drawing his attention back.

"George Harvey was killed last night," Louis said.

"I heard. You think there's some connection?"

"To what?"

Tinker looked out over the crowd. "To that other man who was shot in the woods."

Louis looked at Tinker, surprised. "Why do you think there would be?"

Tinker shrugged. "Two men, two white men, turn up dead within two weeks of each other. . . . That never happened in this town before. Seems kinda strange to me."

Louis stuck his hands in his pockets. "Me too." He paused. "I've been getting anonymous phone calls, someone trying to steer me in some direction that I haven't been able to figure out." He wasn't sure why he was confiding in Tinker, but he knew somehow he could trust him. "George Harvey had my phone number in his wallet," he added.

Tinker turned to face him. "You believe he was your caller?"

Louis nodded slowly.

"And now he's dead," Tinker said.

Louis looked over at the gravesite. The coffin was covered with an extravagant blanket of red and white flowers, paid for out of the city slush fund, no doubt. There were other flowers set about in a semicircle—several large, splashy horseshoe arrangements, a few small bouquets. It looked so bright and colorful, almost cheerful, like a wedding. The coffin was suspended on a frame above the open grave, but it would not be lowered here. After the crowd left, the bones would be transferred to a cheap wooden casket and buried in Black Pool Gardens, the indigent cemetery.

Louis thought of the meager pile of bones lying in the shiny, brass-handled coffin. His chest tightened.

"They're trying to bury it," he said softly.

"Who is?" Tinker asked.

"I don't know," he said. "But it's all connected. I know it now. The bones, Earl Mulcahey, George Harvey . . . they're all connected."

Louis's eyes went back to Walt Kelly. Off in the distance, behind Kelly, Louis spotted Dodie just getting out of his Blazer. The sheriff was also wearing his dress uniform. It made him look different. More like a cop, but also more threatening somehow.

"Detective," Tinker said.

Louis turned to face him.

"You be careful," he said.

Louis nodded. Tinker walked away and was lost in the crowd. Louis watched Dodie, but he was heading away from the canopied grave. He walked a short distance, stopping in front of a headstone under a group of sprawling trees.

Louis watched him, debating whether to interrupt what was obviously a private moment. He knew Larry must have called Dodie seconds after Louis had released Leverette. Louis sighed. It hadn't been a smart move—it went against everything he believed about following procedure—but it had been the right thing to do. He started across the grass. Now he had to pay the price.

He paused several feet from Dodie. "Sheriff?"

Dodie looked up. "So," he said sarcastically, "Leverette make it home okay?"

"Look, Sheriff, I know I should have called you first, but it couldn't wait a minute longer."

"And why the hell not?"

Louis looked back at the crowd. "Can we talk about it later?

"You're damn right we'll talk about it later," Dodie muttered. "That was a right bad move, Kincaid. Judge Eucher ain't gonna like it, and I don't like it." Dodie took a deep breath, then, as if he'd suddenly remembered, he turned to Louis again. "And we'll talk about you going over to Wallace-Pickney to get that necklace and book without telling me."

"I wanted to send them—"

"Enough, Kincaid, Dodie said through clenched teeth. "This ain't the time or place." Dodie shook his head in angry disgust and looked back down at the headstone.

Dodie took off his hat, his face somber. It was quiet, no birds, no rustling of leaves, just faint waves of voices drifting over from the crowd. Chastised, Louis just stood there.

Louis looked down at the engraving on the stone.

Jedidiah Samuel Dodie
1918–1959

"Father?" Louis asked softly, even though he already knew.

"Yeah."

Louis nodded, silent.

"He was a sheriff, too," Dodie said. "Right here in Black Pool."

Louis thought about the FBI report on old Jed. "I saw the picture in the office."

Dodie looked over at him, his gray eyes steely. "That man made this office what it is today. He got the new jail built, and it was pretty damn snazzy in its day." Dodie's eyes went back to the headstone. "He kept this county orderly, and the people here respected him for that."

Louis waited a moment, then asked, "What happened to him?"

"He was shot, doin' his job." Dodie took a long breath. "My father was the kind of man who demanded and got respect. Admiration, too. Jus' before he was killed, they was talking about running him for town board. These folks in this here town . . . to them, Jedidiah Dodie was God."

Louis looked away, suppressing a sigh, seeing again the picture of the teenage Sam Dodie in the annual. "Hard to fill the shoes of a man like that," he said.

Dodie's eyes moved slowly from the grave and settled on Louis's face, and for a second Louis wondered if Dodie had caught the mix of sarcasm and pity in his response.

"Yeah," Dodie replied.

Dodie looked up, over Louis's shoulder, and his eyes hardened. "Here comes the mayor," he said. "He's pissed, Kincaid."

"So what else is new?" Louis muttered.

"Don't smart-mouth me. He's pissed at you, and he's pissed

at me because of you." Dodie hitched up his belt. "And I'm gettin'
pissed about his fuckin' pissin'."

The sheriff headed toward the mayor. Louis knew he was not
invited to participate in the conversation and he waited, watching
them. Louis could not hear them, but they talked fervently, the
mayor glancing in Louis's direction. Dodie kept shaking his head.
After the upbraiding the sheriff had just given him, it had to be
out of frustration.

A realization suddenly hit Louis. Even though he had decided
to stay, he wasn't going to get the chance to finish this. The killer
was getting desperate; George Harvey's murder had proven that.
But would the killer be desperate enough to come after a cop?

Louis looked at Walt Kelly and caught him staring at him.
Killer or not, Walt Kelly would find a way to get rid of him. He
wouldn't drag him to the woods and hang him. He wouldn't even
send someone out to ambush him some night with a gun. Kelly
would find a way to do it nice and legal. Publicly they would
say he resigned. Privately they would say he just couldn't cut it.

The conversation broke up, and the mayor walked to the lectern
under the canopy and looked at his watch. People began to sit
down in the folding chairs, and many had to stand in back. Louis
took a reserved chair near the front. The sheriff sat down next to
him, pulling off his hat and holding it between his knees. After
a few minutes of awkward silence, Louis spoke.

"What did Kelly have to say?"

"He found out about Leverette. And he got the bill for that
damn clay bust—twenty-five hundred dollars. He's had it with
you and your 'fuck everyone' attitude."

"Sheriff—"

Dodie leaned close, too close, to Louis's face. "Kincaid, I don't
want to hear one more damn excuse from you. I'm damn tired
of being the last person to know every damn thing you do." His
eyes locked on Louis. "You're forgetting who's in charge here."

The menacing edge in Dodie's voice made Louis shrink back
in his chair and he focused on the minister preparing to begin
his speech.

"I will see you after this is over," Dodie added.

Louis nodded, looking down.

The minister from Tupelo opened the memorial with a short
speech that lauded "Willie Johnson" as a good man who died

in the heat of unrest, who suffered needlessly in the throes of misfortune. He spoke as if he had known him personally, and after a few minutes, Louis tuned him out, turning his thoughts to last night.

George Harvey was afraid for his life. He had been killed because he knew about the lynching; he was there, he said. But why had Earl been killed? What did he know? Had he been involved in the lynching, too? Louis's eyes wandered idly over the flowers around the coffin as his thoughts swirled. He focused finally on a small arrangement of white flowers, slender lilies that stood out in their simplicity against all the splashy color.

It just didn't fit. Earl Mulcahey, a man respected by everyone, loved by many. A high-school sissy who sold insurance, puttered in his basement, tended a garden, and gave money to black colleges. But what did those scholarships mean? Atonement for a past sin? Louis stared at the flowers. Earl had never really fit in with anything lurid or remotely aggressive. Damn, where did he fit in now?

A shuffling of bodies broke his chain of thought and he looked up to see Kelly thank the minister and take his place behind the lectern.

Time was running out, Louis thought grimly.

"We honor a man today who was a victim," Kelly began, "a victim of life, of society and of himself. This man, Willie Johnson, represents the struggle for freedom in black America. He represents a bravery and a dignity unknown to us until recent years."

Louis sat back. What a joke.

"We mourn for Willie Johnson because he was not given a chance to live a full life. We mourn for Willie Johnson because he died needlessly." The mayor paused, looking down at his script. "We mourn for Willie Johnson because he is a symbol of a time when violence was a way of life and hatred filled the streets of Mississippi. But that time is no more. Willie Johnson died during an era of unrest and we now bury him with the dawn of a new age."

"Bullshit!"

Heads turned to find the source of the booming voice discharged from the crowd.

Kelly frowned, momentarily flustered, and then opened his mouth to speak again.

"I said bullshit!"

Louis spun around, scanning the crowd. It was Tinker's unmistakable baritone. A murmur moved through the crowd. Louis spotted Tinker standing by a tree. He turned to see Kelly's reaction.

Kelly looked over at Dodie then at Tinker. "What is your problem, sir?"

"I say this is bullshit," Tinker said loudly. "You talk real nice, Mayor, but we got some questions here for you."

"I'll be glad to answer your questions after the service."

Tinker stepped forward. "You'll answer them now."

The crowd rumbled softly. The mayor's face was quickly losing its color. He nodded slowly. "All right."

"Who's going to pay for this crime?"

"Well, I . . . I'm not in charge of the investigation."

"*Is* there an investigation?" Tinker asked.

Kelly was gripping the sides of the lectern. "Of course there is."

Both the sheriff and Louis averted their eyes as the mayor looked over at them, his eyes begging for support.

"Look here," Kelly began, "this case is damn near thirty years old. This is not a simple crime with eyewitnesses and fingerprints." He smiled uneasily. "There is no smoking gun, as they say on TV."

"There's a dead man, isn't there?" Tinker said.

The others in the audience looked around and began to whisper. Tinker made his way to the front of the crowd and faced Kelly. He was an impressive figure standing there in his suit and panama hat, his hard, brown eyes focused on the mayor. For a second, they stared each other down, then Mayor Kelly wet his lips.

"We are not here today to pass judgment," he said. "We are here to honor someone."

"We'll do that, in good time," Tinker said, "but first, some of us want to know what you're going to do about finding who it was that killed this Willie Johnson."

"Of course, I'll do what I can, but the Sheriff's Department, well, I have no control over what they do."

Louis listened to the rumbling in the crowd. They knew better.

"Now listen here," Kelly stammered, "we're not going to stand here and talk about this and desecrate the memory of—"

"We want answers, Mayor," Tinker interrupted.

"Look, mister," Kelly said, raising his voice, "why don't you take your seat and we'll discuss—"

"No," Tinker said firmly. "You got any suspects, or are you just gonna bury him and forget about it?"

Kelly looked helplessly at Dodie. "The sheriff will be glad to answer your questions. Sam?"

Dodie was still looking at the grass, unmoving. Kelly waited and all eyes turned to the sheriff. A few people in the back had stood and were craning their necks in Dodie's direction. Dodie didn't move and for several seconds, the crowd was quiet.

"Sam . . ." Kelly repeated.

Dodie stood up and went slowly to the lectern, his hat in his hands. Kelly stepped back, relief washing over his face. Dodie looked out at the expectant faces, and then over at Louis, who was staring at him, also waiting.

"I want to assure you that this is an ongoing investigation," the sheriff said quietly, running his fingers along the brim of his hat. "We've put a lot of effort into this here case, but y'all got to realize how hard it is to investigate something this old."

More murmuring from the crowd. Louis could feel Tinker's eyes on him and he turned toward him. Briefly, he and Tinker locked gazes and suddenly Louis understood where this was heading.

"Look, folks, I'm not the one you should be talking to. Kincaid, come on up here," Dodie said.

Louis looked up in surprise. Part of him just wanted to let Dodie and that bastard Kelly twist in the wind. But he couldn't waste the chance. Louis glanced back at Tinker, then stood up slowly. He set his hat on the metal chair. A hundred pairs of eyes watched him as he took Dodie's place and he gazed back, unsure what to say. In the strange faces he saw hope and suspicion, respect and hostility. And oddly enough, acceptance.

"My name is Louis Kincaid, and I'm the investigator for Greensboro County. I'm in charge of this case."

"And what are you doing about it?" Tinker asked.

Louis hesitated. He glanced at Dodie, but the sheriff's face told him nothing. Well, then he would tell enough to cement his place here for a while. If the public knew enough, it might buy him time to finish.

"We found a few pieces of evidence with the body and that evidence is now in Washington, D.C., at the FBI lab," Louis said. He saw Kelly out of the corner of his eye, saw the surprise flash across his face.

"We know about how old the body is and how the man died," Louis went on. "We've talked to many people. We have only a few leads and they're weak. But . . ." Louis paused. The crowd waited expectantly.

"Allowed enough time and with the assistance of my department," Louis said, glancing at Dodie, "I feel a breakthrough is inevitable. In fact, we feel we already have a suspect." The suspect, George Harvey, was dead, but what the hell, it sounded good. Louis didn't turn but he could imagine the color of Kelly's face.

Louis waited until the buzz from the crowd faded and continued. "If given the opportunity, I feel we may be able to solve this case in the near future."

"Mayor," Tinker demanded, "are you going to give your man that opportunity?"

Louis restrained a smile over Tinker's use of "your man." Kelly stepped up next to Louis and wrapped an arm around Louis's shoulder. Louis stiffened, resisting the urge to shrug it off.

"Of course I am. You have my word."

Tinker locked eyes with Louis. "Mr. Kincaid," he said, "you finish this, man."

"I will, you have *my* word." Louis sighed, wondering just how much his word would mean when Dodie and Kelly got ahold of him after this was over.

Soft amens drifted up from the crowd and Louis moved away, leaving the lectern to the sheriff and Kelly. He walked away from the tent quickly, slapping his hat back on his head, heading down the slope toward his car. He heard the sheriff call to him but he didn't turn.

"Goddammit, Kincaid!"

Louis started to open the car door.

"Kincaid, Jesus Christ, would you wait?"

Louis turned. Dodie stopped several feet from him, glancing back at the casket, then at Louis. "You set that whole thing up?"

"No, Sheriff. Maybe these people aren't as gullible as Kelly thinks."

"Either way, now Kelly's obligated to keep you around."

Louis stared at Dodie, trying to read his face. There was a suggestion of satisfaction there, but Louis had the feeling it came simply from Dodie seeing Kelly embarrassed in public.

"How about you, Sheriff?" Louis demanded. "You want me around? You going to let me finish this, like Kelly said, or was that just some nice little show to keep the folks there off Kelly's ass and him off yours?"

"Kincaid—"

It was time, Louis thought. It was time for Dodie to show his colors one way or another. Louis spotted Kelly coming their way.

"I have to know, Sheriff," Louis said. "Are you going to back me on this or not?"

Dodie didn't have time to answer. Kelly stalked up and stopped inches from Dodie's face, his small black eyes snapping with anger.

"You stupid son of bitch," he hissed at Dodie, his finger jabbing at his chest. "I called you up there to help me and you fucking bury me."

"Walter, you dug your own hole out there," Dodie said, his jaw tight. "I handled it the best way I knew how."

"It wasn't good enough!" Kelly shouted.

Louis sank back again a tree, shaking his head in disgust. "Jesus," he murmured.

Kelly turned to glare at Louis. "And you, I should have you arrested for that stunt with Leverette! All you did today was buy yourself some time. I know people all over this state. I'll crucify you, Kincaid. They'll be screaming for your resignation."

Louis shot up from the tree. "And they'll be screaming for yours, Mayor, as soon as we publish that photo of you wearing your family medallion. The same medallion we found on the dead body."

For a second, Louis thought Kelly would faint. His bony face drained of color and he caught a tree for support.

Dodie's eyes grew large and he parted his lips to speak but nothing came out.

Louis had not wanted to play his hand but it was too late now. The photocopy was in Atlanta with the necklace. It was safe.

Kelly's eyes went even darker and his brows furrowed together. "You son of a bitch," Kelly said, the words sneaking out from tight lips. "How dare you accuse me of having anything to do with that man's death."

"I have the evidence, Mayor," Louis said.

"You have nothing!" Kelly shouted. He turned away and stalked off to his car.

Louis watched him get in the white Cadillac, then turned. Dodie was staring at him, his face flushed with fury.

"Why the *hell* didn't you tell me you had evidence against Kelly?" he demanded.

Louis met his eyes calmly. "I didn't trust you," he said.

Dodie's jaw flexed and he doubled his fist. For a second, Louis thought Dodie was going to hit him.

"I ought to fire your ass right here on the spot!" he hissed.

Louis tensed. He had gone too far. He had broken his own rules now. First with Leverette and now he had disregarded an unspoken code among cops. No matter how suspicious he was of Dodie, a boss was a boss, even here. Shit. He couldn't do this alone, not any longer. He had backed himself into a corner with his rash moves. It was time to trust Dodie.

"Sheriff—"

"Shut your mouth, Kincaid," Dodie said, his voice now a low growl. "You may think we're a bunch of ignorant rednecks down here who couldn't find our asses blindfolded," Dodie went on. "But let me tell you something, Kincaid. You're a smart-ass. And I hate smart-ass cops worse than I hate my mother-in-law. You know why? 'Cause they're not team players, Kincaid."

Louis wet his lips. "Sheriff—"

"And I'll tell you something else, too. You think the other guys hate you 'cause you're black. Maybe that was true in the beginning but you could've overcome that. But no, you had to do it your way, always being the smarter man, treating the rest of us like we're fuckin' imbeciles. The rest of them . . . *they* don't trust *you*."

"And what about you?"

"Right now I wouldn't trust you to hand me the last corn cob in the outhouse."

Dodie turned away in anger, running his hand through his hair. He spun back around. "I should can your ass."

Louis took a deep breath. "So why don't you?"

Dodie was breathing rapidly, still glaring. "I wouldn't give you the satisfaction of screaming 'discrimination'!"

Louis watched Dodie's face carefully. The man looked like he was going to have a stroke. "So you're not firing me," he said slowly.

"No!" Dodie said sharply. "But I'll tell you what I am going to do. You're on suspension, Kincaid. Without pay. Starting now."

Louis gestured toward the gravesite. "But what about this case?"

"Fuck it. You're suspended."

Louis shook his head. "Until when?"

Dodie put on his hat and stalked off. "Until I say so, goddammit," he shot over his shoulder.

CHAPTER 19

Louis got a Dr. Pepper from the fridge and went back to bed. He took a swig and pulled the quilt up over his chest, balancing the can on his belly. He lay there for a long time, listening to the sounds of the street, watching the soda can's rhythmic rise and fall with each breath he took.

He glanced over at the clock. After midnight, and sleep was still a long way off. He had been replaying the scene with Dodie from that afternoon over in his head, but he kept coming back to the same conclusion. He had blown it. Whatever credibility he had had with Dodie was gone now. He should have taken the sheriff into his confidence as soon as he found that picture of Kelly. Regardless of what kind of man Jedidiah Dodie had been, he should have given the sheriff the chance to be a sheriff.

Louis glanced over at the clay head sitting on the table and sighed in frustration. He was suspended—and so was the case. And there was nothing he could do about it until Dodie decided otherwise.

Louis got up and went to the space heater, turning it down a notch. He heard a sound, like a faint thump downstairs, and he froze, straining his ears. He went out into the hall, but Bessie was snoring away. He heard it again. Someone was knocking on the front door.

Slipping on a T-shirt and jeans, he quickly went downstairs. He could see a shadow on the porch, silhouetted in the streetlight and thought of his gun upstairs by his bed.

He hooked a finger around the curtain on the door's small window and looked out. He sank back against the wall. Jesus, it was Abby.

He opened the door. She was bundled up in a parka and a bright blue ski hat. A look of relief washed over her face, fading quickly to chagrin when she saw Louis's disapproving expression.

"Please, Louis," she said softly. "I had to come."

"Abby, we can't do this."

"But, Louis, I've been trying to reach you all day. I—"

"I was at the memorial service."

"Oh, I forgot."

He shook his head, looking at her through the screen door. Man, she looked forlorn, like a lost kid in that silly hat. "Abby, you've got to leave."

She pulled off a glove and dug into her coat pocket. "I found something," she said. "I think it might help you."

Louis looked at the folded paper she was holding out. If it was a ploy to get him to let her stay, it wasn't going to work.

"It's an old article from the newspaper," Abby said. "It's about a missing boy."

Louis blinked. "Boy? What boy?"

"I don't know, exactly—"

Louis opened the screen door and motioned her in. He took the paper and unfolded it. A photograph of a group of women caught his eye first, but then he saw the headline, COLORED BOY MISSING, and his heart stopped. The edge of the page had been cut off with the exception of four lines.

> *A colored boy was reported missing by his grandmother, Annie Graham, of the Sweetwater community late Thursday night. Graham told police her grandson, Eugene . . .*

He could not believe what he was seeing. Eugene. Eugene Graham?

"Abby," he said softly, "where did you get this?"

"At the library, that day you were there looking through the old *Journal* files. You would have found it yourself if you'd kept going." She looked up at him eagerly. "Is it the same man?"

"The date is about right," Louis said, his heart beating faster. "Damn! I need the whole article!"

"I could go get it for you Monday morning," Abby said.

Louis's eyes went from the headline to Abby's face. "Monday? Jesus, today's Sunday. The damn library is closed." When Abby nodded, he began to pace in the foyer, staring at the headline. "Damn it, damn it, damn it . . ."

"Louis?"

"Eugene Graham . . . A name, I finally have a name," Louis said, his voice tinged with excitement. He stopped short. "Wait! I can go to the *Journal* and get it from their files!"

"The newspaper?" Abby frowned. "Louis, they're never open on Sundays."

He stared at her. "Shit, I forgot. It's a weekly." His expression clouded and he sank down on the stairs. "Damn, I can't wait till Monday on this, I just can't," he murmured. He stared at the copy, reading the name over and over.

"Louis?" Abby said softly. When he didn't reply, she sat down on the step next to him. "Louis, maybe I could get Mrs. Jenkins to let us in tomorrow."

He looked up, frowning. "Mrs. Jenkins?"

"The librarian. I think if I asked her, she would do it for me. We're pretty close."

A slow smile spread over Louis's face. "You're wonderful!" he said, taking her face in his hands. He kissed her lightly on the cheek and jumped up, excited again.

"This is incredible," he said. "How in the world did you ever find this?"

Abby was looking up at him, stunned from his kiss. "See that picture? That's my mother," she said softly. "She won the Miss Magnolia contest."

But Louis was reading the four lines again, as if they might somehow reveal more. "I can't believe this," he murmured, grasping the paper.

His mind was racing. He didn't have much time in the morning. Lila's funeral started at one. He looked down at Abby. "How early can you call her?" he asked. "If you got back here by eight, we could be there by nine." He paused, seeing the wounded look on her face.

"Abby? What's the matter?" he asked.

"Nothing," she murmured.

He frowned. Shit, she expected to stay with him tonight. "Abby, look," he said softly. "You can't stay here."

She looked away.

"I'm sorry," he said, "but I thought you understood how I felt about this."

She shook her head. "It's not that."

"Then what?" She was crying softly and he pulled her hands away from her face. "Abby, what's the matter?"

She shook her head again. "He's pulling me out of school."

"What? Your father is? Why?"

"To control me. He wants to control everything, who I see, where I go, what I think."

"Abby, it'll be all right," Louis said weakly. "You don't have to stay there. You're nineteen, free to leave. You know that."

"I can't leave. I can't leave Mother there alone."

"Your mother will be fine, Abby. You need to think about yourself."

"He hits her," she whispered, choking back tears.

"What?"

"He hits her," she repeated. "My mother, he hits her. I couldn't do, I couldn't . . . he . . ."

Louis stared at her. "Who? Your father? Your father hit your mother?"

Abby's eyes flashed angrily. "Yes."

Louis had a vision of Max that night in the bar, drunk and bellicose, and then he saw Grace, so small and pale. A mix of disgust and pity swept through him. Back in Ann Arbor, he had gone out on his share of domestic calls. They were all tragic, senseless violence. And he swore he would never understand why the women remained with their abusers.

"This isn't the first time this has happened, is it?" he said.

She shook her head. "I can't go home," she whispered.

He could hear Bessie snoring upstairs. He stood up, taking her hand. "Come on," he said.

He led her upstairs. She walked into his room ahead of him and yanked off her coat. Her tears had turned to fury and she faced him suddenly.

"I don't understand how she can live with it!"

"Abby, I've seen—"

"You don't know what it's like. You don't know how it feels to watch it. Seeing her, hearing her screaming and not being able to stop it."

"Abby, let me call the sheriff for you."

"No!" She sat down on the bed. He watched as her fingers curled around the spread, her knuckles white. Her eyes drifted to the gun lying on the nightstand and he tensed at the thoughts that started spinning in his mind. She wasn't capable of it; she could never pull the trigger.

He went to the nightstand and put the gun in a drawer, sitting down beside her, taking her hand. "Abby, you can stay for a while. I don't want you driving or going home as angry as you are."

She was staring at the floor. "I hate him," she whispered.

He pulled her into his arms and held her. Her body was a coiled spring against his, tight and unbending. He realized in that moment that he didn't know her at all. He had seen her only as a romantic kid, a kid with a screwed-up homelife who, like all other kids, was looking for a way to break out. But the hatred in her voice and that look in her eyes as she gazed at his gun worried him. Max Lillihouse undoubtedly kept guns in his house. He didn't believe Abby really would do anything, but he knew how these family things could go. No one ever thought it could happen in their family. But it did.

He leaned back against the headboard, pulling her to his chest. He held her, stroking her hair. She seemed content to just lie there. It was only when he finally felt her muscles start to go slack with sleep that he began to relax.

Louis sat in the chair by the window, listening to the sounds filter up from the street below. He looked over at the bed where Abby lay sleeping. She gave a soft moan and turned, but did not wake up. Louis went to the bed and pulled the quilt up over her shoulder.

He should not have let her stay, but he just hadn't had the heart to send her home. He looked at the clock. Three-thirty. He was tired, but surprisingly alert, the name Eugene Graham spinning through his head. Restless, he wandered back to the window and looked out. The street was quiet. A light was on above Tinker's store. Below it, parked under a streetlamp, was a silver car. He had never seen it parked there before.

Suddenly, without turning on its lights, the car moved away. Louis's eyes moved to the front door of the store. It looked secure. The sidewalks were empty. Nothing out of the ordinary.

He went to the refrigerator and popped open a can of Dr. Pepper. Abby stirred, but did not awaken. He moved back to the window for one more look.

The car was back. Louis frowned. There was something familiar about it. He went to the dresser for his binoculars and returned to the window. It was a Monte Carlo and suddenly he knew where he had seen it before. It was Max Lillihouse's car. Fuck, what was this?

He lowered the glasses. Max had followed Abby. That had to be it. Louis looked back at the car. He couldn't see inside the heavily tinted windows. Why was Max just sitting out there? Gathering his courage for a confrontation? Louis had a sudden vision of Max storming up the staircase, waving a loaded gun. He thought briefly about calling the station, but he knew that wouldn't solve anything. Maybe he should go down there himself.

The car began to move away, slowly and silently at first, then with a roar as the taillights faded into the blackness. Louis looked over at Abby. He could imagine what Max Lillihouse was thinking. What he couldn't imagine was what a man like Max Lillihouse would do.

Louis stared out at the street. He was afraid for Abby. Hell, he was afraid for them both.

Louis watched as old Mrs. Jenkins trudged up the steps of the library, keys in hand. She greeted Abby with a hug but had only a cold stare for Louis.

"I don't know why this couldn't wait till Monday, dear," she said as she unlocked the door.

"I told you, Mrs. Jenkins," Abby said gently. "Detective Kincaid has to get a copy of a newspaper article for police business. We really appreciate this."

"Well, I can only stay here ten minutes," the old woman sniffed as Louis and Abby went in. "I'm going to be late for church as it is."

Louis quickly found the reel for 1955 and wound through the pages until he spotted the photograph of the Miss Magnolia pageant. There at the bottom was the article about Eugene Graham. He hit the PRINT key. He and Abby thanked Mrs. Jenkins and left. Back in the Mustang, he read the article.

A colored boy was reported missing by his grandmother, Annie Graham, of the Sweetwater community late Thursday night. Graham told police her grandson, Eugene Graham, a student at Cotton Town High School, never returned home from a sports event that evening.

Eugene Graham was Sweetwater's top baseball player, having helped that team win the Negro High School baseball championship of 1954. It was reported that Eugene was being scouted by the Cleveland Indians as an outfielder.

Sheriff's officials offered no comment on the disappearance.

"I bet they didn't," Louis said softly.

"What?" Abby asked.

"Nothing," he said. But who would have cared about a missing boy, except Annie Graham? Why hadn't anyone remembered this? Jesus, a boy vanished, and this was his only eulogy. But then he realized that maybe no one remembered it because Eugene Graham had eventually shown up, returning home later in the day or week. Louis closed his eyes. What if this was just another dead end?

"Louis, what's the matter?" Abby asked. "Is it the wrong man?"

He shook his head. "I don't know," he said. "I wish there was someone who—" He stopped.

Buford! That crazy old man in Cotton Town. He might remember, now that Louis had a name. Louis looked at his watch again. Less than three hours until the funeral. He put the Mustang in reverse and peeled out of the parking lot.

"Louis! Where are we going?" Abby asked, grabbing the armrest.

"You're going home. I'm taking you back to your car. I have someplace I have to go."

"Where?" Abby demanded.

"I have to go see a man who might remember Eugene Graham."

"Well, I'll go with you."

"Abby—"

She turned in the seat to face him. "Why not? I helped you find his name, Louis. Why can't I go with you?"

"Abby, this is business. Please understand."

She sighed and sat back in the seat. "All right."

After he backtracked to Bessie's and dropped Abby off at her car, Louis headed to Cotton Town. Buford was sitting on the porch of his house, rocking in a chair, enjoying the unseasonable break in the cold weather. Louis introduced himself, grateful the old man remembered him. He held out the copy of the newspaper article.

"I was hoping you might be able to tell me something about this," Louis said.

Buford squinted at the paper then shook his head. "You read it, sonny. I ain't got my glasses."

As Louis read the story, a slow smile spread over Buford's face. "That's him, Detective. That's the young'un I was thinkin' about."

"Do you know if he ever returned home?"

"Nope. Don't reckon he did."

"Mr. Overstreet, are you sure this is the same boy? You said he had a hand missing. How did he play baseball?"

"That's what done made him special. It was only part of a hand missin' . . . jus' a couple fingers. He still done good. He played right field. The big boys was down here lookin' at him."

Louis frowned, looking again at the copy of the article. "Mr. Overstreet, how do you remember this boy if he lived in Sweetwater?"

"Y'all got to know that Sweetwater was only a couple miles from here. Lots of kids lived there went to school here in Cotton Town. Wasn't no other place back then."

"But what about the school?" Louis asked.

"Closed down. This used to be a nice town, Officer. Real nice. Sweetwater, too. Wasn't no trashy streets like now. Most of the Sweetwater folks moved up Tupelo way after the trouble."

"The trouble in Sweetwater, when did it happen?"

"Let's see . . . '65, '66. Klan. Burnt the church. Burnt houses. Run folks outta town."

"This kid, Eugene Graham, vanished before that?"

"Way before. School here done closed in '64."

"Did you know his grandmother?"

"No, sir, not right well. I know she raised them young'uns like they was her own. She done died of the fever way back. I jus' heard about the boy being able to throw a baseball with a hand that had fingers missin'. I thought that was a pretty good trick. I'm glad I 'membered him. I ain't thought about Eugene in years.

You done good, Officer, finding out on your own. Makes me feel poorly I couldn't help you before."

"Don't worry about it." Louis leaned against the porch railing. "Mr. Overstreet, you said most of the Sweetwater families moved up toward Tupelo?"

"That's what I hear, but I can't say real good, if'n they did. They's could be anywheres."

"Anyone else around here from Sweetwater originally?"

"Not that I know of."

"How do I get to Sweetwater?" Louis asked.

"Back to the highway, go left and look for the old wooden sign."

Louis paused and put on his sunglasses. "I have to go. Thank you for your time, Mr. Overstreet."

"I gots lots of time, Officer."

Louis turned to leave. He turned back to Buford. "Cubs play today?"

Buford shook his head. "Damn Cubs. They get more days off than the gov'ment. Pay them fellas a million dollars and they only plays when they feel like it."

"Maybe tomorrow, Mr. Overstreet."

"Mebbe so."

Louis almost missed the faded wooden sign hidden in the weeds. He followed the rutted dirt road about a mile, rounded a curve, and there was Sweetwater.

The first thing he saw was a white steeple against the brilliant blue sky. It rose from mounds of black rubble. He drove slowly down the dirt road, fascinated but saddened by what he saw.

It had been no more than a village, really. A general store, a gas station, a school and some houses. Now most of it was nothing but charred remains. The old store was choked with brown kudzu. Two rusted gas pumps stood in lonely isolation, their gauges frozen at 21¢ a gallon. Tall, thin weeds fluttered in the breeze.

Almost twenty years had passed since the town's destruction. Sweetwater was long dead, but the air was alive with hundreds of voices. Children laughing. Choirs singing. Women weeping. Men screaming.

Eugene Graham had lived here, in one of these old houses. He had disappeared in 1955; the destruction of Sweetwater happened in '65 or '66. It wasn't related, but it sure made the search harder.

Louis parked the Mustang beneath an oak tree. He got out, standing for a moment, then walked around the edge of what once had been a vegetable garden. He stopped in front of a house that was still standing. The windows were busted out and the door hung off its hinges. A twisted chain-link fence surrounded the yard.

Louis moved the rusty gate enough to step through, and walked to the porch. The railing wobbled and Louis stepped carefully, avoiding the rotted planks. He gently pushed open the door. It squeaked and fell to the floor with a muffled thud, spraying Louis with dust.

He ventured inside. Sunlight, speckled with dust, spilled in through the broken windows. The only furniture was a few small tables and a broken ladder-back chair. A tattered T-shirt lay on the floor next to a dead mouse.

In the kitchen beyond was an old refrigerator with a broken door. Something on the wall over the warped counter caught Louis's eye. Moving closer, he saw it was a wooden plaque. Scrawled on the front, in a child's hand, were the words *Black Is Beautiful*. Louis took it off its nail and turned it over. On the back someone had written in pencil: *LaTonya, 1965, 8th Grade*. He wiped the dust off and stared at it, running his hand across the varnished surface.

Louis turned and looked around the lonely old house. "Talk to me, Eugene," he whispered. "Tell me where to go now."

Reluctantly, he looked at his watch. If he didn't hurry, he would be late for the funeral. He started to put the plaque back on the wall then paused. He would keep it.

Back in the car, he glanced at his watch. He backtracked down the dirt road, swung out onto the main highway and hit the accelerator. He came up quickly behind a plodding log truck.

"Damn," he muttered, waiting out the curve in the road so he could pass. Once clear, he hit the accelerator.

Louis let out a long breath. The vibrations of Sweetwater were still coursing through him, almost like an electric current. It was so real now. Eugene Graham was real. The haunting face now had become real, a person with a family and a life. The jumbled pieces of the case bounced in his mind. Earl's murder. George

Harvey's strange phone calls. The photocopy of the mayor and the necklace. The case was finally starting to make sense.

The Mustang, traveling near sixty, rounded the bend near the Lillihouse property.

Jesus Christ! A man in the road!

Louis hit the brakes and the tires screeched as the car skidded across the asphalt. A flash of red plaid dove into the grass. The Mustang slid sideways and came to a jolting stop. Louis exhaled, still gripping the wheel, his heart thundering. He twisted his neck to look back at the road.

A man was crouched in the ditch. Louis shoved open the door and sprinted over to the ditch. A black man was crawling out of the tall grass. Louis extended his hand.

"Man, I'm sorry. I was speeding," Louis said.

The man looked at him, panting. He grabbed his chest and let out a deep breath. " 'Bout scared the shit outta me, you did."

"I'm sorry. You hurt?" Louis asked.

"Nah, I'm okay."

"Can I give you a lift?"

"I jus' live up the road. Y'all slow down some," the man said, "before you kill somebody."

Louis smiled. "I will, thanks."

The man ambled on his way, walking unsteadily along the slanted roadside. Louis jogged back to the car. But then he paused, hand on the handle, as if someone had touched his shoulder. He frowned slightly, looking around.

To his right were rolling yellow pastures. To his left, a thick forest, the same area where the bones had been found. A sign fifty or so feet ahead pointed to Cotton Town.

Louis glanced back at the man, walking slowly west along Road 234. Toward the direction of Sweetwater. Suddenly, Louis knew. He couldn't prove it, but he knew.

Eugene Graham had walked along this road, too. He had walked down this road every day, heading home from Cotton Town High School. Eugene Graham had been walking down this road the day he was murdered.

CHAPTER 20

Flowers . . . so many flowers. They surrounded the black coffin and spilled out of the doors of the small chapel of Collins Funeral Home. Flowers of all colors, shapes, and sizes. Louis had never seen so many flowers in one place, not even in a garden. Where had they all come from?

He sat on a wooden folding chair, next to Bessie, listening as the eulogy for Lila Kincaid began. The chapel was crowded, every seat taken, with people standing in the back. Who were all these people? he wondered. Who had they been to this woman who was his mother?

They had come up to him, one by one, offering their sympathies, their tears, their handshakes and their hugs. He had stood by Bessie's side, quietly thanking them for coming, confused by this parade of strangers who had shared his mother's life more than he had.

He had met Bessie's minister, Reverend Stacey. And as the reverend delivered the eulogy in his soft voice, Louis gazed at the closed casket, filled with an inexplicable sadness. They called a funeral a "going home" here, a phrase he found sweetly ironic. He didn't remember Lila being much of a churchgoer, and he certainly wasn't. But now, there inside him with the sadness, was a calmness, too, of a kind he had never felt before.

He gazed at the beautiful black coffin. He would never know this woman who had given him life. Yet surrounded by all these people, he knew now that her life had not been without some measure of love. These people were Lila's family, unknown brothers and sisters who had gathered because one of their own had died.

After the eulogy, a young girl named Lenette sang "Amazing Grace." Louis listened, thinking of the photograph of Lila at eighteen that Bessie had shown him. Closing his eyes, he vowed to try and remember her that way. He was done judging. It was over.

Afterward, they gathered at Bessie's house to share food, drink, and memories. Louis met a distant cousin, an uncle, and a couple of kind women who never revealed their relationship to Lila, if indeed they had one. The day wore on. Louis laughed along with the stories, listened to the memories, and looked at photographs. When the last people got up to leave, he found himself wishing they would stay.

It was only four o'clock when Bessie closed the door.

"I'll help you clean up," Louis said.

"No, my sister and me'll do that," Bessie insisted. "You go take time for yourself."

Louis nodded and gave Bessie a small hug. She eased him away and ushered him toward his room, watching until he disappeared up the steps.

Up in his room, he stood at the window looking out at the sunny day. He thought about the last week and turned, looking at the head.

"Eugene," he said softly.

The head stared back with its haunting eyes. If only Dodie could see its expression, maybe he would understand what drove Louis to finish this. And what had compelled him to do the stupid things he had done lately.

He had been wrong to go behind Dodie's back on the Leverette thing. He had been wrong not to tell him about Kelly and the medallion. Shit, he had been wrong about a lot of things, and he needed to humble himself and go apologize.

But it was Sunday. Dodie was probably in church. And it wasn't right to disturb him on his day off just because he felt the need for atonement. It could wait until Monday.

Louis walked back to the window and opened it, taking in the warmer air. He saw the Mustang sitting in the sun out at the curb and on impulse decided to go for a drive.

He headed out of town, with no destination in mind. It was not until he saw the interstate sign for Tupelo that he decided he would go. Buford had said that most of the people from Sweetwater had relocated there. Maybe he would get lucky. Maybe somebody up there would come forward for Eugene.

When he got to Tupelo, he found a phone book and looked up every Graham listed. He called all of them, but the few who answered had never heard of Eugene Graham or a young ball player with a deformed hand. Before Louis left town, he found the office of the local newspaper. Sitting in his car under a sprawling elm, he wrote a classified ad:

> To anyone related to or knowing Eugene Graham who disappeared in Greensboro County in 1955: I have information for you. Please contact Det. Kincaid at the Greensboro County Sheriff's Office.

He folded the letter, attaching a note specifying he wanted to place a classified ad, and a ten-dollar bill. He slid it under the door.

Louis came back into town on Road 234. It was past five by the time he rounded the bend in the road and came in sight of the Lillihouse mansion. He pulled off onto the shoulder and sat there, looking at the house. Abby's yellow Firebird wasn't there, but the silver Monte Carlo was. Louis felt himself stiffen as he looked at the car, still angry that Max had been sitting outside Bessie's last night. He must have known Abby was with him. He just hoped Abby had had the sense to stay away from her father.

The door opened suddenly and Max came out, staring into the setting sun at the Mustang, parked down the road. Louis wanted to slide down into the seat, as if that would do any good. Max stood motionless a long time, watching him, then suddenly turned and went back inside.

Louis reached over to start the engine, taking one last look at the house. His heart ached for Abby. So unhappy, and too damn young to really do anything about it.

"Kincaid," his radio blurted. It was Larry.

He grabbed the mike. "What?" he asked, irritated.

"Sheriff says get away from Max's house."

Louis took a deep breath. "I was just sitting—" Louis said tightly.

"Sheriff didn't ask what you was doin'. He just said git your ass outta there."

"Deputy Cutter, don't you know it's a FCC violation to use

profanity over the airwaves?" Louis said. Jesus, he was sinking
to Larry's level.

"Screw you, Kincaid."

Suddenly the radio crackled with static and it sounded like
someone had dropped it. Dodie came on, his voice hard.

"This here is a police radio. It's not to be used for your belly-
achin' and whinin'. Bring it into the station, for cryin' out loud."

The radio went dead. Louis was surprised Dodie was in on
a Sunday. He started the car and headed back. He stopped at
McDonald's and got something to eat and drove home the long
way, through town, past the courthouse. He saw Dodie's Blazer
parked out front and looked at his watch. It was almost seven.
Louis stared at the Blazer as he waited at the light. He thought
about the clay head, and Tinker's words drifted back to him.
"Show him something he cannot ignore."

Impulsively Louis turned right and headed home. Hurrying
upstairs, he wrapped the clay head in a towel and drove back to
the courthouse. Swinging in next to the Blazer, he killed the engine,
thinking, trying to gather his thoughts. It had always been hard
for him to admit he was wrong. Frances Lawrence had instilled
in him a sense of pride, a need to stand up for what he believed
in. But he knew he had a way of sometimes taking it to extremes.
It had gotten him into more than one scrape in grade school, and
he didn't like listening to Frances Lawrence when she tried to
teach him about humility. Louis gathered up the towel-wrapped
bust. Well, maybe it was time to start learning.

Mike was manning the dispatch desk and looked up when
Louis came in. "Thought you was suspended, Louis," Mike said,
swallowing a bite of his sandwich.

"I am. Sheriff alone?"

Mike nodded again. Louis went to the door and knocked. Then
he poked his head in. Dodie was tilted back in his chair, dozing.

"Sheriff."

Dodie pulled his feet off the desk and ran a hand over his face.
"Yeah . . ."

"Could we talk?"

Dodie's eyes flickered as he brought himself awake. Then he
took a long, steady look at Louis. Louis came farther into the
room and set the head on a chair, unsure how to open the conversation. "Are you feeling okay? You look like shit."

"Just tired, Kincaid."

"You should take care of yourself. Take some time off once in a while."

"That's what the wife tells me."

There was an awkward pause. Dodie gazed at him for a moment then pulled a bottle of Jim Beam out of his desk drawer. He unscrewed the top, poured a shot into a Dixie Cup and took a swig. He looked up at Louis, waiting. "You got something to say, Kincaid?"

Louis stuck his hands in his pockets and leaned against the wall. "I was just driving by."

"And you decided to stop in and say hello to your coworkers?"

Louis sighed, looking up at the ceiling fan. Jesus, why was it so hard to apologize to this man?

Dodie poured himself another shot then stuck the bottle on the edge of the desk. "Have a drink."

Louis shook his head.

"Goddammit, have a drink. It'll clear your mind so you can tell me what the hell you came here for."

Louis pushed himself off the wall and walked to the desk. He poured a quarter shot of whiskey in a Dixie Cup and swallowed it.

"I'm sorry," he said quickly.

"Sorry?"

"I was wrong to let Leverette go without talking to you first," Louis said.

"Yup."

"I was wrong to send that stuff off without asking you."

"Yup."

Louis took a breath. "And I was wrong to not tell you what I knew about Kelly."

Dodie screwed the top back on the bottle and gazed up at Louis. "Sit down, Kincaid," he said.

Louis slid into the hard wooden chair across from Dodie's desk. The alcohol was working its way through his muscles and he twisted his neck, suddenly feeling warm.

"Kincaid, I been sheriff here near eight years. I ain't never been so pissed at one of my deputies as I was yesterday afternoon at the damn service."

Louis looked at the floor.

"It's pretty damn embarrassin' not to know what the hell one of my men is doing, especially in this here case. It ain't like folks here ain't upset enough thinkin' this thing is gonna bring shame on this here town."

Louis sat back, stretching his legs out.

"I guess I should be grateful you ain't involved outsiders yet."

Louis closed his eyes against the image of Winston Gibbons.

"Kincaid, I don't think you understand what kind of position you put me in. Not just with this thing but just by you bein' who you are."

Louis looked at Dodie, first angry then softening when he saw the look of empathy in Dodie's eyes.

"You know, when you first got here," Dodie said, "the only thing I could think about was how I was I gonna look to Kelly and this town. I made a mistake, a mistake I coulda fixed that first day you done walked here."

"Why didn't you?"

Dodie looked away, eyes clouded. "I don't know. I had the words all planned out in my head before you came in here, about how the job was no longer available. But when you walked in here in that snappy suit and that goddamn eager look on your face . . . and you stuck out your hand and I knew you had no idea I had just spent the last thirty minutes on the phone with Kelly trying to hold my ass together while he tore it apart. I think maybe I was so pissed at Walt, I just let you stay out of spite."

This honesty on Dodie's part was something new. Louis liked it, and it made his own distrust seem all the more small-minded in contrast. He leaned his elbows on his knees, looking at the floor.

Dodie played with the bottle cap. "You're a good cop, Kincaid. You don't know everything, but you have character and that ain't an easy thing to have, especially in a place like this."

Louis looked up.

"Lots of people here talk about what they believe in until somebody else disagrees with it," Dodie went on. "Then all of a sudden, their opinions change. But yours don't. Once you set your mind to something, you don't let it go." Dodie looked up at him. "I don't gotta agree with how you do things, but I gotta respect that."

"I'm sorry," Louis said again, surprised at how easy the words spilled out. "I should have respected your authority. I just couldn't stand to see it all buried under a phony headstone and lies."

Dodie sighed. "I reckon I understand. Since y'all went and found out some shit, I guess you better let me in on it."

Louis reached into the pocket of his jacket and pulled out the photocopy of Kelly wearing the medallion. He unfolded it and put it on the desk in front of Dodie.

Dodie picked it up and stared at it. His expression did not change. Finally, he set it down, pushing it away slightly like it was tainted. He looked up at Louis.

"I found it in a family history book at the library," Louis said. "The expert I talked to in Vicksburg said these medallions are pretty rare. The book has disappeared from the library."

Dodie shook his head. "Christ, Kincaid. Kelly, of all people."

Louis let the thought settle, then went on, edging forward in his chair. "Earl's murder and the lynching are related. I'm sure of it now."

Dodie's frown deepened. "You lost me."

"Did the report come back on George Harvey yet?" Louis asked.

"Just the prelim. Said he was shot with a .45. Been dead only a couple minutes when we got there. Insurance still going through the loot. You was right about the glass. It was broken from the inside. Whoever shot George was let in."

Louis nodded. The sheriff studied him for a moment. "I think George knew his killer and they were probably discussing the lynching and how to keep it quiet," Louis said.

"This is all assumption, I take it."

Louis shrugged. "That part, yes."

"What makes you think George was killed 'cause of this?"

"I got an anonymous phone call the night before he was killed. I think it was George."

"What did he say?"

"He said he knew who lynched our victim."

Dodie's mouth dropped open. "Who?"

"He didn't tell me. He was supposed to call me back but then turned up dead. He also told me Earl Mulcahey was killed because he knew about the lynching. The caller said he was there. That's why I released Leverette, Sheriff. That kid didn't kill his father."

Dodie was staring at him, dumbfounded. "So you're saying

these two fellas were killed to cover up a thirty-year-old crime. If that's true, who killed them?"

"Right now, my money's on Kelly."

The sheriff rose slowly. He rubbed a hand over his face and turned away from Louis. He was staring out at the dark square. "Is there anything else you know about this lynching, Kincaid?"

Louis hesitated, rubbing his temples. "I know who he was."

The sheriff turned slowly, his expression incredulous.

"His name was Eugene Graham."

Dodie simply stared at Louis while he told him the details.

"And you knowed this for a while?" Dodie asked.

"Only since yesterday."

Dodie ran his fingers through his hair. Louis didn't know if he was angry at him or just stunned by the revelations. His eyes flicked up to the Confederate flag on the wall then quickly back to Dodie.

"Can I show you something?" Louis asked, getting up.

Dodie nodded. Louis unwrapped the clay head and set it in front of Dodie. Dodie looked at it a long time, then sat down in his chair, letting out a tired breath.

"That," Louis said softly, "is why I couldn't let it go."

Dodie unscrewed the top off the Jim Beam and took a swig. Louis let several moments pass.

"What are we going to do, Sheriff?" Louis asked.

Dodie looked up at him. "We're gonna wait for that report you asked for from the FBI. Once they tell us the medallions match, we'll be able to see where we're going with this."

"You going to bring anybody else in on this?"

"No, not yet."

Louis paused. "Sheriff, when can I come back to work?"

Dodie pursed his lips. "Tomorrow soon enough?"

Louis smiled slightly. "Thank you."

"Just a minute, Kincaid. One more thing."

Louis sat back down.

Dodie looked suddenly ill at ease. "I want you to listen to what I'm gonna tell you. And I don't want you getting riled and readin' too much into it."

Louis waited.

"You gotta be careful 'round Miz Abigail."

Louis bristled and Dodie held up a hand. "I ain't passin' no judgment here, but people are talking. You gotta have a clear head about these things."

"Sheriff—"

"I know you think it don't matter, and maybe it shouldn't," Dodie went on, "but look at it from her standpoint. She's young and right stubborn. Maybe, jus' maybe, she just wants to piss off her old man."

Louis shook his head, partly in frustration, partly out of weariness with the whole business. "There's nothing going on between us, Sheriff."

"It don't matter, Kincaid. That's my point." Dodie paused, sitting back in his chair. "You gotta understand. Women here are different."

Louis rested his elbows on his knees, bringing up his hands to cover his face. Good God, now Dodie was going to lecture him on Southern women, and there was no gracious way to escape.

"Black and white just don't mix easy here, Kincaid. But that don't mean that some men don't get a taste for it, or that some women want what they can't have."

Louis stared at the floor. He looked up at the sheriff slowly. "What did you say?"

"I didn't mean no offense there, I—"

"None taken, just repeat what you said."

"I'm just sayin' some women like to play with fire. Messin' with a black man when you have Max Lillihouse for a father is just asking for trouble."

Louis's eyes took on an excited gaze. "Sheriff, I need your permission to talk to someone."

Dodie's eyes narrowed. "Who?"

"Maisey Kelly."

"Maisey?" Dodie said. "What's Maisey got to do with you and Miz Abigail?"

"Nothing," Louis said. "But she may have a lot to do with Eugene Graham."

The color dripped from Dodie's face. He stared at Louis, unblinking. "Kincaid, where are you going with this?"

Louis was trying hard to recall exactly what it was Ethel Mulcahey had said about the young Maisey. "Do you suppose," Louis said, "that Miss Maisey once wanted someone she couldn't have?"

"Jesus, Kincaid . . ."

"Sheriff, I have to talk to her." Louis stood up.

"There you go again," Dodie said.

"Sheriff," Louis said softly, knowing he should just shut up. "I can do this your way. I can be discreet."

Dodie scratched his head, avoiding Louis's eyes. "You ask a lot, Kincaid."

"I won't go without your permission."

Louis watched him. A cloud crossed Dodie's gray eyes and he began to tap his fingers softly on the blotter.

"These people are my friends, Kincaid," Dodie said quietly. "I've known them all my life."

Louis bit his lip. He knew this was causing Dodie pain, but the fact was, these people were killers. He pressed on, trying one last time.

"Please, Sheriff," he said.

Dodie was staring at the clay head. Louis slumped slightly, knowing suddenly the permission would not come. He rose, setting the chair back against the wall.

"I'll wait for the report," Louis said gently. "I'll see you Monday."

He walked toward the closed door.

"Louis."

Louis turned back. Dodie was swaying slightly in the swivel chair, still looking at the clay head.

"Yes sir?"

"You be gentle with Miss Maisey," Dodie said. "She's sicklike."

CHAPTER 21

Max squinted through the thick gray smoke of Big Al's Tavern and watched as Marcus Allen sprinted into the end zone. The bar erupted into cheers and howls, punctuated with an occasional "Ah, shit."

Max looked away from the television and down into his drink, watching the ice cubes bob against the side of the glass. Then he raised the glass and took a quick swig of the scotch. Across the mirror behind the bar was a silver banner that proclaimed WEL-COME TO BUD LITE'S SUPER BOWL XVIII. Balloons shaped like footballs and beer bottles swayed in the dank air. Propped up against the register was a large piece of cardboard with numbers drawn on it, the Football Square, which gave all takers a chance to win an easy $500 by choosing the final total points.

He had bought three, but he had no chance now. Max stared at the cardboard. He didn't care about the $60 he'd bet on the Football Square. What he cared about was the $5,000 he had laid with his bookie for the Redskins to beat the spread. But the Raiders were now ahead 35–3, and Max had been so sure that Theisman had it in him to pull off the upset.

The noise in the bar kicked up a notch as a commercial came on. Max looked up and found himself staring into the face of a handsome black athlete wearing Fruit of the Loom briefs. Max's gaze drifted over the athlete's lean body and he thought of Kincaid. The image mutated and the man in the briefs was lying in a bed with Abby, his Doll Baby

He took a quick drink of the scotch and gagged, sending the scotch down his chin. He grabbed a napkin and angrily wiped his face. He slammed the glass on the bar.

"Billy Ray! Billy Ray! Fill up this damn glass," he yelled.

The bartender set a bottle of Johnny Walker Red on the bar and sauntered away, back to the television. Max grabbed the bottle.

"Hey! Lillihouse!"

Max peered through the cigarette smoke down the bar. Shit. It was Elmer Miller. Cheap, whiny bastard.

"Hey, Lillihouse, still selling lemons at that car lot of yours?"

Max looked away. "You didn't have to buy the damn car."

"Hey," Miller called out, turning on his stool to the knot of men at the pool table. "You guys know what Ford stands for? "Fix Or Repair Daily!"

Laughter rippled through the men.

"Always the clown, aren't you, Elmer?" Max muttered.

"I just think a man oughta make good on a bum product, that's all. That piece of shit you sold me ain't run in near nine months."

Max filled his glass to the rim. "Not my problem."

"Yeah, yeah . . . not your problem. I'm out two thousand bucks and it ain't your problem."

"That's what I said."

Miller licked his lips. "I guess you got bigger problems to worry about. Like trying to keep that daughter of yours in line."

Max was staring at Miller but the man didn't seem to notice. He was huddled with his friends now at the far end of the bar, whispering, and suddenly the group burst into raucous laughter.

Max turned away, gripping the glass. Their sick cackling vibrated in his head, blotting out all the other sounds, all other thoughts.

Billy Ray, the bartender, took a step toward Miller, shaking his head, but Miller ignored him. *"Abby Lillihouse went down the hill to fetch herself a nigger . . ."* Miller said in a singsong voice, just loud enough for Max to hear.

Max bolted from the stool but Miller's friends quickly surrounded him. Max tore at them, trying to get to the cowering man, but two men got their arms around Max's shoulders and pulled him back. Max muscled one off, knocking him against the bar. His hand groped for Miller's flannel shirt.

"Come here, you little fuck!"

Miller jumped off his stool and backed up against the wall, cowering but grinning drunkenly. "C'mon, c'mon," he called.

Two other men had jumped in to hold Max. They pushed him back, wedging him against the bar. One of the men, Jimmy Beechum, worked for Max and was talking to him, trying to calm him down. Everyone in the bar was on their feet, watching. The only sound was that of the television announcer as the Raiders marched down the field.

Billy Ray leaned over the bar and removed Miller's beer. "You better get out of here, Elmer," he said.

"Why?" Miller sputtered. "I ain't done nothin'. I wanna watch the game."

"Let's go, Elmer," one of his friends said in a low voice.

It was only after Miller and his friends had left that the three men holding Max let him go. Max jerked free. He drew in heaving breaths and wiped a shaking hand across his face.

"You okay?" Jimmy Beechum asked.

"Fine."

Max slowly went back to his place at the bar. He refilled his glass and took a quick drink, still standing. He felt a hand on his shoulder.

"I can fix this for you, boss," Beechum said. "If y'all want me to."

Max set down his glass and reached over to the next stool for his coat. "No, I'll take care of it," he said hoarsely.

He went to the door and shoved it open. The Redskins kicked a field goal and cheers from the bar rippled through Max's head as he headed home.

Grace picked up the crystal decanter and slowly poured the sherry into the glass. She watched, mesmerized, as the golden liquid trembled from the lip, then she carefully replaced the stopper and set it aside. She closed her eyes. The room was cold. The fire had died down to a faint orange glow in the black hearth. She shivered and raised the glass to her lips.

The front door banged open, reverberating in the foyer. The glass slipped from Grace's fingers.

"Abigail!"

Max's voice echoed in the foyer. Grace turned stiffly.

He appeared at the archway, his face red, his chest heaving. Grace shrank back into the shadows. Max squinted, focusing on her.

"Where is she?" he demanded.

"I . . . I don't know," Grace whispered.

Max swung toward the stairs. "Abigail!" he bellowed. Then he spun back toward Grace, taking a step into the library. "Where the hell is she?!"

Grace retreated slowly behind one of the wing chairs.

"Answer me, goddammit!" he shouted.

Grace's eyes darted past Max, looking for an escape. But he turned suddenly and started for the staircase.

"Abigail!"

He was gone. She let out a deep shudder, reaching for the chair to stop her body from shaking. She heard his heavy tread going up the stairs and she closed her eyes.

Abby waited, her heart hammering. She had heard him yelling downstairs. And now she heard the heavy footsteps coming up the stairs. She drew in a sharp breath, holding it. Something was wrong tonight. Usually, she would hear him stumbling into his bedroom, followed by the slam of the door. But not tonight. Tonight, something was different.

Her heart was racing and she sank back against the headboard of her bed, waiting, staring at the door. Her brain was screaming: *Lock it! Quick, go lock the door!*

It was too late. He pushed open the door and stood wavering in the hallway, his hands on the doorframe, bracing himself.

"Why didn't you answer me!" he demanded.

In the dim light of her bedside lamp, she could see him. His sparse hair was awry around his flushed face. His tie hung crooked and his wrinkled white dress shirt had pulled free of his pants. Even from this distance, she could smell the sweat and the whiskey.

He staggered over to her bed. She shrank back, pulling her knees up. He was staring at her, his eyes bloodshot, but with something other than just a booze haze. She stiffened, thinking of her mother, whom she had left sitting downstairs in the library just a few minutes before. Whatever it was that had set him off this time, she knew that this time he wasn't going to take it out on Grace.

"Daddy? What's wrong?" She tried to make her voice sound calm.

"You," he said in a low voice.

She froze. Oh dear God, he had heard the talk.

"Daddy, I haven't—"

Max moved quickly, lunging forward and grabbing the front of her sweatshirt. He jerked her toward him and she let out a yelp. Then she felt the sharp sting of his palm on her cheek. Her head was sent spinning back into the pillows.

"You fucking nigger-loving slut!"

She tried to scramble away from him, but his hands clamped down on the back of her shirt. He climbed on the bed and spun her over, drawing back his hand. Abby's hands flew to her face, catching the brunt of his blow. He twisted her shirt around his fist, yanking her closer, slapping at her.

His foul breath flooded her face. He drew back a fist, but she jerked her shirt from his grasp and rolled away from him. He grabbed for her but missed. She slipped off the comforter and dropped to the floor.

Abby scrambled across the room and got to her feet, pressing against the door, blood trickling down her chin.

"I didn't do anything!" she shouted.

"You think I'm stupid?" he yelled. "You think people don't tell me what you and that nigger are doing?"

Abby spun around and jerked open the door. Max's arm shot out and it slammed shut. He backhanded Abby, sending her careening into the bedside table. A small lamp crashed to the floor. She pulled herself up, glaring at him.

"Let me out of here," she said angrily, brushing her hair from her bloody lip.

"You're not going anywhere."

"I'm getting out!" Abby yelled. "You can't treat me like you treat her!"

Max came for her but Abby flung herself at him with a fierce cry, catching him off balance and sending him crashing back against the wall. He toppled over a small bench. She flung open the door and ran out and down the stairs.

Max stumbled after her. "Abigail! Abigail!"

She grabbed the banister and skidded down the stairs, falling at the bottom. She scrambled to her feet and looked back at Max standing at the top, a blur of black-and-white in the shadows.

"Get back here!" he shouted. "I'll find you! Don't you walk out that fucking door!"

Abby heard a sound and turned to see Grace standing at the door of the library. She felt her chest tighten.

"Abby," Grace whispered, "Don't go. . . ."

Abby grabbed her keys off the table in the foyer. Max was stumbling down the staircase, screaming after her. She pulled open the front door and ran out into the cold night.

The Commodores were singing softly on the radio. Louis had almost drifted off to sleep when the telephone rang out in the hallway. It was late and he knew it was probably for him. He pulled himself out from under the warm quilt and went out into the hall.

"Hello?"

"Louis! Louis, it's me, Abby! Come get me, please. I need you!"

He snapped awake. She was crying. "Abby, calm down. What's wrong?"

"Please, come get me! I'm so scared."

"Where are you?"

"I . . . The Texaco. Out near the bypass. Please come!"

"Abby, stop crying. I can barely understand you."

"Oh, Louis, I need you. . . ."

The door of Bessie's room opened and she stuck her head out. "All right, Abby," he said. "Stay there. I'll be there in five minutes."

He hung up and started for his bedroom.

"Louis, where you going?" Bessie asked.

"It's all right, Bessie, go back to bed."

"Don't you go gettin' involved with that girl. It's trouble, you hear?"

But he was already in his room, pulling on his clothes. A knot formed in his gut. This wasn't just another of Abby's ploys to get his attention. He grabbed his jacket and hurried down the steps out into the cold night. The car's heater hadn't even kicked in by the time he got to the Texaco station. He pulled in next to Abby's yellow Firebird. Before he could get out of his car, she yanked open the passenger-side door and jumped in.

"Drive, just drive," she said breathlessly.

He stared at her. She was without a coat and her hair was a tangled mess. Her sweatshirt was ripped and splattered with blood. "Abby, what happened?" he demanded.

She was sobbing. "Just drive!"

He switched on the overhead light. When he reached over to push back her limp hair, she flinched. There was a jagged cut on her right cheek and a bruise was forming on her jaw.

"Dear God," he whispered.

She pulled away, burrowing against the window, away from him. "He'll come after me," she whimpered. "Please, get me out of here."

Louis thrust the Mustang into drive and peeled out of the lot. He headed out of town, into the darkness of the countryside. The road was empty, a gray line that stretched into the tunnel of dark trees. He heard her crying and reached for her hand.

Louis spotted a sign for Great Oaks Park and swung in. Parked cars with steamed windows dotted the road, and Louis drove past them, far back into the trees, parking between two large oaks. He left the engine running and turned to face her.

"Abby, talk to me," he said. "Who did this? Was it your father?"

She nodded.

Louis turned away from her. He stared out the windshield at the dark trees. He clenched his jaw, wanting to hit something, anything. Finally he jerked open the door and got out. He just stood there for several seconds, pulling in deep breaths of the cold air, trying to calm himself. He started walking in a tight circle, toward the back of the car. Suddenly, he kicked the bumper. He kicked it again and again. Damn him! Goddamn him to hell! He wanted to shoot the bastard.

"Louis? Are you all right?"

He came back to the open door and leaned in, breathing heavily. His stomach knotted again at the sight of her face. He let out a long, slow breath, trying to release some of the anger with it. He could be no help to her this way. He had to stay calm.

"You have to report him, Abby," he said.

"God, can't you stop being a cop for once?" she cried. "They know! They've always known!"

Louis was stunned by the bitterness in her voice. "The sheriff?"

She closed her eyes and dropped her head back against the seat. "Yes," she whispered hoarsely.

Louis got back in the car. For a moment, it was silent. Abby had stopped crying, and now she looked exhausted, the blood dried in streaks on her face. She raised her head wearily and stared vacantly out the windshield.

"I was fifteen," she said flatly. "I called the police. That was the last time the sheriff came out to the house. He asked my mother if she was all right. He could see that she wasn't, but it didn't matter. Daddy was there, and he told Sheriff Dodie that they just had a little argument and that everything was okay now."

Abby paused, wiping her mouth with a shaking hand.

"It wasn't the first time they came out," she went on. "But it was the last time. I think they just gave up. Figured if my mother didn't care enough to do something about him, why should they?"

"I care," Louis said softly.

She looked at him, her eyes welling.

"We have to report this," Louis said.

She shook her head slowly. "I don't want to. I just want to get out of this place. I just want to go back to school."

Louis hesitated. "You can't do that on your own, without his money."

She sighed, then looked away, out the window. He took her hand. Her fingers wrapped tightly around his.

"You need somewhere to stay tonight," Louis said.

"Take me to your place," she said, turning to him.

"No."

She pulled her hand away from his, letting it drop into her lap. Again, she looked away out the window. "He thinks I'm sleeping with you," she said.

Louis suppressed a sigh. She was crying again, softly this time. Louis reached for her hand. She fell against him and he wrapped an arm around her, holding her head.

He had to find a place for her to stay tonight. But what would happen to her after that? What were her options? Max would pull her out of school, that much was certain. And given her state of mind, she would probably run away. Maybe Dodie could help straighten this out tomorrow. But right now, he had to take her back to the station and then find somewhere safe for her tonight.

He caught sight of lights in the rearview mirror, red-and-blue lights coming slowly up the trail behind the Mustang. Shit.

"Abby," he said, taking her shoulders. She looked out the back window and he felt her tense.

"He called them," she said. "I knew he would."

"Don't worry," Louis said. He got out of the car and stood by the open door as the police cruiser pulled up behind. He shivered as he waited for Larry to get out.

Larry eyed the Mustang, looked at Louis, then unsnapped his holster.

"That's not necessary, Cutter," Louis said.

"I'll decide what's necessary," Larry answered. "You seen Miz Abigail?"

Louis hesitated. "She's in the car."

Larry came up to the passenger side, opened the door and peered in, shining a flashlight on Abby's face. "You okay, Miz Abigail?"

Abby mumbled something and Larry looked over the car at Louis. "What you do to her?" he demanded.

"He didn't do anything!" Abby said angrily before Louis could answer.

His eyes on Louis, Larry marched back to the cruiser and reached for the radio. "Sheriff, I found him."

Louis heard Dodie's voice answer, "Miz Abigail with him?"

"Yeah, sheriff, she's been knocked around some," Larry said.

"That ain't your concern," Dodie answered. "Just bring her in."

Louis started toward the cruiser. "Let me talk to him," he said.

But Larry had already clicked off. "Miz Abigail," he called out. "Y'all get out of that car now. Come with me. I gotta take you to the station."

Abby got out of the car slowly. She stood there, nervously looking over at Louis, her body shaking. Louis looked hard at Larry. Larry's eyes moved over Abby slowly and Louis cringed in disgust. The bastard was really enjoying this. Suddenly, he didn't want Abby alone in that cruiser with Larry.

"Abby, you don't have to go with him," he said.

Abby backed away from Larry. The car radio crackled back to life. "Cutter!" Dodie demanded. "Let me talk to Kincaid."

Louis came around the car and grabbed the mike from Larry. "Yeah, Sheriff, I'm here."

"Don't go interfering with this, Kincaid," Dodie warned.

"Sheriff, Abby is scared. She called me to come and get her. Let me bring her in."

There was a long silence. "No. You go back home. We'll watch out for her, I promise."

Louis understood. Max was at the station, waiting. Dodie didn't want a bad situation made worse.

"Sheriff?" Louis said, glancing at Abby.

"Yeah?"

"Don't send her home tonight. Please."

Larry reached for the mike but Louis pulled away, sticking his elbow in Larry's ribs. Larry gasped and Louis rekeyed the mike. "Sheriff?"

Louis stared at Larry. He had his hand possessively on Abby's back, stroking her. She was oblivious, just standing there, shivering in the bloody sweatshirt.

"Kincaid, nothing will happen to her," the sheriff said. "You got my word on that."

Louis tossed the mike on the seat. He led Abby around the passenger side of the police cruiser and helped her in.

"Louis?"

"It'll be all right," he said softly. He shut the door and started toward the Mustang. He stopped when he got to where Larry was standing. He leaned close.

"You touch her and I'll break your fucking arms," he whispered.

"Fuck you."

Louis grabbed Larry's jacket. "Listen, you ballless pervert. I'm going to be following you. You make one move in that car and it'll be the last move of any kind you'll ever make, you hear me, cocksucker?"

Louis let him go and Larry stumbled back against the cruiser. As Louis walked off to the Mustang, he heard Larry kicking angrily at the gravel. He got back in his car and followed the cruiser out of the park.

Back at the station, Louis pulled in, several spaces away from the cruiser. He killed the engine and got out, standing by the open car door, watching as Larry led Abby up the steps and inside. He spotted Max's silver Monte Carlo parked nearby. His heart ached for Abby, having to go in there now and face her bastard father. He wanted to go in and talk to Dodie. But he knew the sheriff was right, and he had to trust him to make good on his promise.

Jesus, what a night. He was just about to get back in the car when the door of the station banged open.

Louis turned to see Max coming down the steps, Larry following. Max spotted Louis and started toward the car.

"Kincaid!" he bellowed.

Shit.

"Kincaid! I want to talk to you!"

Max's voice was soggy with booze. Louis turned slowly. The square was empty, the storefronts dark. A traffic light blinked yellow at the corner. Larry was standing back on the steps watching, a small grin on his face. No one else had come out of the station. Louis debated whether to try to get by Max and Larry or whether to just get in the car and leave. Then he saw the glint of metal in the light from the streetlamp.

Max was coming toward him, waving a nickel-plated automatic. Louis took a step away from the car to give himself room to move. He put up his hands. Max's face gleamed with perspiration and the tails of his wrinkled white shirt and tie flapped against his wide belly.

Louis glanced at the door to the station, then back at Max. "Put the gun away," Louis said.

"You black son of a bitch," Max hissed.

"Max—"

The gun went off. Louis ducked. The shot rattled the leaves of a nearby tree and Louis felt his throat constrict.

"I oughta shoot you where you stand!" Max yelled.

The door to the station popped open and Dodie came to an abrupt stop on the top step. Louis's eyes darted from Max to the door and back. Larry was standing behind Max, paralyzed by the sight of the gun.

Max glanced at Dodie, then with a sloppy grin, turned his gaze back to Louis.

"Stay back, Sam. I'm gonna blow his fuckin' head off," Max hollered.

"You're not shooting one of my deputies, Max. Now, put that thing away."

"He's messing with my Doll Baby!" he bellowed.

Dodie wet his lips. "Max, Abby's a growed-up girl, big enough to make her own decisions. You oughta know that."

"And you oughta know I'm only doing what's right."

Louis swallowed, his heart racing. Max waved the gun like a knife, his finger playing with the trigger. Dodie inched closer and Louis tried to calculate whether Dodie could subdue the bigger man. He had his doubts.

The station door opened and Abby came out. When she saw Max and the gun, she froze, her eyes wide. Her scream pierced the air, and Max and Louis both looked up at her.

"Baby . . ." Max said drunkenly.

"Leave him alone!" Abby screamed at Max.

"Larry! Get her back inside!" Dodie yelled. Larry looked lost for a second, then ran up the steps and grabbed Abby. But she fought him off and started down the steps toward Louis. Larry grappled for her arms but she spun away.

Dodie caught her. "Stay back!" he said sharply, shoving her behind him.

Louis turned slowly to look back at Max. "Max," he whispered, spreading his arms, "however you feel about me, Abby doesn't need to see this. She doesn't need to see her father in prison."

Max laughed drunkenly. "For shooting a nigger?"

Louis clenched his jaw, and Dodie motioned for him to relax, still working his way closer to the two of them. "Max," Dodie said, "I'm tellin' ya. Put it down or I'm gonna have to lock you up."

"You just try it, Sam."

"Max," Dodie said sharply. "Look at me!"

Max's eyes scooted to Dodie then to the gun Dodie had drawn.

"Drop the gun," Dodie said, his breath shallow.

Max didn't move.

"I said drop it, Max!" Dodie shouted.

To Louis's shock, Max did. The smack of it on the concrete echoed in the quiet street. Louis moved forward to pick it up, but Max lunged at him, knocking him over onto the grass. The gun skidded along the sidewalk.

Louis felt the crushing weight of Max's body. Max had him pinned and landed two sharp punches. Louis swung wildly, finally slamming his fist into the fleshy face above him.

Dodie was over them, pulling at Max's shirt. Louis felt the air being squeezed from his lungs as Max wrapped his hands around his neck. Louis fought frantically against the bigger man's chest,

Dodie's face a red blur over Max's shoulder. He could hear Abby's screams in the background.

"Stop it, damn it, Max, stop!" Dodie yelled.

Gasping, Louis wedged a knee between himself and Max's belly and with one thrust, he shoved Max back into Dodie's arms. The two of them tumbled backward into a bush.

Louis bolted upright, sucking in air, wiping the blood from his lip. He saw the gun and scrambled toward it, snatching it up. He spun on his knees, knocked Dodie aside, and grabbed Max by the shirt.

He thrust the gun to Max's temple. "Don't you ever pull a fucking gun on me again," Louis whispered into his ear.

"Fuck you," Max hissed.

"Kincaid, don't do this." Dodie spoke softly, rising to his feet.

Max's fingers dug into the grass as he glared defiantly at Louis's glistening face.

"Kincaid . . ." Dodie said, more loudly.

Louis's breathing settled and he loosened his grip on Max's shirt. Max's eyes were so big Louis could see the red veins. It was as if he were daring him to pull the trigger. From the corner of his eye, he saw Abby. She was crying.

Louis let go, thrusting Max backward. He drew himself erect, the gun hanging at his side, and looked down at Max.

"If you ever hit Abby again, I'll kill you," Louis said, his chest heaving. "I swear, I'll kill you."

CHAPTER 22

It was raining, a slow, steady rain. Louis turned off the ignition and rested his head against the steering wheel, closing his eyes. He had slept fitfully, waking up tired and sore. His jaw was swollen, despite the ice Dodie had applied last night, and his side throbbed, the bruised ribs reinjured by Max's weight.

For a few minutes he listened to the rain on the roof, wishing for a moment he could just go back to Bessie's and crawl under the quilt. But he had things to do, things that couldn't wait, and he couldn't let Max's ignorant accusations and threats get in the way. He wanted to see Maisey before Dodie changed his mind. And he wanted to talk with George Harvey's widow or family. He didn't need this shit with Max Lillihouse right now.

He scurried through the rain and yanked open the station door. Junior was pouring a cup of coffee and looked up at Louis questioningly, almost fearfully, like he wasn't sure what to say.

Louis hung up his wet jacket and went to his desk. Junior ambled to his own desk and sat down. Louis looked over, feeling Junior's uneasiness.

"Junior, what's the problem?" he asked finally.

Junior shrugged. "Nothing."

"Where's Mike?"

"Sheriff put him on nights, with Larry."

Louis got up and went to the coffee machine. He slopped some coffee over the edge as he poured, burning himself. "Damn it," he muttered, going back to his desk. "Junior, where's the sheriff?"

"Home. He was up all night with Miz Abigail and Max."

"Where'd Abby stay?"

"With the sheriff."

Louis felt better. Thank God she hadn't been sent home. Jesus, last night seemed like a blur. Afterward, Dodie had spent a few minutes calming everyone down and sent Louis home. Hell, not sent, *ordered*. Louis had no idea what had happened to Max.

"The sheriff say when he'd be in?" Louis asked.

"Nope," Junior replied.

Louis went to the file cabinet, flipping through for George Harvey's file. It wasn't there and he turned to Junior. "Did you take the Harvey file?"

"George's? No. Sheriff had it, I think."

Louis went to the sheriff's office and tried the door. It was locked, and he returned to his desk, looking down at his coffee, thinking. "Junior, you know where George lived?"

"Sure. He's in the phone book. It's on Flowers Street."

Louis sat down, slipped on his glasses and opened the thin phone book.

"Why you wanna go there?"

"I need to talk to his family."

"He ain't got no family."

Louis took off his glasses. "No one?"

"No one. Wife passed a few years back, no kids. He lived alone."

"Then I need to look around the house."

"I guess you could do that. But why?"

"I can't tell you yet."

Junior looked hurt and he turned back to his desk, doodling on the blotter. "It was a shame George got shot like that," he said softly. "I helped him put in that security system. Guess it didn't do any good."

"No, it didn't." Louis rubbed his eyes and glanced at the clock. It was nine-ten. Probably too early to visit Maisey Kelly.

"Louis, you think George was shot by someone he knowed, don't you?"

Louis nodded tiredly.

"I really liked ol' George. He never hurt no one." Junior paused, smiling slightly. "He was an okay guy, for a Yankee."

"Yeah, well, I guess some people adjust better—" Louis stopped, looking over at Junior. "A Yankee?"

"Yeah, a Yankee. He wasn't from here. Him and his wife come

here in . . . I think, like '76 or '77. It says so on the jewelry-store door. Established 1977, I think."

Louis slumped in the chair. Junior was right. He had seen it on the door, right there in big gold letters. How the hell could George have known anything about the lynching? Louis closed his eyes, suddenly depressed. A worse thought crept inside his head. What if George had not been his caller, after all?

"Junior, I need a favor," Louis said, standing. "Call the phone company and pull George's phone calls."

"Okay. Where you going?"

Louis zipped the jacket and finished his coffee. "I got to go talk to someone."

Louis headed toward the door and paused, turning back. Junior was doodling again, a frown on his chubby face.

"Junior," Louis called. "Thanks."

"No problem. Hey, Louis?"

"What?"

"What is a 'DA's citation'?"

"Why do you ask?"

"Sheriff got one."

Louis slumped against the door. Jeez, poor Dodie. The heat was already on. "It's—it's . . ." Louis paused, remembering to keep it simple. "It's like a contempt-of-court citation, only it's issued by the DA when you piss him off. You get called on his carpet, so to speak."

"You mean like contempt of the DA?"

"Kinda."

Junior shrugged. "Seems to me everyone around here gots that."

Louis smiled tiredly. Junior continued to doodle and Louis watched him for a minute, feeling the need to say something else.

"The sheriff'll be okay, Junior," Louis said weakly.

Junior nodded and Louis slipped out the door, heading for the Mustang. He drove the short distance to Kelly's home and sat outside a few minutes before going in. It lacked the grandeur of the Lillihouse place but it had a quiet elegance about it, something that had always suggested "old money" to Louis. It was a two-story wood-frame home with forest-green shutters and a curved asphalt driveway guarded by iron gates. The gates were open and Louis drove through, stopping in front of the veranda. He hustled through the drizzle and shook the raindrops free as he knocked. A light-skinned black maid opened the door and smiled politely at him.

"Is Mrs. Kelly at home?" Louis asked, after introducing himself.

She nodded and stepped back, letting him enter. He paused on the highly polished hardwood floor. There was a staircase in front of him and several dark-wood doors to his right. The foyer was papered in a dark green-and-maroon colonial print. A circular Persian rug was placed in the center. The maid showed him through the first door, leaving him in a library. The focal point was a huge mahogany desk that sat under the bay window, basking in the meager morning light. The shelves surrounding the room were packed with what looked to be legal and political reference books. The room had a leathery, musty smell. Louis walked to the window. Outside was a white gazebo, peeling and cracked, in what looked to be a neglected rose garden.

"Officer, how nice of you to visit."

He turned. Maisey Kelly was coming into the room slowly, swaying slightly. She was dressed in a lime-green sheath with a colorful scarf wrapped loosely around her neck. She wore misty black stockings, but she was barefoot.

"Mrs. Kelly, you have a lovely home here," he said.

"Yes, I do," Maisey said with a wan smile. She turned and snapped her fingers at the maid. "Wilma! Bring me a drink. And bring Officer Kincaid one, too."

"No thanks, Mrs. Kelly."

"Nonsense. You can accept a drink, it won't hurt you. Be sociable, for chrissakes."

Louis watched the maid disappear and then went closer to Maisey, who was leaning over the back of a brown leather chair, arms dangling in front of her.

"My husband isn't home, Officer Kincaid."

"Actually, it's you I wanted to see. I would like to ask you a few questions about this." Louis pulled a copy of the medallion picture from his pocket and handed it to her.

She looked at it, then back at Louis. "That's Gracie's wedding."

"I'm talking about the chain around your husband's neck."

Maisey straightened and the edges of her lips turned up. "Does Walter know you're here?"

"No, ma'am."

"I didn't think so."

Wilma returned with a tray. She handed Maisey her drink and brought the other to Louis. He accepted reluctantly, looking down at the clear liquid and the bobbing lemon wedge. Wilma left, closing the door behind her.

"Do you recognize the medallion?" Louis asked.

"No," Maisey said quickly. "I don't much remember that day very well."

"Have you ever seen it?"

Maisey fingered the paper for a moment. "I vaguely recall seeing it, but I'm not sure when. Could have been last year, or ten years ago."

Louis should have known he would get nowhere with Maisey Kelly. He reached out for the paper but Maisey pulled it back slowly. "This is about those bones, isn't it?" she said.

Louis nodded. Maisey slid into the leather chair, letting her leg dangle over the arm. "That was a long time ago," she said, sipping her drink and still looking at Grace's wedding picture.

"Mrs. Kelly, did you know a Eugene Graham? A young boy who lived in Sweetwater?"

"Was he black?" Maisey asked.

"Yes."

"I wouldn't have known him."

Louis tightened. He couldn't resist it. "That's not what I hear."

Maisey smiled broadly and for a second, she was pretty again the puff of black hair, the large, alluring brown eyes, the sexy tilt of her head. But then the face hardened.

"Walter was right. You are arrogant."

"I apologize," Louis said.

"Hell, what for? It's the truth, everyone in this town knows it. But I didn't know your young man."

Louis set his drink down and pulled out the sketch Marsha Burns had sent with the head. He handed it to her.

"Are you sure?" he asked. "Please look at it."

She took the sketch. "He was a handsome man."

"He was only a boy, sixteen."

"Well, this boy I would remember. If I had met him."

"Would you tell me if you did?" Louis asked.

Maisey dragged her leg off the arm and stood up, handing

Louis back the two papers. "You haven't touched your drink, Officer."

"It's ten A.M., Mrs. Kelly."

"I started at eight. What time do you usually start?"

Louis sighed. Maisey was about nine cents short of a dime. "I'm sorry to have bothered you, Mrs. Kelly."

"Where are you going? You've only asked me two questions."

"Do you have something more to tell me?"

"Depends on what you ask. I am curious—why aren't you talking to Walter? If anyone could kill someone, my husband could."

Louis hesitated, contemplating her words. Ask her something, *anything.* "Are you saying he committed murder?"

"I'm saying *capable.* You should listen to what people say, Officer Kincaid. It's a good quality in a man."

"And also to what they *don't* say, Mrs. Kelly."

"True, so true." She came closer and he could smell her perfume. He took a step back and she smiled, sensing his apprehension. He met her eyes. She knew something, and she wanted to tell him.

"Mrs. Kelly, do you know anything about the bones?"

Her fingers brushed the front of his jacket but he forced himself to remain still.

"Officer, back in 1955 you would have been shot for letting me do what I'm doing now," she said, fingering the zipper of his jacket.

She knew the year. She knew who Eugene was. Louis took a deep breath, knowing that if he moved away from her now, she would turn on him and close up for good. She was drunk. He had to keep her talking.

"Is that what happened to Eugene?" he asked softly.

"Is that what you think?"

"Yes," he said, tensing. The answer was coming. The *why.* She was going to tell him, he could feel it.

Maisey gave him an odd little smile. "I don't know. Could be."

Louis let out a long breath. Damn it, he didn't know whether to believe her or not. He moved past her, brushing her shoulder as he did. She stumbled slightly, catching herself against the chair.

Louis picked up the drink and took a sip to wet his throat. It was only water and he finished it. Damn, it was warm in here.

He turned back to her and saw that she was staring at him with an empty, rejected look. He averted his eyes.

"Mrs. Kelly, I never mentioned the date. How did you know that?" he asked.

"I was told."

"By who?"

She tossed her head, regaining her composure, and walked slowly across the library. "Officer, if I thought you could put Walter away with what I know, I would tell you my whole life story. But you can't do anything." She turned quickly, holding up a hand. "Trust me, you can't. So why should I make the rest of my life more miserable than it's already been?"

Louis followed her to the desk. "I'd be interested in knowing anything you know, anything at all. And I think you do know something."

"Well, knowledge can be a curse," she replied.

"Mrs. Kelly, I have to assume it was your husband who told you something about the lynching of that man."

"Assume what you want." She paused, smiling wanly. "But you apparently know what I was like back then. I was wild and I went with plenty of boys who would tell me just about anything if they thought it would get me into their backseat. Boys, men . . . they'll talk about the strangest stuff, if they think it's gonna impress you."

Louis turned away from Maisey. Maybe it wasn't Kelly. It could be any one of a hundred boys Maisey had slept with. He rubbed his face, trying to think of his next move. Faces went through his mind. Earl? No, Maisey and Earl didn't fit. Not even then. If it wasn't Walter . . .

Louis turned, taking a long shot. "Mrs. Kelly," he asked, "was George Harvey one of those boys?"

She shrugged. "I was with George once or twice. But he was quiet, never said much of anything. I didn't really like him much. He was very . . . selfish. He was a selfish, weird boy, and he never changed."

"Mrs. Kelly, George didn't live here in the fifties. How could you have been with him?"

"His grandfather lived here. He used to come down every

summer." She was watching Louis carefully. "George and Walter were like this," she added, holding up two fingers, knitted together.

Louis sat down, stunned. She was burying her own husband, talking as if she wanted to get rid of him but didn't know how. He looked up at her suddenly.

"Mrs. Kelly, do you think your husband had something to do with this?"

"More wishful thinking than anything, Officer. But I can tell you, if you can show George was there, you can bet your last buck Walter was, too." She sighed, resting against the desk. "But you can't prove that, can you? George is dead."

Louis shook his head. "No, I can't prove it."

"Look, Officer," Maisey said, "if you could put Walter in jail, I'd be eternally grateful. But you can't, because I can't tell you if he was involved in that lynching or not. And if anyone else knows, believe me, they'll never say."

He studied her. She had sobered some, and her face had taken on a softer, flushed look. He almost felt sorry for her. He thought back to what Ethel had told him. How had the town slut ended up with Walter Kelly, son of a congressman? Had she blackmailed him with the whispered secrets of his friend George Harvey—or some other boy Louis had not even considered yet? If she had, he had the feeling that she had spent the last two decades regretting it.

"Mrs. Kelly," Louis said.

"Yes?"

"How much did this boy, whoever it was, tell you?"

"Not much. Just that it happened. A . . . a black boy was dead."

"Did they say who else was there?"

She shook her head. "George—" She stopped, realizing she had slipped the name. Then she smiled wanly, like it didn't matter. "George was bragging that it was all his doing. I think he thought it made him look more macho." Her smile faded. "Or that it got me hot or something."

Louis leaned forward. "How did he put it?"

Maisey sighed loudly. "He had me in the backseat and I was, well, teasing, like I liked to do. He was getting real frustrated and suddenly he just said to me, real tough-like, 'You know, I killed a nigger.' "

Her words hung in the stuffy library a long time. Louis looked down at the floor.

"I let him have sex with me anyway," she added softly. "I didn't know what else to do."

Louis stared at the brown carpet for several long seconds. Then he stood up slowly. "Mrs. Kelly, thank you."

Maisey looked suddenly old again. "What for?" she said flatly.

"I don't know, for being honest. I'll leave you alone now."

"Officer Kincaid . . ."

"Yes?" Louis said, turning from the door.

"Please don't tell Walter we spoke."

Louis drove quickly back to the station, eager to fill in Dodie on what Maisey had told him about George Harvey. The pieces were falling into place and this was coming to an end. He had at least one murderer now, and maybe even a connection to Kelly's involvement. The motive still wasn't as clear-cut as he would have liked. But he was willing to bet that Maisey was lying about knowing Eugene Graham, and that Kelly and his friend George, and maybe Earl, killed Eugene because of her. Louis let out a sigh. A stupid girl wiggles her ass around and a young man dies because of it. Eugene Graham's death wasn't some grand tragedy of evil. It was just a sad, pathetically common melodrama.

When he got back to the office, Louis was disappointed to find that Dodie's door was still locked.

"Junior, the sheriff didn't come in yet?" Louis asked.

Junior looked up from the dispatch desk. "Called and said he wasn't coming in today. Had to drive his wife to Jackson for her appointment. Some female-plumbing thing. Hey, that package there came for you. I signed for it."

Louis saw the FedEx package on his desk. It was from the FBI lab in Washington. Without bothering to take off his jacket, Louis sat down and ripped the package open. Out fell a paper and the necklace and the book, still wrapped in plastic. Louis reached for his glasses and unfolded the report. His heart raced as his eyes hurried down the page until he reached the part about the medallion.

It didn't match! Fucking shit, it didn't match!

Louis stood up quickly, stunned. Two necklaces, two rare medallions in the same damn town.

Junior looked over. "You okay, Louis? You look sick."

Louis dropped back in the chair, shaking his head. He looked again at the paper. Suddenly, he realized the copy and the original wouldn't have matched. Not if the dead man was Eugene Graham.

He threw the paper down and, standing, kicked his chair across the room. It crashed into the file cabinet.

"What the fuck, Louis!" Junior said.

Louis couldn't contain himself. "I can't believe I didn't see it."

"See what?" Junior asked.

"Of course it wouldn't match!" Louis shouted to the walls. "The newspaper said Eugene disappeared in 1955, and the medallion was buried with him. The wedding picture wasn't even taken until 1956!" Louis ran his hand over his hair. "Damn it, I'm stupid!"

"Who the hell is Eugene?" Junior asked.

Louis turned to look at Junior. Suddenly he felt deflated, drained. He had been so sure, even allowing himself to feel a small sense of pride for putting it all together by himself. But he hadn't done shit! He was right back at the beginning, sitting out on a limb alone. No, he reminded himself, he was not alone this time. Dodie was hanging right out there with him, and Walt Kelly was just waiting for the chance to saw both of them down. Jesus, how was he going to tell Dodie about this?

He leaned on the desk, head down. "Junior, did the sheriff say when he was going to be back in town?"

"Late . . . that's all he said. Louis, what's going on? Who's this Eugene guy?"

"No one," Louis muttered. He went over and picked up the chair, returning it to its place. He looked down at the medallion and book lying on the desk. Suppressing a sigh, he stuffed them back into the FedEx envelope along with the report. He felt a gnawing sensation in his stomach and he wasn't sure if it was from disappointment over the report or dread of facing Dodie. Well, there was nothing to do about it until tomorrow. Right now, he didn't want to think about it.

Louis started to the door, the envelope in hand.

"Where ya goin'?" Junior called out.

"Probably straight to hell, Junior," Louis shot back.

* * *

Louis stared at his face in the cloudy mirror. Was there anything more depressing than sitting in a stinking dark bar in the middle of the day? But that was where he had ended up after driving around for a half hour, sitting on a stool at Big Al's, with a half-eaten hamburger and an empty bottle of Bud in front of him.

Billy Ray came up to him. "Another one?"

Louis nodded. He took another bite of the greasy burger then pushed it away, his appetite gone. Billy Ray set the fresh beer in front of him and Louis took a big drink. When he lowered the bottle and looked in the mirror, he caught the eyes of a man standing at the pool table behind him. The man quickly pulled down the brim of his cap and turned back to his buddies. A few seconds later, their whispers drifted over to Louis. They were talking about him and Max and the fight outside the station. Louis quickly took another drink. Shit, the whole town probably knew about it—and why it happened. Louis dipped a hand into his pants pocket, searching for a quarter. He would call Abby; he needed to know she was okay. But then he paused. That was an excuse; he just wanted someone to be with, someone who would listen to him. He withdrew his hand.

A cackle of laughter shot across the bar and Louis tensed. He saw the three men in the mirror looking at him again. He swiveled around to face them.

"What are you staring at?" he said in a low voice.

The men seemed startled by his directness. Then one of them smiled. "Nothin'," he said. "Ain't staring at nothin' at all."

Louis turned back around. He finished the beer in three quick gulps and motioned to Billy Ray.

"Give me one of those," he said pointing to the bottle of Rémy Martin on the shelf.

"It's expensive stuff, man," Billy Ray said, plopping the bottle down.

Louis slapped two twenties down. "That cover it?"

Billy Ray nodded. Louis rose, slipped on his jacket and picked up the bottle of Rémy Martin. Tucking it under his arm, he started for the door. He paused and turned to the three men.

"And a good afternoon to you fine, *fine* gentlemen," he said, with a sharp click of his heels and a deep bow. He turned abruptly and pushed open the door.

Louis awoke with a start. He wasn't sure what had awakened him. A sudden noise somewhere, probably something that came from deep within his restless sleep. He could feel the blood racing through his veins as if he had just woken up from a nightmare he could not remember. The room was dark, a breeze coming from the window. He lay there for several minutes, watching the headlights from below sweep over the walls. Man, his head ached. He looked over at the Rémy Martin bottle on the nightstand. It was almost empty.

Throwing back the quilt, he went to the small refrigerator and pushed aside the remaining two Heinekens. He grabbed a can of Dr. Pepper and held it up against his forehead for a moment. Then he popped it open. The cold liquid felt good going down. The alcohol had left him dehydrated and hungry. He reached for the peanut butter. It was empty.

The bedside clock was flashing twelve. The power had gone off. He picked up his watch. It was 2:21 A.M. He finished the soda and walked to the window, parting the curtains. The street was dark and silent. It was empty—except for a car that had not been there when he went to bed.

Shit. The silver Monte Carlo. Max's car.

Louis leaned back against the wall, closing his eyes against the pounding in his head. He straightened and looked back out the window. *Fuck this.* Enough was enough.

He pulled on a pair of jeans, a sweatshirt, and Nikes. He started for the door then paused. He went back to the dresser and picked up his gun holster. He unsnapped the holster, checked his revolver and stuck it in the waist of his jeans.

Out in the hall, it occurred to him that Max could already be in the house. He pressed himself against the wall, scanning the darkness for movement. Bessie's door was closed, muting the sound of her snores. Louis crept down the stairs, peered at the shadows in the dark parlor for movement, then edged to the front door. He unlocked the door and slipped onto the porch.

Clouds drifted across the moon and a few stars dotted the black sky. It was quiet, except for the rustle of dead leaves skittering across the street. The silver car was parked in front of Tinker's. A bedroom light was on above the store.

The barrel of the gun against his ribs was cold, and he eased it out, clutching it in his hand. He had brought the gun along only to scare Max, but his gut was tight now with apprehension. He scurried across the street coming up behind the Monte Carlo, sliding behind a tree. Slowly he advanced toward the rear of the car, taking in short, tense breaths.

He crouched by a tree. This was nuts . . . he should call the station right now.

But he kept moving, stopping against another tree. A car squealed around the corner, disgorging a blast of rap music, then disappeared. Louis let out a breath.

He squinted at the car's tinted windows, thinking back to the scene outside the station, wondering if Dodie had let Max take his gun home. He could make out a shadow in the driver's seat.

Louis moved slowly to the rear of the car, squatting against the wheel well on the passenger side. He strained to hear a sound, a body moving against the seat or the click of the ignition. Nothing.

Creeping up to the passenger's door, he lifted himself high enough to peek inside. Max was alone, his head turned toward Bessie's house. The moonlight glinted off the gold keychain that dangled from the ignition. The green lights on the dash gave Max's hand, which lay by his thigh, a ghostly look. Inches from the fingers lay the .45 automatic.

Louis sank back down against the car, tensing. *Okay, Kincaid,* he told himself, *if you sit here long enough, he'll hear you and shoot you. Move.*

Holding his gun next to his ear, he sprang to his feet and yanked the door open. The dome light came on.

In one quick move, Louis grabbed Max's gun and tossed it to the grass. With his left hand, he shoved his gun inside the car, pressing the tip to Max's temple hard enough to force his head against the window.

"Okay, you son of a bitch—" Louis hissed.

Max did not move. For a split second, everything was absolutely still. Then a moth fluttered suddenly against the windshield. Louis jumped, his eyes darting to it, then back to Max. Louis held the gun steady, the tip digging deeper into Max's skull. A second passed.

Then the smell came to him. He knew immediately what it was. The thick, metallic smell of blood.

Max did not move. Louis did not breathe. It was so fucking quiet.

Louis backed up from the car and leaned against the rear door, gulping in the cool night air.

CHAPTER 23

Louis folded his arms and sat down on the top step of Tinker's store. He had called the Sheriff's Office and returned to the Monte Carlo to wait.

How could he have been so stupid? God knows what evidence he had blown by his actions. Why didn't he just call it in before coming down? Why did he have to be a fucking hero?

His eyes drifted back to Max's lifeless body sitting behind the steering wheel. He suddenly thought of Abby, then rubbed the chill from his arms, looking around the deserted street. Most of the houses were dark, including Bessie's. He heard the faint wail of the siren. As it screamed closer, windows up and down the street burst with lights. The squad car rounded the corner and screeched to a stop behind Max's car. Mike emerged, gun drawn. Coming off the step, Louis motioned for him to put it away.

"Jesus, Louis," Mike said, looking into the car from the open passenger's door. "What happened?"

"I don't know."

The small hole in Max's head was nearly invisible under his hair. There was very little blood, except for a heavy swath sprayed across the driver's-side window, flecked with bits of brain tissue. The window was shattered in a starburst pattern.

"You think he killed himself?" Mike asked.

Louis shook his head. "The gun was on the seat, nice and neat," he said.

Mike was staring at the bloody window. He spun away suddenly. Louis heard him vomit.

"Mike, you all right?" he called out after a few seconds.

Mike nodded, edging back to the car, his hand on his stomach.

"The neighborhood is going to get curious," Louis said, motioning toward the people who were gathering on their porches. "You got tape in your car?"

Mike nodded again and went to his trunk. Louis heard a second siren and seconds later, Dodie pulled up in the Blazer. He was alone and in streetclothes, the red cap on his head and the badge clipped to a plaid shirt pocket.

Without a word, Dodie walked to the Monte Carlo and looked at the shattered driver's window, then went around and stopped at the open passenger's door. He took out his flashlight and swept it over the inside. He stared at Max for a minute, hung his head, then withdrew.

Louis waited on the curb, watching the sheriff as he went to Mike and instructed him on roping off the scene. Then Dodie came back across Tinker's grass and stopped by Louis, inhaling deeply.

"Jesus Christ, Louis," he muttered.

People were standing in knots on the sidewalks, most dressed in bathrobes and pajamas, covered with jackets. Louis spotted Tinker standing on the porch of the store. Tinker held his eyes for a moment then went back inside.

"I'll help Mike," Louis said.

Dodie caught his arm. "No."

"Why not?" Louis asked.

"I can't let you touch this one."

"But who's going to do it? Who else do you have?"

"I reckon I can remember how to do a crime scene," Dodie said testily.

Louis stared at Dodie. "But this is a homicide. I'm the investigator. It's my job."

Dodie's eyes met his and his expression silenced Louis immediately. It wasn't anger; it was disappointment, a deep disappointment that left Louis hollow.

"No, not this one," Dodie said firmly.

"Sheriff, for chrissake—"

"Kincaid, that's enough," Dodie said loudly.

Mike looked over from where he was working. Louis took another deep breath, glancing around. A second squad car pulled up. Larry jumped out and skidded to a stop next to the Monte

Carlo. He looked at Dodie and started over, but Dodie raised a hand. "Leave us be, Cutter. You help Mike."

Larry stalked away. Louis turned back to Dodie. "Sheriff, I want to be a part of this," he said. "It's important to me."

"You *are* a part of this," Dodie said, walking back to the car.

"What?" Louis said. When Dodie didn't answer, he followed him. "Sheriff, what are you talking about?" he demanded.

Dodie turned to face him. "Look, Kincaid, first the guy thinks you're poppin' his only daughter. Then I have to tell you to stop stalkin' around his house. And not twenty-four hours ago, you threatened this man in front of me and half this town. Max Lilli-house made no damn secret about how he felt about you. Or you about him."

"Sheriff, there was nothing between Abby and me—"

"Don't matter."

"The hell it doesn't!" Louis caught himself, taking a deep breath. "I can't believe you're buying into their bullshit. I thought you were different. I thought—"

Dodie clicked on his flashlight, shining it on the .45 on the grass. "How that get there?"

"I threw it there."

"Why?"

"So the bastard wouldn't shoot me with it."

Dodie faced him. "Did you come out here intending to shoot Max?"

Louis was so shocked he had to take a step back to balance himself. "What?"

"You heard me. When you left that house, carrying your weapon, did you intend to shoot him?"

Louis stared at Dodie, dumbfounded. "Is that what this was about? You think I killed him?"

Dodie looked away. He just stood there for a moment, survey-ing the scene, hands on his hips.

Louis shivered. "Jesus, Sheriff, I just wanted him to leave me alone. I didn't shoot him."

Dodie's hand moved to Louis's shoulder and for a second, Louis could only stare. Dodie's face was slack, his eyes forlorn. "Louis, let's take a walk here," he began.

Louis jerked away. "I didn't kill the son of a bitch!"

Larry and Mike looked over. Dodie glanced around at the

crowd and again reached for Louis. "Nothin' has been assumed yet. But you know as well as me suspects are just that—suspects. Don't mean nothin'."

"The hell it doesn't."

"Kincaid, calm down."

Louis took several quick steps away, walking a tight circle. "I don't believe this. . . ."

Larry's voice came through the air like a knife. "Start believin' it, Kincaid."

"Shut the fuck up!" Louis shouted.

Dodie put a hand on Louis's chest. "That's enough. You're outta line here."

"You believe I did this!" Louis said.

"I don't know what I believe yet. Least not till we gather the evidence."

Louis's eyes hardened. "Well, you damn well better do a paraffin on me," he said angrily.

"You know we ain't got a kit."

Louis stared at Dodie for a moment then laughed. He laughed, raising his head and arms helplessly to the dark sky. "I . . . don't . . . fucking . . . believe this."

The sheriff's face was frozen with anger. "Listen, Kincaid, I could send you to a goddamn lab if I really wanted to."

"Good idea! Brilliant! Send me to Jackson! I need to get away for a while anyway!"

"This ain't no fuckin' joke here, Kincaid," Dodie said, his voice low. "Now you calm down quick, or I'm gonna have to haul your ass off to the station."

Louis turned his back to Dodie. In a rush, everything came surging back. Max's taunting, bloodshot eyes . . . Abby's beaten face . . . Earl's lifeless body . . . Eugene's sad, lonely eyes . . . All of it flooded back, and as it faded, all Louis could see was Max's gun, lying there in the grass, covered with his own prints.

He fell softly against a tree. "I didn't do this," he whispered.

Dodie held his gaze steady. "Go home, Louis."

Louis shook his head, biting back his response. It wasn't worth it. He pushed off the tree and walked across the grass, dipping under the tape. Dodie's voice cut through the darkness.

"Kincaid!"

Louis turned, pausing.

"Leave your weapon."

Louis jerked it from his belt and, taking a step back, slapped it into Dodie's open palm. Without another word, he turned abruptly and stalked across the street to Bessie's house. He jerked open the screen and shoved open the door. It hit the wall behind it with a bang.

Bessie was standing in a robe by the stairs. "Louis! Louis!" she called to him as he hurried by her. "Louis, is you in trouble? Who is that out there?"

He stopped at the top of the stairs. "Max Lillihouse. He's dead."

"What? He's dead? Abigail's daddy? Oh Lordy, Louis, why'd you go and do a thing like that?"

"I didn't kill him!" Louis said loudly. He paused, seeing Bessie's shocked face. "I'm sorry, Bessie."

She stared up at him, her eyes brimming with tears. "I believe you, Louis, I surely do."

Louis looked back at the lights outside. "You might be the only one."

Back in his room, he turned on the lamp and sat down on the edge of the bed, head in hands. God, what had he gotten himself into? He was in deep trouble and there was no one out there to help him. He would have to save himself.

To do that, he would have to incriminate someone else in Max's death, and the first person who came to mind was Abby. In his mind, he placed a gun in her hand and tried to imagine her blowing her father's brains out. He knew what sometimes happened to women who were beaten, how the weak could be pushed to do the unthinkable against a tormentor. He shook his head. No, it just didn't feel right. Emotional, high-strung, immature—whatever she was, Abby wasn't capable of killing someone.

He rose and paced the room, walking to the window. He watched Dodie directing Mike and Larry. Suddenly a white Cadillac swung onto the street and squealed to a stop at an angle against the curb. Kelly got out and walked rigidly to Dodie.

Louis bristled. That son of a bitch was involved in this somehow. He just knew it. Hell, even Maisey knew it.

Maisey . . .

Louis went out to the phone in the hall, grabbed the little phone book and looked up her number. He dialed it and waited, watching the red-and-blue lights swirl against the lace curtain on the door downstairs.

"Hello, goddamn you, whoever you are," she said hoarsely.

"Mrs. Kelly, it's Detective Kincaid."

"What . . . Who? Shit, it's three in the morning."

"I am so sorry to call you so late."

There was a short pause. "Is Walter dead?"

"No." He heard something fall and crash and Maisey's muttered obscenity. "Mrs. Kelly, was Walter home tonight?"

"Hell, I've been asleep since ten or eleven. Why do you ask? What's happened?"

"Max Lillihouse is dead."

"Oh God," she said softly. He heard her cough and adjust the phone. "Officer, I don't know if Walter was here tonight or not."

Louis leaned against the wall. "Thank you, Mrs. Kelly. Go back to sleep."

"Officer . . ."

"Yes?"

"Max was a good friend, too."

"I know, I'm sorry I was so abrupt."

"Not to me, you idiot. To Walter."

"You mean as kids."

"Yes."

"I heard that already, from Ethel Mulcahey."

"Ethel's a nice lady." Maisey said. She paused. "How many do you think are left?"

Louis found the remark odd. "Left?"

"Witnesses to your lynching. How many do you think are left?"

"I don't know. I know there were two for sure." Louis looked back at the curtain. "Three, maybe."

"Officer, do you think Walter is killing them off?"

Louis hesitated. It was an odd question coming from a wife. Maybe he had read Maisey wrong and her disdain for Walter was just a ruse to feel him out on his intentions. No, that was paranoid. His instincts were telling him that Maisey Kelly hated her husband and that what she had told him was the truth. But if Walter was the killer, steadily eliminating anyone who could bring him down, then who was next?

"Officer, are you there?"

How many more lynching witnesses *were* there? And why weren't they all getting as nervous as George had been? Unless there were no others.

"Officer?"

Earl's death had been made to look like an accident. George's murder was a faked burglary. And now Max was dead, his murder carefully constructed to also make it look like something it wasn't.

Louis's stomach began to knot up. Shit. He had walked right into it. He had been set up.

Louis felt a trickle of sweat make its way down his back. The person who had done this knew how Louis felt about Max. The person also knew Max would come here again. Louis hung his head. *And stupidly, I tied it all up in a neat package by going out there tonight.* Dodie was right, oh man, was he right.

He suddenly realized Maisey had hung up on him. He replaced the phone and went back to his room. He saw the FBI evidence envelope, picked it up and went back to sit on the bed. He dumped the necklace, book, report, and photocopy out on the quilt and stared at them.

It was here, somewhere in these things. He just had to start over and look at everything again. He had to go over it all again, a million times if necessary, until he found it.

He grabbed his glasses from the nightstand and picked up the report. Back at the office, once he had read the news about the medallions not matching, his frustration had led him to ignore the rest of the report. Now he read it carefully, going over each word.

The original medallion was estimated to be about 122 years old. The embossing showed a sword, a Confederate flag, and the small cross. The one in the photocopy was blurry but showed the scales of justice. They definitely did not match.

Louis kept reading. The book's title was *100 Years of American Poetry, Volume II*. It was originally published in 1934. Damn, here was something new: The FBI lab also had been able to lift two prints from inside the old book. Talk about miracles!

Louis flipped through the pages, looking for a list of possible suspects based on the print, praying the lab had gone to those lengths. They had. Louis knew that print comparisons were based on a complex point system and that any names were merely possibles. But this was more than he would expect for such a poor-quality print. He scanned the list. Jesus, there were more than twenty possible matches.

Then he smiled. There was Earl Mulchaey's name.

The rest were strangers to him. But it was Earl's print that was important, positive proof that he had been present at the lynching of Eugene Graham—or at the very least, that he had touched the poetry book found with the bones.

The thought brought a sigh and Louis lowered the paper, taking a second to enjoy the moment. In the long run, it meant little to the Eugene Graham case. But at least it would help Leverette. This would show that Earl could have had an enemy, someone who thought he was enough of a threat to kill him.

Louis turned his attention to the second print. It was of better quality but not good enough to make an exact match. Who did that one belong to—George Harvey, Walter Kelly? Louis flipped back to the first page of the report. The list of possibles for this print contained only seven names, none of whom he recognized. Damn. He had wanted to see Walt Kelly's name there. Kelly must have been printed at some point for his civil-service record, so if the second print was his, he would have shown up on this list. Louis still had nothing concrete to connect Kelly with Eugene Graham.

And the print didn't belong to George, either. His prints were definitely on file, not just the standard postmortem prints taken at the jewelry-store murder scene, but also prints from his military service. It was possible the second print belonged to Max, but there was no way to prove it without knowing if Max had ever been fingerprinted. Tomorrow Max's postmortem prints would be available, and Louis could have them compared. Louis looked back at the window awash with red-and-blue lights. But that didn't do him any good tonight.

He sighed, staring at the meaningless names. It was possible this second print belonged to someone who had since moved away, or even died. And the only way to eliminate all seven names on the list would be to track them down one by one and find out if any one of them had even lived in Black Pool in the fifties. Damn, he didn't have that much time.

He took off his glasses, pinching the bridge of his nose. Think god damn it, he told himself.

He dug through the other papers that had come back with the

FBI report, unearthing the small cards showing the exact images of the prints lifted from the books. He put his glasses back on and held the two cards side by side, peering at the two prints. The larger one, the one that matched Earl Mulcahey, was a thumbprint. The other was from a finger and was much smaller.

Who did it belong to? Who else had touched that poetry book?

All his instincts were telling him that the print didn't belong to Max. He had a feeling in his gut that the print belonged to another man in their circle of friends, someone who knew who Louis was, someone who knew Max would be sitting outside this house tonight. It had to be someone close to him.

Louis stared at the two prints. One large and round. The other small and slender.

Then it hit him, and he threw back his head, clenching his teeth in frustration over his blindness. "God," he whispered, "it's a woman."

He stared at the delicate fingerprint, letting out a long breath. Maisey. She had lied about knowing Eugene Graham. But why? He shook his head slowly. What difference did it make now, especially if she wanted to get rid of her husband? If she had been involved with Eugene, and if Kelly had killed him because of it, why wouldn't she want to cooperate now? She had nothing to lose and everything to gain. Louis climbed off the bed and started toward the phone to call her, then stopped abruptly, his hand on the door.

No. . . .

He turned back to the bed and looked down at the book, *100 Years of American Poetry*. The young Maisey had probably never even opened a book, let alone gone in for such genteel pastimes as reading poetry.

Slowly, a face came to him, serene and cool. Grace Lillihouse. He drew in a long, deep breath and let it out slowly as he looked down at the tattered book on the bed. His mind sifted through the things Ethel had said about Max and Grace, settling finally on their wedding picture and Grace's sad face. Maybe a part of him, deep down, had known all along, but he had not really wanted to face the fact that a woman like Grace could be involved, even indirectly, in something as grotesque as Eugene Graham's murder. He didn't want to face it now, really.

His eyes went to the lights at the window. But if Max had

murdered Eugene over some perverted notion of protecting Grace Lillihouse's honor, why was he now sitting out there with a bullet in his head?

Louis went to his nightstand drawer. He opened the drawer and carefully took out the book Grace had given him, Eudora Welty's *The Golden Apples*, holding it by the tip of one corner. He was glad he had never opened it. It held a pristine set of prints, Grace's prints, ripe for comparison.

He went to the hall phone, dialing Winston Gibbons at home. Gibbons answered sleepily and Louis waited for him to struggle into consciousness before going into detail.

"What is so urgent, Louis?"

"I have a book I need prints from. Immediately."

"Immediately—as in now, or tomorrow?"

"Tomorrow."

"I can do it, if you bring it to me. Might take some muscle around the lab here but I'll swing it." Gibbons paused. "You sound agitated. How is everything else?"

Louis slid down against the wall. "I have another dead man. And reason to believe someone is killing off witnesses."

"Witnesses to your lynching?"

"Yes."

Gibbons let out a long breath.

"I have a hunch about something," Louis said, "and I hope to God I'm right. If I'm wrong . . ." He paused, not wanting to tell Gibbons that he was a possible suspect in Max's murder. Not yet. Maybe a few days from now, if things turned bad, but not now.

"Louis?" Gibbons said.

"I'm all right. Things are just bad right now, Mr. Gibbons. I feel like I've lost control. The bad guys are winning."

Gibbons chuckled. Louis was relieved he didn't know just how serious he was.

"Do you want some help?" Gibbons asked.

Louis thought of Dodie and how things would look for him if Gibbons and the feds marched into town. And he wanted to try to finish this. Right or wrong, it was his. He had taken possession of this case that rainy day in December and until he put it down, it belonged to him.

"Not yet," Louis replied. "I'll let you know."

"You're stubborn, Louis."

"So I'm told."

"Don't be afraid to ask for it when you need it."

"I won't, believe me."

"When can I expect your book?"

"Give me three hours."

"I'll be waiting for you. Drive carefully."

"Yes, I will."

Louis packaged up the items, slipping *The Golden Apples* into a paper bag. He quickly changed clothes and grabbed his jacket off the bed, tucking the precious bag under his arm as he started down the steps.

Bessie was standing by the door, peeking out the curtain at the scene outside. She heard his footsteps and turned.

"Where you goin'?" she asked.

Louis stopped in front of her. "I need to deliver something. Please don't tell anyone anything."

Bessie sighed heavily and reached up, touching his cheek. "Louis, please be careful. I don't like what's happenin' here."

"I'm sorry about all this, Bessie, I really am."

"Louis, you ain't runnin', are you?" she asked.

Louis shook his head, stepping by her. "I'll be back by morning. I'll be going into work. I swear."

On the porch, Louis paused, looking at the lights. A portable floodlight had been set up, brightening the entire neighborhood. An ambulance had arrived, and someone was crawling around inside the Monte Carlo. Louis saw Dodie turn toward him and he walked quickly across the grass to the Mustang. Dodie started over. Louis was tempted to just get in the car and back out; but he waited, hand on the door.

"Where you think you're going?" Dodie asked.

"Unless I'm under arrest, anywhere I want to, Sheriff."

"Kincaid, don't be stupid."

Louis thought about saying something to Dodie about what he had discovered in the FBI report, but he couldn't force it out. Dodie's accusation rang in his ears and he swallowed back his anger, opening the door.

"Kincaid."

"Move out of my way."

Dodie stepped back, watching him. Louis climbed in the car and closed the door, refusing to look at him. He started the car and shoved it into reverse, backing out of the drive. When he reached the street, he finally looked back. He could see Dodie standing in the reflection of the headlights, chewing on that cigar.

It was nine-twenty when Louis got back from Jackson. When he walked into the station, only Larry was there, sitting at the typewriter, unshaven and glassy-eyed as he agonized over Max Lillihouse's homicide report. He looked at Louis then turned back to the paper sticking out of the typewriter.

"Long night, Cutter?"

"Yeah, thanks to you. I was supposed to be off four hours ago." Larry stopped typing. "Didn't think I'd see you today. Thought maybe you was on suspension—or somethin' worse."

"Not yet." Louis sat down at his desk. "What did you guys find out last night?"

"I ain't tellin' you shit."

"Cut the crap and just tell me."

Larry eyed him for a minute, then spoke. "The mobile CSU from Jackson showed up about daybreak. Sheriff stayed with 'em for a while. Had me and Mike talkin' to fuckin' neighbors, see if anyone heard anything," Larry added disgustedly.

"What else?"

"They figure Max was shot with his own .45, close range, over the ear. A couple people heard the shot, anywheres from two-fifteen to two-thirty. You called it in at two-forty."

Louis ran a hand over his tired eyes and down over his own prickly jaw. He hadn't heard a shot. Or had he? Is that what had awakened him?

"Nobody saw nothin'," Larry went on bitterly. "No other cars, nobody walkin' around. 'Cept we got a couple guys cruisin', say they saw a tall, slender black guy lurkin' around the car about two-thirty." Larry let his words dangle.

Louis ignored the insinuation. "Where's the body?"

"Jackson." Larry looked at his watch. "The autopsy's probably 'bout done. Sheriff should be coming back anytime. He's over there, too."

Louis thought about the bones and how long it had taken anyone to look at those. Hell, Max hadn't been dead twelve hours and already somebody was cutting him apart.

"They do the car?" Louis asked.

"How the fuck do I know? I followed the damn thing to the garage and they ran me off. Like we're not fuckin' good enough to even look at them bastards."

"You're not," Louis said dryly.

"Fuck you, Kincaid," Larry said sharply. "What are you even doin' here anyways?"

Louis had his back to Larry and he forced himself to remain calm. He took a deep breath and tried to focus his thoughts. He waited for Larry to say something else, and when he didn't, Louis let the next few minutes pass in silence. He heard the tapping of the typewriter keys resume, and looked over his shoulder.

"Who notified the family?" Louis asked.

"Sheriff did it himself, about five A.M." Larry turned in his chair. "I hear Miz Abigail took it *real* hard. Guess maybe I ought to go over and console her, you think?"

Louis ignored him, his eyes drifting to a hand-scrawled note that said: *Ethel Mulcahey called.* Louis picked it up and faced Larry. "What did Mrs. Mulcahey want?"

"Mike took the call. Ask him."

Louis glared at the back of Larry's head, wanting to knock him off the chair. Suddenly Larry spoke again. "Probably wanted to ask you why we arrested Leverette again."

"What?" Louis asked.

When Larry didn't answer, Louis bolted from the chair and walked angrily to the back, grabbing the keys off Larry's desk as he passed him. He jerked open the broken front door to the cells and stalked down the corridor. Willis, the jail sergeant, glanced at Louis, then back down at his magazine.

Louis stopped in front of Leverette's cell. Larry hurried up behind him and placed himself between Louis and the bars.

"Don't you dare, Kincaid. Give me them keys."

"I just want to talk to him. Privately."

"Give me the keys and you can talk all day if you want. But this dirtbag ain't going nowhere. Not with you."

Louis threw the keys at him. Larry caught them and glared at Louis, then turned and left the cellblock.

Louis faced Leverette. The young man sat on the edge of his bunk, elbows on his knees. It occurred to Louis that he might be praying, so he didn't speak immediately.

Leverette finally looked up. "Detective . . ."

"Leverette, I'm sorry."

"I just don't understand what's going on."

"I need to tell you something. But you can't share it with anyone, not even your mother, not yet."

"Yes sir."

"I think your father knew something about the bones we found last December. Do you remember that?"

"Yes sir."

"And I think someone killed him for it."

Leverette lowered his head. Louis put his hand through the bars and touched Leverette's arm. "I need you to tell me about your father."

"Like what kinda stuff, Detective?"

"Why did he give scholarships to black students?"

"He always said they needed education worse than the rest of us. Said they didn't always get a fair shake and that somebody ought to lend a helping hand."

"Did you know George Harvey, the jeweler?"

Leverette nodded. "Everybody knew George."

"Were he and your father close?"

"No sir. Don't think they talked for years." A strange look passed Leverette's brown eyes. "Except last Christmas. Dad went over to George's before Christmas, about a week after y'all found the bones. He told us he was getting something special for Mom's birthday. That was December twelfth. I remember now because I was home that weekend and we were suppose to go hunting. But he was late and when he got back, said he didn't feel like it. I was kinda angry at him." Leverette faced Louis again. "But he didn't get anything for her. Mom got the usual stuff . . . slippers, bathrobe, but no jewelry."

"Did he seem upset about anything?"

"Dad was upset lots. He was kind of depressed-like sometimes."

"Depressed?"

"Yeah. He saw a doctor in town about it, a psychiatrist named Eckles."

"Why didn't your mother tell me that?"

"She was probably ashamed."

Louis heard the metal door clang and looked down the corridor to see Larry standing at the end, leaning against the wall.

"Do you think Eckles would talk to me?" Louis asked in a low voice.

"If I called him, he might."

"I'll get you a phone. Do you remember your father having any contact with Max Lillihouse last December?"

Leverette looked up sadly. "Dad hated Max."

"Did he ever say why?"

"No, just that he was an evil man and he'd go to Hell one day. Said he could really get him, if he wanted."

Louis gripped the bars, taking a quick glance at Larry, still standing by the door. "Did he ever say how?"

"No, except to say it wouldn't be worth it."

Louis looked at his watch. He had to see Dr. Eckles. He told Leverette he'd get back to him, and asked Willis to bring him a phone. Louis pushed past Larry.

Larry watched Louis go, his mouth slowly working on a chaw of tobacco. He waited until Louis put on his coat and left, then spat on the concrete floor and walked back to Willis's desk.

"What'd he ask you for?" Larry demanded.

"He wanted Leverette there to get a phone."

Larry glanced at Leverette. "He don't need no phone. What else did they talk about?"

Willis shrugged, not looking up from his magazine. "Max and George. Louis is goin' to see some guy named Eckles."

Larry's facial muscles tightened and he stormed from the corridor. "Watch the radio," he hollered back to Willis. "I'll be right back!"

Larry slammed out the station door and hurried up the courthouse steps. On the second floor, he strode boldly through the reception area, past the sputtering secretary and into Kelly's office. He closed the door loudly behind him.

Kelly looked up from his desk. "What do you want?"

"He's on his way to see Eckles."

"Earl's shrink?" Kelly asked. He rose and went to the window. He watched Louis go down the block and turn a corner at Mulberry Avenue. He picked up the phone and dialed the DA's office.

"Bob?" he said tersely. "I want Kincaid suspended. Immediately. And if that imbecile Dodie gives you any lip, hit him with everything you got.''

Kelly slammed the phone down. Larry turned from the window.

''The son of a bitch is the prime suspect in Max's murder and he's still chasin' those damn bones,'' Larry said with a snicker. ''Is he fuckin' stupid or what?''

''He's not stupid, Cutter,'' Kelly said. ''He's trying to find a patsy for Max's murder, that's all. He thinks if he can tie Max to the bones, he'll be off the hook.''

Larry wrinkled his face. ''You ain't gonna fall for that, are you? You don't know how hard it was just to be civil to him this morning, knowing he killed Max. For pussy. For fucking pussy.''

''It's immaterial. By sundown he'll be in jail.''

''That's not enough.''

Kelly glanced at Larry. ''Justice is funny, Cutter. It comes when you least expect it.''

''Yeah, well, sometimes you got to go out and get it yourself.''

Kelly smiled tightly and went back to his desk. He opened a drawer and pulled out an envelope. ''How long have you and I been doing business?''

''It's fixin' to be a year. Since Dodie started getting senile and weird.''

''And you have been very good about providing me with little tidbits you felt I ought to know. But things have changed. This is a different ball game now, and I need your help.''

Larry's eyes drifted to the envelope and Kelly held it up. ''You remember what this is?''

Larry shrugged.

''It's that envelope your two friends got off Kincaid on the Trace that night. You delivered it to me the next day.''

''Yeah, I remember. I didn't read it, though.''

''The hell you didn't.'' Kelly tossed it on the desk and put his hands in his pockets. ''The information in that envelope is a lie, a bold-faced lie.''

Larry grinned. ''Hell, I thought it was great. Gave me a whole new image of you, Mayor.''

Kelly stared at him in disgust.

"I wish I coulda been there, ridin' along with you guys," Larry said, with a low whistle, "Riders in the night, ghost riders, that's what you guys were, only the ghosts belonged to—"

"Shut up!" Kelly snapped.

Larry's smile melted.

"You don't know what they did to us, the damn FBI and their so-called ..." Kelly stopped, took a breath and tugged at the lapels of his suit. "It was a long time ago," he said, more calmly. "It's all lies anyway."

"Then why you so worried about it?"

"I'm a politician, Cutter," Kelly said slowly, as if explaining to a child. "And politics is all about perception. It doesn't really matter who I am, what I do—or what I did. Image is everything."

Larry frowned, shifting from one foot to the other.

Kelly smiled stiffly. "My father used to tell me something about being a politician. It's a lot like being a Mississippian. Both have bad images. There are always people trying to dig up your old dirt, sniffing around for scandals and ugliness. Liberals, Northern-ers, the FBI ... they all think they have the right to tell you how to do things—whether it's running the country, a town, the schools—or what you can put on the damn state flag."

"Like Kincaid," Larry said.

Kelly pointed a finger at Larry. "Don't underestimate him, Cutter. Kincaid read that FBI report."

Larry edged forward. "You think he'd use it? Like, give it to some big newspapers or something?"

"He's trying to cover his ass right now. He would do anything to detract from his own guilt." Kelly walked around his desk and stood at the window, staring out at the square. "This town is sixty-seven percent black."

"Yeah, tell me about it."

"Don't you see what I'm getting at?" Kelly said impatiently, turning. "Perception, you idiot. What would happen to me if they read the lies in that FBI report? I'd be out of here, Cutter, and you'd lose that nice little allowance I give you that I'm sure you've never bothered to tell the wife about."

Larry just stood there. Kelly turned back to the window, stuffing his hands in his pants pocket. He began to jingle the loose change in his pocket, staring down at the street.

Larry shifted uneasily. "Mayor," he said quietly, after a few seconds.

"What?"

"What do you want me to do?" Larry asked.

Kelly didn't turn around. "Whatever it takes, Deputy Cutter. Whatever it takes."

CHAPTER 24

Howard Eckles was a young man, with thin blond hair and adolescent features, appearing barely old enough to have any kind of degree, let alone a doctorate. He told Louis he had not received a call from Leverette, but after some cajoling agreed to talk to Louis.

Louis sat down on a comfortable sofa in his office and waited while Eckles settled into his chair and told the receptionist to hold his calls. There were several orchids growing in pots on the sill and a bold Matisse print on the pale blue walls. The soothing sound of ocean waves played from a hidden stereo. Louis could imagine Earl in this sanctuary, baring his secrets.

"Earl Mulcahey was a troubled man," Eckles began. "But that's all I can say."

"I am familiar with privilege, believe me, I am," Louis said, "but Earl Mulcahey's dead and I need some help here."

"Detective, you know I can't share anything specific."

"I think Earl knew something, or may even have been involved in the lynching of a young man many years ago."

Eckles face revealed nothing.

Louis let out a deep breath. "Doctor, Leverette Mulcahey did not kill his father. I'm trying to help him."

"I agree. But I can't confirm anything."

"All right. Let's put it this way: If Earl was involved, and regretted it, how might he act?"

Eckles shook his head, smiling. "Sorry."

Louis sat back in the chair, sighing. He tried another tactic. "Okay, if any man, a sensitive, weak man, prone to depression, did something terrible he regretted, how might such a man atone for this crime?"

"People who commit crimes, people who would normally never do such a thing on their own, generally remain deeply penitent, always searching for ways to erase the act from their lives. Sometimes they kill themselves."

"And the ones who don't?"

"They suffer every day. Some might move away, change the scenery."

Earl had sold his land. Louis needed more. "How would such a person act if he or she thought, after many years, their sin would be revealed?"

"It would depend," Eckles said quietly, tapping a pencil. "To some, it would be a relief."

Louis sat back. Earl had wanted to come forward. There was no question in his mind that the unearthing of Eugene Graham had forced Earl to confront his crime.

"Doctor, how might a stronger man act, maybe an irrational man, one who had a lot to lose?"

"I think that's easy, Detective. He would do anything to prevent exposure."

"Including more killing?"

"Possibly. If he thought he could get away with it."

The receptionist buzzed, saying the doctor's next patient was waiting. Eckles rose and Louis knew the psychiatrist would reveal no more. He thanked him and extended his hand. Eckles shook it and sat back down, swinging casually in his chair as Louis turned to leave.

"Detective . . ." Eckles said softly.

Louis turned and waited for him to speak. The psychiatrist's eyes glinted as he stuffed the pencil into a holder. "You know, a common therapeutic technique is to have a patient write down their thoughts."

Louis paused, his hand on the doorknob. "You mean like a journal? Are you telling me you advised Earl to keep a journal?"

The psychologist smiled slightly. "I don't know if Earl did or didn't. And that, Detective, is really all I can tell you."

* * *

Louis had to talk to Ethel Mulcahey. As he headed the car toward the Texaco station, the radio squawked to life. Junior was trying to reach him again.

"Louis? Louis! You out there? Sheriff wants to see you now. Louis?"

Louis pulled up next to the pay phone, letting out a long breath. He had a bad feeling about Dodie. The man really had no choice but to suspend an officer who was a suspect in a murder case. But once he was suspended, the case was over. Louis keyed the mike.

"Can't copy you, Junior. You're breaking up."

"Lou—"

Louis turned the radio off, feeling like shit. But he needed to buy some time, even if it was only hours. He slipped into the phone booth and dialed Ethel. Six rings, seven . . . Damn, where was she? He was just about to give up when she answered.

She barely gave him enough time to identify himself. "How could you arrest Leverette again?" she cried.

"Please, calm down. Listen to me—"

"I can't talk to you, my lawyer—"

"Mrs. Mulcahey, please, just take a second and listen to me. I'm trying to help your son. I don't think he did anything."

"Then why is he back in jail?"

"The sheriff is trying to take the easy way out. Please, I think I can help."

She was crying. Louis let out a breath and it clouded in the chilly, damp air. He pulled up the collar of his jacket. Man, it was getting cold all of a sudden.

"Mrs. Mulcahey, I need you to do something for me."

She did not answer. But she hadn't hung up.

"Look around the house for a notebook or journal your husband might have written."

"Detective, I don't understand what all this has to do with Leverette."

"Trust me, Mrs. Mulcahey, please."

He asked Mrs. Mulcahey to call if she found anything, and she hung up without another word. Louis stood at the phone for a second, debating his next move. He knew he should just go home and get some sleep. He had been awake since discovering Max outside Bessie's, and had driven straight to Jackson and back after that. He had forgotten to eat, too, as his rumbling stomach now reminded him. He went inside the Texaco, picked up a bag of chips and a Dr. Pepper and headed to the counter.

There were two hunters in camouflage gear ahead of him. Louis paid for his soda and pushed open the glass door, stopping abruptly. One of the hunters had taken out his rifle and was pointing it toward the store across the street.

Louis stepped up to him quickly. "Hey, what do you think you're doing?" he asked sharply.

The hunter looked at his friend then looked back at Louis, a dumbfounded look on his face. Louis yanked out his badge, flipping it open.

The hunter lowered the gun to his side. "I was just showing Roy here my new gun, that's all."

"You shouldn't be pointing a gun out on the street like that," Louis said. "C'mon, man, you guys are suppose to know what you're doing. Put the damn thing away."

"Sorry," he said. "But it ain't loaded."

"That's right," his friend said. "He just bought it. Ain't even got bullets for it yet."

The first hunter stroked the barrel of the rifle proudly. "Paid 600 bucks. Can pick a buck off from a quarter mile away."

"Well, be careful," Louis said, walking away.

"Will do, Officer," Roy said.

Louis headed toward the Mustang then stopped, turning. The hunters were getting in their truck and Louis hurried back to them, tapping on the window. Roy rolled his down.

"What kind of gun is that?" Louis asked.

"A Remington DBL 700."

"What caliber?"

".30-.30."

Louis stared at the rifle, but in his mind he was seeing the spread-eagled body of Earl Mulcahey. Someone else owned one of these rifles, said it had cost a month's pay. Who was that? Larry. No, Larry didn't own it; he had said his friend Max owned it. Jesus . . .

Louis watched the truck pull out, and walked slowly back to the Mustang. Lots of men owned rifles. What was nagging at him about this one? He stopped by the car, shivering in the cold, thinking now of the tire tracks out near the deer stand. A Monte

Carlo could produce a wide radial tread like that. Could Max have been Earl's killer? But that didn't make sense; Max was a victim, too—of the same killer who was eliminating the lynching witnesses.

Max had no reason to kill Earl. Or did he? God knows, the bastard probably would have done anything to protect the life he had built for himself. He had married into an old-money family and climbed his way to respectability and power. He threatened to kill Louis when he thought his daughter's honor was being compromised. Would he have killed Earl to keep a damaging secret from getting out?

Louis got in the car and started the heater, slowly munching on the potato chips. If Max had killed Earl, then it followed that he killed George Harvey, too. But George was shot with—

Louis bolted upright. A fucking .45! The same damn kind of gun that Max had threatened Louis with. The same kind of gun Max himself had been shot with.

He had to get a ballistics comparison on Max's gun and the bullet taken out of George Harvey. But the .45 had been taken into evidence and was in the state crime lab in Jackson by now.

Louis got out of the car, hurried to the phone booth and placed a call to the Mississippi State Crime Lab. He hoped Jacob Armstrong was there. The young medical examiner who had handled the bones was the only person at the state lab who might be willing to do him a favor. While he waited, he watched the clouds slowly moving in. They were dark and heavy.

"Armstrong here."

"Armstrong!" Louis replied. "This is Detective Kincaid, the one with the bones up here in Black Pool."

"Yes, I remember you. How's your case coming?"

"Good, but I need some help on something and you're the only one I know I can ask."

"Well, this is your lucky day, Detective. Slow day for corpses here. I'd be glad to help if I can."

"You have a man there by the name of Lillihouse."

He heard Armstrong shuffling through some papers. "Yeah, came in last night."

"There will also be prints, fibers, whatever, from his car. And his gun, a nickle-plated .45. Do you have access to those?"

"No, but I can ask someone upstairs. What do you need?"

"We had a man shot here last week, a George Harvey. You guys did his autopsy. Do you still have the report?"

"I don't suppose you have a case number, Detective? It sure would—"

"No, I don't, sorry. But I need you to see if Lillihouse's gun matches the bullet taken from Harvey."

"I'll try, Detective." Armstrong paused. "Why do I have the feeling that's not all?"

Louis smiled slightly, cradling the phone. "Actually, I could use one other thing. Tire casts of a car. They should be with Earl Mulcahey's file—"

"Mulcahey? Who's Mulcahey? I thought you wanted me to look at some guy named Harvey?"

"No, this second one is a separate case. Earl Mulcahey, shot with a rifle on . . . Damn, it was a Sunday." Louis rubbed his eyes.

"Wait a minute, Detective. I don't even know if we have your reports," Armstrong said. "Did we do this Mulcahey guy? And even if we did, casts and ballistics are another department. I'm a doctor, Detective, not a cop. Why don't you just bring whatever you got and we'll run it for you when we get the stuff back on Lillihouse?"

"I can't, Mr. Armstrong, please."

Armstrong sighed. "Who did the post on this Mulcahey guy?"

Louis tried to remember the examiner who had done Earl's autopsy but couldn't. "I don't know. It was last month, before Christmas, around the twentieth." There was a long pause on Armstrong's end of the line. Louis leaned against the phone, watching the clouds. "Mr. Armstrong, I need some help here and I need it in a hurry."

"Detective, does all this have anything to do with those bones?"

"I hope so, Mr. Armstrong."

There was a pause on the other end of the line. "All right, give me the info again," Armstrong muttered. "It might be fun playing Quincy for a change."

Louis repeated the names and days as Armstrong wrote them down. When Louis asked the Medical Examiner what time he could call back, Armstrong told him he needed at least four hours.

"Mr. Armstrong?" Louis said before hanging up. "I owe you a big one."

"Well, those bones you brought in kinda got under my skin, Detective," Armstrong said. "You know what I mean?"

"I sure do," Louis said.

Ethel Mulcahey sat on the edge of her bed across from the mahogany chest. It had been Earl's dresser, and once belonged to his mother, God rest her soul. Now Earl was gone, too. And Leverette was in jail, charged with the murder of his father. What had happened to her family? How could God be so cruel as to take both from her in such a short time?

She stared at the dresser. The detective wanted her to look for notebooks, but Earl had never hid anything from her, and it didn't feel right invading his privacy like this, even if he was gone.

Ethel rose slowly from the bed and opened the first drawer. The sight of Earl's underwear lying in neat stacks brought a catch to her throat. She didn't understand how this could help Leverette, but she was ready to grasp any thread of hope. She opened the second drawer, then the next and the next. Nothing but clothes, golf shirts, hunting shirts, fishing shirts. Tube socks, argyle socks for church, and a small selection of ties given to him over the years by the children.

She closed the last drawer, and walked on slippered feet to the bathroom. She checked the small cedar towel cupboard and his drawer. Nothing but a razor, blades, his prostate pills and the like.

She would have to throw his things away soon. Or maybe she could donate them to the Goodwill. Earl would want somebody to use them. Earl hated waste.

The den was a small, oak-pancled room Earl had decorated with a stuffed armadillo and a deerhead his father had shot. It was his room, and she seldom went inside. He had paid the bills in here, talked about fatherly things with Leverette. He watched football games and fishing shows here.

The desk was as he left it, papers stacked on top, most concerning insurance or his side business of roofing. The gray television screen was covered with dust. She would have to tend to that soon, too. She sat behind the desk and placed her hands flat on the top. It was the first time she remembered sitting here. She inhaled; Earl's smell was in the old leather chair.

She opened the desk drawers, one by one. There were old

bills, insurance papers, photographs of his cousins and sister. She stopped, knowing she could go no farther.

Ethel closed the drawer and stood up. It wasn't right to intrude. Detective Kincaid had no right. She had no right. She would not do it.

Louis shifted in the hard plastic chair, picking at his french fries. He glanced at his watch. It was almost four, too soon to call Armstrong back. He gulped down the last of his Big Mac and drained the Dr. Pepper, barely tasting either. He looked up at the girl behind the counter who had been watching him suspiciously for the last hour. After calling Armstrong, he had cruised by Bessie's, only to see Junior's squad car sitting at the corner. He had done a quick U-turn and headed the other way. He was beginning to feel like a federal fugitive.

He looked at his watch again. He couldn't wait another minute. Scooping up a handful of quarters, he hurried to the pay phone and dialed Winston Gibbons's office. When the agent came on the line, Louis asked if the results were back.

"Let me ask you this first," Gibbons said. "Are you positive you are okay? You don't sound like it."

"I'm very tired, Mr. Gibbons," Louis said. "And truth is, I'm beginning to feel a little like that guy Damocles, watching that sword dangling over his head."

"Well, I'm heading to Atlanta tomorrow for a conference. Let us come down when I get back."

"I'll call you if I need you."

Winston paused again. "Louis, you can't let yourself get tangled up in this."

Louis leaned his forehead against the phone. "Eugene, the victim . . . he was just a kid, Mr. Gibbons, a kid who wanted to be a pro ball player."

"You're too involved."

"I know."

Gibbons was quiet on the other end of the line for a moment. "Be careful, Louis."

"I will. About the book . . ."

"Well, as you know, there are two prints on the old poetry book. There are three prints on *The Golden Apples*. One's yours, and the others didn't come up in the data bank. According to our man here, who is the best there is, they both very likely belong either to a child or female."

"Because of the size," Louis said.

"Yes, but here's what's interesting," Gibbons said. "One of these unidentified prints matches the unknown print on your old poetry book."

Louis clutched the phone. "So the same person handled the old poetry book and *The Golden Apples*?"

"Looks like it. Do you know who owns this second book?"

"Yes, I do." Louis sighed, suddenly feeling drained. He had hoped that Grace would prove to be the owner of the poetry book, but now that he knew, the expected feeling of exhilaration did not come. Instead, a sadness passed over him. Grace Lillihouse was the catalyst in Eugene Graham's lynching. Somehow, some way, she was part of it.

Louis said good-bye to Gibbons and hung up. He dialed the crime lab in Jackson.

"Kincaid," Jacob Armstrong greeted him.

"Did you do it?" Louis asked.

"Sure did. Man, you don't know what it took to get these results together. I owe donuts and beers all over the place."

"I'll send you a dozen of each." Louis shifted the phone to his other ear impatiently. "So?"

"The ballistics matched. Lillihouse's .45 killed your man Harvey," Armstrong said.

"And the tire tracks?"

"The guy who did the comparison said the Monte Carlo tread is rare, too expensive a tire for most folks," Armstrong said. "And the tread you lifted from the field matches the Monte Carlo. Looks like you got yourself a killer, Kincaid."

A dead killer, Louis thought. It was finally all starting to fall together, even if he still didn't know who had stalked and killed Max.

"Do me a favor," he told Armstrong. "Hold on to the results. I'll come down and get them. Things are a little shaky here."

"Sorry, Detective," Armstrong said. "I thought you needed them quick. I just overnighted them to your office."

"Damn," Louis muttered.

* * *

Louis came around the corner of Water Street and craned his neck, looking for Junior. The street was empty. It was after four; they had probably given up on finding him today. But at least now when he did go in, he would have something concrete to tell Dodie.

He pulled up in front of Bessie's house and killed the engine. Inside, he called for Bessie, but there was no answer. The house was cold and he flipped on the thermostat and headed upstairs. As excited as he was about the news from Gibbons and Armstrong, he was drained. He had been running on adrenaline, and right now the thought of crawling under the quilt for a quick nap seemed pretty good.

The old furnace kicked on. Louis undressed, pulling on a pair of old blue sweatpants. Barefoot and bare-chested, he grabbed a Dr. Pepper from the refrigerator and moved to the window to watch the street.

It was too cold for the kids to be outside. But Tinker was on his porch, rocking, bundled in a blue parka. The wind was kicking up dervishes of dead leaves in the gutters, and the exhaust pipes of passing cars coughed out white clouds. The sky was a block of gray granite. It reminded him of a February sky in Michigan.

A squad car rounded the corner slowly, and Louis watched it cruise down the street. It was the car Larry usually drove. They hadn't given up, after all. The squad car stopped at the intersection. Tinker watched the car, then looked up at Louis's window as if he knew there was something more to this visit. Louis felt it, too, as a knot formed in his gut.

Louis watched the squad car. It had pulled over to the side of the curb. Louis took a swig of the Dr. Pepper, thinking about Dodie again. Once he confronted him with the evidence about Max killing George and Earl, Dodie would have to realize that Max's murderer also must have had something to do with the lynching. A fourth man was still out there somewhere, and for some reason he had felt threatened enough to kill Max. Louis was still betting it was Kelly. The knot in Louis's stomach tightened as he thought of Kelly—and Bob Roberts. The two men were close allies and would be hard to beat. If he expected Dodie to go to bat for him against those two, he would need as much ammunition as possible.

Louis had a sudden idea. He went to the phone in the hall and dialed the Jackson Medical Examiner's Office, asking to be connected to whoever was in charge of the Max Lillihouse shooting. As he waited, he heard the front door open and looked down to see Bessie come in, arms full of grocery bags from the Piggly Wiggly. He waved to her.

"Yo, this is Victor," came a voice over the phone.

Louis turned his attention back to the phone. "Victor, this is Deputy Resnick, Greensboro County Sheriff's Department." He couldn't risk giving his own name.

"I was told y'all was going to be calling," the other man said. "In a big damn hurry for those results, are ya?"

"Yeah, we are. Got anything for me?"

"Hold on, got to get the file."

Louis waited impatiently, listening to Bessie singing softly down in the kitchen. Victor came back on the phone a few minutes later.

"Sorry, Deputy, I can't help you."

"Why not? Aren't they back?"

"Some are, but I can't release it to you."

"Why not?"

"The file's been sealed. Says here, 'To be released only to the Greensboro County District Attorney.'"

Louis slumped against the wall. "That's crazy," he muttered.

"I'm just doing what I'm told. Sorry, Deputy."

Louis slammed down the phone. Roberts again. Hell, for Roberts to put a seal on that file meant two things: He was leaving Dodie out of the loop and he was after Louis's ass. There was only one thing left to do now: Call Winston Gibbons.

He reached for the phone, but then stopped. Sirens. . . .

Bessie appeared in the foyer, looking up at him, fear in her eyes. The phone rang and Louis jumped, his eyes darting from it to the front door.

"Louis?" Bessie said.

The sirens were coming closer; the phone's shrill ring filled the house. Louis grabbed for it, knocking it off its cradle.

"Hello?" he said sharply.

"Lou . . . Lou! This is Charles."

"What?"

"Cousin Charles. . . . Lou, you ain't gonna believe this, I almost didn't my own self until I seen it. Jesus, Louis, I can't believe all this shit is coming down."

"Charles, talk to me, man!"

The sirens were right outside. Bessie spread the curtain, mumbling something.

"Charles, what the hell's happening?"

"I'll lose my job for sure now, I know it."

Louis could see the red lights flashing outside the front window. The sirens fell silent. Charles's voice was barely audible.

"A clerk in the D.A.'s office done called me. Louis, they's issued a warrant for your arrest."

CHAPTER 25

L ouis waited at the top of the stairs. In one sense, he felt calm, almost invincible. He had done nothing wrong, and he was a cop. Cops took care of other cops. But another part of him was terrified because he knew a lot of things weren't right in this miserable town.

His heart quickened as he heard footsteps out on the porch. When they pounded on the door, Bessie looked up at Louis and he nodded for her to let them in. She opened the door wide, standing behind it.

Larry was standing behind the screen, Junior and Mike behind him. Each man wore his tan uniform and brown felt hat. Larry held a black nightstick in his right hand and was tapping it against the wood slat of the screen door. He opened the screen and it banged against the house, snapping back to catch Mike in the shoulder as the three men entered the vestibule.

Larry looked at Bessie. She returned his stare with such abomination that he turned away.

Junior stepped forward and looked up the stairs. "C'mon, Louis, we gotta take you in," he said.

"I'd like to see the warrant," Louis said. "And I want to make a phone call."

"At the jail, Kincaid," Larry said.

Junior pulled a folded piece of paper from his shirt pocket and held it out. When Louis didn't move, he put it away. "Now, come on down here, Louis," he said. "Let's keep this easy-like."

Junior sounded almost apologetic, but the look in Larry's eyes was unnerving. Louis tried to swallow but his throat was tight.

"What are you 'resting him for?" Bessie cried. "What's he done?"

Mike was the only one who looked at her. "For killing Max Lillihouse, Miz Bessie," he said quietly.

She let loose with a wail. Larry yanked the cuffs off his belt and took a step up. "Git your ass down here, boy. Now."

"Jesus, Larry, this is Louis you're talking to," Mike said.

Larry ignored him. "Kincaid, don't make us come up there and get you."

Bessie was crying and Louis was afraid she would do something that might get her hurt. "Let me get dressed," he said.

"We'll just take you the way you are," Larry said quickly.

"Y'all can't take him like that!" Bessie said, "Let Louis get dressed. What's wrong with you?"

Mike touched her arm. "You leave things be, Miz Bessie. Go on."

She jerked away from Mike and backed against the wall.

Louis stepped forward. "Don't touch her."

"You come on down here and we won't have to," Junior said.

Louis came down the stairs. Larry shoved the nightstick in his belt, and when Louis reached the third step, Larry grabbed his arm, jerking him down. He pushed him up against the wall, bracing the back of his head with his forearm while he wrenched Louis's left arm up behind him. Louis did not fight. He closed his eyes, feeling Larry's hot breath on his neck.

"You're really enjoying this, aren't you, asshole?" Louis hissed.

Larry slammed his forearm against the back of Louis's neck, forcing his face roughly to the wall. Louis jerked instinctively in defense, but Larry's hand tightened on his shoulder.

"Hey, hey!" Junior shouted. "Calm the fuck down here."

Larry snapped Louis's wrists in the handcuffs and spun him around. "You have the right to keep your mouth shut," Larry began.

"Jesus, Lar, you don't need to do all that," Mike said.

"You have the right to a lawyer. If you can't afford a lawyer on that big-ass salary of yours, then we'll git you one. . . ."

Larry wheeled Louis around, and Louis tripped on the throw rug and fell. He heard Bessie cry out and felt warm hands on his bare arms. He struggled to his feet, balanced by Mike.

The door opened and the cold air rushed in. Mike had a steadying hand on one arm, Larry was jerking on the other. Junior walked on ahead. As he was led down the sidewalk, Louis scanned the faces of the neighbors standing outside their homes watching. His stomach churned with humiliation, and he felt color rise to his cheeks. Where the hell was Dodie? he thought angrily. Why wasn't he here?

Larry gave him a subtle push, and Louis fell forward, scrambling for balance. He spun around and planted both feet, glaring.

"Don't even think it, nigger," Larry hissed.

Mike pulled on Louis's arm. "C'mon, man."

The concrete was cold on Louis's feet and the frigid wind cut across his bare chest. Louis wanted to look down, look away from the staring eyes, but he forced himself to hold his head up, stealing a look back at Bonnie. She stood gripping the porch rail, her shoulders heaving. Louis spotted Tinker standing on his porch, watching. Then, with a shake of his head, he went inside.

Mike put a hand to Louis's head, guiding him into the backseat. The door slammed behind him. Larry and Junior got in front, and Junior started the car with an unnecessary flood of power and kicked on the lights.

Louis sat back against the seat. The leather was cold against his skin and the cuffs cut into his wrists. He shifted to lessen the pressure and leaned his head back, closing his eyes.

The cell was cold and smelled of mildew washed over with disinfectant. Gray—everything was gray. The cell walls were peeling gray paint. The bars were gray, as were the metal bunk and its thin wool blanket. Across the ceiling were large gray water pipes, pocked with rust. It was the only spot of color except for the red line on the corridor floor, painted exactly one foot from the cell door. Even the light was gray. No windows and just an empty socket hanging from the ceiling of the cell. The only light came from the dim corridor lights and the desk sergeant's lamp.

Louis couldn't stop shivering. He still wore only the blue sweatpants. He pulled the blanket from the bunk and wrapped himself in it, walking to the front of the cell. He stepped in some icy water and looked up. The pipe above was leaking. He had been placed in a cell nearest the door to the office, and he pushed his head against the bars, trying to see down the corridor.

"Hey, Willis," he called out.

There was no answer. Louis knew the desk sergeant was there. He could hear him turning the pages of his magazine.

"Detective Kincaid. That you?" Leverette Mulcahey called, his voice echoing from several cells away.

"Yes," he replied.

"What happened? What are you doing in here?"

"Long story."

"What's happening around here?"

"I don't know," Louis said. "Leverette, do they let you make phone calls?"

"Yes, but they listen in on them."

Shit. He'd been here four hours now and they had yet to bring him a phone. He needed to call Gibbons. And where the hell was Dodie?

"Hey, Willis," Louis shouted again. "Tell Junior I want a phone."

No response. Louis sat down on the bed and stared at the floor. A roach scurried across the cement and disappeared into the drain.

Mike backed through the door to the station, arms loaded with to-go containers from the Burnt Bun Diner across the street. Slipping them onto the desk, he opened one, and the steam from the biscuits and gravy curled upward.

Larry came over and lifted a lid. "What's the third one for?" he asked.

"I thought maybe Louis would be hungry. He's been here since four o'clock with nothing to eat." The eggs were plastered to the top of the container, and Mike carefully peeled them loose with a plastic fork.

"You pay for it?"

Mike shrugged. "It was only a buck ninety-nine."

"That nigger don't need no food. We'll feed him in the morning."

"It's already paid for, Larry. Let's just give it to him."

"I'll give it to him, all right," Larry said, scooping up the white container. For a second Mike thought he was going to throw it away, but Larry started toward the back, then stopped abruptly. Larry looked around the office. It was after ten P.M. and no one was there except Mike and himself. He pulled a paper cup from the dispenser on the wall and unzipped his trousers.

"Christ, Larry," Mike said.

"I heard about cops doin' this before," Larry said, turning his back to Mike, "but never thought I'd get to."

Mike heard the tinkle of urine hit the cup. It disgusted him what Larry was about to do, but he said nothing.

Larry poured the urine onto the top of the gravy and stirred it in with the plastic fork. He wiped the fork on the side of his pants and placed it on top of the box. He was chuckling as he went through the door to the cellblock.

Early the following morning, Louis awoke to the bang of the broken lock of the office door slamming up against the bars of his cell. He opened his eyes to see Junior holding a phone.

Louis stood up and took the phone through the bars. Junior pushed a bundle of orange cloth through the bars. "Here, get dressed," he said. "You got your arraignment this morning."

Louis took the orange jumpsuit and tossed it on the bunk. The phone did not reach to the bunk, so Louis cradled it in his forearm while he dialed. He dialed Gibbons's direct line at the FBI in Jackson. Junior stood near the bars, chewing on a toothpick, watching him. There was no answer.

"Junior, what time is it?" he asked.

"Ten after six." Junior replied.

Too early, and Gibbons's home phone number was back in his room. Louis wanted to call Charles but couldn't remember that number, either. The thought of calling Frances or Phillip Lawrence crossed his mind, but he quickly dismissed it. He couldn't call them at six in the morning to tell them he'd been arrested for murder.

"Y'all didn't eat much," Junior said, his eyes indicating the open container of untouched food.

Louis didn't answer. He dialed Bessie's number. It took several minutes to calm her down enough to ask her to bring him shoes, socks, and underwear. He thought of asking her to search for Gibbons's home number, but he had scribbled it on an envelope and didn't know where it might be. When he asked Bessie if she knew an attorney, she said she would see what she could do. She told him she was praying for him before she hung up.

"You done?" Junior asked.

Louis nodded and Junior took the phone. Louis watched him

as he turned away. He had always known Junior did not really like or accept him. But something had developed between them in the last month, a vague kinship created by the uniform. But now that was gone, and though he couldn't believe it, he felt a chilling loneliness in Junior's aloofness. He went back to the bunk and sat down, putting his head in his hands. He hadn't slept more than a few minutes at a stretch, and he knew he should be exhausted but he felt wide-awake, tense with adrenaline. Or fear.

And he couldn't keep warm. The cold, damp air had seeped clean through to his bones.

" 'Morning."

Louis looked up. Dodie's face was shadowed by his cattleman's hat and the bars. Louis rose slowly and went to the bars. "You can't believe I did this," he whispered.

Dodie looked down the corridor and back to Louis. "Louis, I don't know what to believe," he said wearily. "Hardly anything you told me seems to have panned out. Now this. I jus' don't know."

"Max was killed for the same reason the others were."

Dodie sighed. "Yeah."

"Sheriff, listen to me. Max killed George and Earl, and I can prove it."

"Just like you proved the medallion belonged to Kelly." Dodie hesitated. "I saw that FBI report. Junior found it in your room. When were you gonna tell me that they didn't match?"

Louis gripped the bars. "I was wrong about that, but I'm not wrong about this. There is evidence to prove—"

"Where is it?"

"You'll have it today. It's coming, from Jackson."

Dodie's disappointment was etched deeply in his haggard face. It occurred to Louis that he looked like he hadn't slept much, either.

"Give it up, Louis," Dodie said quietly.

"Sheriff . . ."

"Forget about them damn bones and start worrying about your own skin." Dodie hesitated then placed a hand on Louis's. "They want to nail you on this thing and it looks like they have enough to do it."

" 'They'? Who? Kelly?" Louis asked.

Dodie pulled his hand away. "Get yourself a good lawyer, Louis." Dodie turned and started back toward the office.

"Sheriff! Wait!" Louis called out. "Listen to me, damn it!"

Dodie turned. "It's outta my hands, Louis," he said. "There ain't nothin' I can do. It's outta my hands."

Louis grabbed his sleeve again. "When are you gonna get a backbone?"

Dodie jerked away this time and disappeared through the door. Louis slapped angrily at the bars, and turned, snatching up the orange jumpsuit. He slumped down in the bunk, turning the suit over in his hands. He read the block letters on the back: GREENS-BORO COUNTY JAIL.

Before taking him upstairs to court, they chained him.

Louis had to walk carefully, shuffling his feet no more than five or six inches with each step. His hands were cuffed in front, attached to a short length of chain that circled his waist. The orange jumpsuit was too large and the cuffs dragged on the floor as he walked. He wore the white sneakers Bessie had brought him. He could smell the stench of the cell on his body.

Larry opened the prisoners' entrance door at the back of the small courtroom and pulled him along a bench. Louis found himself seated next to a man dressed in street clothes who smelled of whiskey. Louis looked around. He had expected more of a crowd; small-town arraignments always attracted a regular pack of local gossips. But his hearing had been scheduled quickly, and the weekly *Journal* didn't hit the streets until tomorrow.

Bob Roberts was at his table, shuffling through his briefcase. The last time he had seen the district attorney was when they had discussed arresting Leverette. Louis stared at Roberts, remembering how Dodie had buckled under to Roberts's pressure then. How much convincing did the district attorney have to do this time to get Louis arrested?

Louis lowered his head, the mix of anger and humiliation coursing through him again. He had to stay focused, try to direct his thoughts back to Earl, Max, and Eugene Graham. It was only through them that he could hope to clear himself. But the weight of his situation had dulled his ability to reason and as long as he was confined, he couldn't make any progress.

Louis felt someone's eyes on him and looked up to see Roberts staring at him. The district attorney's expression remained impassive, with just a hint of contempt. Louis looked away, a knot forming in his stomach. He knew he already had been judged. It was just a matter of going through the motions to make it all look legal.

The bailiff announced the judge's arrival, and Louis looked up to see old Judge Eucher come through the chamber door.

The bailiff called forth the case. "The People versus Louis Washington Kincaid. Case number 67-45790. The charge is murder in the first degree."

Larry pulled Louis to his feet, and Louis jerked his arm away. He shuffled to the center of the courtroom and faced the judge. Eucher's face was set in a scowl of displeasure.

"Are you represented by counsel?" Eucher asked.

"No sir." Louis said firmly.

"Do you need a court-appointed attorney?"

"No sir."

Louis heard the doors of the courtroom open and some mumbling behind him. He did not turn. Eucher paused and his eyes followed the commotion. When it was quiet, he resumed speaking to Louis in his raspy voice. "Do you wish to enter a plea at this time?"

"Yes."

"The charge against you is murder in the first degree. How do you plead?"

"Not guilty, Your Honor."

Eucher looked at Bob Roberts. "Bail?"

"No bail, Your Honor, due to the nature of the charge, the defendant's familiarity with the legal system, *and* the fact we feel he is a flight risk. He is not a long-term resident of Greensboro County and has no ties to the community. The offense is so heinous in nature, the crime so brutal—to cut down one of Black Pool's most notable citizens—we cannot find it within our prudence to recommend bail of any amount, Your Honor."

Louis shot the district attorney an angry look. "Think you made your point there, Bob?" he muttered.

Eucher pounded his gavel. "Defendant is held without bail. Preliminary hearing is set for February 25."

Larry came forward and pulled Louis back away from the judge. "I jus' thought of something, Kincaid," Larry whispered.

"This here state has the death penalty. But hell, you won't have to wait for that. You know how long cops live in prison."

"You got to be guilty first, asshole."

"Not if you're black," Larry said softly.

Louis locked eyes with Roberts. A trickle of fear traveled up his spine as Roberts's eyes began to waver. The D.A. finally looked away, stuffing papers in his briefcase. As Larry led him back across the courtroom, Louis looked toward the gallery. He knew she was there; he could feel her presence.

Larry tugged on the chain but Louis resisted. Then he saw her.

Abby stared back at him from the third row. Her face was a pale blur against the black of her dress. It was shadowed by a brimmed hat, but he could see the tears in her eyes.

CHAPTER 26

Mike stopped in front of Louis's cell, holding a tray, a newspaper tucked under his arm.

"Want some food, Louis?"

Louis didn't look at him. He lay still on the bed, hands folded behind his head, staring at the wire supports on the upper bunk.

"It's chicken-fried steak," Mike said.

When he still didn't answer, Mike set the tray on the floor, then stood up. "I got the paper here. You made the front page. Wanna read it?"

Louis slid off the bunk and took the paper from Mike. The entire front page had been given over to Max's murder and Louis's arrest. A bold two-inch headline was stripped across the top.

COP HELD IN LILLIHOUSE MURDER
Interracial Affair Alleged as Motive

There was a picture of him being escorted into the jail, flanked by Larry and Junior. He hadn't even noticed the photographer. He didn't want to read the story but knew he had to. He got his glasses off the top mattress and put them on.

> Louis Kincaid, a black investigator with the Greensboro County Sheriff's Office, was arrested Tuesday afternoon for the murder of Maxwell E. Lillihouse of Route 8, Box 123, Black Pool.
>
> Police believe Mr. Lillihouse was shot in the head in his car at approximately 2:30 A.M. Monday. Sheriff's officials say the body had been there only minutes before being reported by Kincaid.
>
> Kincaid, twenty-four, was arrested at the home of Bessie Lloyd,

314 Water Street, where he was a boarder. He was arrested when it was found that Kincaid was romantically involved with Mr. Lillihouse's daughter, Abigail Elizabeth, nineteen, a student at the University of Florida.

Said Greensboro County District Attorney Bob Roberts, "We have good reason to believe this was a crime of passion."

Unnamed sources at the sheriff's department have told the Journal *that Kincaid threatened to kill Mr. Lillihouse only days before, and that Kincaid had recently been suspended from the department for insubordination.*

Louis folded the paper. Sweet Jesus.

"Louis."

He lifted his eyes to see Mike.

"You going to eat something? You ain't eaten all day."

Louis didn't feel like eating. The newspaper article had made him sick.

"Well, I'll leave it, if you want it," Mike said, walking away.

Louis set the newspaper on the bunk, went to the bars and crouched, lifting the lid of the to-go container. He stared at the greasy food, then reached between the bars and grabbed a roll. He had to eat; he had to keep up his energy. Crossing his legs, he sat down on the concrete floor and scooped up some mashed potatoes. He tasted them cautiously; cold, but no weird taste this time.

As he chewed, he thought about the attorney Bessie had found. The moment he had set eyes on Linus Grimm this morning, he knew his fate was in the hands of the wrong man. Grimm was a cipher of a man. A nondescript suit hung on his sticklike frame. His bleached-blue eyes were devoid of any passion, and his voice had an annoying way of trailing off at the end of every sentence. To Louis, he was the quintessential deep-rooted Southern man who did not want to make waves.

Mike returned with a tray for Leverette. On his way back, Louis called to him. Mike stopped, squatting down so he was even with Louis. Mike's bland young face was colored by a gloominess that made him look older.

"Mike, tell the sheriff I want to see him."

"Sheriff's with Mayor Kelly."

"Figures," Louis sighed. Any last hope he had that Dodie would suddenly grow a spine was fast dissipating.

"Can I get you something?"

"I need a phone," Louis said.

"Junior says you get a phone in the morning and you get one call, and you used that one already today."

"Mike, you know I used it to call Bessie to bring my glasses. C'mon. I need to call someone."

"I'll call them for you," Mike said. "But I ain't callin' Abby, Louis. I just can't."

"Jesus, I don't want you to call Abby. Give me your pen."

"Can't do it, man."

"For chrissakes, Mike. If I wanted to stab you with something, I could use this damn plastic fork. Give me your pen, please."

Mike shrugged helplessly.

Louis sighed. "All right, write this number down, then."

Mike took a pen from his shirt pocket and spread his palm to use as paper. In between bites of the chicken steak, Louis gave him Winston Gibbons's name and office number.

Louis thought about Gibbons's trip to Atlanta. "If he's there, tell him where I am."

"Who is this?"

"A friend."

"You want I should hand you that tray through the hole?" Mike asked.

Louis dropped the fork. "I'm done."

Mike nodded and looked at Louis sadly. He seemed to want to say something, but he didn't. Louis stood up and Mike followed suit, picking up the tray.

"Thanks, Mike," Louis said.

Mike nodded again, and left the cell area.

Back in the office, Mike eyed the other deputies and slid over to Louis's desk. He sat down, started to push a large FedEx envelope aside, then hesitated. He stared at the envelope. It was addressed to Louis, from the Mississippi Crime Lab in Jackson.

Mike glanced over at Larry. He didn't trust Larry anymore. Max had been Larry's friend, and ever since Max was killed, Larry had kind of gone berserk over this whole thing. Besides, no one deserved to have piss put in their food. Mike poked at the envelope with his finger, debating whether to open it. No, he couldn't do that. But this letter could be something important, maybe even something that could help Louis. Mike looked back at Larry. He'd best hide it for now, and show it to the sheriff when he got back.

He went to open Louis's drawer but it stuck. Larry heard the rattling and looked up. "What are you doing?"

"Uh, just sitting here."

Larry came over. He saw the return address on the FedEx envelope and snatched it up. "I'll be damned," he said. He took the envelope to his desk and ripped it open. After several seconds, Larry bolted from his chair and hurried over to Junior, a paper in hand. After some intense whispering, the two of them got up and disappeared into the men's room.

Mike looked at the telephone number in his palm. His hand was sweaty, and the ink was starting to blur. He dialed the number.

A female answered the phone. "Federal Bureau of Investigation, Winston Gibbons's office."

Mike slammed down the phone. Jesus, what the hell was Louis involved in?

"Man, it stinks in here."

Larry pushed open both stall doors and finding them empty, turned back to Junior. "Look at this," he said.

Junior unfolded the report from the crime lab. Larry drummed his fingers on the top of the urinal while Junior read.

Junior looked up with a frown. "I don't get it."

Larry grabbed the paper from Junior. "Can't you fuckin' read?"

"Yeah, I can fuckin' read. But what does it say?"

"It says," Larry started. "It says . . . This is saying Max killed Earl and George."

Junior shrugged. "Why would he do that?"

"How the hell do I know?"

Larry looked back at the paper in disbelief. Then his eyes glazed over. "Shit . . ."

"What?" Junior asked. "What?"

"We fucked up, man."

"How?"

Larry gaped at Junior. "Leverette. Leverette. We arrested the wrong guy. We arrested the wrong guy twice! Shit, shit, shit."

"If Leverette didn't kill Earl, and Max did . . ." Junior hesitated. "Do you think this has anything to do with Louis?"

Larry's eyes darted to Junior. "No. That fucker killed Max and I know it. This is something else." Larry walked a small circle. "This can't be right. No way Max would kill anyone."

"Larry, that report can't be wrong. I mean, these guys are experts, for chrissakes."

"I'm tellin' you, it's wrong."

Junior leaned against the sink. "Maybe we better ask the sheriff."

"No way."

"Why not?"

"I bet he doesn't know about this. You know, last week when the sheriff suspended Kincaid, it was 'cuz he was mad at something Kincaid was doin' . . . something like this." Larry started pacing in front of the urinal. "I think Kincaid wanted to use this against the sheriff."

"Why would Louis—"

Larry spun around. "Do you know what would happen if this got out?"

Junior shook his head.

"It would look like the sheriff suppressed evidence to protect Max, and all the while lettin' Leverette rot in jail."

"Sheriff wouldn't do that."

"Dammit, Junior, stay with me on this! Do you know what arrestin' a man like Max for murder would look like?"

"But if he was guilty   "

"It's an election year, idiot!"

The color rose in Junior's cheeks. "Larry, don't go callin'—"

"Shut up. I'm thinkin'." Larry resumed his pacing. "If the sheriff didn't do something with this information, he must've had a good reason. And we need to respect that."

"Are you goin' to show him this here report?"

"No way. 'Cuz if he knew that we knew he was coverin' something up, then he would be embarrassed to have us know that. We can't let the sheriff look like a fool to his own men."

Junior ran a hand through his hair. "I guess," he said softly. "I sure wouldn't wanna do nothin' to hurt Uncle Dodie."

"No, you sure wouldn't," Larry said.

* * *

Ethel Mulcahey started the engine of her pristine 1972 Chevrolet Impala, turning on the headlights. She sighed heavily, looking down at the spiral notebook laying on the passenger seat.

She had found it in his office, in a bottom drawer of his filing cabinet, buried far beneath some old tax returns. At first she had resisted opening it; she felt bad enough just for having unearthed it from his hiding place. And it was hidden. She knew that. Earl hadn't meant for anyone to see what he had written in it.

She didn't know why she resumed her search. Maybe it was because Leverette had looked so sad during her last visit to the jail. All she knew was that she wanted her son to come home, and that if Detective Kincaid could use what was in this notebook to help, then so be it.

She glanced down at the faded blue notebook. Last night she had read it, beginning to end. First, it had horrified her. Then it had made her sad; how could she have not known the depth of her husband's pain? But finally it had left her feeling only confused. This was not Earl, this man who poured out his agony on page after page.

But it was Earl. It was his handwriting there in the notebook, the same cramped, straight up-down handwriting he used to write checks and greetings on the kids' birthday cards. It was Earl . . . her husband, a stranger.

Ethel closed her eyes, leaning her head against the wheel. If she took the notebook to Detective Kincaid, Earl's crime would become public, casting shame on her and her children. Earl had been a good man, respected and admired. How could she destroy that?

But if she did not, this poor man named Eugene would never rest in peace, and evil people would go unpunished.

Ethel turned off the ignition and sat hunched over the wheel. Maybe, just maybe, if the sheriff read the journal he would understand that Leverette did not kill his own father. Maybe Detective Kincaid was right. Maybe they did kill Earl out of fear he would reveal their secret.

She started the car again and drove slowly toward Black Pool, her thoughts turning to Detective Kincaid. She had read in the newspaper that he had been arrested for murdering Max Lillihouse. She couldn't believe that he did it. Maybe the journal would help him, too.

She had been to the courthouse many times in the last few weeks to visit Leverette, but it was a different kind of visit she made now. She didn't even intend to see him this time. It would be hard to face him knowing what she knew about his father.

Parking in front, she picked up the journal with trembling hands. Glancing around the square, she started up the walk, the notebook clutched against her chest.

Larry, the deputy who always escorted her to the back to see Leverette, looked up when she came in. He rolled his eyes, like it pained him to see her.

"Evenin', Miz Mulcahey," he said, standing up. "Kinda late for a visit, isn't it?"

"I was passing by," she said softly. "May I go in back?"

Larry walked around the desk and headed toward the cell. Ethel followed him to the metal door and paused while he shoved it open. Larry noticed the notebook in her hand. "Miz Mulcahey, you can't take Leverette that book, ma'am. It's got that spiral wire in it."

Ethel looked at him and summoned her courage. "Deputy, this is of extreme sentimental value to my son. He's not going to stab himself, or you, with a puny little wire."

"What are you going to do with the book?" Larry asked.

"These are poems my husband wrote," she said. "I plan to read them to him. Or you could, if you want to."

Larry wrinkled his lip. "I suppose it'd be all right. Don't leave that book with him, though. Y'all take it home when you're finished."

"Yes, Deputy." Ethel walked past him. When he didn't move, she turned. "Could you leave us alone, please?"

"I'm not supposed to do that, either, ma'am."

"Please, Officer, allow my son and I this time."

Larry looked down the dim corridor. On the right was a solid gray wall. On the left were four cells. Leverette was in the fourth. Louis was in the first. Larry nodded. "All right, but I gotta leave the door open."

"That will be fine."

Ethel waited until Larry walked back to his desk before she moved into the hall. Louis was in his cell doing push-ups. He seemed to sense her presence and he stopped, arms extended, and lifted his head. For a moment, they gazed at each other.

When she did not move away, he slowly stood up, keeping his eyes on her face. She blinked twice and sighed heavily, putting a finger to her lip.

He went to her, glancing at the open door. She showed him the notebook, looking like she was about to give away her firstborn.

Ethel opened the notebook to the back, ripped out the last six or seven pages and held the tattered papers through the bars.

Louis took them, touching her fingers as he gathered the papers in his hand. A tear rolled down her powdered cheek and she turned away, hurrying through the open door. Louis heard Larry call something to her about this being a short visit. He stuffed the papers under the bunk then dropped to the floor and resumed his push-ups.

Larry came through the door, glanced at Louis and walked down to Leverette's cell. Louis heard Larry coming back up the hall.

"He's asleep," Larry said, as if he felt the need to explain something. Louis ignored him, lowering his chest to the floor and raising himself back up.

When Larry left, Louis sat on the floor, drawing up his knees. He listened for more footsteps, and when he thought it safe, pulled the papers from under the mattress.

Sitting against the bed, he unfolded them and began to read. When he finished the first page, he paused, dropping his head back against the cold metal railing of the bunk. Looking up at the empty light socket, he let out a long breath.

"Jesus," he whispered.

A clank woke Louis from his sleep. He threw a hand over his eyes. The cell was flooded with light.

Then, suddenly, the light went out. Louis heard the familiar sound of the broken lock rattling in the door to the outer office.

The cell door banged closed again. He could hear someone breathing. Someone was in the cell with him. Louis slowly stood up and eased back into the corner near the toilet. His hands groped for a weapon of some sort, anything. But there was nothing. He slipped around the edge of the bunk, backing deeper into the corner. He held his breath, waiting.

He heard the shuffle of feet near the bunk and could see shadows patting his mattress. There was a muffled thud, followed by a quick guttural mutter. Louis's fingers curled around the rail of the top bunk.

His eyes adjusted to the darkness, and he saw them more clearly. Two men were moving across the cell toward him. An arm stretched out at him through the darkness. Fingers touched his face and he bolted forward, ducking under the groping hands. He flattened himself against the bars.

They turned and came at him again, a solid wall of muscle. Gripping the bars he kicked at them and missed. A laugh echoed through the cell. Cold, strong fingers gripped his upper arms and he was shoved downward. Louis went rigid with fear. He arched back, fighting. They drove him to his knees and dragged him to the center of the cell.

"Willis! Leverette!" Louis shouted.

He felt the sharp sting of an open palm across his mouth.

A heavy hand covered the back of his head and he was thrust forward. He could smell the sewer drain and he twisted his head to the side. His arms were yanked behind him. He jerked one free. They grabbed it and tightened their grip, squeezing his wrists together. A cloth was quickly wrapped around them. Louis gagged against the stench, straining to see through the darkness, terror racing through him.

He heard the bedsprings squeak. He tried to stand but a large hand on his shoulder forced him back to his knees. A punch to the back of his head sent him forward again. He fought for breath, his arms fighting furiously with the rag that bound them.

Something rough scraped his face. Dear God . . . it was a rope . . . a noose.

He twisted violently. A fierce kick to his rib cage doubled him over. Coughing and gagging, he gasped for breath, choking as his head was forced back by the tug of the rope.

Slowly he was pulled up to his knees.

He tried to cry out but nothing came. The rope tore into his flesh as he was hoisted up. "Jesus . . . God . . ." he whispered.

He balanced on his toes, swaying slightly. Everything was fuzzy. He could hear his heart. The air was being sucked from his lungs.

He felt a breath, hot on his cheek. He weakly twisted his head and came eye-to-eye with Larry.

"Bastard," Louis rasped.

His toes left the cold floor.

Louis fought violently with the rag, wrenching his arms free. Gagging, he grabbed at the noose, digging his fingers between the rope and his neck. He started to kick, sucking in air.

"Motherfucker," Larry hissed, grappling frantically for Louis's arms. Louis twisted away from him, beginning to swing. Larry pulled at his body, unable to get a grip, cursing through his teeth.

Louis thrust his legs out at him, catching him squarely in the chest, knocking him back against the toilet.

"Fuck, man," the other man said.

Louis felt the rope slacken just a little and pulled on it as his toes touched the floor. Larry staggered toward him and Louis pushed off again and kicked out. His heel caught Larry's head, slamming him against the bottom bunk, rattling the bed frame.

A loud crack split the darkness.

Louis gasped as the icy water poured down over him. He dropped to the floor with a thud, the rope trailing after him. Water was flooding into the cell from the broken pipe above. Louis heard the cell door clang open and, still on his knees, spun around. The man on the bunk jumped to the floor and bolted out the cell door, knocking Louis back to the floor.

Louis grabbed the bars, struggling to stand on the slippery floor, jerking furiously at the rope. He yanked it off over his head and threw it aside. Panting, his heart hammering, he searched the darkness for Larry.

He saw him. Crawling out the cell door.

Louis jumped on him and Larry groaned as his chest slammed against the concrete floor. Locking a leg around Larry's waist, and his hands wrenching Larry's shirt, Louis roughly flipped him over. Larry looked up at Louis, shaking his head. Louis wrapped the collar of his shirt in his fist.

"Stop, stop," Larry moaned. "We wasn't really going to do it, I swear."

"You sonofabitch!" Louis hit him across the face, his knuckles cracking as they hit bone.

"We were just gonna scare ya!" Larry cried.

Louis paused, his fist in mid-air. Water dripped from Louis's

head to Larry's quivering face. Louis clenched his fist tighter.
Larry raised his hands.

"You fucking son of a bitch!"

Louis smashed his fist into Larry's face again and again until
it became a bloody blur. Then suddenly, he stopped, the rage
waning. He let go, drawing a deep, tremulous breath. Larry's
head fell to one side.

Louis crawled off him and slumped against the wall, still
trembling. Water spewed from the broken pipe, running like a
river out the open cell door and down the hall. The metal door
to the office was ajar.

Louis grabbed the bars and pulled himself upright, leaning his
head against the cool steel. He drew a hand across his mouth,
and slowly stepped over Larry, into the corridor

He touched the rope burn on his neck and thought about
Eugene. Standing in the forest that day last December, he had
wondered what Eugene's last moments were like. Now he knew.

He staggered out into the outer office. It was deserted. Whoever
the second man was, he was long gone. The radio was silent.
Louis looked at Dodie's closed door and wiped a hand across his
mouth. His eyes fell for a second on the phone, then to the open
door.

A moan came from deep within the cell area. A short burst of
static crackled up from the radio. Louis went back to the cell.
Larry was still sprawled out in a pool of water. Louis stepped
over him, grabbed his shoes and the journal papers from under
his bunk and hurried back to the outer office. He spotted a used
Ziploc sandwich bag in the trash and snatched it up. He put the
papers in the bag and stuffed it in the waistband of his underwear
under the jumpsuit. He looked back at the cell and headed for
the open door.

Outside, atop the steps, he paused, the cold night air hitting
him in the chest like a fist. He glanced around at the empty street,
pulled the collar of the sodden orange jumpsuit up around his
raw neck and began to run.

CHAPTER 27

Louis huddled in the shadows of a large shrub. He was only a block from the jail. The square was empty, its storefronts dark. A lone traffic light at the intersection blinked yellow. He could see the old clock on the courthouse, glowing in the darkness like a full yellow moon. It was 1:45 A.M.

Louis felt for the Ziploc bag under the jumpsuit. It was still there. He started to shiver. Jesus, it was cold. His sneakers were heavy with water and the jumpsuit clung to his skin, the cuffs and sleeves crisp from the cold. He cupped his hands together and blew into them, his breath clouding the still air. He rubbed his face and neck, wincing as he touched the spot where the rope had left its mark.

He was scared. Afraid to run, more afraid to go back. He stood up slowly, the muscles in his legs stiff. Lurching across the street, he slipped into an alley behind Benson's Furniture.

As he climbed over cardboard boxes and around trash cans, his mind reeled. This was insane. He should go back, call Dodie, tell him what had happened. Dodie couldn't turn his back on this. At the very least, he would transfer him to another jail. But then the feel of the rope around his neck came back to him, and he almost gagged. He kept going, cutting through another alley.

Halfway through, he stopped, falling back against a brick wall. His feet stung, a prickling pain eating away at his toes. A car came rattling down the street, its broken muffler piercing the quiet. Louis sank down into the shadows until it passed.

The streets were quiet again. Where the hell were they? Sleeping? He knew Mike was on patrol and wouldn't bother to find out why Larry didn't answer his calls; he'd just keep on driving and try again later. He was shaking violently now from the cold, and knew he had to find someone to help him.

Winston Gibbons . . . he was the only one who could help him now. He had to get to a phone. Bessie's was only about a mile away. Maybe there was time to get home. He had to try.

"Larry! Larry!" Mike shouted, pulling at Larry's shirt. When Larry didn't move, Mike dragged him down the flooded, dark corridor and out into the bright lights of the office.

"Goddamn," he muttered, seeing Larry's bruised and bloody face. Mike looked frantically around the office, unsure what to do.

Call the sheriff. He was gonna really be pissed at all this. He ran to the phone and dialed Dodie's home. The call roused Dodie from his sleep.

"Sheriff, this is Deputy Mike Peterson."

"What's goin' on? What time is it?"

"It's after one, sir. We got a bad situation here, Sheriff."

"What happened?"

"Larry's bad hurt, sir. He's bleeding. I think he needs an ambulance."

"What the hell happened to him?" Dodie shouted.

"I don't know. I just came in and found him like this. All beat-up."

"Jesus Christ, Mike. Is there anything missing?"

"Just Louis, sir."

Louis kept to the alleys, making his way across town. By the time he reached the tracks, he was exhausted. His feet throbbed and he could no longer feel his fingers. The frosted jumpsuit chafed his skin. He stepped over the rails and slipped, falling onto the gravel embankment. The jagged edge of a broken bottle ripped into his left arm.

He cursed softly and pulled a piece of glass from his arm, grimacing. He put his hand over the cut and felt a warm liquid ooze through his fingers.

He staggered to his feet, stumbling on. He skidded down the

loose gravel, his momentum carrying him down the grassy slope that led to the back of Tinker's store. Leaning against the shingled building, he inhaled deeply, fighting for breath. He could feel the blood oozing through his fingers.

Louis slumped down the wall to the sidewalk, tears of hopelessness in his eyes. He brushed them away with his forearm, and looked down at his throbbing arm. He wiped the blood on the leg of the suit and returned pressure to the wound.

He heard a squeal of tires and he craned his neck to see a squad car come to a stop in front of Bessie's house. He struggled to stand only to fall back weakly against the building. He was too late. They were looking for him.

He slowly got up and made his way toward the shadows at the end of the building. Another car pulled up in front of Bessie's house and he watched as a deputy sprang from it, joined by two state troopers from a third. The policemen hurried up the walk to Bessie's house and, finding the door locked, kicked it in. Louis looked away, praying Bessie would be all right. He ran an arm across his frozen nose, and tried to think.

Even if he got away, where would he go? Jackson? To Gibbons? Jesus, this was getting so screwed-up even Gibbons wouldn't be able to straighten it out. Louis hobbled to the back of the building toward the tracks. A cold, heavy fear began to ferment in his belly. He stared at the squad cars, trying to pick out Dodie. There was nothing to do but surrender; he had no choice.

He faced the lights, taking a crooked step in their direction. "Mister Kincaid."

A spasm of fright paralyzed him until he recognized the deep voice. Louis turned around. Alfred Tinker stood in the dimness of the streetlamp, dressed in a robe and slippers. He looked over Louis's shoulder at the police cars then back at Louis's bloody sleeve.

"Come," Tinker said. He walked toward the rear entrance of the store. Louis limped along after him.

Dodie pushed open the double doors to the office and stopped, the doors banging closed behind him. His eyes hardened as they moved around the office. The dispatcher's desk was empty. The radio spewed out a cacophony of codes, static, and cries for acknowledgment.

Larry was sprawled in a swivel chair in the center of the room, his uniform unbuttoned, his white undershirt splattered with blood. Mike hovered over him. A widening pool of water was puddled near the cellblock door.

"Sheriff! Sheriff! Anyone there?" the radio blurted.

Dodie looked at the radio then back at Mike. "Peterson, man the desk."

Mike nodded and hurried to the radio. Dodie went to Larry, stopping by his outstretched leg. He put his hands on his hips and stared down at Larry's shredded face.

"You need an ambulance?" Dodie asked.

"Fuck no," Larry muttered. He picked up a cotton ball from the first-aid kit and dabbed at his split lip. Dodie glanced at the pool of water, then back at Larry.

"How did this happen?"

"The fucker jumped me."

"What the *fuck* were you doing in the cell?"

Larry's fingers began to shake as he dabbed at his cuts. "The water pipe broke. I went in to look at it."

Dodie stared at him for a minute then turned and walked into the cellblock.

Larry began to rummage through the first-aid kit for a Band-Aid. He rose unsteadily from the chair and moved to the mirror on the wall. He grimaced.

"Fuck . . . Look at me. . . . Fuck . . ."

Larry leaned closer to the mirror, pressing the Band-Aid against his forehead. He saw the sheriff's reflection behind him.

"Cutter . . ."

Larry turned.

The sheriff held up the dripping noose. "What the fuck were you gonna do with this?" he asked through clenched teeth. "Tie the pipe back together?"

Larry opened his mouth and without saying a word, closed it again. A small puddle was forming under the rope. Larry swallowed dryly.

"It was a joke."

"A joke?" Dodie repeated.

"A joke, yeah."

Dodie threw the rope at Larry. Larry ducked, batting it away.

"I don't like your kind of jokes, mister. Get out. You're fired," Dodie said.

"What?" Larry croaked.

"You heard me. Get out."

Larry stood up and took a step toward Dodie. "You wanna hear about jokes?" he shouted, pointing at Dodie. "You're the fuckin' joke! You know what they call you upstairs? 'Do-do bird' Dodie . . . Screw-up Sam . . . and that's just a few."

Dodie squinted at him. "Move it, mister. Out of this office."

Larry just stared.

"Now!" Dodie thundered.

Larry glanced at Mike then back at Dodie. The veins rippled down his temples and he stepped around the sheriff, grabbing his jacket off the chair. He stormed out the door, shoving it open with both hands.

Dodie looked down at the rope and slowly bent to pick it up.

Junior came in, his eyes trailing after Larry. "What's with him?" Junior asked, motioning toward Larry.

Dodie threw the rope on a desk. His eyes moved to Mike, who quickly turned back to the radio. "What's going on out at Bessie's?" Dodie asked.

Junior shook his head. "No sign of him, sir."

"Who's out there?"

"Our guys. A couple of troopers. Sheriff Vance wanted to know if we needed help. They want to know if Louis is dangerous."

Dodie rubbed the bridge of his nose and looked down at the rope. "Tell them no," he said softly.

Dodie walked to his office and Junior could hear him searching the drawers for the Jim Beam. He sidled over to Mike.

"What the fuck happened here?"

Mike eyes darted nervously. "Sheriff fired Larry."

"Why?"

Mike pointed to the rope on the desk. "He tried to hang Louis."

Junior walked over to Larry's desk and stared down at the noose. He felt a wave of queasiness as he thought about that cold December morning in the woods. He let out a long breath.

He looked at the rope dangling in front of the top drawer. Picking up a pencil, he flipped the rope out of the way and opened the top drawer. He took out the Federal Express envelope and headed toward Dodie's office.

Louis was sitting on the couch, wearing a pair of Tinker's size 44 pants, a quilt over his bare shoulders. Stretching his legs out toward the fireplace, he took a sip of the steaming cup of coffee. He glanced at the phone, thinking about the message he had just left on Gibbons's machine. *"The shit hit the fan. I need you."* He knew it was enough.

Tinker brought the coffeepot to the small living room, spread a tattered kitchen towel on the end table, and set the pot down. He gingerly pulled the quilt off Louis's shoulder and examined the freshly-cleaned cut on his arm. "It'll be fine."

"Hurts like the devil," Louis said.

"It's very deep. You should really get a tetanus."

Louis almost laughed. "When I get time."

"You want ice for that eye?"

Louis touched the bruised cheek but shook his head.

"So, what are you going to do?" Tinker asked, sitting down next to him.

"I need to call the sheriff."

"There's the phone."

Louis looked at it. Then he lifted his eyes to the kitchen window, watching the flashes of red and blue travel across the curtains. He rose stiffly, went into the dark kitchen and peered through the curtains.

The kitchen faced the street and below he could see Junior, two troopers, and a strange man in streetclothes standing in front of Bessie's. Three squad cars were parked at angles in the street. God, what a mess this was.

Tinker came up behind him.

"Mr. Tinker, I better leave. They'll probably come over here and I don't want you involved in this."

"You did not involve me, I involved myself," Tinker said. "When I saw them take you away the other day, I got mad. I've been angry a long time, angry at almost everything. But I just sat on the porch and watched." Tinker paused. "I thought it was time I did something."

Tinker fell silent. The squawk of a squad-car radio filtered up to them.

"Did you kill that girl's father?" Tinker asked quietly.

"No," Louis said.

"Then why did you escape from that jail?"

Louis hesitated, then tilted his head back. Even in the dim light of the street lamp, Tinker could see the rope burn under Louis's jaw. He closed his eyes for a moment.

"Mr. Tinker," Louis said, "I didn't kill Max Lillihouse. I think he was killed because he was involved in the lynching."

"So you know who killed that boy, then," Tinker said.

Louis looked at Tinker then nodded. Pulling the quilt tighter, Louis hobbled back to the sofa and sat down. Tinker followed him.

"Yeah, I know who did it," Louis said quietly. "Max Lillihouse, George Harvey the jeweler, and Earl Mulcahey. They were all involved."

"So you did it," Tinker said. "You said you would solve it and you did."

Louis shook his head slowly. "I didn't do anything, really. I didn't even know what I was doing half the time. Hell, at one point, I thought it was these men's *fathers* who lynched Eugene Graham."

"But you still found your answers," Tinker said.

"I suppose, but you know what's funny? The answers didn't come from the men, they came from the women. Grace Lillihouse, Ethel Mulcahey, and even Maisey Kelly."

Tinker's eyes grew distant. "But there's no justice for that boy. The men who killed him are all dead," he said.

"No," Louis said. His gaze drifted to the Ziploc bag on the end table. "There was a fourth man, too."

"Who?"

"I'm not sure." Louis took a sip of coffee. "But if Max was trying to eliminate his partners in crime, then he had one to go."

"But then he was killed," Tinker said. "By the fourth man?"

"That's what I suspect, but I can't prove it. Not yet, anyway."

Tinker shook his head. "If you knew who killed Mr. Lillihouse, then your puzzle would really be solved."

"I know who did it," said a small voice from the door.

Louis and Tinker looked at Teesha standing in the hall. Her skinny arms hung from the limp lace sleeves of her cotton nightgown. All the braids were gone and her hair formed a fuzzy black aureole around her small face. Tinker rose slowly, moving to his granddaughter. He gently took her shoulders.

"How do you know?"

Teesha spoke with a teenager's arrogance. "I saw it," she said. "I saw it from my window."

CHAPTER 28

L ouis parted the curtains on Teesha's bedroom window and looked down into the street.

"I was standing right here," Teesha said softly at his side.

There was a streetlight just to the left of the window, which illuminated the street. Louis knew Teesha had had a better view of Max's car than he did from his own window. From where she stood, she would have seen the passenger-side door, a good portion of the roof, and the entire block from the intersection to the corner.

Louis turned to face Teesha. Louis could tell from her eyes she was scared, only a trace of her usual insolence visible in the set of her lips.

"Teesha," Tinker said quietly. "You need to tell Mr. Kincaid what you saw."

She bit her lip and looked up at her grandfather. "Then the police will come."

"Mr. Kincaid *is* the police," Tinker said.

"Not anymore, I done seen him get arrested."

"Teesha," Tinker urged.

Teesha nodded. "All right."

Louis gently pulled her to the window and let her look out, keeping a reassuring hand on her back. Louis felt Teesha's shoulder rise and fall with a heavy sigh.

"I was awake, listening to music. The only light I had on was that one there, near the bed," she said. "I heard a car door close. I wondered who was out there. So I went and looked." She glanced back at Tinker.

"Teesha, why did you wonder? It was just a car," Louis asked. He needed to make sure she was telling him the truth.

She shrugged. "I jus' did." Her eyes flicked to Tinker but she said nothing.

"I can tell you why she looked," Tinker said. "There's a boy, works at the Texaco in town. Gets off at two in the morning," Tinker said. "She's snuck out to meet him before."

Louis looked back at her. "Is that true?"

Teesha nodded. Tinker gave her a firm pat on her shoulder. "Tell him the rest, girl."

"Well, I looked outside. There was two cars out there. That big silver one and another one, a smaller one. The silver one was in front. I could see a man sitting in there."

"What about the other one?" Louis asked.

"The door opened and a woman got out."

Louis took Teesha's arms and turned her to face him. "A woman?"

"Yeah, a woman," Teesha repeated, looking at Louis like he was stupid.

"What did she look like?" Louis asked.

Teesha jerked her shoulders away and resumed looking out the window. "She was a white woman, wearing a dark coat and a hat. I didn't see all of her."

"What color of hair?"

Teesha sighed. "I told ya, she was wearing a hat!"

"What kind of hat, what color?" Louis pressed.

"I don't know . . . like a blue thing."

"What happened then?" Louis asked.

"The woman got into the big car."

"And?"

Teesha looked back at Louis. "She was in there 'bout ten minutes. Then the inside of the car looked like a firecracker went off. Sounded like it, too."

Louis put a hand on the windowsill. "What happened then?"

"The woman got out of the big car," Teesha said, turning from the window, indicating her story was over. Louis watched her walk back toward the living room.

"Teesha," Louis called. "What did she do then?"

"The white woman?" Teesha asked.

Louis nodded.

Teesha put her hand on her hip. "She got back into that yellow car and left."

Louis sat on the edge of Tinker's bed, his hands clasped. Tinker brought him a neatly folded set of tan sweats, a long-sleeved T-shirt, and a pair of rolled socks.

"This is the only thing I have that will fit you," Tinker said. "Take this, too," he said, holding up a huge parka. "It's supposed to snow."

Louis looked up, frowning. "Snow?"

"It does, once or twice every couple years."

"No thanks. I'm going to be running. It'll slow me down."

Louis stared absently at the floor. Tinker sat down next to him. Louis could hear the clock on the nightstand ticking away the minutes.

"You don't really think that girl killed her father, do you?" Tinker asked.

Louis shook his head, reaching for the clothes. "Abby drives a yellow car. But I can't imagine it. I just can't."

"What will you do if you find out she did?" Tinker asked.

Louis pulled on the hooded sweatshirt. "I don't know." If Abby did kill her father, he wanted to know why. He wanted to know what she was thinking. Was it to go back to school? Was it to stop the abuse? Or worse yet, was it so she could be with him? No, she couldn't do it. No matter what Teesha had seen, he just couldn't see Abby pulling the trigger of a gun pointed at the head of her father. But he knew one thing for sure: No matter what had happened in that Monte Carlo, Abby needed his help. He had to go to her.

"Where are you going?" Tinker asked when Louis stood up.

"To see her."

"Why?"

"Because she'll tell me the truth."

Tinker came closer. "You'll never make it. Call your sheriff."

Louis shook his head. "I can't."

"You told me you trusted your sheriff."

Louis stood up, shaking his head. "It's not that simple anymore. Now it's *my* life we're talking about. And I won't spend it in some damn Southern prison for a crime I didn't commit." The anger passed and Louis rubbed his face. "Right now I don't trust anyone."

Tinker stared at him silently. Louis picked up the plastic bag with the journal pages and tucked it in his pants.

"If anything happens to me," Louis continued, "please call the number I left by the phone. His name is Gibbons, with the FBI in Jackson. Tell him everything I told you."

Tinker nodded again. "There's a window you can climb out that will put you on the roof. There are trees to get down on the other side."

Tinker led Louis to the back of the apartment and opened a small window that looked out onto a flat roof. Tinker pushed out the screen, and Louis stuck his head out into the cold night air. He could see the police on the street below. Louis turned back to Tinker. He could think of nothing else to say.

Tinker extended a hand and Louis took it. Tinker squeezed tightly. Louis pulled him to him and gave him a quick hug.

"God be with you," Tinker said.

Louis nodded and hopped out onto the roof. He scurried across the tarred roof to the other side. There were three sprawling oaks, and Louis jumped the small gap to the nearest tree, swinging himself over to a thick limb. There was a familiar smell to the air, heavy and wet. Snow was coming.

CHAPTER 29

L ouis ran along the empty blacktop road. Despite the cold, he was sweating. He had come nearly five miles and still had one to go. It gave him time to think and he didn't like the thoughts that rumbled around in his head.

One way or another, it was almost over for him. He could feel the end coming, an end to the last two disastrous months, and an end to this strange part of his life that had begun that day last December when he stood in the mud staring down at Eugene Graham's yellowed skull.

After a quarter of a mile, he spotted the porch light of the Lillihouse mansion and it spurred him onward. He cut across the grass and hopped the white brick wall on the east side of the house. A light was on downstairs and another one on the second floor. He estimated it was about three A.M.

He paused near the door, trying to remember if he had seen a security system on his visits. He edged across the long porch toward the front door. It was locked. He moved off the porch to the bushes, going to the first window. It, too, was locked. He crept around to the back of the house to the patio. The curtains on the French doors to the dining area were open and Louis could see inside. A wall sconce burned faintly in the dining room.

He tried the door, and it opened with a squeak. There were more of the sconces to guide his way through the hallway and out into the foyer. He paused, looking into the dark library. The two wing chairs were black silhouettes against the orange glow of the dying fire in the hearth.

Louis held his breath, listening. Silence. He looked up the staircase. There was a light on in one of the bedrooms. He put a hand on the bannister and started up. The stair creaked loudly under his weight.

"Mother?"

Louis froze. It was Abby; her voice had come from the library. "Mother? Is that you?"

With a quick glance up the stairs, he descended quietly. She was sitting in one of the chairs by the fire. Her face had been hidden from him by the chair's wing, but as she rose slowly now, he saw it in the faint firelight. Her look of apprehension quickly faded when she recognized him.

"Louis," she said. "What are you doing here?"

"I had to see you."

Her eyes swept over his sweatsuit, returning to his sweaty face as she shook her head in confusion. "I thought, I thought you were—"

"I was." It crossed his mind to tell her what had happened, but he quickly dismissed it. He ventured closer, seeing her more clearly now. She was wearing a nightgown, an unbelted robe hanging loosely over her slender body. Her hair was bedraggled and she looked dazed, almost drugged. It occurred to him that she might have taken a sedative, but there was something else in her expression, a strangely passive, almost resigned look, as if all the energy had been drained out of her. It was quiet and a part of his brain was alert for the sounds of sirens outside. How long would it take Dodie to figure out Louis would come here?

"Abby . . ." He started toward her and she took a step back. He paused, surprised. The look on her face the day of his arraignment came back to him in that moment. God, did she believe he had killed Max? "Abby," he said softly. "I didn't kill your father."

"I know," she said, the words coming out in a strained whisper. She drew her arms up around herself and looked away. She started to cry softly. "Oh, Louis, I never meant . . . I didn't want . . ." Her voice trailed off.

Louis couldn't move. *Oh no, dear God. Please—she didn't do it, she couldn't kill him.* His brain was reeling, a million thoughts and images rushing through. Abby's beaten face, her hand on his gun. Red blood, a yellow car. Temporary insanity, diminished capacity . . . all those damn legal names that could be put on murder to make it sound like something it wasn't.

He went to her, enfolding her in his arms. She slumped against him, crying. "Abby, it's all right," he whispered. "It will be all right. You didn't mean it. I won't let them hurt you. It will be all right, I promise. There are—"

"Detective . . ."

Louis's head shot up in the direction of the soft voice. Grace was standing under the archway.

"Mrs. Lillihouse, Abby—"

"My daughter will be all right."

Louis stared at Grace, shocked at the woman's utter calm in the face of Abby's pain. "How can you say that?" he demanded. "After what she's been through, how can you just stand there and say that?"

"Louis, no," Abby said.

Grace's eyes were locked on Louis's. She shook her head sadly. "Abby didn't kill her father, Detective."

Abby pushed away from Louis's chest. "Mother, don't—"

"I killed him," Grace said.

Louis just stood there, too shocked to move. Finally he turned to look at Abby, who had drifted away to stand at the fireplace. "You knew?" he whispered.

Abby nodded numbly. Tears fell silently down her face.

"How long?" he asked hoarsely.

"I just told her, Detective, only about an hour ago," Grace said.

Louis looked back at Grace, dumbfounded. Grace shivered slightly and walked slowly toward the fire, stopping several feet away from Abby. Louis watched her, wanting to spin her around, shout at her, shake her in anger. How long had she expected him to rot in that damn jail? How long had she intended to let him take the blame?

Grace turned to face him. Her mouth quivered and she shook her head. "I've called the sheriff," she said.

"What?"

Her fingers curled over the top of the chair. "When I heard you downstairs, I called them." Her shoulders were shaking. She was trying so hard to maintain her composure. "Don't worry, Detective. I'll tell them the truth." She paused, lifting her chin. "Believe me, I wouldn't have let you go to prison. I'm . . . sorry."

Louis came around the chair and slumped into it. He pulled in a deep breath and ran a trembling hand over his face and down over his raw neck. He closed his eyes. "Sorry," he repeated in a whisper.

He felt a touch on his arm. He looked up into Grace's pale blue eyes. She blinked rapidly and let her arm fall. She moved away into the shadows. Louis looked up at Abby, but she was staring down into the fire as if mesmerized.

"Why?" Louis asked. When Grace didn't answer, he turned to look at her. "You didn't have to kill him. There were other ways."

Grace was standing at the window, holding back the drapes, seeming to look out at the falling snow. She shook her head without looking back at Louis. "You don't understand," she said softly.

"Yes, I do, Mrs. Lillihouse," he said. "I've seen this situation before. I've seen women who've been abused who manage to get out, who—"

"I didn't do it for me," Grace interrupted. Her eyes went quickly to Abby. "I did it for her." She looked back at Louis. "I did it for you."

Louis waited, unmoving.

"He was going to kill you that night," Grace said. "He told me before he left. He told me he was going to find you and kill you. He hated you, hated the thought of you and Abigail together." Grace put out a hand to the piano to steady herself. "I . . . I followed him," she went on, her voice quavering. "I thought I could talk to him. I thought . . . I don't know, I thought . . ."

Grace brought up a trembling hand to her forehead. Louis watched her, ready to catch her if she fainted. But she drew in a deep breath and with an unsteady step, went to a bookcase. She pulled out a book and came over to him, holding it out. Louis looked up at her questioningly.

"Do you recognize it?" she asked.

It was a poetry book, the one Abby had brought to his room that night. He took it, turning it over in his hands. Suddenly it was all clear. "It's a copy," he said slowly. "It's a copy of the book we found with Eugene Graham." He looked up at her. "You replaced it, didn't you, after he disappeared with it?"

"Yes," Grace said. "So my mother would not know I lent it to him."

Louis shook his head. "Mrs. Lillihouse, why did you show me this? What does this have to do with you killing your husband?"

"Nothing," she whispered. "Everything."

Grace drifted away, returning to the window. Louis looked over at Abby. She was dry-eyed now and was watching Grace carefully. As if coming out of a trance, she went to the window, put an arm around Grace's shoulder and led her back to the wing chair. Grace sat down heavily, closing her eyes.

"Tell him, Mother," Abby said gently. "Tell him what you told me."

Grace did not move. Louis waited, holding the book between his hands. The room was growing cold.

"Gene took care of the horses," Grace said softly. "He came every week, on Friday. He would walk over from Sweetwater."

Louis fingered the book, letting her talk.

Grace opened her eyes, but her gaze was distant. "Gene was different, different from the other Negroes . . ." She focused on Louis and smiled gently. "I'm sorry . . . from the other black men we had working here. He loved books, any kind of book. But especially poetry."

Louis glanced up at Abby, standing over the chair.

"We used to talk," Grace went on. "About the poems, about life. I loved Emily Dickinson." She smiled slightly. " 'I'm Nobody / Who are you? Are you Nobody, too? Then there's a pair of us / Don't tell! They'd advertise, you know . . .' Gene loved that poem."

A log fell in the hearth, briefly bathing Grace in gold.

"We talked about what we were going to be when we grew up and got away from this place," Grace said. "He wanted to be a baseball player." She looked at Louis. "Did you know that?"

Louis nodded.

"He said he would become rich and then he would come back and be a teacher."

Louis leaned forward, elbows on knees, staring blankly at the book.

"Gene didn't deserve to die," she whispered.

Louis shook his head. "Mrs. Lillihouse, you had to have known what this would lead to. You had to know what would happen if you and Eugene—"

Grace closed her eyes. "I didn't . . . We didn't." She drew in a deep, shuddering breath. "You're right, of course," she whispered. "I should have known."

She twisted back to look at Abby. "But we did nothing wrong," she said, her voice pleading. "You have to believe that. We did nothing wrong."

Louis saw the tears welling in her eyes. He rose and went to the bar, returning with a small glass of sherry. Grace took it, gripping it with trembling hands.

"Thank you," she whispered.

Louis sat back down in the chair, watching Grace's wan face as she sipped the sherry. He suddenly thought of the two photographs of Grace, from her high-school annual and her wedding. Two photos, taken just a year apart, but so different.

"Mrs. Lillihouse," he said softly. "Do you know what happened to Eugene?"

Grace stared at him for a moment, gripping the tiny glass. Suddenly her face crumbled. She began to weep softly. The glass fell to the carpet.

Abby knelt in front of her. "Mother, don't. You don't have to."

Grace shook her head. "No, I'm tired of it," she said. "I'm tired of holding it inside me. It has made me ill and I want it out, I want it out!"

Grace took several deep breaths and brushed a strand of hair back from her face.

"One night my father came to my room," she said. "It was just before my seventeenth birthday. He said he had heard that I had been with the Negro Eugene Graham." Grace's eyes glistened as she looked at Louis. " *'Been with'* . . . that was the words he used."

Louis watched Grace's face harden as the memories came into focus. "I told him it wasn't true, that Gene was just my friend. But Daddy . . . he wouldn't believe me, and he said things. Things about his only child, his daughter, disgracing the family." Grace's voice had become a low monotone. "Daddy never talked to me like that before, he had never looked so sad. He said he was *'disappointed'* in me. It was so . . . ugly."

Louis looked up at Abby. It was obvious from her pale face that Grace had not told her this part.

"But then Daddy told me that everything was going to be all

right," Grace continued. "He said he was going to take care of 'the *situation*'. He said that I was going to marry Max."

"Your father arranged your marriage?" Louis asked.

Grace nodded woodenly. "Daddy said that no decent man would have me if they found out about Gene." She lowered her head. "But Max didn't care, Daddy said. Max said he'd marry me no matter what I had done."

Louis closed his eyes, now seeing the faded newspaper photograph of Grace Ketcher just after she was crowned Miss Magnolia. She had looked like a princess, and that's the way her life had been, carefully laid out for her by her father, right down to the prince who would come to her rescue. Grace Ketcher had been just a girl, a weak girl who trusted Daddy to chart out her life and then allowed Max to destroy whatever was left of it. Grace's wedding portrait came back to him, and the sad *blankness* in her pretty young face. He looked at her now. He could see an echo of it still, as if someone had just erased her.

"I wanted to talk to someone, I needed to talk to someone," Grace said. "I waited that Friday for Gene to come, but he didn't. I thought Daddy had fired him. And then when Gene disappeared, I thought he finally had just left, gone to play ball like he said he would."

Louis's eyes dropped to the book in his hands; he couldn't bring himself to look at Grace.

"Max was the one who told me," Grace said suddenly.

Louis looked up at her. Her face was streaked with tears.

"Max told me that Gene had been killed," she said. "He told me that Daddy had arranged it."

"What?" Louis said.

Grace shook her head slowly. "I didn't believe him. I didn't want to believe Daddy could hurt someone." She paused, wiping at her face. "But I knew how Daddy got his way about things he wanted done." Tears fell down Grace's face. "And I knew that Gene never would have left without saying good-bye."

Louis shook his head in disbelief. "And you never spoke to your father about it? You never asked him if Max was telling the truth?"

Grace's shoulders slumped. "I couldn't. . . . I couldn't. I was seventeen, don't you see? He died two years later."

Louis's eyes went up to the portrait of Colonel Ketcher that hung above the fireplace. The man's handsome face was inscrutable in the dark. Louis looked down into Abby's eyes. *No more,* they pleaded, *no more, let her be.*

"I hated him," Grace said quietly. She was looking up at the portrait now. "I hated him until the day he died for killing Gene."

Louis sighed, leaning forward and resting his elbows on his knees. He hung his head, bringing the poetry book up to his forehead. He closed his eyes. For a moment it was so quiet he could hear Grace's ragged breathing.

"Mrs. Lillihouse," he whispered.

Slowly he looked up. Abby was watching him, her hand on Grace's shoulder. He set the poetry book on the table.

"Mrs. Lillihouse, your father didn't kill Eugene," he said gently. "Max did."

For several seconds, Grace didn't move. Then she blinked rapidly and her hand fluttered up toward her neck as if she were choking. Abby grabbed her hand, holding it tight.

"How do you know this?" Grace whispered.

Louis hesitated. "I have proof," he said softly, hoping she wouldn't ask anything else. "I have proof that Max killed Eugene, with the help of . . . other men."

"Who?" Grace demanded.

"Mrs. Lillihouse—"

"Who? Tell me, please!"

Louis let out a deep breath. "George Harvey, Earl Mulcahey, and one other. . . . I don't know who for sure."

A strange look came over Grace's eyes, as if she had suddenly been carried off somewhere. She closed her eyes, but her hand was still gripping Abby's.

"What happened?" Grace said.

"No, Mother," Abby said, her eyes frantically going to Louis's.

"Mrs. Lillihouse, I don't really know how—"

"Yes, you do," Grace said. She let go of Abby and sat forward in the chair. Her eyes burned into Louis, glistening with tears.

Louis could feel the plastic bag against his skin beneath his waistband. How could he tell her the truth? She was far too fragile.

Grace reached out for his hand. Her fingers, cold and soft, closed tightly around his. "Tell me," she said. "Tell me the truth."

"Mrs. Lillihouse—"

"I want to know!" she said, her eyes bright with tears. "I was never told anything but lies. After thirty years, I have a right to know. I want to know what happened to Gene. Tell me the truth, please!"

Louis slowly withdrew his hand. He reached under his sweatshirt and pulled out the plastic bag. He took out the journal papers and handed them to Grace.

CHAPTER 30

From the Journal of Earl Mulcahey, August 25, 1976:

I have to tell this about what happened that night. I don't know if anyone will ever read it but I figure if I write it down maybe it will mean something.

It was June 9, 1955. The sky was real black and it was a warm, sticky night. I remember the frogs chirping like there was a million of them. There was four of us. Max was driving a big black convertible he got from his daddy's car lot. It was in there for repairs and the muffler was real loud. We were drinking Dixies and we tossed the beer bottles out of the car. I remember the wind in our faces and us laughing and the bottles crashing on the road behind us as we drove down old 234 by my house. I never drunk much before that night and I never touched a drop since but that night it just seemed like the right thing to do. It was the only way I could be one of them.

We were rounding the curve by the creek when we saw him. He was walking home toward Sweetwater from his school in Cotton Town. Max saw him first and his face got all twisted up and his eyes got all fire-like because Max hated Gene. You got to know Gene sometimes did some horse-grooming stuff for Grace Kelcher. Grace was a real nice girl with a soft heart and she liked Gene because he was one of the few Negroes around who went to school and could read the stuff Grace liked.

Anyway, Max thought Gene had a crush on Grace or maybe vice versa and that made Max real mad. Whether she did or didn't I didn't know but either way Max thought so and to Max that's all that mattered.

Then Wallie says something like, "Let's play with him." So Max pulls the car over and all the sudden we're all in this circle around Gene and his eyes get big and he's acting real nervous-like. Now, Gene wasn't stupid and he knew he couldn't fight all of us so he tries to reason with us. But Max and Wallie were pretty tanked-up, and there was no reason. So they started shoving him and finally Max grabs him and starts shaking him and telling him to keep his eyes off Grace.

Gene got scareder and started throwing wild punches. By now I was scared too because I had decided this wasn't what I had in mind when I went along on the ride.

Well, Gene decides he ain't going to win this fight no way, no how, so he takes off into the woods. Now, Gene is a pretty good runner but Max was our school's best sprinter and he caught him a quarter mile or so into the trees. I couldn't keep up with the others so good, the branches and everything cutting me when I ran. When I got there Wallie was kicking him but Max was doing most of the hitting, smacking him on the head. Gene was bleeding pretty good when Max pulled out his pocketknife. I knew things was getting crazy but I couldn't talk. I just couldn't. Wallie took a piece of the tree and was hitting Gene with it and all Gene could do was scream and hold his hands over his head. Max and Wallie kept yelling things at him like "white woman fucker" and "nigger filth" and Gene just kept screaming.

Max stabbed him around the shoulders and on the arms but Gene was still yelling. George hit him a few times with a branch but mostly George stayed back just watching. His eyes was strange-looking and he was sweating real heavy. Then Max says we need to do this right. He tells George to go back to the Olds and get the rope out of the trunk. Max pulls Gene to his feet and sets him up against a tree, slapping at his face. Max used his lighter to see better and it was then I could see Gene's face. His eyes was half closed and he was crying.

Gene was wearing a rope around his waist for a belt and Wallie unties this and jerks Gene's pants down and Max puts his knife right up to Gene's penis. Gene is crying real loud now and tries to protect himself and Max just keeps slashing away at his hands. Gene's only got one good hand but he doesn't pull them away and they both get all sliced up. Max keeps cutting and cutting but Gene doesn't pull them away.

George comes back with the rope and Wallie makes a noose. I think I said something then but I can't remember. Nobody was listening anyhow. They tied his hands first with the rope from his pants. Then they put the noose over his head and jerked it up so Gene stood on his toes. Gene looked right at me quiet for a second like he was asking me to do something. But it was like I was frozen.

Then Max cuts off his pecker. It wasn't a clean cut cuz the knife wasn't real sharp and it took a long time and blood got all over. I knew someone would hear the screaming. They had to because it was the loudest screaming I ever heard.

Max held the penis with a piece torn off Gene's shirt and threw it at Wallie, laughing about not wanting to touch it and be a homo. Then they threw it in the trees. They told Gene he wasn't such a big boy now and that it wasn't true that niggers had bigger dicks than white boys and now Gene was living proof of that.

I think Gene passed out by now because it was so quiet I could hear the rope scraping against the tree as they hefted Gene higher in the air. They tied the rope off somewhere and we all stood around for a minute, the leaves blowing around our feet and a dog howling somewhere far off. The wind was blowing and it moved Gene's body back and forth real slow.

Then it was like all of a sudden they realized what they had done because Max and Wallie took off whooping and disappeared in the woods. George and I looked at each other and then ran, too. Max dropped me off at the road to our farm and I remember puking on the way up to the house. See, I only lived a quarter mile or so from the place where we stopped, and my daddy owned the land on both sides of 234 so it was my daddy's property they killed him on.

The next morning as the sun was just coming into view I got up and went back. I knew where it was because I knew those woods real good and I walked through the trees till I found him and cut him down. I had a small shovel and a tarp with me and I dug him a grave but I couldn't dig far because the ground was so hard. But I dressed him back up proper and took his shoes off because my daddy always said people aren't buried with their shoes. So I took them with me.

On the ground I saw a book and I picked it up. There was writing inside—To my friend Gene, from Grace. I figured borrowing this book was what helped get him killed so I tucked it in his shirt.

There was this funny-looking necklace there and I remembered seeing Max with it. Max bragged about having it and liked to pretend it was some important medal but I think he stole it from Grace's father when he was at their house. I thought about taking it back to Colonel Ketcher but I couldn't, because I would have to explain how I got it and I surely didn't want to do that. So I buried the necklace with him too. After I got him all covered up I said a prayer.

A few days later I know that Max and Wallie went back. Exactly for what I don't know except to maybe look for that necklace. Max must have been in a panic about it but they was so drunk that night they couldn't remember exactly where the place was. But I put so many leaves over the grave there was no way they could ever find it anyway.

I didn't talk to any of them after that. I never told Grace or anyone what happened that night. Not even my wife. I sold the farm. Seemed haunted to me and it was easier than living there every day. Sold it to Max. He didn't seem to have any trouble owning it.

Gene was sixteen when we murdered him. And all he did was be nice to Grace Ketcher and borrow a book. I still think about Gene sometimes late at night when Ethel is asleep and the kids are fussing at each other downstairs. I can still see the hopelessness in his eyes.

And sometimes, when the night is real dark and real cold and the wind starts howling, and I'm alone, I can still hear him screaming.

CHAPTER 31

Grace had taken the pages and read them without moving. Louis watched her, looking for some emotion, some sign of distress. But there had been nothing.

Now she was just sitting there, the papers in her lap, staring into the fire. Louis glanced to the window. It was so quiet he felt he could almost hear the snow falling.

Grace let out a small whimper. Louis looked back.

Her eyes were closed, and she was rocking gently back and forth in the chair, the pages clutched to her chest. The whimpering came out in one soft, long stream, like the sounds of a baby too exhausted to cry anymore.

"God, God . . . oh God," she whispered, rocking back and forth.

"Mother?" Abby took a step toward Grace, but Louis held up a hand to stop her. Louis dropped to one knee in front of Grace.

Grace let out a guttural shudder and began to cry, huge choking sobs that shook her body. She wrapped her arms around herself, as if trying to hold herself together. The papers floated to the floor.

"Mrs. Lillihouse," Louis said gently. He felt a tingle of fear run down his back. She was having a breakdown, right before his eyes.

"No, no, no," she murmured, rocking back and forth. "Oh dear God, no."

He grabbed her wrists, pulling her to a stop. "Mrs. Lillihouse!"

She froze, her eyes locked on his. Then her face crumbled. "Gene, oh my God, Gene . . ." she whispered. She collapsed against his chest.

Louis hesitated then awkwardly wrapped his arms around her.

He held her for several minutes, letting her cry. Over her shoulder, he met Abby's frightened eyes.

"Mrs. Lillihouse," he whispered. "Mrs. Lillihouse, please . . ."

He felt her pull in a deep breath. Slowly, she sat back in the chair. As he studied her pale, tear-streaked face, he felt his throat tighten.

"I'm sorry," he said softly.

"For what?" she said.

"For showing it to you. For . . . I don't know." Louis shook his head. "I'm just sorry."

Grace smoothed back her hair and wiped her face. She looked away, as if suddenly embarrassed to meet Louis's eyes.

"If I had known . . ." Grace said softly. "If I had known . . ." Her eyes drifted up to the portrait of the colonel. "I'm so sorry, Daddy. I'm sorry for everything."

Louis sat back and looked up at Abby. The fear was gone from her face. In its place was a new strength, a strength that came from knowing that her mother needed her. Abby knelt by the chair and took Grace's hand. To Louis, it was as if daughter had become mother.

Louis gathered up the journal papers. He looked at them for a moment then slipped them back in the bag. He stood and returned it to his pants.

"I'm not sorry anymore," Grace said.

Louis looked down at her. "Sorry?"

"I did it for you, but—"

"Mrs. Lillihouse," Louis said gently. "You didn't have to kill your husband. Not to protect me."

Grace stood up and walked slowly to the fireplace. "But I was so sure he was going to kill you," she went on, her voice taking on an urgency. "I believed him because . . . because . . . I could see it, I could see it in his eyes. He was changing so quickly. Your finding Gene started it and . . . it just got worse. Oh God, he hated you. He hated you because of Abigail and he hated you because you scared him. I didn't know why then. Now I do."

Louis hung his head slightly, listening.

"And then, that night, that night he hit Abigail . . ." Grace's eyes were bright with tears and she was shaking. "I heard her screaming. And I saw it in her face, the terror of her father." She paused. "And the disappointment in me."

"Oh, Mother," Abby whispered.

Grace didn't seem to hear her. "I didn't plan it. I didn't plan to shoot him. I just went there to talk," she said, the words tumbling out. "But he was drunk, and when I got in the car he told me to go home. He said I had no business interfering. He said he was going to save Abigail."

She took a step back, toward the bookcases, her hands suddenly balled-up in front of her. "And then he hit me. I reached for the door and he grabbed my neck. I couldn't get out. I couldn't get out."

She was breathing hard, her back against the bookcase. "And . . . and I looked at the gun. I looked at the gun on the seat. . . . It smelled, the car smelled like whiskey . . . and I saw his face, his ugly, ugly face and I couldn't stop, I couldn't stop—"

Louis heard a faint sound, something outside, like a distant cry.

"I picked it up," Grace said, her words pouring out over her sobs. "I picked it up, I picked up the gun and I shot him, I shot him." Grace bent slightly, clutching her stomach. "I picked up the gun and shot him. I shot him and I'm not sorry!"

Louis heard the sirens and looked toward the windows. The red-and-blue lights were moving toward them.

Abby went to her mother and wrapped her arms around her. The fire was dead and the room was dark and quiet. From outside came the sound of car doors slamming and the muted call of the police radio. Louis's eyes went from Abby and Grace huddled in the corner to the lights in the window.

"Abigail," Grace said, her words muffled in Abby's shoulder. "I'm not sorry. . . . I'm not sorry."

"It's all right, Mother," Abby said softly. "It's all right now."

Dodie's eyes moved from window to window of the mansion. There had been no sounds or sign of movement within. There was one light on upstairs, but the ground floor was dark. He had sent Mike around to look at the back, but there was no sign of anything wrong, not even one footprint in the snow. Dodie chewed on his cigar, debating what to do. Grace's call had come as a shock. He felt a tightening in his gut, an instinct he couldn't ignore. He knew Kincaid was inside; why else would Grace call?

Snowflakes fluttered across the top of the squad car. Dodie

brushed them away with his hand. He heard Junior's boots crunch on the gravel behind him but he did not turn.

"Sheriff, mayor's here."

"Christ. I told you to keep this quiet. Who called him?"

"He heard on his scanner."

Dodie looked over his shoulder. There were four cars, six policemen, two of them troopers from the highway patrol. He had wanted to handle this himself but word had gotten out, probably from Kelly. Dodie watched the troopers nervously. He didn't want them here; he didn't need them here.

Dodie saw the white Cadillac pulled up to the end of the drive. Kelly was hustling toward them, his long wool overcoat over his pants and pajama top. Dodie looked back toward the house.

"What are we going to do, Sheriff?" Junior asked.

"We're going to wait."

Junior leaned against the car. Kelly came up behind them and grabbed Dodie's arm, turning him. "How the hell could you let this happen?"

"I didn't let anything happen," Dodie replied, shrugging him off.

"You incompetent son of a bitch!" Kelly spit, grabbing Dodie again. "You really fucked this one up."

Dodie jerked away from him. "I didn't fuck anything up! You wanna blame somebody, go talk to that slimy snitch of yours, Cutter," Dodie said.

Kelly's eyes blazed. "If you did your job, I wouldn't have to have someone watching your ass."

Dodie took a deep breath. "Walt, if I was twenty years younger I'd take a swing at you. But it just ain't worth the effort. I just don't have the energy." Dodie turned to Junior. "Go get that bullhorn over there. I'm calling Kincaid out."

Walter Kelly glared at the back of Dodie's police parka. He rubbed his hands together then stuck them up in his armpits, trying to warm them. "Sam," he began, "we've always been friends."

Dodie shot him a look, but Kelly ignored it. "This is my town, and my people. Your people, too," he went on. "The man is an escaped murderer. You could justify anything you do—"

"Shut up, Walt."

"Do you understand the repercussions of a trial? Any kind of trial? Do you really want that? Don't you understand what's happening here?"

"I reckon maybe I don't."

"Then you're stupid. Your father would have never let him get to trial."

Dodie took off his cap and slapped it against his thigh to shake off the snow. He put it back on, tugging it down.

Junior hurried to them with the bullhorn. Dodie took it and turned away from Walter Kelly. "You'd better get back, Mayor," he said. "The shit might hit the fan here."

"Kincaid!"

Louis turned, his heart quickening at the sound of the sheriff's voice. He went to the window and peered out around the draperies.

Snow floated from a black sky, iridescent in the twirling, colorful lights of the police cars. Blazing white headlights formed blurry circles in the darkness. Shadows darted. Men shouted. Radio traffic was nasal and erratic. None of it looked real. But nothing seemed real now.

Louis could make out Dodie, Junior, and several other deputies positioned behind the cars. Louis stepped back from the window. Hell, he didn't even have his gun.

"Kincaid, don't make us come in there and get you," Dodie bellowed. "You caused me enough fuckin' trouble tonight."

Louis leaned against the wall. He parted the curtains again, watching as the troopers crept around the cars like a SWAT team. They were getting nervous. He had to do something to calm this whole situation down. He had to talk to the sheriff before he took the chance of opening the door. He tried the window but it wouldn't move. It wasn't locked; it was old and painted shut. Louis looked around and picked up a bronze horse. With a glance back at Abby and Grace, he banged it against the window, shattering one of the panes.

A volley of shots sent Louis to the floor, covering his head. Louis heard Abby scream.

"Get down!" he yelled back at her and Grace. This was bad, this was really bad, and someone was going to get hurt if he didn't do something quick.

Louis heard Dodie shouting. "Goddammit, you assholes, did

I say shoot? Did any one of you hear me say anything about fuckin' shooting?"

Silence. Louis lifted his head. "Sheriff! I want to talk!" he shouted.

"Just come out, Kincaid," Dodie yelled back.

"I will. I just don't want to get shot when I walk out of here."

Waiting for an answer, Louis glanced back at Abby and Grace. They were huddled on the floor in the corner, Abby's arms over Grace's shoulders. Abby was looking at him nervously. He held up a hand to assure her and turned back to the window.

"Sheriff!" he called again.

"You get your ass out here, Kincaid. Now."

Louis rose slowly. A cold wind blew in through the broken window. He glanced back to see Abby helping Grace to her feet.

"Mr. Kincaid," Grace said weakly. "I'll explain to them."

Louis motioned for her to sit down. He crept out to the foyer, and went cautiously to the double doors. He unlocked the door and cracked it open. A cold wind poured in, swirling snowflakes over the black-and-white marble floor.

"Sheriff," Louis called. "I'm coming out."

"Open that door wide, Kincaid. I want to see you."

Louis hit a switch and the foyer was flooded in light from the chandelier. He swung the door open and positioned himself in the center of the foyer, his hands on his head.

"Stay there, Kincaid," Junior said, coming around the car, shoving his gun into his belt. Louis could see Dodie behind him, slowly moving forward.

A wave of relief washed over Louis. It was over.

He let out a breath, meeting Junior's eyes as he started up the walk. Junior's gaze was steady but there was no hostility.

"Detective . . ."

Louis turned. Grace was wobbling toward him, grabbing at the skirt of her satin robe.

"Mother!" Abby said.

"Abby, get her!" Louis called.

Grace was almost to the foyer, trembling so badly she had to catch the wall for support. Louis took a step toward her.

"Kincaid!"

"Mrs. Lilli—"

An explosion ripped through Louis's side, spinning him against the wall. He staggered, falling against the wall of the foyer. His legs crumpled under him.

"What the fuck?" Dodie shouted, spinning. "Who did that?"

Louis grabbed at his middle, gasping. Blood poured out from between his fingers. He stared at Junior in disbelief, parting his lips to speak. Junior watched in shock as Louis slipped to the floor.

"Jesus!" Junior said. He turned back to the front yard, his face ashen.

"No!" Abby screamed, running toward Louis.

Junior moved to catch her but she dropped to her knees next to Louis, pulling him to her chest. "God no," she whimpered. "Please, no . . ."

"Who fired that shot?" Dodie screamed. From the blur of headlights and darkness came silence.

"Somebody get on the horn and call an ambulance. Now!" Dodie yelled.

Junior took several steps farther into the house. Grace pressed herself against the wall, weakly holding on.

Dodie ran up the porch steps then paused, bracing himself in the doorframe, his eyes darting from Louis and Abby to Grace, and then back to Louis.

"Junior! Go get the first-aid kit. Now!" Dodie shouted.

Dodie knelt by Abby, who was cradling Louis in her lap. Her nightgown was stained dark with blood. A pool was forming under Louis. Louis looked up at Dodie, his eyes wide with confusion and fear.

Junior returned with the kit and Dodie grabbed it, popping it open and pulling out a handful of trauma dressings. With shaking fingers, he tried to rip them open, fumbled and cursed. Junior dropped to his knees, grabbed the packs from Dodie's shaking hands and tore them open. As fast as Junior handed the dressings over, the ones under Dodie's hands turned crimson.

"Junior," Dodie said. "Go get everything they got out there."

"Yes sir." Junior hopped to his feet and disappeared.

"Sheriff, I'm cold," Louis whispered. He was trembling, his skin a dull gray.

"Hold on, Louis," Dodie said. "Just hold on."

Abby grabbed Dodie's hand, tears in her eyes. He squeezed

it, then placed it under his, sitting back. "You keep him turned that way and keep pressure on this dressing. Real tight, now."

Abby nodded and bit her lip. Dodie took off his jacket and laid it over Louis, looking back at the door.

"Where's that fuckin' ambulance?" he bellowed.

The next few minutes ticked off slowly. Abby continued to rock Louis, who was unconscious. She was crying softly, one hand on his wound, the other stroking his hair. Dodie stood at the door, watching the snow swirl in the blue-and-red lights. It reminded him of one of those stupid plastic snow-dome toys. He started to shiver, finally hearing the wail of the ambulance in the cold night.

It swung into the drive, and within seconds the doors slammed shut with Louis inside and it was gone. Dodie watched Abby bolt up the stairs and then he turned toward the door, looking out at the lights. He saw Kelly coming up the walk and bristled in contempt.

Grace appeared from the shadows of the library, moving slowly toward the door. She stepped in front of Dodie in the open doorway, facing Kelly. He came to an abrupt halt on the porch.

"You are not welcome here," she said, so softly Dodie barely heard it.

Kelly smiled. "Grace, now . . ."

Grace met Kelly's eyes coldly. "Please leave my home."

Kelly looked over her shoulder at Dodie, stunned. When Dodie did not move, Kelly turned away, stalking down the porch steps. Dodie leaned against the banister, then slid onto the second step tiredly. He looked at the pool of blood that had formed on the floor. His jacket lay in the middle of it. He hung his head, rubbing his eyes.

"Sam?"

He looked up. Grace was standing in front of him. She looked so tiny and frail. But her expression was calm.

"Sam," she repeated softly, "I have to tell you something."

"Grace, this can wait."

"No, it can't. It's important, Sam," she said. "I have to tell you the truth. Please."

"All right, Grace." He rose, took her arm and led her slowly into the library.

CHAPTER 32

The fluorescent light overhead flickered and went out, plunging the small waiting room into darkness. Junior came off his chair and reached up, tapping on it lightly. It vibrated and came back to life dimly. Dodie stood near the door, a silhouette against the bright red-and-white lights of the Coca-Cola machine, chewing on an unlit cigar.

He looked at his watch. "Christ, you'd think they know something by now."

"What time is it?" Junior asked.

"Almost six."

A small, pitiful voice came from the corner. "Sheriff, fire my ass . . . just fire me."

"Mike, shut up."

Mike slumped forward, head in his hands. "Man, I didn't mean to shoot Louis."

"Enough, Mike." Dodie turned to Junior. "Go on home. I'll be needin' you later. Get some rest."

Junior ambled to the door and stopped. "Sheriff?"

"Yeah?"

"You think he's gonna make it?"

"Say a prayer, Junior."

Junior nodded and left the room. Dodie's eyes followed him through the large glass window and out the double doors of the emergency room. A second later, the doors opened again and Bob Roberts and Kelly strode in, shoulder to shoulder. They came around the corner and Kelly shoved open the swinging door with the palm of his hand.

"Is he dead?" Kelly asked.

"Fuckin' Christ," Dodie mumbled, turning away.

"They ain't said yet," Mike offered.

"Mike, shut up."

"What's wrong with *him?*" Kelly asked, gesturing toward Mike.

"I'm a piece of shit, a no-good piece of shit," Mike said.

"Mike, shut up," Dodie said. "Walt, what the hell are you doin' here?"

Kelly unbuttoned his overcoat. "We have some things to talk about, Sam."

"Like what?"

Kelly looked at Mike then pulled Dodie into a corner. Roberts followed. "In a few hours, this place will be swarming with reporters and TV cameras," he said. "I want to make sure we have everything straight."

Dodie's eyes went from Kelly to Roberts's bland face and back to Kelly. "Like what?" he repeated.

"I understand Grace made a full confession to you."

"We talked," Dodie said, shifting his cigar to his other cheek.

"Look, Sam, don't pull any shit with me," Kelly said. "What did she say, exactly?"

"The woman killed her husband, Walt. We all know what he was like. He was a sorry S.O.B., the worst kind. What do you want her to say? That she's sorry?

"It doesn't matter what she told you," Roberts interjected. "We've already decided to call it justifiable homicide. Self-defense, for her and Abigail. And that's the way it'll read."

Roberts and Kelly exchanged glances. Dodie watched them carefully. There was something going on here, something he wasn't able to read. These two had cooked up something and it was starting to smell.

"What about Kincaid?" Dodie asked.

Kelly pursed his mouth. "If he makes it, the murder charge will be dropped, of course. We'll leave it with felony escape and assault on a police officer."

"What?"

"Sam, Deputy Cutter is upstairs getting twenty stitches as we speak."

Dodie took the cigar from his mouth. "Ex-deputy Cutter."

"Whatever. Kincaid assaulted him in the commission of another felony."

"For chrissakes, Walt—"

Kelly leaned closer. "I don't want any lip from you on this, Sam. Kincaid will be charged *and* rearrested."

"I suppose you two already done made that decision, too," Dodie said angrily.

Roberts nodded. "Innocent or guilty, Kincaid committed a felony. He escaped from a county jail." Roberts shrugged. "If we let everyone who says they're innocent escape, what kind of system would we have going?"

"Cutter tried to kill him, for God's sake!"

"Oh, come on, Sam," Kelly said derisively. "Deputy Cutter is guilty of being stupid, that's all. To make anything more of it would be ridiculous. He wouldn't try to kill anyone." Kelly smiled. "He doesn't have the brains, for God's sake."

Dodie stared at Kelly.

Kelly's smile faded. Dodie shook his head then turned away, running a hand through his hair. He saw Mike watching from his place on the bench. The young deputy sniffed, running a hand under his nose, and looked away.

Dodie spit into the trash can and turned back to face Kelly. "This'll ruin him as a cop, you know that."

Roberts's gaze wandered away, out the window. Kelly shook his head. "That's the price he'll have to pay."

Before Dodie could answer, the door opened and a nurse poked her head in.

"Sheriff Dodie?"

"Yeah?"

"Would you come with me, please?"

Dodie tossed his cigar in the trash and started across the room. Kelly stepped forward but Dodie put up a hand. "He's my deputy."

Dodie followed the nurse down the empty corridor and around a corner. He was met by a weary-looking doctor in surgical scrubs.

"Mornin', Sam," the doctor said, pulling off his green cap.

"Mornin', Doc." Dodie took a deep breath. "Well?"

"He's going to be okay. Bullet didn't do a lot of damage. He's strong, and very lucky."

Dodie blinked rapidly several times and let out his breath. "Thank you."

"He'll be in recovery for a while. You might as well go home."

Dodie nodded. "Thanks again. I appreciate it, Doc." Dodie started back down the hall.

"Sheriff?" the nurse called.

She came up to him and handed him a large plastic bag.

"What's this?"

"Mr. Kincaid's personal items. We figured you might need them."

Dodie took the bag from the nurse and started back down the hall to the waiting room. He paused in the empty corridor, listening to the soft *ping* of the hospital paging system, thinking about Louis lying on an operating table somewhere nearby. Louis would live, and that was all that really mattered. Dodie let out a long, tired breath. But it wasn't all that mattered to Louis. If Kelly took away his career now, it would be as if that bullet had passed right through his heart.

Dodie hoisted up the plastic bag and opened it. He looked at the tan sweats, stained with dark brown dried blood. The sight brought a catch to Dodie's throat.

"Sheriff! He okay?" Mike called from the door.

Dodie closed the bag and took a deep breath. "Yeah, he's fine. Go on home now, Mike."

Mike's head dropped in relief then shot back up. "I'd like to hang around, if it's okay with you. I'll head on upstairs and just wait a spell."

Dodie watched Mike hurry off to the elevator. "Mike!" he shouted.

Mike skidded to a stop. "Yes, sir?"

Dodie tossed him the bag. "Get rid of this, will ya?"

Mike caught it, nodded, and disappeared into the elevator. Dodie pulled open the door of the waiting room. He faced Roberts and Kelly, who abruptly ended their conversation. Dodie reached into his pocket for a fresh cigar.

Kelly came over to him. "So, we got everything straight, Sam?"

Dodie met his eyes and slowly began to shake his head. "I don't think so, Walt."

Kelly glanced back at Roberts. "What do you mean?"

"It ain't right."

"Right? *What* 'ain't right'?" Kelly said impatiently.

"This whole shitty mess, Walt. Nothing sets right about any of it. Grace goin' free, Louis locked back up."

"Are you suggesting that Grace Lillihouse be arrested for murder?" Kelly demanded. "You have any idea how that would look? And what about Abigail? You want to take away both her parents?"

"I ain't suggestin' anything," Dodie said, "other than the fact that Kincaid don't deserve to lose his job over all this." Dodie pulled the Zippo out of his pants pocket and flipped it open, his eyes locked on Kelly. "You hear what I'm saying, Walt?"

Dodie flicked at the lighter but it sparked and died. He tried again, then shoved it back in his pocket. Kelly's jaw tightened and he turned away, walking silently past Roberts to stand at the window. "I can't believe you pick this point in your fucking career to grow balls, Sam Dodie."

Kelly turned. "Do it, Bob."

Roberts walked to Dodie, slipping a folded paper from his suit pocket. "I'm serving you with this action, effective immediately."

Dodie looked down at the paper. He took it, unfolded it and read it. Slowly, he looked up, taking the cigar from his mouth.

" 'Malfeasance of duty'?" Dodie said, incredulous.

"It's not hard to understand, Sam," Kelly said from his spot at the window. "You had three—no, make it four—unsolved murders. You arrested the wrong man twice. You let a prisoner escape from your jail. You allowed that same prisoner to nearly kill a law enforcement officer as well as break into the Lillihouse home with unauthorized use of force. On top of all that, one of your own deputies then turns around and shoots the prisoner, who was unarmed."

Dodie stared at Kelly's back.

"If that isn't malfeasance, I don't know what is," Kelly said.

Dodie looked again at the paper. "I could fight this, Walt," he said. "I could blow everything wide open, cause a hell of a stink."

Kelly turned. "But you won't, Sam. Will you?"

The words lay in the air like thick smoke. Dodie stared at the paper in his hands, at the three ugly words . . . *malfeasance of duty.* He knew what it meant—misconduct, wrongdoing. Kelly was going to paint him as an incompetent, a sheriff too stupid even to keep his deputies from shooting each other. Kelly wasn't just going to drive him from the job he loved—the only thing in the world he truly cared about—he was going to publicly humiliate him. Dodie's hands began to tremble. Squeezing the paper in his fist, he stuck the unlit cigar back in his mouth and pulled out the lighter again. He clicked it with nervous hands but it was dead. Dodie removed the cigar slowly, facing Kelly.

"So here's the story," Kelly said flatly. "Grace will plead 'no contest' to justifiable homicide and she and Abby will quietly go on with their lives. . . ."

"No," Dodie whispered.

"The case against Max will be closed and he will be officially charged with the deaths of Earl and George. However, no one ever needs to know his motive."

"No," Dodie said.

"Kincaid will be arrested on felony escape and assault. . . ."

"No," Dodie said, looking up.

"And those damn bones will be forever buried under the damn name of Willie Johnson so this town can have some peace and quiet."

"No!" Dodie said.

Kelly and Roberts looked over at him. "What did you say?" Kelly said.

"I said no." Dodie crumpled the summons and tossed it on the floor.

Kelly let out an angry sigh. "Sam, it's over."

"Not yet, Walt," Dodie said. "Not until I say it is. You want my ass? Well, you can have it. You've damn well had it for years anyway. But I ain't givin' you Kincaid's, too."

"Sam, listen to me," Kelly said slowly. "The rest of the board of commissioners won't—"

"No, Walt, you listen to *me*, dammit." Dodie threw the cigar in the trash and took three steps, standing only inches from Kelly. "You think you're holding all the cards here, but I got a few of my own. You're so fuckin' worried about this town's image. Well, the last thing you want is Grace Lillihouse sitting on a stand being grilled by some prosecutor while some punk camera guy's filmin' it for CNN. And I don't think you wanna take the chance that some hot-shot NAACP lawyer is gonna get wind of Cutter's little stunt." Dodie glared at Kelly. "Think if they tossed Cutter in jail that he might have some interesting things to say about how you run this town?"

Roberts stepped forward. "Now, look—"

"Back off!" Dodie ordered. "This is between me and him. And another thing about you," Dodie said, jabbing a finger at Kelly. "Kincaid was on to something. He was close to pinning you to that lynching."

"You fucking—" Kelly sputtered.

"I don't know if you killed that boy, Walt," Dodie said. "But I sure as hell am gettin' a lot more willin' to listen. And maybe other folks would be, too."

"You wouldn't do this to Grace and this town." Kelly said.

"Try me."

Kelly had backed up against the wall, his face red. With a grunt of anger, he pushed aside Dodie's arm and escaped. He retreated to the other side of the small room, running his hand through his hair. When he turned around, he was icy-calm.

"What do you want, Sam?" he said.

Dodie reached down and picked up the crumpled summons. "A deal."

"What kind of deal?"

"You let Kincaid go, all charges dropped, the arrest expunged, and I'll keep my mouth shut." He fingered the paper nervously.

"I don't know if I have the connections to do that," Kelly said quickly.

"Bullshit, Walt."

Kelly's eyes darted to Roberts. Roberts nodded subtly.

"What about Cutter?" Kelly asked.

"I won't touch him," Dodie said bitterly.

"What guarantee do I have you'll keep your end of the deal?" Kelly said.

"You'd have my word, Walt."

"It's not enough."

Dodie drew in a deep breath. "What more can I give you?"

"Your resignation."

Dodie stared at Kelly.

"I'll give you Kincaid," Kelly said, "but I'm tired of your attitude, Sam. We're all tired of it, all the board members. You're not the kind of man we want in this job. You never were, really.

But I thought we could mold the man to the job. I thought the name was enough. I was wrong."

Dodie turned away. The faint buzz of the fluorescent light echoed in his head.

"Sam," Kelly said quietly. "Take the deal. You've lost anyway."

"All right."

"What?"

"All right," Dodie said softly, without turning. "You'll have it after Kincaid gets out of here and on his way."

Kelly's eyes slipped to Roberts and then back to Dodie.

"Done," Kelly said.

Dodie walked slowly to the window. A few moments later, he heard the door close. It was quiet. He stood, looking out at the gray parking lot. The snow had melted already, leaving ugly rivers of mud and water running through the pocked asphalt. Dodie watched Kelly and Roberts hurry to their cars and pull away, the exhaust pipes belching out gray plumes of smoke in the cold air.

He reached into his pocket for a cigar. The pocket was empty. He padded his other pockets. Nothing. His fingers closed around the Zippo lighter in his left pants pocket and he pulled it out. He looked at its scratched steel then idly turned it over in his hand, until his fingers found the initials etched there. He stared out the window, gently rubbing the *J.D.* etched in the dull metal.

The small white room was dark, except for the moonlight and the ghostly green lights on the monitors over the bed. Dodie was sprawled in a plastic chair to the left of Louis's bed, his head back, his eyes closed. But he was awake, as he had been for hours, listening to the beeps of the machines behind Louis's bed.

"Oh, Jesus . . ."

Dodie sat up, grabbing the bed's rail. "Louis?"

Louis opened his eyes and tried to focus, blinking in the near darkness. Dodie touched his shoulder. "You want I should turn on the light?"

"No."

Louis closed his eyes again, wincing. "Jesus Christ . . . it hurts."

"You want the nurse, Louis?"

Louis took a deep breath and nodded. Dodie pressed the call

button. Louis looked at the ceiling, waiting for the pain to lessen. "Man, who shot me?" Louis whispered.

"Mike did."

Louis laughed softly, then winced again, his palm on his belly. "God . . ."

"I'm sorry, Louis."

"I didn't know you gave Mike bullets."

"He feels real bad, Louis. Jus' got excited, that's all. I had to pry him off that there chair a few hours ago. Been here for hours."

Louis looked up at Dodie. For a second, neither spoke, and finally Dodie looked down, both hands on the rail. "What a sorry mess I made of this," Dodie said.

"I didn't help, running like that."

"No, you didn't. But I can't say I blame you."

They were quiet again for a second. The nurse came in and asked Louis if he was in pain. When he nodded, she said she would return with a painkiller and a sleeping pill. After she left, Louis closed his eyes and took a shallow breath.

"They're going to charge me, aren't they?" he said.

Dodie hesitated. "They talked about it, but then decided to drop the charges. I think they just decided maybe it wasn't worth it. They was more worried about Grace, I reckon."

Louis swallowed dryly. "Sheriff, can I have some water?"

Dodie looked around, saw the plastic pitcher and poured Louis a small cup. "You don't want much. Just wet your lips."

When Louis tried to sit up, Dodie slipped a hand behind his neck and held the cup to his lips. He took a sip and lay back down, grimacing.

"What about Grace? How's she doing?"

"She's okay, I reckon. She told us everything. She also sent them flowers there."

Louis looked over to see a vase of white lilies on the table. The same flowers he had seen at Eugene's memorial.

"What's going to happen to her, Sheriff?"

"Ain't nothin' going to happen to her. And I suppose that's okay, too." Dodie met Louis's eyes. "That okay with you?"

"Part of me says no. But the other part . . . Jesus, Sheriff, I don't know why she didn't kill that bastard years ago." Louis closed his eyes. The pain had subsided some and he let his mind wander.

Last night was a blur of lights and tears. He saw Abby and

Grace, pitiful in their embrace, he could hear Junior shouting at him and could still feel the cold air on his face when he opened the door. The crack of the shot echoed through him and he forced his eyes open.

The journal. Dodie had to know about it. "Sheriff . . ."

"Yeah?"

"Where are my clothes?"

"Why?"

"I need them. Check the cabinet." Louis moved gingerly, pointing to the cupboard.

Dodie frowned. "Louis, we threw them away."

Louis fell back, grimacing in pain, his fist doubled. "No, goddamn it, no."

"What the hell do you need bloody clothes for?"

"I had proof, Sheriff. I had Kelly nailed."

"For the lynching?"

Louis nodded, pain shooting through his abdomen. He tightened, gritting his teeth.

"You all right?" Dodie asked.

"I don't believe this."

"It was just a bunch of bloody clothes, Louis."

"No, no, there were some papers. Earl kept a journal. He wrote it all down."

"He admitted to it? On paper?"

"The whole thing. Him, Max, George and Kelly. They killed Eugene Graham in the summer of '55."

Dodie sat back down with a thud. "Jesus Christ . . ."

The nurse returned with a paper cup. She helped Louis take the two pills, straightened his blanket, checked his IV, then slipped back out.

"Louis," Dodie said. "You know some 30-year-old piece of paper won't get anyone convicted. Especially since there ain't no witnesses left. Plus, they was minors in '55. Ain't no court could touch 'em."

"Still," Louis said softly. "I wanted people to know. I wanted you to know."

"Why, Louis? It was over. Why?"

Louis looked at him. But before he could answer, Dodie held up a hand, shaking his head slowly.

"I know why," he said. "It was because it was the truth."

Louis closed his eyes with a sigh. Dodie looked at him for a long time, thinking back to his conversation with Kelly. He started to speak when his eyes drifted to the fading scar on Louis's neck. He cleared his throat.

"I fired Larry. Kelly gave him a job."

"Figures."

"He took twenty stitches in the face."

"Should've been a hundred and twenty."

"Yeah, well, you did a number on him."

Louis didn't reply. The sleeping pill was kicking in. Dodie stood up. "I reckon you need your rest. I'll be headin' home."

Louis nodded sleepily. Dodie touched his arm. "I'll stop back tomorrow and see if you need anything."

"Yeah, thanks," Louis said, closing his eyes.

Dodie went to the door then paused, turning around. "Louis, you're a good cop. I've been meaning to tell you that for some time now," he said. "I always knowed it. I knew it since that day in the woods last December."

Louis didn't reply.

"Louis?"

Dodie pulled on his cap and left.

CHAPTER 33

Louis got out of his car and waited while the black Lincoln cruised to a stop in the next parking place. He looked at his watch. Right on time.

Winston Gibbons and a second black man got out of the Lincoln. They straightened their dark overcoats, shared a smile, and looked over at Louis.

Louis moved up the walk of the courthouse, bypassing the sidewalk that led to the station. Although the wound in his side was still sore, there was a spring to his step.

Mayor Kelly was coming out of the double doors, and both of them stopped. For a second, the two men eyed each other warily.

The two FBI agents stopped a few steps behind Louis. Kelly slowly came down to Louis. Louis felt his muscles tighten but he wasn't sure why. Maybe it was just being in the presence of Kelly and knowing what he had done.

"Good morning, Kincaid."

Louis nodded.

"Glad to see you're all right."

Louis didn't reply as he stared at Kelly. Finally Kelly cleared his throat. "Look, Kincaid, I know what you think of me, but you're wrong."

"I am not wrong," Louis said, shaking his head.

Kelly offered a half smile. "You still think I'm guilty of something. I assure you I am not. This whole mess with Max and Grace . . . and that boy . . . What's his name again?"

Louis clenched his jaw. "Eugene Graham."

Kelly nodded. "It's all very tragic. And although I don't agree with your methods and the end result, I have to commend you on your determination. If it were up to me, though, innocent or not, I'd still have you in jail for assault on a police officer."

"It wasn't up to you. It was up to Sheriff Dodie."

"Well, the man never did have very good judgment."

Louis took a deep breath. "Mayor, were you aware Earl Mulcahey kept a journal?"

"No. Why would I care?"

"He wrote it all down."

"I'm afraid you've lost me, Kincaid. Wrote all what down?"

Kelly's face remained impassive. Louis hesitated. Was it possible the "Wallie" in the journal was a different Walt? Was Kelly innocent after all?

"The whole story of the lynching. How Earl and Max and George . . ." Louis stopped. "How they lynched Eugene Graham."

Kelly sighed. "Just another story that somebody will use to disgrace the fine state of Mississippi."

"You folks don't need help doing that."

"Kincaid, let me tell you something," Kelly said. "This whole thing never had to end like it did. You think I stonewalled you because of my beliefs. My feelings about race played no part in my desire to see this case closed quietly." Kelly stopped, taking a breath. "Do you know where Neshoba County is, Kincaid?"

"Yes."

"And how do you know of it?"

"That's where the three civil-rights workers were killed in 1964."

Kelly met his eyes. "Twenty years later, they still talk about it. Tourists who drive into that town ask where the earthen dam is. They stop to have their pictures taken in front of the jail. That is that town's sad legacy, Kincaid, a shadow cast forever. I didn't want the same thing to happen here."

"It's not the crime that casts the shadow, Mayor, it's the absence of justice," Louis said tightly. "Maybe if you recognized that, then people *would* begin to forget. And maybe forgive."

Kelly's eyes hardened. "Look, Kincaid, we know better than anybody what our sad history is. We're working hard to put it behind us. But people like you, with your self-righteous vendettas, you keep kicking up the same old dirt. And one day it has to stop."

Louis remained silent.

"I'm proud to be a Southerner, Kincaid," Kelly said quietly. "I know who I am and what I stand for. Do you?"

Louis smiled. "Yes, I do. And the strange part is, I have you and your friends to thank for it."

Kelly blinked several times then gave him a tight smile of his own. "Then at least one good thing has come out of all this." Kelly turned away from Louis and continued down the walk, eyeing the two FBI agents as he passed.

"Kelly," Louis called.

The mayor turned, squinting into the sun.

"You might want to watch this," Louis said, continuing up the steps.

Gibbons and his partner followed Louis through the door and up the marble steps to the second floor. Louis and the two distinguished black men parading through the courthouse corridors drew stares from curious clerks and receptionists. Louis heard the door below open and knew Kelly had come back in the building.

Louis pushed open the door labeled Mayor's Office, and strode by the wide-eyed clerk to the secretary's desk. The woman's eyes moved nervously across the faces of the three men. Louis saw his cousin Charles glance up, his eyes widening.

Larry, dressed in a cheap suit and thin tie, was standing by the window, feeding papers into a noisy shredder. As if he sensed trouble, Larry raised his head slowly.

His flecked green eyes grew dark as they settled on Louis, then changed abruptly, glazing over with apprehension as they shifted to Gibbons and his partner. The two FBI agents walked as a pair to Larry, looked at each other, then at Larry.

"What the fuck's goin' on here?" Larry asked.

"Are you Lawrence Cutter?"

Larry's eyes darted to Louis. Louis smiled, folding his arms over his chest. "Yeah, I'm Cutter," Larry said, looking back at Gibbons. "Who wants to know?"

"Agent Gibbons and Agent Marks. Federal Bureau of Investigation."

"That's the FBI, Larry," the secretary said softly.

"I know who the hell it is."

"You are under arrest for violating the civil rights of Louis Washington Kincaid on the night of January twentieth."

"What?"

Gibbons took out his handcuffs. He looked at Marks and smiled. "I haven't done this since 1969." He looked back at Larry. "Turn around. You have the right to remain silent. . . ."

"This is a fuckin' joke," Larry said, turning slowly.

Gibbons cuffed Larry; Marks grabbed his arm and pulled him away from the window.

"Wait! Somebody call Kelly," Larry yelled.

Marks led Larry to the door, jerking him to a halt in front of Louis. "Don't worry," Louis said, "cops don't live long in prison."

"Fuck you, Kincaid."

Marks pulled Larry out the door. Louis took a second to scan the astonished faces and when he reached Charles, he grinned. Charles looked as if he had seen a ghost. Then slowly he began to smile.

Louis hurried down the steps after Gibbons and Marks. The two agents shoved by Kelly, yanking Larry along. Louis stopped at the bottom step.

Kelly gripped the bannister. "We had a deal, Kincaid."

Louis looked at him. "Deal? I don't make deals, Kelly."

Kelly pointed toward the stationhouse, sputtered something and hurried past Louis and up the stairs. Louis continued on down the steps, shoving open the courthouse door. He watched as Agent Marks put Larry in the backseat of the Lincoln. He waited until the car pulled away then made a sharp right to the sheriff's office.

He stopped at the entrance. He had been out of the hospital less than a week and this was the first time he had set foot back inside the office. He thought it would feel odd, but strangely, he found it comforting.

Inside, Junior was coming out of Dodie's office, coffee in hand. Louis went to his desk, feeling Junior's eyes following him. On top of the desk was a cardboard box, which held all his personal items. Louis picked up the small wooden box that was sitting on top, turning it over in his hands.

Junior ambled over. "How ya doin', Louis?"

"It's still sore."

"Louis, I want you to know I didn't have anythin' to do with what happened in your cell that night."

"I never thought that, Junior."

"Good. I wouldn't want you to."

Louis looked back at the cardboard box, realizing in that moment there was nothing he really wanted to keep. He pulled out his glasses and stuck them inside his shirt pocket, under the Michigan jacket and looked back at Junior.

"Where you goin' now?" Junior asked.

"Back to Michigan."

"Gonna be a cop there, too?"

Louis smiled faintly, thinking of his application still on file with the Detroit police force. "I hope so."

Junior's eyes wavered and he looked away. "You could stay here."

Louis was so stunned at first he couldn't think of a reply. Before he could say anything, Junior added, "I guess maybe that's not a very good idea, is it?"

Louis shook his head. "No, Junior, I guess not."

Junior sighed and the radio crackled with the voice of a deputy Louis did not recognize. Junior wandered off and Louis looked toward Dodie's closed door. Tucking the small wood box under his arm, he went to the door, knocked softly and poked his head in.

"Sheriff?"

Dodie was standing at the desk, bent over a cardboard box. He looked up in surprise. "I thought you were gone."

"I wouldn't leave without talking to you—you know that." Louis noticed the clutter on Dodie's desk, stacks of papers, notebooks, the bottle of Jim Beam, and a picture of Margaret. "What is all this?" he asked.

"I've resigned." Dodie said.

"Resigned? Why?" Louis asked.

"It was time."

"But you love this job."

Dodie took a deep breath. "I used to love it, Louis. It ain't the job it used to be. Things are different. These are different times and the rules changed on me. I reckon it's time I bowed out gracefully."

"They applied pressure, didn't they?"

"No, this was my decision, Louis. I didn't have to do it."

Louis suddenly thought back to Kelly and what he said outside. *A deal?* Had Dodie made some kind of deal with Kelly about

Larry? If this was part of a deal, what was Dodie getting out of it?

"Sheriff—"

Dodie held up a hand. "It's over, Louis. Let it be."

Louis watched him for a minute. Dodie blinked back the hurt in his eyes. Louis looked away, not knowing what to say. "You heard anything about Leverette?" he asked finally.

"Yeah," Dodie said. "He's stayin' home with Ethel. They're doin' okay, I guess." He smiled slightly. "Looks like she's gonna let him go ahead with that Laundromat idea."

Louis nodded. He hesitated, then set the wood box down on the desk and reached in the back pocket of his jeans. He removed his badge from the leather holder and held it out to Dodie.

"I need to give you this."

Dodie looked at the badge for a moment, then took it. He sat down in the chair, swinging slightly, rubbing the badge with his thumb.

Louis found it hard to look at him and he let his gaze wander. The wall to the sheriff's right was bare.

"You took the flag down," Louis said.

"Seemed time."

Louis let out a breath and stepped forward, extending his hand. Dodie stood up and shook it, and Louis met his eyes. They were empty gray pools. Louis forced himself to pull his hand away.

"So what are you going to do?"

"Hell, I dunno. Maybe me and Margaret will move to Florida."

Louis laughed softly. "You'll never leave this place."

Dodie smiled. "You're right. But I'll be okay."

Louis nodded. "Oh, I almost forgot," he said, picking up the wood box. "I got you something."

Dodie's brows knitted together as he looked at the flat wood box. He took it, opening the lid gingerly. Nestled inside, in a bed of red felt and ribbon, were eight glass cylinders, each holding a cigar.

"Macanudo? Never heard of 'em," Dodie said, looking up at Louis.

"I had Agent Gibbons bring them up from Jackson," Louis said. "Supposed to be the best you can buy. Thought it was time for you to move up from those damn El Productos."

Dodie smiled awkwardly. "Well, thank you, Louis. I'll keep

'em for a special occasion." He carefully closed the box and set it down on the desk.

"I better get going," Louis said quietly.

Dodie nodded quickly. "Yeah. You have a good trip, you hear?"

"Thanks, Sheriff."

Louis hesitated, wanting to say more but knowing there was nothing else. He left the office, closing the door softly behind him. He walked through the station, waving at Junior who returned the acknowledgment with a nod of his head. He paused at the door, taking a final look.

The door burst open behind him, catching him in the back and making him wince. Mike squeezed through.

"Oh, man, sorry, Louis."

Louis tensed at the sight of Mike's bland young face. For a second, he thought about slamming him up against the wall and putting a gun up to his head just so the kid would think twice the next time he pulled out his gun. But the penitent look in Mike's eyes stopped him.

"Jesus, Louis, I'm glad you're not gone yet," Mike said quickly. "I—I wanted to tell you, I mean, I didn't mean to . . . I prayed that—" Mike's face was flushed. "Aw shit, Louis, I'm so sorry, man."

Louis sighed. He nodded toward the holster on Mike's hip. "Be careful with that the next time you have to pull it," he said.

Mike nodded furiously and held out a box to Louis.

"What's this?"

"It's nothin' great. But I thought it was the least I could do."

Louis opened the flaps of the box and looked down to see a sweatshirt. He lifted it and noticed the small off-color patch on the front. "Mike, these are my sweats. I thought—"

Mike grinned. "I patched up the bullethole there. Man, I betcha I washed them things twenty times. Pressed 'em, too."

Louis lifted out the sweats. Underneath was the Ziploc bag. A slow smile spread across Louis's face.

Mike's own smile faded. "I didn't read it, Louis, I swear."

Louis looked at him. "What?"

"I didn't read it. I figured maybe it was some love letter from Abigail, and I wouldn't do that, I swear."

Louis laughed. "Jesus, Mike, you are a piece of work. And I love you for it."

Junior looked up and groaned. "Louis, don't you be saying that shit to him."

Louis headed back to Dodie's office. He walked in without knocking and Dodie looked up at him from his chair.

"I have something else for you," Louis said, popping open the bag. He pulled out the papers, unfolded them and laid them on the desk. Dodie picked them up and winced.

"Smells like bad tuna fish. What is it?"

Louis grinned. "Don't read it now. Read it one night when you're laying in bed next to Margaret and drinking a beer and thinking about what a rotten son of a bitch Kelly is."

Dodie sifted through the papers, his brows knitted. He looked up at Louis. "This here's Earl's journal, isn't it?"

"Yes."

The corners of Dodie's mouth twitched into the beginnings of a smile.

Louis leaned over the desk. "Sheriff, I don't know what they said to you to get you to resign, but whatever it was, maybe you can fight it with this."

Dodie stood up. He pulled an envelope from a drawer, carefully folded the papers and put them inside. He hesitated, then flipped open the cigar box. He pulled one of the Macanudos out of its glass cylinder and stuck it in his mouth.

"You can't convict him with it, you know," Louis said.

Dodie pulled the Zippo out of his pocket and smiled. "Yeah, but I don't have to. I only gotta scare him, Louis," he said. "That's all. Just scare him."

Dodie snapped open the Zippo. He flicked it and flame shot up. He sucked on the fat black cigar several times, sending a blue plume of fragrant smoke up into the ceiling fan.

CHAPTER 34

Teesha watched Louis come through the front door. "I thought you was shot," she said.

Louis patted his middle. "I was but I'm not dead, Teesha. Where's your grandfather?"

"He back there. Granddad!" she hollered.

Tinker came out of the back room and Louis moved to him, hand outstretched. Tinker shook it.

"I'm glad to see you're well." Tinker said.

"I'm kind of glad to be here, too."

"Bessie tells me you're leaving," Tinker said.

Louis nodded. "I'll miss you."

Tinker gave him a rare smile. "Why would you miss me? We barely knew each other."

"True, true. But I feel like I've known you all my life."

"Or maybe in another life," Tinker said.

Louis smiled. "Plus, I owe you something."

"What?" Tinker said, frowning.

"I wanted to thank you for sticking your neck out."

Tinker's eyes held his. "It was your neck at stake, not mine. No pun intended," he added.

Louis laughed softly, then the smile faded and he met Tinker's rich brown eyes.

"Are you satisfied with the outcome?" Tinker asked.

Louis shook his head slowly. "No. I just wish the men responsible had paid for their crime."

"They did pay, Kincaid. With their lives."

"It's still not enough."

Tinker sighed. "You're trying to satisfy yourself. You see justice as only a legal issue. There are many kinds of justice. Some kinds are a lot more fair than a prison term."

"Maybe," Louis said. "But one man didn't pay. The fourth man, whoever he was, is still walking around free." Louis thought of the smug smile Kelly had given him at the courthouse. "I hate the thought of that man getting away with it."

"But you don't even know for sure who it is, do you?" Tinker said.

Louis let out a long breath, his eyes wandering to the street outside. "No, I don't."

"What does it really matter?" Tinker said softly. "He could be any man. Anyplace. In any time."

Louis nodded woodenly, staring at the kids outside at the bus stop.

"Louis . . ."

Louis looked back at Tinker.

"Let it go," Tinker said.

Louis held the old man's eyes for a moment then extended his hand. "I'd better be going," he said softly. He hesitated, looking around the store.

"What's the matter? I thought you couldn't wait to get out of here." Tinker said.

Louis shrugged. "I don't know. There's just something about this place." Louis shook his head, smiling. "God knows, I hate it here."

" *'The place is dignified by the doer's deed,'* " Tinker replied.

Louis held up a finger. "Not *Hamlet*, right?"

Tinker smiled. "Have a safe trip. May God be with you."

"You, too, Mr. Tinker," Louis replied.

Louis started toward the door.

"Louis," Tinker called out.

"Yeah?" Louis asked, pausing, hand on the screen door.

"You ever decide what world you're going to walk in?"

Louis hesitated then smiled. "Mine."

Louis closed the car door and paused, looking up at the Lillihouse mansion. The trees were still bare, but pale green crocus shoots were peeking out of the dirt near the porch.

He knocked lightly and waited, shifting the small box under his arm. The door swung open and Abby stood in front of him.

He had seen her only once in the last ten days, while he was still at the hospital. Though the memory was fuzzy, he could recall her sad eyes, dark-circled in her pale face. He could remember, too, the feel of her hand on his as he drifted off to sleep.

She was wearing the yellow sweatshirt again, barefoot with her hair pulled back in a haphazard ponytail. She looked very young and content. It pleased him to see her that way again.

"Louis," she said with a smile.

He took her hand and let her pull him inside. His eyes swept the foyer, stopping briefly at the spot where he had fallen. The wall and tile were polished clean. He looked beyond to the library. There were sheets covering the furniture.

"I didn't think I'd get to see you again," she said. "The sheriff told me you had resigned."

"I couldn't leave without saying good-bye to you," he said.

When she didn't reply right away, he set the box on a table and touched her shoulder. "How are you doing?"

"I'm okay, we're okay, Louis. Really we are." She nodded toward the covered furniture. "We're going away together for a while. What about you? How are you feeling?"

"Good as new . . . almost," he said, touching his side.

She brushed her bangs from her eyes. "I don't know what to say, Louis. I feel like I need to say a million things, but nothing seems right."

"I know."

"Can I give you a hug?" she asked.

He hesitated then held out his arms. "Gently."

She moved into his arms and laid her head against his chest. He wrapped his arms around her. He pressed his cheek into her neck and closed his eyes, smelling the lilacs.

When he finally drew away, he saw Grace standing at the bottom of the staircase. He tensed slightly, then let out his breath. Abby saw her mother and broke away from Louis, smiling.

"Mother, I didn't know you were awake."

"I have been for a while. I was listening to music." Grace met Louis's eyes and smiled tentatively as she came into the room.

Louis picked up the box and opened it. He cupped something in his hand and held it out to Grace. "Mrs. Lillihouse, I thought you might want this back."

Grace looked down at his palm then slowly took the medallion.

Her expression didn't change as she gazed at it. But when she looked up at Louis, there was warmth in her pale eyes. She went slowly to a cherrywood cabinet in a corner of the library, took out a blue velvet box and set it on a table.

Louis and Abby followed her and watched as she opened it. Nestled inside were the two other pieces of the set. The sun glinted off the pristine silver bracelet and ring, making the tarnished necklace look ugly by comparison. Grace laid the necklace in the empty depression. She touched it lightly then closed the box.

She looked up at Louis. "Thank you," she said. "My father would be pleased."

"I brought you this, too."

Grace looked down at the moldy book in his hands. She started to reach for it but then quickly withdrew her hand, lifting her eyes to Louis. "Gene should have that," she said softly.

Louis shook his head. "You should have it."

She took the book and closed her eyes. It was only for a second but Louis felt she had regressed thirty years and he looked away, embarrassed. Abby was watching them, and when she saw Louis looking at her, she brushed quickly at her eyes and smiled. It was quiet, the moment stretching awkwardly. It was time to go.

Grace came over to him and held out her hand. He took it, unsure why it was being offered. "I'll let you and Abby say good-bye in private," she said. "Take care of yourself, Mr. Kincaid."

Her hand was cool, but there was a flicker of affection in her eyes. She went quietly up the staircase, clutching the book to her chest.

Louis looked down at Abby. "I have to go," he said.

"I know," she murmured, looking down and pulling at the edge of her sweatshirt.

He took her face in his hands, kissing her softly on the lips. He could feel them trembling as she tried not to cry. He drew back, his hands lingering on her face. Finally, he stepped back.

Abby opened her eyes. "I bet it would have been beautiful," she said softly.

"I *know* it would have been," he said. "Good-bye, Abby."

He walked toward the door, leaving her standing in the middle of the room. He opened it and stepped into the sunlight, letting the door close softly behind him.

* * *

Louis slowed the Mustang to a stop on the shoulder of the narrow blacktop road and turned off the ignition. It was quiet. He could hear the wind whistling through the crack in the window. Leaning back in the seat, he looked out at the cloudy sky, then to his left, letting his eyes wander over the cemetery. He reached for the flowers on the passenger seat and got out.

He headed up a small hill, pausing at the top. Gray headstones were scattered across the yellow, lifeless grass. The colorful bouquets of plastic flowers on the graves were an odd contrast to the bleakness of the grounds. This cemetery was smaller than Black Pool Gardens and not as well maintained. But it was here Eugene Graham rested.

As soon as Louis got out of the hospital, he had ordered a headstone for Eugene. It wasn't right that a small plate with the wrong name marked the grave of a man who had changed so many lives.

As Louis walked on, he thought about how hard it had been to say good-bye to Bessie. She had cried and hugged him like he was her own, and for a minute he almost felt he was. She had packed a suitcase for him this morning. Not one of his, but an old leather one she had kept since her honeymoon. In it, she had put the picture of Lila, the snapshots of his family, the quilt from his bed, and four peanut-butter sandwiches. He hadn't seen the suitcase until he had stopped for gas at the Texaco in town.

Louis paused, looking down at a small marble headstone.

Lila Louise Coleman
1931—1984
Mother of Yolanda, Robert, and Louis

It seemed an odd epitaph, but Louis didn't mind. He had let Bessie pick out the headstone and the words she saw most fitting, including Lila's legal name. She had never legally been a Kincaid and Louis guessed Bessie thought it ought to stay that way.

He knelt and put some flowers in the plastic holder. Still on his knees, he said good-bye, knowing he would never set foot in Greensboro County again.

He moved on up the slope and stopped again. He had not seen the headstone before now. It was a small, square piece of granite with a barren tree etched in the corner. He stared at the epitaph. He had composed it while he still lay in the hospital, inspired by a poem he had found during his days of research in the library. It wasn't much, but he thought it appropriate.

Eugene Graham
1939—1955
"Died in the Dark of the Moon"

Louis put flowers on the grave and stood up. A breeze chilled him and he shivered. He was about to turn away when he heard a voice.

"Are you Detective Kincaid?"

He turned to face a black woman. She was pretty, with cocoa-brown eyes, high cheekbones, and full red lips. A colorful purple-and-black scarf covered her hair and she wore a knee-length white cardigan sweater.

"Yes, I'm Kincaid," Louis replied.

She smiled and came up to him. She looked down at the head-stone.

"They told me I would find him here. They didn't tell me I would find you. I'm very pleased to meet you."

Louis looked at her curiously. She caught his gaze and she laughed softly. "I am sorry. My name is Charlotte. Charlotte Graham."

Louis glanced at the headstone then back at Charlotte. Her eyes drifted to the granite stone.

"Gene was my brother."

"How did you . . . ?"

"The ad in the Tupelo paper. An aunt called me and . . . well, I had to see for myself what all this was about. I called a few weeks ago but they said you were in the hospital. No one at your office knew anything about Gene so I decided to come down."

"From where?"

"Norfolk, Virginia."

Louis smiled, nodding. He waited, feeling awkward, as Char-lotte turned to look back at Gene's grave.

"I want to know the details," she said quietly after several moments. "Can you tell me?"

Earl's description of the murder flashed through his mind and he knew he could not tell her everything.

"Are you sure you want to know?"

Charlotte met his eyes, her own dimming. "Maybe not," she said softly. She took a minute to let the emotion pass. "I was nine when Gene disappeared. He was the light of my life. He taught me to read, to ride a bike. He held my hand when we walked to Sunday school. He was all I had, really." She took a deep breath. "I owe all that I am to Gene. He changed my life."

Louis looked at the grave. "Mine too."

Charlotte touched his arm. "Thank you for finding him," she said.

Louis nodded stiffly, not trusting his voice.

Charlotte knelt down and reached out, putting a hand on the cold stone. She closed her eyes and Louis could see her lips move in prayer. He waited for a moment then turned away from the grave. He started back down the hill. At his car, he opened the door. There on the floor of the passenger side was a book. It was *The Golden Apples*, the book Grace had given to him months ago, the first day he saw her. He had brought it along to give back to her, but had forgotten. He hesitated, considering driving back. But then he smiled slightly. He would keep it, knowing she would not mind.

He got in the car and started the engine. He paused for a moment, looking out over the cemetery, then slowly he pulled away. Out on the highway, he turned the Mustang north. He rolled down the window. The wind blew in against his face, warmer, with a hint of honeysuckle.